The Power of Disturbance
Elsa Morante's *Aracoeli*

LEGENDA

LEGENDA, founded in 1995 by the European Humanities Research Centre of the University of Oxford, is now a joint imprint of the Modern Humanities Research Association and Maney Publishing. Titles range from medieval texts to contemporary cinema and form a widely comparative view of the modern humanities, including works on Arabic, Catalan, English, French, German, Greek, Italian, Portuguese, Russian, Spanish, and Yiddish literature. An Editorial Board of distinguished academic specialists works in collaboration with leading scholarly bodies such as the Society for French Studies and the British Comparative Literature Association.

MHRA

The Modern Humanities Research Association (MHRA) encourages and promotes advanced study and research in the field of the modern humanities, especially modern European languages and literature, including English, and also cinema. It also aims to break down the barriers between scholars working in different disciplines and to maintain the unity of humanistic scholarship in the face of increasing specialization. The Association fulfils this purpose primarily through the publication of journals, bibliographies, monographs and other aids to research.

Maney Publishing is one of the few remaining independent British academic publishers. Founded in 1900 the company has offices both in the UK, in Leeds and London, and in North America, in Boston. Since 1945 Maney Publishing has worked closely with learned societies, their editors, authors, and members, in publishing academic books and journals to the highest traditional standards of materials and production.

EDITORIAL BOARD

Chairman
Professor Colin Davis, Royal Holloway, University of London

Professor Malcolm Cook, University of Exeter (French)
Professor Robin Fiddian, Wadham College, Oxford (Spanish)
Professor Paul Garner, University of Leeds (Spanish)
Professor Marian Hobson Jeanneret,
Queen Mary University of London (French)
Professor Catriona Kelly, New College, Oxford (Russian)
Professor Martin McLaughlin, Magdalen College, Oxford (Italian)
Professor Martin Maiden, Trinity College, Oxford (Linguistics)
Professor Peter Matthews, St John's College, Cambridge (Linguistics)
Dr Stephen Parkinson, Linacre College, Oxford (Portuguese)
Professor Ritchie Robertson, St John's College, Oxford (German)
Professor Lesley Sharpe, University of Exeter (German)
Professor David Shepherd, University of Sheffield (Russian)
Professor Michael Sheringham, All Soul's College, Oxford (French)
Professor Alison Sinclair, Clare College, Cambridge (Spanish)
Professor David Treece, King's College London (Portuguese)

Managing Editor
Dr Graham Nelson
41 Wellington Square, Oxford OX1 2JF, UK

legenda@mhra.org.uk
www.legenda.mhra.org.uk

The Power of Disturbance

Elsa Morante's *Aracoeli*

Edited by Manuele Gragnolati and Sara Fortuna

Modern Humanities Research Association and Maney Publishing
2009

Published by the
Modern Humanities Research Association and Maney Publishing
1 Carlton House Terrace
London SW1Y 5AF
United Kingdom

LEGENDA is an imprint of the
Modern Humanities Research Association and Maney Publishing

Maney Publishing is the trading name of W. S. Maney & Son Ltd,
whose registered office is at Suite 1C, Joseph's Well, Hanover Walk, Leeds LS3 1AB

ISBN 978-1-906540-50-0

First published 2009

All rights reserved. No part of this publication may be reproduced or disseminated or transmitted in any form or by any means, electronic, mechanical, photocopying, recording or otherwise, or stored in any retrieval system, or otherwise used in any manner whatsoever without the express permission of the copyright owner

© *Modern Humanities Research Association and W. S. Maney & Son Ltd 2009*

Printed in Great Britain

Cover: 875 Design

Copy-Editor: Nigel Hope

CONTENTS

Acknowledgements ix
Notes on the Contributors x

1 Introduction 1
   SARA FORTUNA and MANUELE GRAGNOLATI

PART I: LANGUAGE AND (INTER–)SUBJECTIVITY

2 Between Affection and Discipline: Exploring Linguistic Tensions from
   Dante to *Aracoeli* 8
   SARA FORTUNA and MANUELE GRAGNOLATI

3 Seeing and Telling: Anamorphosis, Relational Identity, and Other
   Perspectival Perplexities in *Aracoeli* 20
   REBECCA WEST

4 Resisting Paranoia: Poesis and Politics in *Aracoeli* 30
   FLORIAN MUSSGNUG

PART II: PSYCHOANALYSIS

5 'The Lover of a Hybrid': Memory and Fantasy in *Aracoeli* 42
   CHRISTOPH F. E. HOLZHEY

6 *Scene madri*: Psychoanalytic Visions from *Aracoeli* to *Volver* 59
   VITTORIO LINGIARDI

7 Baubo — Another and Additional Name of Aracoeli: Morante's Queer
   Feminism 73
   ASTRID DEUBER-MANKOWSKY

INTERMEZZO

8 Staging the Passion of Aracoeli 86
   AGNESE GRIECO

PART III: ELSA E GLI ALTRI

9 *Aracoeli* and Gadda's *La cognizione del dolore*: Disturbed Sons, Disturbing
   Mothers 96
   GIUSEPPE STELLARDI

10 Politics and Sexuality in Pasolini's *Petrolio* 107
   FRANCESCA CADEL

11 Between Italy and Spain: The Tragedy of History and the Salvific Power
   of Love in Elsa Morante and María Zambrano 118
   ELISA MARTÍNEZ GARRIDO

PART IV: RELIGION

12 The Womb of Dreams: Cabbalistic Themes and Images in Elsa Morante's *Aracoeli* 130
    SERGIO PARUSSA

13 Morante and Weil: The Aporiae of History and the End of the Fairy Tale 145
    CLAUDE CAZALÉ BÉRARD

14 Indian Traces: *Aracoeli*, Pasolini's *L'odore dell'India*, and Moravia's *Un'idea dell'India* 161
    MIMMA CONGEDO

Bibliography 177
Index 185

ACKNOWLEDGEMENTS

The symposium on Elsa Morante at which the essays contained in this volume were first presented took place on 11–12 April 2008 at the Berlin Institute for Cultural Inquiry (ICI), and we would like to thank the ICI and its staff for its full support, and to show our gratitude to all of those who from many places and in many ways took part in the symposium and contributed to its success. We are also grateful to the Istituto Italiano di Cultura a Berlino for funding the *Szenische Lesung* from *Aracoeli* and thereby allowing for one more perspective on the complexity of Morante's last novel. We would also like to thank wholeheartedly the poet Patrizia Cavalli, whose personal, intelligent, and passionate reflections on her friend and first mentor Elsa Morante opened a broader perspective to all of us from which to reconsider her work also in the light of Cavalli's remarkable poetry. In addition, we would like to express our gratitude to Francesca Southerden for the care and insightfulness of her help, and to thank Martin McLaughlin and Graham Nelson for their professional and generous advice. Finally we would also like to thank Somerville College, Oxford, and the ICI Berlin for their generosity in supporting the publication of this volume.

NOTES ON THE CONTRIBUTORS

Francesca Cadel teaches Italian Literature at Yale and Columbia Universities. She has published a book on Pasolini, *La lingua dei desideri: il dialetto secondo Pier Paolo Pasolini* (Lecce: Manni, 2002), and articles on poetry and political thought in Post-World-War Italy and France. She is currently working on a book entitled *Italian Cultural Landscapes in Post Fascist Italy: Umberto Saba, Pier Paolo Pasolini and Elsa Morante*.

Claude Cazalé Bérard is Professor of Italian Literature at the Université Paris Ouest-Nanterre-La Défense. She has published widely on Elsa Morante and twentieth-century Italian literature, and edited several books and proceedings, including *Quatre poétesses juives de langue allemande: Else Lasker-Schüler, Gertrud Kolmar, Rose Ausländer, Nelly Sachs* (Lille: UL3, 2003); *Présence et culture des Juifs en Italie* ('Tsafon', 2005); *Femmes et Tradition du Livre* (Lille: UL3, 2006); *Scritture di maternità, paternità e infanzia* ('Écritures', 2–2006); *Venise sauvée dans la tradition européenne historique, littéraire et philosophique* ('Écritures', 3–2007); *Nelly Sachs. Ethique et modernité* (Lille: UL3, 2007).

Mimma Congedo (University of Milan) has a Ph.D. in Indology. She has written on Hinduism and comparative philosophy and is completing a book on the work of Ananda K. Coomaraswamy.

Astrid Deuber-Mankowsky is Professor of Media Theory at the University of Bochum and has published books on Benjamin, Kant, Cohen, Nietzsche and gender theory, including *Der frühe Walter Benjamin und Hermann Cohen. Jüdische Werte. Kritische Philosophie. Vergängliche Erfahrung* (Berlin: Verlag Vorwerk 8, 2000); *Lara Croft: Cyber Heroine* (Minneapolis and London: University of Minnesota Press, 2005); *Praktiken der Illusion. Kant, Nietzsche, Cohen, Benjamin bis Donna J.Haraway* (Berlin: Verlag Vorwerk 8, 2007).

Sara Fortuna teaches Philosophy of Language at the Università Telematica Guglielmo Marconi in Rome. She has published the books *A un secondo sguardo. Il mobile confine tra percezione e linguaggio* (Roma: manifestolibri, 2002) and *Il laboratorio del simbolico. Fisiognomica, percezione, linguaggio da Kant a Steinthal* (Perugia: Guerra, 2005), co-edited two books of feminist theory, and written articles on Vico, Wittgenstein, Herder, Humboldt, psychoanalysis and gender.

Manuele Gragnolati is Reader in Italian Literature at Oxford, where he is Fellow of Somerville College. He has published a book on Dante and medieval eschatology (*Experiencing the Afterlife: Soul and Body in Dante and Medieval Culture* [Notre Dame and London: Notre Dame University Press, 2005]), co-edited two books on embodiment in the Middle Ages, and published several articles on Italian literature from the Middle Ages to the present. He has collaborated with Teodolinda Barolini on an edition of Dante's *Rime* (Milan: Rizzoli, 2009) and is co-editing a volume on performance in the Middle Ages with Almut Suerbaum. He serves as Adviser to the Director at the Berlin Institute for Cultural Inquiry.

Agnese Grieco received a Doctorate in Philosophy from the Freie Universität Berlin and works in Berlin as an essayist and a theatre director. Her publications include *Die ethische Übung* (Berlin: Lukas Verlag, 1996), *Wittgenstein* (Milan: Il Saggiatore, 1998), and *Per amore. Fedra e Alcesti* (Milan: Il Saggiatore, 2005). She co-edited Girolamo Cardano's *Somniorum Synesiorum* (Venice: Marsiglio, 1989 and 1993; with Silvia Montiglio), Hans Georg Gadamer's *Dove si nasconde la salute* (Milan: Cortina, 1994; with Vittorio Lingiardi), *Goethe scienziato* (Turin: Einaudi, 1998; with Giulio Giorello).

Christoph F. E. Holzhey holds a Ph.D. in theoretical physics from Princeton University and one in German literature and critical theory from Columbia University, and is the founding Director of the Berlin Institute for Cultural Inquiry. He has edited the books *Biomystik: Natur — Gehirn — Geist* (Munich: Fink, 2007) and *Der Einsatz des Lebens. Lebenswissen, Medialisierung, Geschlecht* (Berlin: bbooks, 2008; with Astrid Deuber-Mankowsky and Anja Michaelsen), and published several articles on science and the relationship between science, psychoanalysis, and literature.

Vittorio Lingiardi is Full Professor of Psychology at the University of Rome 'La Sapienza' as well as a practising psychoanalyst in Milan. He has published several books, including *I disturbi della personalità* (Milan: Il Saggiatore, 1996; French tr. *Les troubles de la personnalité*, Paris: Flammarion, 1996); *Compagni d'amore* (Milan: Raffaello Cortina Editore, 1997; English tr. *Men in Love*, Chicago: Open Court, 2002); *La personalità e i suoi disturbi* (Milan: Il Saggiatore, 2004); *Citizen gay: Famiglie, diritti negati e salute mentale* (Milan: Il Saggiatore, 2007).

Elisa Martínez Garrido is Professor of Italian literature at the Universitad Computense de Madrid. She has written several articles on twentieth-century Italian authors and edited the volume *Elsa Morante. La voce di una scrittrice e di un'intellettuale rivolta al secolo XXI* (Madrid: Departamento de Filología Italiana de la Universidad Complutense de Madrid, 2003) as well as books on Italo Svevo, Luigi Pirandello, and Dino Buzzati.

Florian Mussgnug is Lecturer in Italian Literature and Convener of the MA in Comparative Literature at University College London. His publications include articles on Primo Levi, Ludwig Wittgenstein, Italian postmodernism and literary theory, the volume *Lutero e la riforma protestante* (Firenze: Giunti, 2003), and two forthcoming monographs on Giorgio Manganelli and Umberto Eco. He is the editor of 'Contemporanea. Rivista di studi sulla letteratura e sulla comunicazione' and a member of the BCLA executive committee and of the 'Réseau Européen d'Études Littéraires Comparées'. He is currently working on a comparative study of twentieth-century European apocalypse fiction.

Sergio Parussa is Associate Professor of Italian at Wellesley College. He is the author of *L'eros onnipotente: erotismo, letteratura e impegno nell'opera di Pier Paolo Pasolini e Jean Genet* (Turin: Tirrenia Stampatori, 2003) and of *Writing as Freedom, Writing as Testimony: Four Writers and Judaism in Twentieth Century Italy* (Syracuse, NY: Syracuse University Press, 2008). His work also includes the translation of *Simonetta Perkins* by L. P. Hartley (Rome: Nottetempo, 2008) and of *L'orso maggiore* by Ginerva Bompiani (*The Great Bear*, New York: Italica Press, November 2000).

Giuseppe Stellardi is Lecturer in Italian Literature at Oxford, where he is Fellow of St Hugh's College. He has written on Dossi, Tarchetti, Michelstaedter, Svevo, Gadda, Moravia, Eco; also, on Deconstruction (Derrida), and on metaphor. He has published a book on metaphor in Derrida and Heidegger, *Heidegger and Derrida on Philosophy and Metaphor. Imperfect Thought* (Amherst: Humanity Books, 2000), and one on the work of Carlo Emilio Gadda, *Gadda: miseria e grandezza della letteratura* (Florence: Franco Cesati Editore, 2006), as well as a translation in English of Carlo Michelstaedter's *La persuasione e la rettorica*.

Rebecca West is the William R. Kenan, Jr. Distinguished Service Professor in the Department of Romance Languages and Literatures and in the Department of Cinema/Media Studies of the University of Chicago. She has published widely on Italian literature and cinema, including *Eugenio Montale: Poet on the Edge* (Cambridge, MA: Harvard University Press, 1981) and *Gianni Celati: The Craft of Everyday Storytelling* (Toronto: University of Toronto Press, 2000); she has edited or co-edited several volumes including *The Cambridge Companion to Modern Italian Culture*; *Italian Feminist Theory and Practice: Equality and Sexual Difference*; and *Pagina, pratica, pellicola: Studi sul cinema italiano*.

CHAPTER 1

Introduction

Sara Fortuna and Manuele Gragnolati

Aracoeli (1982) is the last novel written by Elsa Morante (1912–85), one of the most significant Italian writers of the twentieth century. From *Menzogna e sortilegio* (1948) and *L'isola di Arturo* (1957) to *La Storia* (1974), Morante became an increasingly important author, provoking animated debates in the Italian and European literary and cultural milieux. Her final novel, by contrast, was received with profound aversion and almost unanimously dismissed as a desperate writer's self-destructive attempt at a tragic parody of everything she had previously written.

If it is indeed true that *Aracoeli* returns to topics fundamental to all of Morante's texts and questions them in an often disturbing manner, the hypothesis informing this volume is that the novel cannot be reduced to a deep expression of despair, but, rather, succeeds in confronting crucial philosophical and epistemological questions in an original and profound way: through its narrative inquiry into the relationship between mother and child, Morante's text creates a 'hallucinatory' representation of the original mother–child dyad, questioning the classical distinction between subject and object and offering a theory for the genesis of language and meaning. The protagonist's journey to Spain in search of his dead mother forms the poetic and theoretical nucleus for the novel's manifold perspectives and motifs that contaminate and disrupt literary, psychoanalytic, and political paradigms as well as categories of identity, gender, and sexuality. In particular, the novel's intricate structure allows different levels to interact with one another, producing asymmetries and contrasts that represent a form of resistance to the hegemonic and totalizing claims of the *logos*.

The Power of Disturbance, which originates from an international conference held at the Berlin Institute for Cultural Inquiry in April 2008 within its core project on *Tension/Spannung*, combines literary scholars and Morante experts with scholars from other disciplines — such as Jewish Studies, Psychoanalysis, Theatre, Philosophy, and Indology — who accepted the challenge of engaging with Morante's last novel. The result is a truly interdisciplinary enterprise seeking to re-evaluate the complexity of *Aracoeli* and reflect on the manifold tensions that it stages and that are also present in contemporary philosophical discourse (from feminist to queer to political theory) and authors (such as Carlo Emilio Gadda, Pier Paolo Pasolini, and Pedro Almodóvar).

Part I, entitled 'Language and (Inter-)Subjectivity', explores the original way in which the corporeal and relational concept of subjectivity staged in *Aracoeli* challenges the conventional vision of the world based on binary and disembodied categories.

Fortuna and Gragnolati's 'Between Affection and Discipline: Exploring Linguistic Tensions from Dante to *Aracoeli*' (Chapter 2) deals with a central image in Dante and Morante's meditation on corporeality and language: that of the infant suckling at the mother's breast. While several critics have noted that in *Aracoeli* Manuele's journey to Spain in search of his dead mother is modelled upon Dante's *Divine Comedy*, they have especially placed emphasis on the difference between the two texts, reading Morante's last novel as a sort of anti-*Divine Comedy*, thereby agreeing with the common interpretation of *Aracoeli* as a dark and desperate text. According to Fortuna and Gragnolati's interpretation, the dialogue with Dante's oeuvre allows for a different reading of Morante's novel, which is not only less negative but also — and especially — more interested in the novel's philosophical and linguistic meditation. It is against the background of Dante's discourse of language and corporeality that they propose to use Julia Kristeva's psycho-linguistic concept of the 'semiotic' to explore *Aracoeli*'s complexity and suggest that it elaborates a theoretical model for a corporeal relationship between language and subjectivity.

Rebecca West's 'Seeing and Telling: Anamorphosis, Relational Identity, and Other Perspectival Perplexities in *Aracoeli*' (Chapter 3) argues that in her final novel, Elsa Morante problematizes the sense of sight, and concomitantly complicates issues pertaining to self-identity as well as to narrative point of view, the truth-value of a first-person narration, and the essential bond between mother and son. West explores the symbolic meaning of the protagonist Manuele's bad eyesight, which she links to the visual technique of anamorphosis. The unconventionality of Manuele's distorted/anamorphic vision, on account of which he is incapable of seeing himself, the world, others, and especially his mother Aracoeli in a straightforward manner, is explored as an emblem of the modern author himself or herself, who can no longer use a mimetic or realist style in order to convey the complexities of both the outer world and inner subjective identity. West further explores problems of identity and self-representation by turning to the theory of 'relational identity' as defined by the feminist philosopher Adriana Cavarero, in her work that brings philosophical and literary issues together.

Florian Mussgnug's 'Resisting Paranoia: Poesis and Politics in *Aracoeli*' (Chapter 4) begins with the claim that *Aracoeli*, set against a background of massive political disappointment, is defined by a sense of directionlessness and despair. In the violently unjust world of Morante's novel there is no transcendent basis for moral action. Nihilism therefore appears to be the only legitimate response to a profound anguish, which floods into all areas of life. Yet, Mussgnug argues, *Aracoeli* resists the temptation of absolute nihilism, and against the tragic force of existential despair — the narcissistic *reductio ad unum* of paranoia — Morante's novel advances a different, less heroic vision of ethical subjectivity, suggesting that *Aracoeli* is best approached as a comic acknowledgement — rather than a tragic affirmation — of human finitude. Inauthenticity (the experience of an essentially divided self) is not an obstacle to ethical and political expression, but a necessary basis for the invention of new political subjectivities.

The essays in Part II, 'Psychoanalysis', argue that psychoanalytic models inform *Aracoeli*'s narrative and thereby deconstruct classical concepts of subjectivity. In particular, scholars show how by problematizing traditional ways of conceiving of the relationship between mother and child, Morante's novel becomes a space for the articulation of 'queer' and hybrid subjectivities.

Christoph Holzhey's '"The Lover of a Hybrid": Memory and Fantasy in *Aracoeli*' (Chapter 5) deals with the many tensions in Morante's novel, claiming in particular that in Manuele's ambivalent actions, sentiments, and fantasies there is also a considerable consistency that points to a different kind of logic beyond binary oppositions and the principle of non-contradiction. The essay focuses on the relation between memory and fantasy, upon which the novel reflects in a central scene where Manuele imagines a trial in which he is accused of a 'pathological confusion of the imagination and memory' that contrasts with the supposedly 'healthy' way to use memory as a 'teacher of life'. Drawing upon Laplanche and Pontalis's interpretation of Freud's seduction theories, Holzhey argues that Manuele's memory, rather than being pathologically confused, is thoroughly sexualized, making the whole narrative less of a description than an actualization or even fulfilment of Manuele's sexuality — a pre-oedipal sexuality that emerges through traumatizing seduction and is not univocally painful except within a normative order of reason.

Vittorio Lingiardi's '*Scene madri*: Psychoanalytic Visions from *Aracoeli* to *Volver*' (Chapter 6) engages Morante's novel in a dialogue both with some filmic representations on the theme of the mother (to which the phrase 'Scene madri' refers) and with some fundamental concepts of contemporary infant research and psychoanalysis. The essay starts by looking at some mothers in Pasolini's films (from the Mater Dolorosa of the *Vangelo* to the Mediterranean Mothers of *Mamma Roma* and *Medea*), and claims that Morante was pushed by an almost ancestral urge to move away from the model of the mother of Pasolini's Classical, Greek, and Christian iconography and to enter a dimension which goes beyond the reassuring polarity between good and bad mother. Aracoeli's maternal aspects *always and at the same time* express themselves in the form of a barbaric polytheism and paganism that combines and mixes different genders: hereby their power of disturbance. The essay concludes by exploring the similarities and the differences between this unsettling and queer feature in Morante's novels and Almodóvar's films, focusing in particular on *Aracoeli* and *Volver*, which both deal with stories of lost mothers who come back and inhabit their children's life like ghosts.

Astrid Deuber-Mankowsky's 'Baubo — Another and Additional Name of Aracoeli: Morante's Queer Feminism' (Chapter 7) proposes an interpretation of Morante's novel which prevents the reader from losing him/herself in the labyrinth of the text's meanings on the one hand and from bypassing the complexity of this baroque writing on the other. In order to do so, Deuber-Mankowsky proposes to add one further name to the many names by which Aracoeli's son refers to her ('Shepherdess. Hidalga. Thorn. Death. Immortal. Victim. Tyrant. Doll. Goddess. Slave. Mother. Dancer'): that of *Baubo*. By referring to Nietzsche's affirmation in *The Gay Science* that the name *Baubo* stands for truth and life and that the will to truth is shameless and indecent, this essay argues that Morante's feminism is queer and consists in the fact that in constructing the couple mother and son, Morante superimposes the appearance of the Virgin Mary and her child with the image of the obscene Baubo, from whose vulva protrudes the head and the hand of Iacchus/Bacchus. The battle among these different traditions and meanings is also a battle for the meaning of life and death. Aracoeli can thus be considered the figure in which Morante gives expression to the ambivalence, the abysmal and the indifference reacting to which life responds to the search for meaning. One could also say, with reference to Nietzsche, that Aracoeli is another name for life.

An *intermezzo*, represented by Agnese Grieco's 'Staging the Passion of Aracoeli' (Chapter 8), investigates some theoretical and aesthetic aspects connected with Grieco's work on a 'stage interpretation' of Morante's *Aracoeli*, which she adapted as a dialogue between two actors on the occasion of the Berlin symposium. Grieco explicitly declares that the idea to structure her dramatic project as a dialogue between two actors was based upon an evident challenge, inasmuch as Morante's book is written, from beginning to end, as a classical *monological narration* in the first person. Therefore her hypothesis of a dialogical, transgender presentation of *Aracoeli* cannot find its justification in the first level of the written text or in the formal construction of the narration. It depends, rather, on a deeper analysis of the sources of the narration itself: the possibility of a dialogical perspective is based upon a non-dualistic theory of knowledge according to which the language, experience, and biography of the son's character create the language of his mother Aracoeli.

Part III, entitled 'Elsa e gli altri', explores the richness of *Aracoeli*'s literary world with a contrastive, comparative, and intertextual approach that illuminates its take on sexuality, politics, and ethics.

Giuseppe Stellardi's '*Aracoeli* and Gadda's *La cognizione del dolore*: Disturbed Sons, Disturbing Mothers' (Chapter 9) offers a comparative analysis of these novels, which both tell the story of a single male character, whose life and destiny seem to have been profoundly and permanently affected during his childhood by the influence of a powerful and disturbing maternal figure. The two mothers are antithetical: if Aracoeli is unable (also in her educational methods) to abide by the rules of middle-class decorum, and at first swamps Manuele in unbounded maternal love (only to subject him subsequently to a traumatic rejection), *la Signora* seems to have internalized the strictest demands of the paternal-symbolic order and, in the pursuit of an almost inhuman pedagogical ideal, deprives young Gonzalo of any real affection. But the effect on the two men is similar: an emotionally pathological mother–son relationship in the early years leads to disastrous consequences later on. Ultimately, however, the conclusion is different: if Gonzalo, in his Hamletic pursuit of truth and justice, seems destined to a nihilistic rejection of life and ultimately to self-destruction, Manuele's indelible memories of Aracoeli's boundless love seem to provide a path to some sort of salvation, supplying him with a puzzling but indestructible potential for human empathy. The divide separating Gonzalo from Manuele is also reflected linguistically and stylistically: whereas *La Cognizione* constantly oscillates between implosion and explosion (silence and logorrhoea, lyricism and the baroque), *Aracoeli* is clearly dominated by an anamnestic (in both the philosophical and medical meaning), linear-circular and almost Dantesque orientation, 'saving' the text from the destiny of internal incompleteness and infinite deferral that affects all of Gadda's narrative writing.

Francesca Cadel's 'Politics and Sexuality in Pasolini's *Petrolio*' (Chapter 10) explores Pasolini's posthumous novel in relationship to the last novel by Morante, Pasolini's contemporary and friend. In particular, the essay reads the Mattei Affair as an *exemplum* through which *Petrolio* elaborated his representation of the mutational process — involving both politics and sexuality — taking place in Italy in the 1960s and early 1970s. These were the years in which 'la strategia della tensione' (a strategy of tension) between Italy's Red and Black entities became constitutive of politics and society, and *Petrolio* represents it within a key symbolism indicative of both politics and sexuality: 'il misto' (the mixed), a symbolism also used by Morante in *Aracoeli*. Cadel argues that there is a deep dialogue that can be inferred between these two texts, and that in *Petrolio* the reader can experience a similar tension to that represented in *Aracoeli*. But, although dissociation is the form of the search for identity in both novels, and Manuele and Carlos are the final characters used by Morante and Pasolini to express — as in a powerful dystopia — their analysis of the self and society after the Second World War, their proposed vision is peculiarly and significantly different: the tension in *Aracoeli* engages with the maternal dimension and seems to be finally directed towards an asymptotic allusion to paternal love/order, while in *Petrolio* it is embodied by a different understanding and representation of the normative process which leads to a dismemberment of both paternal and maternal love/order.

Elisa Martínez Garrido's 'Between Italy and Spain: The Tragedy of History and the Salvific Power of Love in Elsa Morante and María Zambrano' (Chapter 11) argues that the theme of the journey to Spain in Morante's novel can be read as an *anabasis* that crosses borders, and that the novel is structured as a path towards the frontier; at the end of it, the protagonist arrives at a salvific union with the father, in the mythical scenario of El Almendral. Martínez Garrido shows that in *Aracoeli*, Elsa Morante shares some philosophical reflections with María Zambrano's ethical and political commitments in *L'agonía de Europa* (1945) and in *El Hombre y Lo divino* (1955). In particular, Manuele's 'retrieval' of his father at the end of the novel can be read in connection with Zambrano's concepts of the sacred and mercy: love represents for Manuele a possibility to find the way out from his tragic condition. Martínez Garrido also argues that Aracoeli is a victim of history, too, and that it is her sacrifice that allows Manuele to attain his final salvation.

Part IV, 'Religion', focuses on the several references to the non-Christian traditions of religious thought that are scattered throughout the novel and convey a mystical concept of knowledge and experience. The essays show how these references, which question the Western idea of rationality, reflect and symbolize the novel's epistemological project.

Sergio Parussa's 'The Womb of Dreams: Cabbalistic Themes and Images in Elsa Morante's *Aracoeli*' (Chapter 12) focuses on Morante's relationship with Judaism and explores the cabbalistic theme of death and rebirth starting with the analysis of 'Il ladro dei lumi', a juvenile prose published in 1963 in *Lo scialle andaluso*. The story — the first one by Morante openly dealing with a Jewish theme — is told by a first-person narrator who remembers herself as a girl living in the Jewish ghetto of an unspecified city at an unspecified time in history. 'I am dead and reborn', says the girl at the end of 'Il ladro dei lumi', 'and at every birth a new uncertain process begins'. Parussa proposes to interpret this voice as an echo of *Gilgul Neshamot*, the principle in Jewish Cabbala that describes the cycle of life of the souls and their reincarnation in different bodies. This issue hints at a spiritual depth that, Parussa argues, comes to the surface again in *Aracoeli*. Indeed, like the girl in 'Il ladro dei lumi', Manuele in *Aracoeli* wonders if he bears in himself the imprint of a previous existence. Parussa claims that the narrative texture of these two stories is woven with deeper spiritual meanings that seem to allude to images, notions, and symbols of Jewish Cabbala and explores how these images help reveal that a secret texture of hope lies behind Manuele's seemingly desperate journey.

The hypothesis of Claude Cazalé Bérard's 'Morante and Weil: The Aporiae of History and the End of the Fairy Tale' (Chapter 13) is that Morante's last novel brings to maturation and fruition the themes, narrative, and meta-narrative procedures of her previous works, deepening their intellectual and ethical engagement. Cazalé argues that Simone Weil's religious thinking plays a major role in the development of Morante's tormented interest in the question of God, already present in her youthful writings and deepened and dramatized in the temporal arc from *Senza i conforti della religione* to *Il mondo salvato dai ragazzini*, where the name of Simone Weil appears explicitly numbered among the 'Felici Pochi'. As in case of Weil's thought, *Aracoeli* also represents a conclusive statement against a modernity confronted with the aporiae of history and challenged by witnessing the end of fairy tales and myths. However, in Cazalé's reading, *Aracoeli* takes a different position from Weil's mystical asceticism — that 'uncreation' which leads to the obliteration of the 'I' in an act of love, in the free acceptance of the void, death, and even of God's silence. Manuele's regression '*ad uterum*' and the renunciation of his own individualization would not allow him to escape the '*pesanteur*' — as Weil would put it — but would make him lose all possibilities of salvation.

Mimma Congedo's 'Indian Traces: *Aracoeli*, Pasolini's *L'odore dell'India*, and Moravia's *Un'idea dell'India*' (Chapter 14) analyses the Indian or Oriental traces which can be found in *Aracoeli*, both by exploring the motifs common to *Aracoeli* and the two other works and by commenting upon the way in which some references to the Oriental world are presented in the text. The three texts taken into consideration share the motif of the journey, and the essay shows that there is an interesting assonance between *Aracoeli* on the one hand and Pasolini and Moravia's texts on the other: they all somehow stage a journey towards the *diverso*, the 'Other', represented as a disturbing and puzzling dimension, which contrasts with the rational/bourgeois/European and Western order. The references to the Oriental world analysed in the essay are the symbol of the stairs, the mention of the brahmanical revelation, and the figure of the Indian dancer. By referring to Morante's *Il mondo salvato dai ragazzini*, the symbol of the stairs is brought into relation with the Buddhist tradition and to the representation of a spiritual path of knowledge, while the other references are analysed in connection to the theme of the coexistence and union of opposites.

PART I

Language and (Inter-)Subjectivity

CHAPTER 2

Between Affection and Discipline: Exploring Linguistic Tensions from Dante to *Aracoeli*

Sara Fortuna and Manuele Gragnolati

Dante and Language

Dante is acknowledged to be an important interlocutor for Morante and several critics have highlighted that Manuele's journey to Spain in search of his dead mother in *Aracoeli* is modelled upon Dante's *Divine Comedy*. However, scholars have emphasized especially the difference between the two texts, reading Morante's last novel as a sort of anti-*Divine Comedy*, that is, as a journey to the otherworld that does not conclude happily with the attainment of God in the luminous splendour of the Empyrean, but rather with a sort of faint and meaningless apparition of the dead mother in a desolate landscape that is more reminiscent of the infernal desert of the circle of violence. In agreement with the frequent interpretation of Morante's novel as a dark and desperate text, Manuele's journey would therefore be a journey towards nothingness, or — using Concetta D'Angelis's words — 'un ribaltamento del Paradiso sperato nella dannazione infernale'.[1]

Our analysis takes a different course and focuses on the image of the infant suckling at the mother's breast, which plays a central role in Dante and Morante's meditation on corporeality and language. According to our interpretation, the dialogue with Dante allows for another perspective and for a very different reading of Morante's novel — a reading that is not only less negative but also more interested in the novel's philosophical and linguistic meditation.

Our point of departure has been some recent scholarship on Dante, which has shown that the image of the baby suckling at the mother's breast informs Dante's reflection on desire, language, and subjectivity. Especially interesting for us has been Gary Cestaro's *Dante and the Grammar of the Nursing Body*, which draws on Julia Kristeva's *La Révolution du language poétique* and its meditation on the relationship between language-learning and the development of subjectivity.[2] In particular, Cestaro focuses on Kristeva's theory of what she calls the 'semiotic', which designates a pre- or proto-linguistic mode of signification that takes place in the body. Kristeva associates the *semiotic* with the intermediate condition that in *Timaeus* Plato calls the '*chora*'. She conceives of the 'semiotic *chora*' as a kind of spatial and temporal realm where the individual human subject — one with language — begins to emerge, symbolizing perceptual inputs and bodily drives and focusing his/her desire on the nursing body, which is not yet perceived as a discrete object. In her reflection on the ontogenesis of language, Kristeva characterizes *chora* as the form of multiple signification expressed in vocal and rhythmic motility that precedes and underlies adult verbal language.[3]

Although Kristeva claims that the semiotic *chora* is lost in the symbolic order of adult verbal language, considered by her as a symbolic system that is superimposed on the semiotic, she argues that a form of poetic praxis can subvert this order at all its levels (morpho-syntactic, semantic, and phonologic) and let the *semiotic* re-emerge — as in the case of nineteenth- and twentieth-century avant-guard movements that Kristeva considers in her essay.

With this Kristevan theoretical framework, Cestaro's analysis focuses on the relationship between the vernacular, which Dante conceives as maternal language learned spontaneously and received 'by imitating the wet-nurse without the need of any rule', and Latin, which is 'gramatica', that is, an abstract language, artificially constructed and learned through rules, discipline, and assiduous effort (*De vulgari eloquentia* 1.1.2–3).[4]

Cestaro begins by following Dante's theory and praxis of language in *Convivio* and *De vulgari eloquentia*, arguing that while they acknowledge the natural character of the vernacular, they both end up conforming to the 'classical' paradigm of linguistic subjectivity, according to which the image of the child suckling at the mother's breast represents the initial phase of development which needs eventually to be left behind for the rational formation of the subject and adult language to take place. It is a non-corporeal model of subjectivity, in which the subject's rational development implies a movement away from the mother towards the realm of the father, and which is best exemplified by the following passage from the *Convivio*: 'Onde sì come nato, tosto lo figlio a la tetta de la madre s'apprende, così tosto come alcuno lume d'animo in esso appare, si dee volgere a la correzione del padre, e lo padre lui ammaestrare' (4.24.14).

Dante's *De vulgari eloquentia*, his theoretical treatise on the vernacular language proposing to identify an illustrious vernacular within the Italian peninsula, is also characterized by some significant tensions: on the one hand, the natural character of the vernacular, its universality, and the fact that it was the language originally spoken by Adam, would seem to make the vernacular nobler than Latin's artificiality ('nobilior est vulgaris'; 1.1.4); on the other hand, however, Dante indicates that after Babel the vernacular is inevitably corrupted and constantly mutable in space and time. For this reason, Dante's search for an illustrious vernacular (which inasmuch as vernacular should be natural and learnt without rules) turns into an attempt to fix rules limiting the vernacular's extension (with respect to words, accents, structures, and so on) and giving it a ruled and normative structure that assimilates it to the rationality and immutability of Latin and its 'paternal', rational character as *gramatica*.

Particularly exemplary of this move away from the maternal, natural, open aspect of language towards paternal, rational normativity, is the fact that the language originally spoken by Adam, which is an ideal model for the illustrious vernacular sought by Dante, is presented as a natural language but, at the same time, Adam is defined as the man who never had a mother or drank her milk, the man who never saw either childhood or maturity: 'vir sine matre, vir sine lacte, qui nec pupillarem etatem nec vidit adultam' (1.6.1). Like *Convivio*, *De vulgari eloquentia* also acknowledges the maternal aspect of language and subjectivity, but ultimately falls into the classical model of development that prescribes a progressive, complete movement away from a maternal and corporeal space and a shift towards a paternal and rational space or, with the image of the *Convivio* mentioned above, from 'la tetta della madre' to 'l'ammaestramento del padre'.

According to Cestaro, the *Divine Comedy* produces a major change with respect to the classical, incorporeal paradigm of *Convivio* and *De vulgari eloquentia* and deploys a more significant presence of corporeality with respect to both identity and language. Two crucial points of this change are represented by the recovery of the image of suckling and the continuous shift and interaction of gender that characterize one of the most important scenes of the whole poem, that is, Dante's recovery of Beatrice and her replacement of Virgil in the Garden of Eden.[5] As we shall see, it is precisely these issues (suckling at the mother's breast and the shift of gender) that also play a central role in *Aracoeli*.

On the one hand, the transition from the first to the second guide on the top of Purgatory (*Purg*. 30.40 ff.) re-enacts the classical paradigm from mother to father, from the protective figure of Virgil (towards whom Dante turns 'col respitto | col quale il fantolin corre a la mamma') to the authoritarian and harsh figure of Beatrice who is in fact presented as the male figure of a commander ('ammiraglio'). On the other hand, Beatrice's arrival can also be understood as an integration of the paternal figure (which Virgil recovers right after his disappearance: 'Ma Virgilio n'avea lasciati scemi | di sé, Virgilio dolcissimo patre, | Virgilio a cui per mia salute die'mi', *Purg*. 30.49–51) with the maternal one, which, in spite of her initial harshness, Beatrice acquires in the rest of the *Purgatorio* and throughout the *Paradiso* as the symbol of Christian charity.

Here the formation of a new Christian subject would be staged, which integrates the classical model of rational development with the recovery of the corporeal and maternal sphere connected with the image of suckling. Indeed, the image of suckling at the mother's breast recurs frequently in *Paradiso*.[6]

The corporeality connected with the image of suckling and recovered in the *Commedia* is best symbolized by the motif of the resurrection of the body, which, as several recent studies have shown, plays a significant role in Dante's understanding of human identity as embodied and relational.[7] What matters to our argument is the poem's linguistic performance, which reflects this new, corporeal understanding of identity: the linguistic choice of the *Divine Comedy* is no more that of Dante's previous works, but rather, as Erich Auerbach has defined it, a 'sermo humilis', which through its extension, wideness, and malleability goes beyond any conventional category of medieval rhetoric and can thereby encompass the whole spectrum of reality that the poems aims at describing. In other words, it is that plurilingualism — variety of languages and styles — which is universally considered to be the greatest linguistic achievement of the *Divine Comedy*.[8] It is also significant that the image of the baby suckling at the mother's breast appears again at the very end of the *Paradiso*, which conveys the final vision and ultimate bliss with a 'revolution of poetic language' engaging a different kind of textuality, which — as Teodolinda Barolini has shown — is 'nondiscursive, nonlinear or circular, dechronologized and affective'.[9]

It is against the background of Dante's discourse of language and corporeality that we propose to use Kristeva's theory to explore *Aracoeli*'s complexity and to suggest that Morante's novel elaborates an interesting model for the relationship between corporeality, language, and subjectivity. Considered from this perspective, *Aracoeli* appears as a text thought of and consciously written as a farewell novel, which doesn't merely reflect the deep personal crisis of the writer (a fact which is undeniable), but rather proposes to confront the theoretical issues mentioned above in a specifically narrative way, *sub specie narrativa* one could say.

Aracoeli

The act of suckling that rejoins the baby with his mother is ubiquitous in *Aracoeli*, where it undergoes significant metamorphoses.[10] Our hypothesis is that this image is the sign of the radical way in which Morante's writing stages the creation of a new linguistic subjectivity that deconstructs and challenges the discourse of patriarchy and its binary oppositions.

What we could call Morante's 'revolution of poetic language' operates above all by interrupting the linearity of the narrative structure through continuous breaks, ruptures, and temporal shifts and by overcoming the monolingualism of paternal language in favour of a plurilingualism marked by the mixture of Italian and Spanish, the prelapsarian language spoken by Manuele and his mother in their personal Eden.

The following analysis distinguishes and reorganizes three moments that in the novel are constantly interwoven: the first is Manuele's Edenic phase in the first years of his life, which is characterized by a language originating from the mutual desire that joins mother and child; the second moment begins with the departure from Eden and the Fall into the language of the Father, that is, with the arrival at the Quartieri Alti, and continues through Manuele's desperate adult life; and the last moment begins with the trip to Spain, which marks the recovery of Spanish and opens up the possibility of new, more positive developments.

Totetaco's Maternal Eden

Totetaco is the name which the little Manuele in his baby talk gives to Monte Sacro, the Roman neighbourhood where he lived alone with his mother for 1,400 days of heavenly happiness. Here the spontaneous act of suckling milk from the mother's breast is provocatively presented both as a 'primal scene' that corresponds to the originary moment of language learning and as the first 'apocryphal memory'.[11] This event, which joins the baby with his mother right after his birth, is the point of departure for the organization of a space of signification that coincides with what Kristeva calls the semiotic *chora*. Morante's text deploys a double connection between voice and suckling and between language and milk. It is a connection that recalls that kind of vocal expression that Hélène Cixous calls *languelait,* namely '*voice and milk*'.[12] In an analogous way to Cixous's *languelait*, Morante presents the maternal voice and the affectionate phrases addressed by the mother to her child as a space evoking, precisely as an original semantic substratum, the act of suckling milk mingled with saliva and the pleasure associated with it:

> Con le sue prime nenie di culla [. . .], essa accompagna, invariabilmente in queste mie 'rimembranze apocrife', l'atto di porgermi il petto o di dondolarmi. È proprio la sua tenera voce di gola, intrisa di saliva, che mi ricanta all'orecchio quelle sue canzoncine di paese.[13]

In Totetaco, Morante also follows the phase of subsequent language learning, of which the *languelait* somehow represents the origin, a powerful 'matrix', thereby dealing again with the origin of language, which was also present in Morante's previous novels. However, while *Menzogna e sortilegio* and above all *L'isola di Arturo* and *La Storia* seem more influenced by Classical glotto-genetic accounts, Morante's last novel assumes a psychoanalytic, post-Freudian approach.[14]

In this respect we consider Kristeva's theoretical framework and its Lacanian and Kleinian background highly productive for our analysis. But we also see an important difference between Kristeva and Morante in their descriptions of the development of human language. Kristeva presupposes a caesura between semiotic and symbolic and considers it as necessary for a non-pathological development of language. Morante by contrast seems to suggest the possibility of a different kind of linguistic evolution, which does not consist of discontinuous phases and is not marked by the loss of the semiotic: the learning situation in Totetaco does not present a dual model that, like Dante and Kristeva's, opposes maternal and paternal language. Manuele and his mother Aracoeli speak at once Italian and Spanish, and the child learns both from Aracoeli, who teaches Italian to her son while she is learning it herself. Very interestingly, learning refers at once to how to speak and to how to read and write, and is for both languages — for speaking, reading, and writing — spontaneous and playful (*Aracoeli*, p. 1191). This form of learning corresponds to the discovery of a world structured according to fluid categories, marked by continuous metamorphoses and perceived through a magic dimension — that of the acts of magic which are often performed by Aracoeli in the joyous interaction with her son. Briefly put, it is a model of learning very different from that of the father's correction and discipline that we have mentioned a propos Dante's concept of *gramatica*.

What follows directly from this corporeal fullness of symbolization is that Edenic state that according to Morante is the period of very early childhood. This enchanted condition finds its fulfilment also in the androgynous structure of subjectivity: on the one hand, Manuele is not aware of being male; on the other, he does not consider Aracoeli's womanhood as a trait not allowed to him:

> Per me fra l'unità e i suoi multipli non esistevano confini precisi, così come ancora l'io non si distingueva chiaramente dal tu e dall'altro né i sessi uno dall'altro. Per tutto il tempo di Totetaco, io non ebbi nozione di essere maschio, ossia uno che mai poteva diventare donna come Aracoeli. (p. 1186)

For what concerns Manuele's subjectivity, gender categories are not yet activated and Manuele is not yet inserted within an order that forces him to assume either one in a normativization process acting above all on the body.[15]

Quartieri Alti: The Fall into Paternal Order

The Fall away from the maternal Eden of Totetaco into the order of the Father begins with the arrival at the Quartieri Alti. Contrary to Totetaco's fluidity, affectivity, and corporeality, this new space is characterized by a normative order conforming to the model of a society rigidly organized in classes and to its norm that the paradigmatic subject is a male adult belonging to the dominating class. Inserting herself into the tradition of Dante's meditation on language, here Morante creatively adopts the dichotomy between maternal and paternal: Dante's opposition between vernacular and Latin becomes, in *Aracoeli* at the moment of entrance into the Quartieri Alti, the opposition between Italian and Spanish.[16] This linguistic normativization is accomplished and eventually leads to the catastrophic evolution of the novel's main characters: whereas Aracoeli abandons Spanish and surrenders to Zia Monda's apprenticeship to become a lady (which Morante ironically calls 'tirocinio da signora'), not only does she return to Spanish during the arguably positive anarchic phase of her second pregnancy, but her body also expresses through her illness a paradoxical rebellion that is both passive and self-destructive.[17]

Things end up almost equally badly for Manuele: forced to relinquish his Edenic language of Totetaco and his originary androgyny, he seems to adapt well to the new order but eventually initiates a series of acts of resistance, which recover the originary attachment to the mother's breast. Paradigmatic is the scene when Manuele tries to suckle it after the birth and death of his sister: 'E non esitai: badando a non destarla, rampai vicino a lei sul letto, attaccando al suo capezzolo le mie labbra ingorde' (p. 1301). After Aracoeli's death, Manuele develops a melancholia that on the one hand is fixed on the lost mother and on the other is pushed to reproduce the trauma of abandonment in his sexual intercourses, which are characterized by an oral aspect, in Freudian terms, that is clearly experienced as a substitution for the relationship with the mother's breast. This aspect is evident in the scenes of oral sex between Manuele and his young, paid lovers (p. 1159) and in the oniric encounter with his uncle Manuel (p. 1175).

Linguistically, Manuele's disturbed subjectivity corresponds to a reduction of Spanish to a merely semiotic element à la Kristeva, that is, it is mere sound, rhythm, and affection as in the lullabies of childhood, and is severed from the semantic field (and indeed at the beginning of his journey to Spain, Spanish is for Manuele 'poco più che un rumore incomprensibile'; p. 1064). Furthermore Manuele's pathological state also affects his use of Italian: as soon as he enters the completely unaffective world of the fatherly grandparents, his speech loses fluidity and fragments itself as the boy is affected by a stutter which he will get rid of only after his grandparents' death.

Back to the Origins: the Journey to El Almendral

The trip to Andalusia, which is transfigured into a sort of Dantesque realm of the dead, initiates the third moment of the novel. Manuele's journey represents the search not only for his lost mother but also for a memorial substratum that would allow his Edenic childhood in Totetaco to emerge again. For the protagonist, the choice itself to go on this journey (see pp. 1043–48) equates to getting out of a deep amnesia (pp. 1044–45).

This act of recollection is explicitly deemed the only practicable form of 'a carnal resurrection of the dead' (p. 1049), and the journey to Andalusia has the primary goal of recovering bodily memory and a bunch of sensations long since lost. Contrary to Manuele's previous pathologic experiences, which are symptoms of his condition as a melancholic subject, the journey allows him to move to a further stage, which enhances a veritable re-elaboration of the suffered loss and is attained through the retrieval of the semiotic dimension. This re-elaboration is made possible through several dreams and visions, which allow Manuele to meet his dead uncle and mother. A common pattern of these meetings is the striking tension between Manuele's rational and philosophical language discussing political and metaphysical issues, and the affective, 'semiotic' language spoken by his two relatives. This happens for instance when Manuele compares human existence with that in the *Lager* (concentration camp) and the uncle Manuel derides him lovingly, claiming that he doesn't understand his nephew's language. In a sort of affectionate joke, the word *Lager* is turned into the babble 'LAG LAG' by the uncle, who reproaches his nephew for not speaking the proper language and addressing the wrong divinity: 'Ma che lingua parli tu, Manuel?! E chi è el Señor?' (p. 1256).

'LAG LAG' is exemplary of the maternal aspect of language and evokes the playful sounds of lallation. It contains the first syllable of milk, which recalls the affectivity and sweetness of suckling, but it connects it with a guttural, harsh sound, thereby creating a phonosymbolic oxymoron that could represent the possibility of going beyond binary oppositions. Uncle Manuel's babbling also indicates the necessity of retrieving the maternal language, and thereby calls — in Spanish — Manuele 'Manuel', and God 'el Señor'. Moreover, the passage ends by referring to the immortal sphere of a female Goddess, 'dove regna, irrimediabile, la mia Signora la Macarena, con le lacrime impietrite sulla sua faccia di rosa vermiglia sempre fresca' (p. 1254).

The final stage of Manuele's journey is represented by the encounter with the mother and marks a first point of arrival leading to the retrieval of the lost maternal dimension and to the reconciliation with the most troublesome figure of Aracoeli:

> 'Mama! mama!'
> 'Sono io — mi vedi?'
> (In verità scorgo — o pretendo scorgere — appena una sorta di minuscolo sacco d'ombra. La voce, strappata, mista di risa cortissime, somiglia a un rantolo futile di animale).
> 'Sì. Mi hai sentito?'
> 'Sì, Ma che fatica raggiungerti — raccattare quell'ultimo infimo residuo

d'energia viva nella mia poca polvere — e produrla in questa forma senza forma — che poi dovrò pagarla — ogni forma è una merce che costa'.

'Pagherò io per te, mama'.

'Nada nada — e trasportarmi a questa distanza. Ma tu dove vai'.

'Manca molto, ancora per El Almendral?'

'Non capisco — però da queste parti devo esserci passata — in un'altra agonia'.

'Quale altra?'

'Una. A un certo grado della febbre, il conto si perde — bisogna passare molte agonie, mica una sola — per guarire'.

'Ma si guarisce?'.

'Si dice per finta'.

'E lo Zenit?'

'Quale lingua parli — non ti capisco — ma che devi dirmi — affréttati — è già tardi'.

(Dunque lei pure, come Cenerentola) 'Volevo dirti che tutto mi fa paura'.

'E più di tutto, che?'

'Aver peccato'.

'Tu! E dove hai peccato tu povero niño?!'

'Dovunque, ho peccato. Nelle intenzioni e nei fini e negli atti ma peggio di tutto nell'intelligenza. L'intelligenza si dà per capire. E a me si è data, ma io non capisco niente. E non ho mai capito e non capirò mai niente'.

'Ma, niño mio chiquito, non c'è niente da capire'.

La sento che manda un riso, tenero. E questo è l'addio. Vedo il sacchetto d'ombra afflosciarsi e sciogliersi nel vuoto. (pp. 1427–28)

Whereas scholars have primarily pointed out the infernal character of this meeting, we want, rather, to suggest that in the economy of the novel's narrative Aracoeli's apparition represents a moment of solution and positive progression, which shows significant analogies with the end of Dante's *Commedia*.[18]

The opening invocation, 'Mama! mama!', introduces the bodily and affective component of language and subjectivity that, as we have seen, is radically different from the paternal symbolic realm. Also in this case Manuele uses a term — Zenith — which is paradigmatic of rational language and of an attempt to grasp reality in a geometric and scientific way; and also, as does uncle Manuel before her, Aracoeli complains that she doesn't understand her son. As at the end of *Paradiso*, where Dante the pilgrim's mind must relinquish the rational struggle to understand like the 'geomètra che tutto s'affige | per misurar lo cerchio, e non ritrova, | pensando, quel principio ond'egli indige' (33. 133–35), in the same way, pushed by his mother's complaint, Manuele transforms his merely intellectual attitude into a negative form of affection — fear, guilt, and a sense of persecution — which is typical of the melancholic subject.

It is through this movement that the novel succeeds — like a psychoanalytic therapy– in granting Manuele the possibility of getting rid of the inclination always to define (negatively) his own life and to see it obsessively under the aspect of not being loved and being abandoned.[19] Manuele's complete retrieval of Spanish can be interpreted as a progression of a specifically linguistic nature, which overcomes the stage of a language blocked at the condition of a *languelait* and moves towards a fully grown-up language (which also preserves the bodily aspect of the semiotic). It is not by chance that the protagonist's recovery of Spanish (p. 162) is presented as one of the prophetic signs announcing the forthcoming meeting with his mother.

Returning to Rome: An Epilogue under the Sign of the Father

In the conclusion of *Aracoeli*, the progression of language and subjectivity also coincides with the recovery of the father. The narrative epilogue, in fact, doesn't stop with the reunion with the female and maternal dimension but, after the attainment of the symbolic sphere of maternal language, it stages a confrontation with, and an integration of, the paternal side.

This final achievement is accomplished in the last part of the novel entitled 'TORNARE A CASA', an epilogue suggesting precisely the possibility of recovering affection for the father. The novel takes the reader back to the time of Manuele's teenage years, when the boy ran away from his boarding school near Turin and came back to Rome passing through a destroyed country that had just emerged from the Second World War.

Manuele's search for his father in Rome culminates with the encounter with a man who, like him, is suffering from a sort of melancholic block that chains him to the memory of Aracoeli: after deserting from the Navy, Eugenio moved into an ugly building in San Lorenzo next to the Verano, the cemetery where Aracoeli is buried, and let himself be consumed by alcohol. Eugenio's breakdown clearly symbolizes the breakdown of the Fascist universe and appears as the necessary condition to overcome the binary model that opposes male and female and reserves different and incompatible emotions to each: respect and admiration for the father conceived of as a hero, and love for the mother seen as an almost divine figure.

The reintegration of both spheres is announced by a creature hanging between fairy tale and myth, a hybrid figure whom Manuele meets on the staircase of his father's house where she fell on her back and could not stand up again. This creature is called 'orca', a female ogre, and can be considered emblematic of the extreme and radical operation performed by Morante's novel: as Morante subverted the paternal language by going back to the roots of maternal language and deploying it in her narrative, in a similar way the old hybrid creature is in an upside-down position and manifests her condition through a paradoxical laughter.[20]

Morante's narrative operation and its destabilizing character are symbolized by not only the ogress's laughter, but also by tears as a sign of transformation and release; indeed tears and their relationship with body and language are the last point that the novel makes, and tears are deemed able to break down and smash what the writer calls Manuele's inner dam, 'la sua diga'.

It is through his bursting into tears that Manuele (re-)discovers his love for Eugenio: 'piangevo per amore', he says at the end and imagines that if during their last meeting his father had been able to manifest his affection for him with caressing he could have cried to him 'Ti amo!' (p. 1453). Manuele's hypothetical 'Ti amo!' to his father refers to another theoretical nucleus which, also through the figure of Eugenio, the novel connects to the motif of resurrection, that is, the poetic performance that revitalizes language and recovers the corporeality that is normally lost in the transition from the semiotic to the symbolic stage:

> dette da lui a lei, le due comuni scadute parole riprendevano integro il loro valore primigenio. *Amore* significava proprio AMORE, e così *mio* voleva dire MIO. Nel secolo della degradazione, che noi viviamo, le parole sono ridotte a spoglie esanimi: restituire una parola alla sua vita primigenia si avvicina quasi, per l'atto miracoloso, alla resurrezione dei corpi. (pp. 1339–40; italics in the original)

Morante's narrative seems to associate Manuele's recovery of the love for his father with the possibility of having words emerge again in their affective corporeality, thereby rescuing their originary value, their 'vita primigenia'.

While the novel evokes this possibility, it also focuses on the loss of the affective aspect of language and the traumatic block it produces in Manuele. It shows how the power of poetic language vanishes within the social order that produces an opposition between a maternal language of body and affection and a paternal language of reason and discipline — a separation which coincides with a hierarchical system of mutually self-excluding categories.

Morante's novel indicates that this separation is not unavoidable and that the task of poetic discourse is to trace new possible intersections between different symbolic expressions. The writer seems convinced that a necessary condition for this to happen is to dissolve what her essay *Sul romanzo* calls 'simulacri convenzionali', 'conventional simulacra' of reality. By dissolving these simulacra, her last novel demonstrates at least three points: the monstrous aspects of the contemporary world and of the subjectivities produced by the socio-symbolic order; the way in which this order has progressively subdued the originary component of language and subjectivity; the operations which allow the overcoming of the subjugation that has taken place, and the reintegration of the removed semiotic texture of language.

One could then affirm that the feeling of unease and irritation produced by the novel (which is so common when the reader approaches *Aracoeli* and which was also our experience, at least when we first confronted it) is the symptom that it achieves its aim at a narrative level by not conforming to the reader's expectations stemming from deeply interiorized norms. In this sense the protagonist's condition, though exceptional (that is, exceptionally negative) in its melancholic traits and pathological linguistic expression, reveals an emblematic character and encourages the reader to share Manuele's distance from a normative order and a language that have lost all sort of corporeality: with Manuele, the reader is given the possibility of experiencing and recognizing the blocks that forbid her or him from having access to a different form of language and knowledge of the world.

Notes to Chapter 2

1. Concetta D'Angeli, *Leggere Elsa Morante: 'Aracoeli', 'La Storia', e 'Il mondo salvato dai ragazzini'* (Rome: Carocci, 2003), p. 28. See also Anna Maria di Pascale, *Senza i conforti di alcuna religione*, in *Vent'anni dopo 'La Storia': Omaggio a Elsa Morante. Atti del Convegno (Pisa, 24–26 gennaio 1994)*, ed. by Concetta D'Angeli and Giacomo Magrini, *Studi novecenteschi* [Special Issue], 47–48 (June–December 1994), p. 299. On *Aracoeli* as a dark, hopeless text, see Cesare Garboli, *Il gioco segreto: Nove immagini di Elsa Morante* (Milan: Adelphi, 1995), pp. 193–200.

2. Gary Cestaro, *Dante and the Grammar of the Nursing Body* (Notre Dame and London: Notre Dame University Press, 2003). See also Id., '". . . quanquam Sarnum biberimus ante dentes. . .": The Primal Scene of Suckling in Dante's *De vulgari eloquentia*', *Dante Studies*, 109 (1991), 119–47.
3. Julia Kristeva, *La Révolution du langage poétique: l'avant-garde à la fin du XIXe siècle. Lautréamont et Mallarmé* (Paris: Flammarion, 1974).
4. 'Vulgarem locutionem appellamus eam qua infantes assuefiunt ab assistentibus cum primitus distinguere voces incipiunt; vel, quod brevius dici potest, vulgarem locutionem asserimus quam sine omni regula nutricem imitantes accipimus. Est et inde alia locutio secundaria nobis, quam Romani gramaticam vocaverunt. Hanc quidem secundariam Greci habent et alii, sed non omnes: ad habitum vero huius pauci perveniunt, quia non nisi per spatium temporis et studii assiduitatem regulamur et doctrinamur in illa.'

We quote Dante's *De vulgari eloquentia* and *Convivio* from Dante Alighieri, *Opere minori*, 2 vols (Milan and Naples: Ricciardi, 1984–89), and the *Divine Comedy* from Dante Alighieri, *Commedia*, ed. by Anna Maria Chiavacci Leonardi, 3 vols (Milan: Mondadori, 1991–97).
5. Cestaro, *Dante and the Grammar of the Nursing Body*, pp. 109–34.
6. See Cestaro, *Dante and the Grammar of the Nursing Body*, pp. 154–66. See at least, *Paradiso* 23.55–60 and 121–24, 30.82–90 and 33.106–08.
7. Manuele Gragnolati, *Experiencing the Afterlife: Soul and Body in Dante and Medieval Culture* (Notre Dame: Notre Dame University Press, 2005), pp. 139–60; id., 'Nostalgia in Heaven: Embraces, Affection and Identity in Dante's *Comedy*', in *Dante and the Human Body*, ed. by John Barnes and Jennifer Petrie (Dublin: Four Courts Press, 2007), pp. 91–111; Anna Maria Chiavacci Leonardi, '"Le bianche stole": il tema della resurrezione nel *Paradiso*', in *Dante e la Bibbia*, ed. by Giovanni Barblan (Florence: Olschki, 1988), pp. 249–71; Caroline Walker Bynum, 'Faith Imagining the Self: Somatomorphic Soul and Resurrection Body in Dante's *Divine Comedy*', in *Faithful Imagining: Essays in Honor of Richard R. Niebuhr*, ed. by Sang Hyun Lee, Wayne Proudfoot, and Albert Blackwell (Atlanta: Scholars Press, 1995), pp. 81–104.
8. Erich Auerbach, 'Sermo Humilis', in *Literary Language and its Public in Late Latin Antiquity and in the Middle Ages*, trans. by Ralph Manheim (New York: Pantheon Books, 1965), pp. 25–66. See also Zygmunt Barański, 'I trionfi del volgare: Dante e il plurilinguismo', in *'Sole nuovo, luce nuova': Saggi sul rinnovamento culturale in Dante* (Turin: Scriptorium, 1996), pp. 41–78.
9. Teodolinda Barolini, *The Undivine 'Comedy': Detheologizing Dante* (Princeton: Princeton University Press, 1992), p. 221.
10. See our article '"Attaccando al suo capezzolo le mie labbra ingorde": corpo, linguaggio e soggettività da Dante ad *Aracoeli* di Elsa Morante', *Nuova Corrente*, 55 (2008), 85–123.
11. It is Cestaro who refers to suckling as the 'primal scene' in the case of Dante (*Dante and the Grammar of the Nursing Body*, pp. 49–76), and we believe that the foundational character of this image in *Aracoeli* justifies the same phrase. It should be noted that in *Aracoeli* one also finds the motif, which is significantly less important in the novel, of the primal scene in Freudian terms, that is, the child's looking at the parents' sexual intercourse.
12. On Cixous's concept of *languelait*, see Adriana Cavarero, *A più voci: Filosofia dell'espressione vocale* (Milan: Feltrinelli, 2003), pp. 154–55.
13. Elsa Morante, *Aracoeli*, in *Opere*, ed. by Carlo Cecchi and Cesare Garboli, 2 vols (Milan: Mondadori, 1988–90), II (1990), pp. 1039–1454 (p. 1051–52). Further references to this edition will be given after quotations in the text.
14. It is the so-called physiognomic or pathognomic paradigm, which originates from late eighteenth-century German philosophy; see Sara Fortuna, *Il laboratorio del simbolico* (Perugia: Guerra, 2005), pp. 169–75. For an analysis of the origin of language in Elsa Morante's works, see our 'Allattamento e origine del linguaggio tra la *Commedia* dantesca e *Aracoeli* di Elsa Morante', in *Parole di donne*, ed. by Francesca Maria Dovetto (Milan: Aracne, 2009), pp. 271–303.
15. On the significance of androgyny in Morante's works and in particular in *Aracoeli*, where it is presented as spiritual fullness transcending the binaries of patriarchal order, see Hanna Serkowska, *Uscire da una camera delle favole: I romanzi di Elsa Morante* (Krakow: Rabid, 2002), pp. 158–66, and 'The Maternal Boy: Manuele, or The Last Portrait of Morante's Androgyny', in *Under Arturo's Star: The Cultural Legacies of Elsa Morante*, ed. by Stefania Lucamante and Sharon Wood (West Lafayette, IN: Purdue University Press, 2006), pp. 157–87.

16. See Giacomo Magrini's point that, 'quasi dantescamente', Spanish is considered as 'un volgare opposto alla grammatica', although he claims that in Morante's novel Spanish is both originary and mortally corrupted ('Un paragone con Lowry', in *Per Elsa Morante*, ed. by Giorgio Agamben and others [Milan: Linea d'ombra, 1993], pp. 153–66 [p. 165]).
17. On Morante's particular concept of feminism, see Adalgisa Giorgio, 'Nature vs Culture: Repression, Rebellion and Madness in Elsa Morante's *Aracoeli*', *MLN*, 109.1, Italian Issue (January 1994), 93–116.
18. For a more detailed analysis of this complex passage, see our '"Attaccando al suo capezzolo. . .".
19. On Freud's presence in Morante's works, see Marco Bardini, *Morante Elsa. Italiana. Di professione poeta* (Pisa: Nistri-Lischi, 1999), and id., 'Dei "fantastici Doppi" ovvero la mimesi narrativa dello spostamento psichico', in *Per Elisa: Studi su 'Menzogna e sortilegio'*, ed. by Lucio Lugnani and others (Pisa: Nistri-Lischi, 1990), pp. 173–299. For an interesting analysis of the pre-oedipal condition of many of Morante's characters, and of their marginal position within the symbolic order, see Lucia Re, 'Utopian Longing and the Constraints of Racial and Sexual Difference in Elsa Morante's *La Storia*', *Italica*, 70.3 (Autumn 1993), 361–75, and especially pp. 363–67, where Re indicates significant analogies between Morante's text and Kristeva's paradigm of the semiotic *chora*.
20. On the ogress as a conclusive figure that exemplifies the novel's attempt to combine opposites, with respect to both language and corporeality, see Marco Bazzocchi, *Corpi che parlano: Il nudo nella letteratura italiana del Novecento* (Milan: B. Mondadori, 2005), pp. 129–61.

CHAPTER 3

Seeing and Telling: Anamorphosis, Relational Identity, and Other Perspectival Perplexities in *Aracoeli*

Rebecca West

Manuele, the narrator of Elsa Morante's *Aracoeli*, brings into play all of his senses in recounting the story of his obsessive love for his mother. His earliest memories are rendered in extraordinarily sensual detail, as he explores remembered touches, smells, tastes, and sounds associated with the adored Aracoeli. It is, however, the sense of sight that dominates, and it is to sight, understood both literally and metaphorically, that I want to devote my exploration of Manuele's voyage — again, literal and metaphorical — into the perplexing territories of self-identity, the Other, and the relation between them. In this novel, Elsa Morante problematizes not only sight and relational identity but also the very act of narrating, which, in this novel as in her other works, activates quandaries associated with such issues of continuing relevance in modern and postmodern literature as the function and meaning of point of view, art's truth value, narrational reliability, and the relation between the fictional and the real.

On a literal level, Manuele's bad eyesight and his need for eyeglasses are specified more than once, yet this literal level morphs into a highly resonant metaphorical (indeed metaphysical) significance that permeates the novel. As the tradition has it, to see is to know. But to know how? And to know what? Let me begin with reference to Manuele's first experience of seeing clearly with the aid of his new eyeglasses as he and Aracoeli go out onto the street from the optician's shop:

> Ma il peggio mi aspettava fuori dalla bottega: dove la strada affollata, rutilante di neon e di fanali, m'investí col suo mai veduto spettacolo di orrore. Gli aspetti del mondo avevano preso, ai miei occhi, una chiarezza e un rilievo inusitati, che me li accusavano come un'unica violenza proteiforme. Non m'ero accorto mai, prima, di quanto fossero duri e brutali i segni sulle facce umane.[1]

This episode inevitably recalls Anna Maria Ortese's story 'Un paio di occhiali' that opens the 1953 volume *Il mare non bagna Napoli*. The young girl Eugenia has a similarly negative reaction upon donning eyeglasses and seeing the world clearly for the first time, filled as it is with 'cristiani cenciosi e deformi, coi visi butterati dalla miseria e dalla rassegnazione', she is so overwhelmed by the ugliness she sees that she vomits. Manuele, however, is saved from further trauma at that moment of negative epiphany when Aracoeli quickly removes his eyeglasses. Nonetheless, he has already informed us before he recounts this episode that he himself dates Aracoeli's growing repugnance toward him to when he put on eyeglasses for the first time — 'Io lo so, quando cominciai a piacerle di meno: fu quando, per la prima volta, mi vennero messi gli occhiali' (p. 1254) — thus reversing the emphasis from what he sees to how he himself is seen. The eyeglasses focalize his own ugliness as well as the ugliness of the world around him. Aracoeli insists that he must 'accostumbrarsi' to wearing eyeglasses, yet he invests the banal fact of needing corrective lenses with powerful psychological meaning. As he tries on the glasses, Aracoeli exclaims: 'Non gli stanno bene' and Manuele comments:

> Nella sua protesta, impigliata fra la timidezza e la passione, fiatava un'autentica, furente ferocia; e qua, d'un tratto, una percezione strana mi avvertí che non l'occhialaio soltanto era oggetto della sua rabbia; ma anch'io! Fu un avvertimento inaudito e sensazionale, che mi vibrò nei nervi quasi me lo trasmettesse un'antenna di là da un'artide diaccia; mentre una veggenza lacerante (non certo il senso proprio delle mie pupille, troppo abbagliate dalle lenti nuove) mi esponeva di fronte, in pieno, la faccia di Aracoeli. Per una violenza — si direbbe — fuori dalla sua volontà, essa mi scrutava, e i suoi tratti parevano scomporsi, quasi invecchiati dalla sorpresa e dalla delusione, come alla scoperta d un tradimento. Difatti (io credo) per la prima volta nella nostra vita, essa mi vedeva brutto; [. . .] Senz'altro allora essa dovette rendersi conto, invincibilmente, che suo figlio, crescendo, s'imbruttiva; e che accusarne soltanto gli occhiali sarebbe, in parte almeno, un falso alibi. In verità, sullo stampo primitivo del mio viso, che tanto la innamorava, già cominciava a lavorare quel pollice oscuro e maligno che doveva deformarlo senza rimedio, per la mia eterna disgrazia. (pp. 1257–58)

In this remarkable episode, sight becomes the locus of perceptual shifts regarding the external world, the self, and the Other; what had appeared to be beautiful and wonderfully positive is transformed into malignant ugliness and negativity, and an abyss opens up between Manuele and the now-lost beatitude of perfect love and belonging, which is felt to be as irrevocable as the fracture that rends all of postlapsarian humanity. The 'pollice oscuro e maligno' and the 'eterna disgrazia' resonate with echoes of original sin, just as the references to passing time ('che suo figlio, *crescendo*', or '*cominciava a lavorare* quel pollice'; italics mine) point to the fall from childhood innocence and plenitude to adult guilt and lack that is universally experienced, and that is one of Morante's *leitmotifs* throughout her novels, poetry, and essays.

There are numerous references to Manuele's defective physical sense of sight throughout the novel, just as his eyeglasses are often brought into play, mainly when he removes them in order not to be able to see or, it is implied, to be seen in all of his sheer ugliness. A salient example of his preference for flawed sight occurs in the Madrid airport where he waits for his connecting flight to Almeria. As he searches in his pocket for his eyeglasses, he decides not to put them on since 'non c'è niente da vedere'. He sees a distorted play of lights, a woman who appears to have two heads, and people waiting in line 'che al posto della faccia hanno una proboscide'.

Manuele concludes that 'simili scherzi ottici per me sono effetti abituali già scontati, e non mi curo di smascherarli' (p. 1064, *passim*). (Parenthetically, this passage is followed by a discussion of his lack of understanding of his mother's language, Spanish, which is for him little more than 'un rumore incomprensibile' (p. 1064). This linguistic 'blindness' is, I believe, allied to his flawed eyesight, in that both block the usual straightforward methods by which we comprehend the world and others.) It is, however, to another object that is tied to literal sight — the mirror — that I now wish to devote some attention. The mirror plays a recurrent role in the economy of the novel *Aracoeli* (as it also does in Morante's first novel, *Menzogna e sortilegio*). Presumably a mirror gives back to us an accurate image of ourselves, but it is also the case that we see in it both what we wish to see and what we wish not to see, depending on our perceptual and psychic positioning. 'Mirror, mirror on the wall; who's the fairest one of all?' And, although it is not known for sure how much Lacanian psychoanalytic theory Morante knew, it would seem that she uses his concept of the 'mirror stage' of self-identity in her many elaborations on the mirror. Manuele's earliest memory occurs as a mirror image that returns to him, although he is not sure if he has remembered or imagined it. The mirror itself is described in detail; it has a frame 'vecchia e impallidita nelle dorature, [e] era di uno stile secentesco maestoso', and was in the 'prima stanza clandestina' that Aracoeli and Manuele shared in Rome, following them to their newer and nicer habitation, 'la nuova casa legittima dei Quartieri Alti', subsequently disappearing to an unknown place, perhaps a relative or an antiquarian shop (pp. 1048–49). Manuele's memory is of seeing himself as a baby and his young mother Aracoeli as she nursed him, both reflected in the mirror: 'Secondo certi negromanti, gli specchi sarebbero delle voragini senza fondo, che inghiottono, per non consumarle mai, le luci del passato (e forse anche del futuro)' (p. 1049). Manuele admits that his memory may be a 'pseudo-memoria' or 'uno dei miei ricordi apocrifi', but, he continues,

> Nel suo lavoro continuo, la macchina inquieta del mio cervello è capace di fabbricarmi delle costruzioni visionarie-a volte remote e fittizie come morgane, e a volte prossime e possessive, al punto che io m'incarno in loro. Succede, a ogni modo, che certi ricordi apocrifi dopo mi si scoprono piú veri del vero. (p. 1050)

The salient terms here are 'visionarie' and 'piú veri del vero': vision transcends the merely visual and enters the realm of the visionary and of poetic truth in all of Manuele's remembered experience, so that there is no firm line between the literal and the metaphorical, memory and imagination, waking and dream states. On his flight to Spain in search of his mother's hometown, Manuele learns from a tourist pamphlet he finds in the seat pocket in front of him that the word *almeria* means mirror in Arabic. Almeria is the region in which Aracoeli's town, El Almendral, is located, although Manuele cannot find it on any map. His discovery of the meaning of the word *almeria* leads him to think that this is 'un nuovo segno del destino', since it is a 'chiaro simbolo della specchiera da cui sempre mi riaffiora, viva e presente, Aracoeli' (p. 1087). But he then goes on to comment:

> Sono i soliti prodotti della mia testa in disordine: dove la miscredenza gaglioffa s'impasta con fedi superstiziose; e le opposte visioni si sovrappongono e, nei

> ricordi (autentici? apocrifi?) una stampa lucida e minuziosa, da documentario o da trattato, si avvicenda a sequenze sfocate, abbagliate e mútile. (p. 1087)

Thus his memory of seeing himself and Aracoeli in the mirror may be a true memory or an imagined vision. In either case, it does not help him in the end to find again either his lost mother or himself.

Many critics have underlined Morante's preference for poetic truth over mimetic realism, as she herself did in her essay, 'Sul romanzo', where she wrote:

> *Romanzo* sarebbe ogni opera poetica, nella quale l'autore [. . .] dà *intera* una propria immagine dell'universo reale [. . .]. Non occorre far notare, evidentemente, che *opera poetica* significa, per definizione, un'opera che, attraverso la *realtà* degli oggetti, renda la loro *verità* poetica.[2]

She adds that 'la realtà corruttibile dev'essere tramutata [. . .] in una verità poetica incorruttibile. Questa è l'unica ragione dell'arte: e questo è il suo necessario *realismo*' (pp. 49–50). Manuele's bad eyesight as well as his tendency to mix memories with fantasies are attributes that aid him in perceiving (or at least in attempting to perceive) the poetic truth that lies beyond the surface of reality. Both the visual and the visionary play a major role in his narrative, as they do in Morante's poetics as expressed in her essays as well as in her practice as a writer who is unafraid of embracing such elements as the dream, the fairy tale, anachronism, and space as otherness ('altri tempi' and 'altrove'). In her unpublished talk 'La bestia che parla', delivered at a conference on Gender and Italian Literary History held at New York University in February 2008, the writer Elisabetta Rasy discussed the work of Anna Maria Ortese, Cristina Campo, and Elsa Morante. She pointed out that these three writers' works all share an interest in the 'favola', the 'sogno', and a kind of 'sonnambulismo': 'parole [che] disegnano un altrove, una lontananza', that is, a distance from the concepts of documentary realism, progressive historical linearity, and 'attualità'. Yet, by refusing to 'indossare la maschera del femminile', instead remaining true to their search for poetic truth, these writers' works have not been 'depotenziati dal passaggio del tempo' as the works of many women writers throughout the Novecento who wrote mainly about the position of women in society have been (although these works remain interesting documents of a kind of sociological or political nature). Rasy concludes that in the territories of the 'altrove' in which Morante (and also Ortese and Campo) dwelt, 'lo spazio del testo è luogo e materia di una metamorfosi dove la posizione femminile deve riversarsi nello stile, e la differenza sessuale deve prismaticamente dare luogo all'espansione di ogni altra differenza possibile'.[3] Nowhere is this more clear than in the novel *Aracoeli*, in which Manuele's radical difference — his deep alterity — is represented in great part by means of the perspectival perplexities that attach not only to his way of seeing and imagining the world and others, but also to the way in which he himself is seen (or, at least, how he remembers being seen, first by Aracoeli and then by others in his adult life).

To investigate Manuele's very particular vision, it may prove useful to consider the visual technique known as anamorphosis. Anamorphosis is 'a deformed image that appears in its true shape when viewed in some "unconventional" way', according to Webster's Dictionary. In general, there are two forms of anamorphosis: oblique and catoptric. In the first form, the image in question must be viewed from a position that is not the usual 'from the front' and 'straight-on' position from which images are most conventionally viewed. In the second form, the image must be viewed through a distorting mirror. Although anamorphosis has some practical applications, such as road markings, which drivers must view from the 'unconventional' position of a shallow angle, or cinematic anamorphosis, which squeezes the image horizontally, and then subsequently 'unsqueezes' it back to its wide-screen size, anamorphic designs have been employed historically as an artistic technique for creating secret images that hid erotic or politically sensitive messages. Popular among Early Modern and Baroque artists, anamorphic images were also quite often playful, and aided in creating an element of surprise and delight for viewers, much like *trompe-l'œil*. Most applicable to Manuele's way of seeing are the elements of unconventionality and distortion inherent in anamorphic effects. He is incapable of perceiving himself or his mother Aracoeli 'straight-on', but rather he must navigate through the distortions of memory as well as the limitations of bad eyesight by taking on and taking off corrective lenses, by seeing through a glass darkly, or by giving himself over to the inner eye of dreams and fantasies. How does this thematically elaborated anamorphosis, expressed in the literal 'bad eyesight' of Manuele, in the mirror theme, and in the interplay of memory and fantasies, tie in with broader issues of narrational point of view and representation? Here, I believe that a brief consideration of *the* proto-modern novel *par excellence*, Cervantes' masterwork *Don Quixote*, may help to unearth the importance and relevance of Morante's novel to the development of the genre as it stood in the latter years of the twentieth century, and as it continues to evolve in the twenty-first.

In her essay 'Sul romanzo', Morante listed Cervantes among her favourite novelists, and in another essay, 'I personaggi', Don Quixote is one of the three 'personaggi fondamentali, i quali rappresentano, per l'appunto, i tre possibili atteggiamenti dell'uomo di fronte alla realtà'. She defines Don Quixote as the type for whom 'la realtà non lo soddisfa e gli ispira ripugnanza, e lui cerca salvezza nella finzione'.[4] Morante's other two types are Achilles and Hamlet, the first finding reality fresh, vivacious, and completely natural, the second feeling repugnance for reality as does Don Quixote, but unable to find salvation in fiction, and choosing instead non-being. She notes that there can be 'hybrid' characters, made up of attributes taken from two or more of these basic types. Manuele is most like Don Quixote in his repugnance for reality and his search for salvation in fantasy and apocryphal memory (in fiction, in short), although he also shares attributes with Hamlet in his push toward self-obliteration. In Cervantes' novel, there are many characters who are particularized by attention to their eyes, which are often weak, deformed, or missing. According to Roberto González Echevarría, this results in an 'anamorphic' character such as Pandafilando, the cross-eyed giant who is a disproportionate and deformed being (owing to his size), anamorphic both in his appearance and in how he sees the world. Ginés de Pasamonte is also cross-eyed, and sees the world aslant rather than 'straight-on'. I do not have the space here to present the subtle argumentation by which González Echevarría arrives at the conclusion that this kind of oblique and complex gaze, represented by the crossed eyes of Cervantes' characters, is 'by extension or analogy [. . .] that of the modern author',[5] but the following portion of his summing up of his claim is very clear:

> Being cross-eyed, then, may be called the modern condition of artistic or literary vision: double, distorting, anamorphic [. . .] it is the new model for being, in conflict with and within itself, capable of seeing up close and afar at the same time, like a dialogue of interior visions that cannot be resolved or harmonized. It is moreover [. . .] a being driven by desire.[6]

Manuele is not literally cross-eyed; in fact, he is 'miope e presbite al tempo stesso' (*Aracoeli*, p. 1060), but his weak eyesight similarly brings to him conflictual, inharmonious images, both close and far away, and his is an existence utterly driven by desire.

Pirandello's radically modern novel, *Il fu Mattia Pascal*, also makes use of the metaphor of deformed eyes. Mattia Pascal is characterized by his wandering eye, which singles him out and marks him as different, both seeing and being seen in ways that men with normal eyes are not. More recently, the writer Patricia Highsmith, who has been called 'one of our greatest modernist writers' by Gore Vidal, has created works in which many readers and critics detect a warped or skewed view of reality. Accused by her own mother of not facing the world 'Highsmith replied that she did indeed view the world "sideways", but since the world faces reality sideways, sideways is the only way the world can be looked at in true perspective'. 'The problem', Highsmith said, 'was that her psychic optics were different to those around her'.[7] In Cervantes, in Pirandello, in Highsmith, and in Morante, the dilemmas associated with modernity — the loss of foundational certainties, the fracturing of the self, and what can be called (with a historically resonant but somewhat out-of-date term) alienation, are reflected in the very details of their texts, as the narrationally 'unconventional' perspective needed to decipher reality is embedded in the narration itself by means of the perspectival entanglements generated by their characters' aslant, off-skew looks (both in the sense of 'sguardo' and of 'apparenza'). In her reading of *Aracoeli*, Anna Maria Zampolini interprets the fractured, distorted, and discontinuous images that characterize Manuele's perspective as indicative of '*ciò che è stato disgregato*' (italics are Zampolini's), and she links this concept of disgregation to 'il tema affine dell'incapacità di percepire la continuità di una storia o la saldezza di un'identità'.[8] In the same article, Zampolini writes that 'lo sguardo di Manuele pare evocare un mondo in mutazione incontrollata, sia quando egli da adulto toglie gli occhiali, sia quando da piccolo li mette per la prima volta'.[9] Yet, although art is 'il contrario della disintegrazione' for Morante (at least when she wrote the essay 'Pro o contro la bomba atomica' in 1965), this does not mean that art cannot express within its integrative structures the forces of disintegration — whether corporeal, psychical, or social — as they act upon individuals and human collectivities. Her last novel, *Aracoeli*, reflects more intensely than her earlier novels the shattering power of those forces, and I believe that it remains an open question whether the book is fundamentally an expression of defeat of long-held beliefs in the vitalistic, integrative essence of art, no matter how tragic or fractured the content, or a sort of last challenge to the downward, disintegrating pull of age, disillusionment, and the silence of death. (I think that the same sort of question can be asked about Pasolini's *Petrolio*.)

The theme of vision can be linked to other salient preoccupations in *Aracoeli*, which include most intensely the relationship between the mother and the child, and the construction of self-identity. A useful approach to this link can be found in Adriana Cavarero's work on relational identity, developed extensively in her book *Tu che mi guardi, tu che mi racconti: filosofia della narrazione*. As her very title indicates, looking at and narrating are inextricably bound up one with the other in the construction of identity. According to Cavarero, identity is always relational, in that we depend on how we are seen and then recounted by others as we develop a sense of ourselves. Attempting to construct and to narrate ourselves without this relational element is doomed to failure, for we cannot reach a hold on *who* we are, but only on *what* we are (based on social or biological or national characteristics) without the reflecting mirror of others who are close to us, who love us, and who see us in our uniqueness and complete differentiation from any other human being. The mother is the first giver of the look, 'lo sguardo', that sees the child as a unique *chi*, and thus she is also the first 'other'. Cavarero sums up:

> Fin dalla nascita ciascuno, in quanto è un esistente unico, mostra agli altri *chi* è [. . .]. Il carattere espositivo e quello relazionale dell'identità sono perciò indisgiungibili: si appare sempre a qualcuno, non si può apparire se non c'è nessun altro [. . .] oltre a essere colei da cui l'esistente viene, la madre è anche l'*altra* alla quale, per prima, l'esistente appare.[10]

Just as Manuele's literal sight is flawed, and just as the mirror reflects possibly fictional images that have their origin in fantasy rather than in brute reality, however, so too relational identity for Manuele is infused with ambiguities, doublings, and even gender confusions. In *Aracoeli*, it is clear that Manuele's mother's perception of him as unique and irrepeatable (as well as beautiful) is the foundation of his sense of self-identity, and that this sense of self-identity begins to fracture and dissolve upon the loss of Aracoeli's positive looking at and recounting of his being. His extreme solitude as an adult contributes as well to his sense of non-identity or negative identity, and his only recourse is to his memories, which by his own admission are often apocryphal, and to outright fantasies. These perplexities of identity cluster primarily around his relationship with Aracoeli, but they extend to his ostensible 'double' — his uncle Manuele — and to his stand-in mother, the servant Daniele, among others. They are also tied to his own 'maternal' feelings towards those who evoke his tenderness. At different moments in his narrative he feels himself to be a doll, an extension of his mother's body, a child in a man's body, a man who should have been a woman, a mother, an ugly, awkward, unloved homosexual or 'deviant', and an outcast without any place in which he is able to feel at home or at ease. Is Manuele, as Zampolini argues, incapable of internalizing 'a solid identity', a unified sense of his own whoness? Is the ultimate origin of his fractured sense of himself to be found in his mother, whose own identity is profoundly unstable? Whether explainable by means of a psychoanalytic approach, or a metaphysical one (the loss of prelapsarian wholeness that is inevitable for the entire human race), Manuele's shattered self cannot be entirely clarified or healed by recourse to grids or systems of explication, including that of relational identity, for the terms of his self-presentation through self-narration are bound up in ambiguity, distortion, and the blurring of the line between literal vision and transformative visions. In Sharon Wood's analysis of *Menzogna e sortilegio* and of *L'isola di Arturo*, she highlights the thematic and stylistic techniques by which Morante expresses her view of the profoundly mysterious and ultimately unreachable essence of identity, and her conclusion applies as well to *Aracoeli*:

> Morante [. . .] cannot be classified simply as either straightforward realist or lucid insomniac. Her perception of the instability of the subject is reflected in a narrative in which ambiguity and uncertainty provides [*sic*] the dynamic both of text and subjectivity. If narrative becomes the mirror to reflect not so much the world as the mind-in-the-world, then that mirror is indeed bewitched.[11]

In the last brief part of this essay, I would like to suggest some ways of thinking about the broad question of Morante's placement along the continuum known as 'writing by women'. Although Morante enjoyed critical attention by some prominent male literary critics during her lifetime (Sgorlon, Garboli, Venturi), it was only after her death in 1985 that more widespread and intense analyses of her work began to flourish, owing largely to the interest of so-called feminist critics both in Italy and abroad. Elisabetta Rasy writes:

> Sono assolutamente convinta che nella emarginazione o nella incomprensione o negli equivoci sperimentati da Morante, abbia giocato un ruolo importante la radicata misoginia della società italiana in generale e quella letteraria in particolare. E tale convinzione è confermata dalla beatificazione di cui [Morante ha goduto] *post mortem*, quando cioè il [suo] vivo e contraddittorio corpo di donna non esisteva più.[12]

This assertion is, I think, applicable to any number of dead women writers who have been 'rediscovered' in recent years by a large number of critics both male and female: discoveries motivated by the feminist passion for restoring women writers to their proper place in the history of Italian literature. Yet Morante does not fit smoothly or unproblematically into the niche defined as 'women's writing'. Her work confounds and frustrates feminist critical approaches, intensifying ever multiplying additional 'perspectival perplexities' of a literary historical or critical nature. Looking back to the reception of another strong and unclassifiable writer, Grazia Deledda, might provide us with some useful analogies. Like Morante, Deledda was essentially an autodidact who could not be comfortably slotted into the prevailing categories of genre or schools of her time: *decadentismo*, *verismo*, *scrittura femminile*. Like Morante, she privileged the theme of motherhood in many of her novels, and this emphasis has led contemporary feminist critics to have trouble with what they perceive to be an 'essentializing' tendency and a definition of Woman and women that is too tied to a patriarchal conception of the proper female role in the family and in society. Such concerns have also entered into analyses of Morante's work in recent times. There is, however, a powerful critique of traditional definitions of maternity in both of these 'bestie che parlano'. I have no way of knowing if Morante had any of Deledda's work in mind as she wrote *Aracoeli*, but I see a possible allusion to it, and specifically to *Cenere*, a novel about filial obsession with the absent mother that resonates strongly with the main theme of Morante's novel.[13] In *Cenere*, the unwed peasant mother Olì gives up her little son Anania, taking him to his father's household and then disappearing. The trauma of what is felt as abandonment by Anania colours his entire existence, and sets him on an endless search for his lost mother, for whom he feels both intense longing and furious anger as he imagines at different times that she is dead, or that she has become a shameless harlot. Before leaving Anania, Olì puts an amulet around his neck, which he wears throughout the novel. In *Aracoeli*, the young mother also puts an amulet around Manuele's neck, after a street gypsy predicts that he will die of love before attaining the age of fifteen. In *Cenere*, after Olì's suicide (which I read as expressing her tenacious love of freedom and self-determination more than self-sacrifice; see Heyer-Caput for a similar reading),[14] Anania has an epiphany:

> Come un velo gli cadde dagli occhi; egli vide tutta la meschinità delle sue passioni, dei suoi odi e dei suoi dolori passati. Egli aveva sofferto perché sua madre aveva peccato, perché lo aveva abbandonato ed era vissuta nella colpa! Sciocco! Che importava tutto ciò? Che importavano queste sfumature nel quadro grandioso della vita? Non bastava che Olì lo avesse fatto nascere, perché ella rappresentasse la più meritevole delle creature, la madre, ed egli dovesse amarla ed esserle riconoscente?

These words of Anania are presciently similar to Luisa Muraro's concept of maternal authority — that is, the need to recognize the mother as the first 'author' of all human beings — as elaborated in her philosophical study, *L'ordine simbolico della madre*.[15] Anania finally opens the amulet, a little sack that he had worn around his neck all his life, and discovers nothing but ashes, 'cenere annerita dal tempo', which he suspects may be 'l'avanzo di qualche ricordo d'amore di sua madre'. He then posits that the ashes are 'un simbolo del destino. Sì, tutto era cenere: la vita, la morte, l'uomo; il destino stesso che la produceva'. But, in an uplifting final sentence, Deledda writes that 'egli ricordò che fra la cenere cova spesso la scintilla, seme della fiamma luminosa e purificatrice, e sperò, e amò ancora la vita'. Morante makes a similar connection between the amulet, love, and death: the little wooden figure of a man holding up a little bow over its head was a 'garante della [mia] vita' for Manuele, and Aracoeli's faith in its power consecrated his own faith in it. In the 'last summer of his childhood', he throws it into a trash bin, and he comments that 'non c'è dubbio che la mia intenzione, in quel gesto, era di rinnegare Aracoeli, e di amputarmi da lei, e del mio troppo amore, come di un oggetto di vergogna'. But he also notes that his gesture of denying Aracoeli was also a way of consigning himself to his own death: 'Ma chi era, da sempre, l'amore mio? e chi, dunque, la mia morte? E quale gioco sia questo, di ripudiare una femmina infame, nell'atto stesso in cui, come un martire, le si getta ai piedi la propria vita?' (*Aracoeli*, p. 1066). Both Anania and Manuele are in thrall to conflicting emotions towards their mothers, who hold the key to life and to death. These 'phallic mothers', of enormous psychic power, are far from the passive, self-sacrificial mothers of tradition. They are the positive givers of life, but they are also transgressive, abject, 'female grotesques', as Mary Russo defines and uses this category in her eponymous book, and profoundly mysterious figures of the Other in which our own inherent 'otherness' is confusedly reflected. Along with Manuele, we see his mother 'anamorphically', sometimes as a distorted and grotesque figure, sometimes as a vision of absolute beauty. The perplexities generated by this moving and disturbing last work originate in and put into question the human ability to see and, in seeing, to understand our existences and the world in which we live them. Morante leaves us with more questions than answers, which is the legacy of the greatest writers, of which she is one.

Notes to Chapter 3

1. Elsa Morante, *Aracoeli*, in *Opere*, ed. by Carlo Cecchi and Cesare Garboli, 2 vols (Milan: Mondadori, 1988–1990), II (1990), pp. 1039–1454 (pp. 1258–59). Further references to this edition will be given after quotations in the text.
2. Elsa Morante, 'Sul romanzo', in *Pro o contro la bomba atomica e altri scritti* (Milan: Adelphi, 1987), pp. 44–45.
3. All quotations are taken from an unpublished manuscript of 'La bestia che parla'.
4. Morante, *Pro o contro la bomba atomica*, both quotations from p. 12.
5. Roberto González Echevarría, '*Don Quixote*: Crossed Eyes and Vision', *Cervantes' 'Don Quixote': A Casebook*, ed. by Roberto González Echevarría (Oxford: Oxford University Press, 2005), pp. 217–39 (p. 227).
6. González Echevarría, p. 228.
7. Quoted in Andrew Wilson, *Beautiful Shadow: A Life of Patricia Highsmith* (New York and London: Bloomsbury, 2003), p. 130.
8. Anna Maria Zampolini, 'Aracoeli: Morte di Narciso', in Gruppo la luna, *Letture di Elsa Morante* (Turin: Rosenberg and Sellier, 1987), pp. 55–58 (p. 55).
9. 'Aracoeli: Morte di Narciso', p. 175.
10. Adriana Cavarero, *Tu che mi guardi, tu che mi racconti: Filosofia della narrazione* (Milan: Feltrinelli, 1997), p. 32.
11. Sharon Wood, 'The Bewitched Mirror: Imagination and Narration in Elsa Morante', *The Modern Language Review*, 86.2 (April 1991), 310–21 (p. 321).
12. Rasy, 'La bestia che parla'.
13. Quotations are from the online version of *Cenere* that is available at <http://www.liberliber.it>.
14. Margherita Heyer-Caput, *Grazia Deledda's Dance of Modernity* (Toronto and London: University of Toronto Press, 2008).
15. Luisa Muraro, *L'ordine simbolico della madre* (Rome: Editori Riuniti, 1991).

CHAPTER 4

Resisting Paranoia: Poesis and Politics in *Aracoeli*

Florian Mussgnug

> Then it is easy to dance, for the thought
> of death is a good dancing partner
>
> SØREN KIERKEGAARD[1]

How does literature contemplate the complexity of ordinary life? In her essay *Sul romanzo*, Elsa Morante gives a surprising answer:

> Al momento della sua massima attenzione verso le cose reali (al momento, cioè, in cui si dispone a scrivere) lo scrittore dovrà fare il silenzio intorno a se stesso, e liberarsi da ogni schema culturale, da ogni feticcio, da ogni vizio conformistico.[2]

True literature invites silence; it resists rules, defers knowledge, and suspends meaning. There is a crude, rhetorical force to Morante's polemic against cultural conformism, but her call for silence is subtle, unexpected, and, it seems to me, deeply unsettling. When a writer chooses silence, she renounces her place at the centre of life and goes in search of a deeper, hidden truth: 'Col puro esercizio delle parole — dove queste parole non siano confidate dalle cose, e discusse attraverso il dialogo con le cose — si potrà magari combinare un artificio elegante; ma non si inventa nulla'.[3] But is literature ever completely disentangled from other human affairs? How can the art of writing — with its many allusions, its subtle hints and verbal gestures, its ways of engaging our knowledge of the world, our sense of inquiry, and our desire for interpretation — survive the awareness that art discloses nothing, that it is a path towards silence, which offers no value or guidance? In Elsa Morante's last novel, *Aracoeli*, there is no revelation. Literature does not tell us what do next. It is simply there, hanging in the air like the memory of an old mood. This is not to say that writing has become a form of meaningless play. On the contrary, what could be more important than the obliquity of an unexpected, prolonged silence?

First and Last Words

Aracoeli begins with the nostalgic recollection of a period of unspeakable (and unspoken) happiness. Before language, there were the unconscious satisfactions of early infancy: emotionally abundant times without coherent verbal expression.

Before words, there were experiences that escaped the language of adults, memories that could only be prompted by physical experience. 'Non è stata una trascrizione astratta della memoria a restituirmi le sue primissime canzoncine, già seppellite, ma proprio la voce fisica di lei, col suo sapore tenero di gola e di saliva'.[4] Totetaco, the mysterious, enchanted kingdom of childhood, offers shelter to mother and child, and grants them a joyful language of laughter and song, which barely crosses the boundaries of articulation:

> Mi torna all'orecchio una canzoncina speciale delle sere di plenilunio, della quale non volevo mai saziarmi. E lei me la replicava allegrissima, sbalzandomi su verso la luna, come per fare sfoggio di me verso una mia gemellina in cielo:
>
> > Luna lunera,
> > cascabelera,
> > los ojos azules,
> > la cara morena.
> > (*Aracoeli*, p. 1039)

Lullabies, with their steady rhythm and simple melodies, settle the child to sleep and dispel his fears of darkness and the unknown. But this is only one of their many functions. As Marina Warner remarks, cradle songs also calm the singer; they can bring time to a standstill and create an atmosphere of warmth and comfort, of uneventful atemporality:

> Space and time coincide in the lullaby: the place where the song is sung, that secure place of the breast, the lap, the crib, intersects with the dreams and forebodings of the future, drawn by the singer from the blank of the infant's life.[5]

According to Kaja Silverman, the mother's voice acts as an 'acoustic mirror', a natural frame for the child's first experience of himself and of his relation to the outside world.[6] Unlike Jacques Lacan's mirror phase, this description of early childhood does not postulate individual separateness as a precondition for identity, expressiveness, and thought. For the infant, self-recognition does not start when he sees himself in the mirror as separate from his mother, but when he joins her in a tender, comforting duet of crooning, cooing, and song. Manuele's insistence on visual memory and on the alleged authenticity of images therefore reminds us, paradoxically, that every attempt to evoke the child's original relation to the maternal body is inevitably based on revision and reinscription. Memory is not simply a recovery of the past, but a re-presentation that involves the distortion and displacement of earlier desires — a manipulation that is unconscious, but always purposeful and deliberate. When Manuele recalls his earliest memories — the infant held by Aracoeli and reflected in a large mirror — his vision, *pace* Lacan, is already tainted by shame, uncertainty, and nostalgic desire:

> Secondo certi negromanti, gli specchi sarebbero delle voragini senza fondo, che inghiottono, per non consumarle mai, le luci del passato (e forse anche del futuro). Ora, la primissima visione postuma di me stesso, che fa da sfondo a tutti i miei anni, si presenta alla mia memoria (o magari pseudo-memoria?) non direttamente ma riflessa dentro quella specchiera, e inquadrata nella nota

> cornice. [. . .] Siamo, difatti, soli noi due nella camera; e sono io quel lattante dalla testolina nera, che ogni tanto leva gli occhi verso di lei. (*Aracoeli*, p. 1049)

Uncertainty also affects Manuele's memories (or pseudo-memories?) of the language of childhood. 'Learning to talk', writes Adam Phillips, 'entails keeping alive the inarticulate self [. . .]. As the young child becomes gradually more verbally coherent — less impressed by her uncivil self — she is forever crossing and recrossing the borders of articulation'.[7] For Manuele, however, the delightful to and fro between wordlessness and language soon becomes a traumatic experience of exclusion and loss. Bourgeois education — the dreaded 'condizione borghese [che brucia] la pelle, come un marchio di razza inferiore' (*Aracoeli*, p. 1391) — puts an end to primordial harmony, turning mother and son into dilettante speakers, into amateurs of the sentence. Gradually, grace turns into ugliness, and the joyful play with syntax and diction becomes a frustrating experience of inadequacy. Spanish, the language of infancy, is replaced by the new idiom of the 'Quartieri Alti' and thus transformed into a buried, repressed language, which Manuele, the adult, is no longer able to understand.

> Questa parlata doveva pure suonarmi chiara nei giorni che, analfabeta, imparavo le prime canzoncine di Aracoeli; ma in seguito — salvo il ritorno ossessivo di quelle canzoncine da culla — essa è piombata in un qualche impervio, oscuro dirupo della mia conoscenza. E adesso il rumore quasi estraneo, intorno al mio scalino solitario, mi si rivolta in una nostalgia negativa, di rigetto, come lo stormire di un albero abbattuto a un passero che, prima, ci teneva il nido. (p. 1065)

As Manuele discovers during a stay with his grandparents, there is no way back to the less resourceful but emotionally abundant time of early childhood. Fear and humiliation can make it difficult to speak, and wordlessness can be a powerful defence against shame. Even deliberate silence, however, does not connect us with the experiences of the pre-linguistic self. Manuele's sudden, unsettling speech impediment — the experience of being struck dumb — is an incomplete reversal and a tragic parody of the child's formative path from inarticulacy to fluency: a loss of words without the delights of pre-linguistic expression.[8] Many years later, in one of his most tormented inner dialogues, Manuele looks once again for words to describe the happiness of his inarticulate childhood self. In the mind of the 43-year-old, the journey to Spain becomes a promised return to Totetaco, the lost domain of a necessary, universal language of grace: 'Bisogna dire che esisteva una parentela stretta fra tutte le cose: tutte apparentate dalla luce. Era un segno universale grandissimo, ma delicato' (*Aracoeli*, p. 1183). For a brief moment, the novel seems to endorse this fantasy: when Manuele arrives at El Almendral, he suddenly finds himself able to communicate in the lost idiom of his early childhood: 'E il vecchio non tarda affatto a capirmi' (p. 1429). But Manuele's achievement appears in a very ambivalent light. As Sara Fortuna and Manuele Gragnolati point out, Spanish is both the language of Manuele's mother and his *languelait*, his primordial, pre-oedipal mother tongue.[9] But Spanish is also a public language, and its apparently natural association with unique, personal memory presupposes collective linguistic practice. Like the proper name 'Muñoz Muñoz', the language of childhood is both tantalizingly familiar and, because of its dependence on organized public life, frustratingly alien. As the old man in El Almendral remarks, with a laconic smile: 'Qua in giro tutta la gente porta questo cognome' (p. 1430).

Like Manuele's idea of a harmonious and universal, prelapsarian language, his overwhelming desire for the maternal body needs to be understood as a retroactive fantasy: a powerful myth, supported by an aura of nostalgia and pathos.[10] Throughout Morante's novel, the ghost of Aracoeli — 'la mia ragazza Aracoeli' — appears to her son in different visions, finally as a mocking, disembodied voice: 'appena una sorta di minuscolo sacco d'ombra' (p. 1427). But this imagined metamorphosis is not the most disturbing of Aracoeli's transformations. During their final encounter in a Roman hospital, days before Aracoeli's death, Manuele sees his mother as a body devastated by violence and pain, a wretched animal, blind to its human surroundings and almost offensive in its absolute helplessness:

> E la faccia, chiusa fra le bende, appariva tanto rimpicciolita da rendersi quasi irriconoscibile. Smangiata dalla magrezza, fra gli zigomi prominenti e il mento minuscolo, somigliava al muso triangolare di una bestiola. E al pari delle bestiole inselvatichite quando cadono inferme, sembrava assente a tutto l'universo fuorché al proprio male. (p. 1415)

Aracoeli's atrocious suffering demands an explanation. Like the four bourgeois observers gathered around the deathbed, Morante's reader feels compelled to articulate a response, to transform Aracoeli's dying into a meaningful event. But Eugenio's predictable 'amore mio, amore mio' and Manuele's hesitant and self-conscious 'Mama mama' are as inadequate and superficially ritualistic as Raimonda's helpless anguish or the false optimism of her acquaintance, 'la sua amica dal sorriso egizio' (p. 1415). Only Aracoeli's mother, an inscrutable peasant woman sitting by herself in silence, does not betray the meaningless agony of the dying woman. Like the mother of Manuele's childhood memories, she expresses herself in few basic utterances, which make no assumption about how the world should be. 'Ah, Manuelito', her only words, bring no consolation and rest suspended, without a response. Aracoeli, in the meantime, has progressed beyond language: 'Ma lei non conosceva più nomi o voci, né si curava di nessuno, intenta a un colloquio elementare impercettibile con se stessa' (p. 1417). Her last words, 'sangre, sangre' resonate like a bleak reflection of the incomplete, fragmented idiom of Totetaco, pointing not towards other words but towards the terrifying reality of the wordless body: 'la nostra materia corporale' (p. 1048).

Empty Transgression

Unlike Aracoeli, Manuele cannot escape language. His existence knows no sublimation, not even the tragic dignity associated with self-destruction. Manuele's journey to El Almendral is an interminable descent into agony, a prolonged dying without any real hope for redemption. By contrast, Aracoeli's death appears — at least in the eyes of her son — like a mythical rebellion against history, a suicide in complete union with nature. The discrepancy between such consolatory fantasies and the real dread of dying is nowhere more evident than in Manuele's celebration of the mysterious force of his mother's 'beautiful' death: 'È stata la tua misteriosa ambiguità, Aracoeli, che ti ha reso immortale [. . .] Solo una morte prematura può escludere i corpi adorati dai sordidi sepolcreti della norma e salvare la verità dell'assurdo contro i falsi della logica' (p. 1404). We are at the ambivalent core of Morante's novel. Manuele's puerile fantasy of heroic transgression does not capture the true horror of Aracoeli's suffering — its contingency, its arbitrariness. In Manuele's obsessive musings, meaninglessness gives way to a Romantic belief in suicide as the highest realization of the human will; a final, resolute decision to assert the power of the 'I'. For the reader, it is difficult to resist this perspective, since the novel provides no positive model of ethical subjectivity to counter Manuele's nihilistic fascination with self-destruction. And yet, the disturbing beauty of *Aracoeli* hinges precisely on what Manuelito cannot understand and on what Manuele, the adult, refuses to accept: Raimonda is almost certainly right — and she appeals to all the right authorities — when she remarks about Aracoeli that 'quella sua condotta. . . strana degli ultimi tempi era un sintomo. . . una conseguenza della sua malattia' (p. 1441). Aracoeli's suffering is not an act of meaningful resistance or transgression; it reveals nothing but the vulnerability and directionlessness of human life: 'Si direbbe, in realtà, all'epilogo di certi destini, che noi stessi, per una nostra legge organica, fin dall'inizio, insieme con la vita, abbiamo scelto anche il modo della nostra morte' (p. 1056). Manuele's affirmation, right at the beginning of Morante's novel, recalls a basic convention of narrative prose: the idea of meaningful closure, of a sense of an ending, which is implicit from the beginning and which gives order and significance to the plot.[11] *Aracoeli*, however, resists this apparent necessity. Death is repeatedly described as the only absolute source of meaning — 'Solo a quest'atto finale il disegno, che ciascuno di voi va tracciando col proprio vivere quotidiano, prenderà una forma coerente e compiuta, nella quale ogni atto precedente avrà spiegazione' (p. 1056) — but Aracoeli's suffering ends in a disturbing silence, whose meaning remains inaccessible to the narrator. Aracoeli withdraws into a space before language.[12] The lingering movements of Manuele's interminable confession, by contrast, recall the interminable agony of prolonged dying, not the abruptness of violent death. Verbal excess appears to be the only possible response to an inescapable present defined by physical violence, but also by more subtle forms of coercion, domination, and exploitation. Living means being inside language and, therefore, being one with history: 'quello scandalo che dura da diecimila anni'.[13] Morante's reflections on politics, too, need to be understood in this light.

Is *Aracoeli* a political novel? The question, I believe, needs to be answered on more than one level. First, there is the expressionistic force of Morante's descriptions. The 'Quartieri Alti', with their wild array of sycophants, conformists, and hypocrites are a masterpiece of fierce, political satire. As Bruno Pischedda rightly observes, a few, well-chosen words are sufficient to conjure up the strident pomp of Fascist Rome, the belated *fin-de-siècle* puritanism of 1930s Turin, the ambiguity of Milan's post-war bohemia, and the shallow self-righteousness of 1968.[14] Morante's meticulous, often disturbingly deterministic descriptions of characters, actions, and beliefs give the impression of a world over-determined by political ideology — and populated by men and women with an insufficient grasp of politics. Her petty, smaller-than-life characters operate against the background of a vast, deeply pessimistic metanarrative of social decay — a truly epic setting for Morante's bitter parody, which Giorgio Agamben describes as a most extreme form of realism.[15] Seventeen years before the publication of *Aracoeli*, in *Pro o contro la bomba atomica* Morante clarifies the terms of her pessimistic and apocalyptic anthropology with the remark that 'la nostra bomba è il fiore, ossia l'espressione naturale della nostra società contemporanea, così come [. . .] i campi di sterminio [lo sono] della cultura piccolo-borghese burocratica già infetta da una rabbia di suicidio atomico'.[16] The narrative present of *Aracoeli* is suspended between these two paradigms, that is, between memories of Fascist and bourgeois oppression and visions of a contemporary wasteland, accompanied by the sterile, passionless, and meaningless sounds of loudspeaker music:

> Di sopra, esso mi presenta un cielo che non somiglia a una volta d'aria, ma a una crosta di ceneri giallicce, forse depositate da astri in decomposizione già spenti da millennii. E sotto a questo cielo, si stende una regione desertica e rovinosa da macigni, che mi si fa credere, a certi segni esterni, una qualche necropoli fossile di tempi preumani. (p. 1199)

In this bleak, apocalyptic landscape, dominated by violence and desolation, Manuele stands out as a character without recognizable political identity. Indifference to politics is his one distinguishing feature, which links the incongruent parts of his life, and which ties him to his mother, who is repeatedly described as a creature of absolute political ignorance. In striking contrast with the novel's many grotesque masks of power ('Il Notaio', 'La Contessa', 'L'Eccellenza', 'La Doppia Statua') Manuele depicts himself as a victim of history, a beast literally squashed by the violence of the symbolic order:

> La mia natura è negata alla politica e alla storia: miseri e vani i miei tentativi di smentirlo. Io sono un animale schiacciato sulla schiena da una grossa pietra. Con le zampe disperate raspo la terra, e scorgo al di sopra, mezzo cieco, degli azzurri vapori. Non so perché sono incollato alla terra. Non so quale sostanza siano quei vapori. Non so chi mi ha scaricato addosso la pietra. Non so che animale sono. (p. 1217)

Like Manuele's later, heroic vision of Aracoeli's death, this tragic self-portrait manifests an underlying dilemma. Fantasies of sacrifice and alienation are themselves part of the dominant language of power, whose boundaries coincide with the boundaries of meaning. Morante's bitterly ironic plot leaves no doubt that subjectivity — including the desire for redemption — is subordinated to power. Politics, in *Aracoeli*, is not simply what Manuele opposes but also, in a stronger sense, what defines him: it is the very condition of his existence and of his desires. In Manuele's melancholy reflections, this idea of the political manifests itself in a persistent spatial metaphor, the inescapable path of human life: 'Neppure i dodici Angeli della Morte tutti assieme potranno dirottare un mortale dal corso del suo proprio adempimento' (p. 1056). Anarchism — represented in the novel by Manuele's uncle and heroic double Manuel — is mentioned as an apparent alternative, but one that is tragically linked to the nostalgic recollection of an irretrievable past. In Manuele's own fantasies of heroic rebellion, by contrast, utopian longing is invariably haunted by a deeper awareness of the inescapable force of political power. Transgression, according to Manuele, does not lead to a more meaningful system, and self-awareness only makes us more vulnerable to the intrinsic and overt violence of social regimentation:[17]

> Inconsapevoli: questa è la norma voluta. Ma pure, in qualche occasione, una certezza innominata batte alla nostra coscienza con un fragore assordante: come i passi di un esercito straniero in marcia verso i nostri confini per una devastazione inaudita, che non sappiamo spiegarci; mentre sottovoce un spia ci insinua che noi stessi lo abbiamo chiamato. (p. 1057)

When Manuele returns to Rome after the war, he finds the oppressive 'Quartieri Alti' literally torn apart by the greater violence of political change: each of his former neighbours has suffered extreme, often grotesque forms of punishment and humiliation. And yet, there is no relief, no sense of a new beginning. The ideological edifice of Fascism has collapsed, but its trans-ideological kernel survives, decades later, not only in the actual violence of the eternal 'razza propria dei Duci e dei Caudilli' (p. 1423) but also in Manuele's fantasies of conspiracy and persecution. Unlike the caricature-like 'razza borghese' of his childhood, Manuele recognizes the dangers of ideological identification: he maintains a critical distance from the centres of power and an awareness of the complexity of the human psyche. His opposition to ideology, however, appears in itself profoundly problematic. The overzealous, all too literal identification with power in the 'Quartieri Alti' ultimately provokes the collapse of the ideological edifice of Fascism. Its violence, however, survives — paradoxically — in the outsider's fantasies of universal destruction.

Resisting Paranoia

During his long journey to El Almendral, Manuele's awareness of the surrounding world becomes increasingly distorted. Self-reproach — the painful sense of being marked by the ugliness of the despicable 'razza borghese' — is repressed and projected onto a persecutory world, which threatens to engulf and physically destroy him:

> Il vento che corre la città di Almeria diventa adesso, nel mio cervello, i clamori di una moltitudine urlante (slogan? minacce? singhiozzo? kyrie? forse il Generalissimo è morto stanotte? guerriglia a Milano fra i Rossi e i Neri? saltano le banche? bombe contro il Duomo?) E mi s'impone d'un tratto, con panico, una legge geometrica naturale, che i miei sensi ascoltano — non per la prima volta — come una sentenza: di essere io, dovunque mi sposti, il centro dell'universo: il quale infallibilmente gira le sue ruote rabbiose intorno a questo mio punto. Il nodo della croce. L'occhio del ciclone. Non mi resta, allora, che rifugiarmi dentro il letto. (p. 1174)

Auditory hallucinations — the experience of unidentified sounds as invasive, alien voices and the perception of these voices as somehow coming from the 'inside' — are commonly treated as a primary indicator of schizophrenia.[18] Similarly, Manuele's impression of being at the centre of a hostile universe recalls psycho-analytic definitions of paranoia: the unconscious projection of unintegrated psychological content onto an exterior world and its supposedly hostile agents. As

Victoria Nelson has shown, externalization is also a distinctive feature of many literary reworkings of psychosis: 'The barriers between inner and outer, subject and object dissolve so entirely that no boundary remains to protect the ego from the onslaught of this projected, unconscious material'.[19] In *Aracoeli*, this essentially paranoid world-view culminates in terrifying fantasies of annihilation and absolute solitude. When Manuele thinks of his office in Milan, he sees a squalid, desolate world in ruins:

> L'ufficio mi si mostra abbandonato da settimane, mesi, anni. I ragni vi hanno tessuto le loro tele da una parete all'altra. Le scansie, gli schedari e i volumi sono coperti da un soffice muschio di polvere. E le bozze da correggere, rimaste sul mio tavolino, sono mangiucchiate dalle tarme.
> Per me che corro verso El Almendral, i tempi si riducono a un unico punto sfavillante: uno specchio, dentro il quale precipitano tutti i soli e le lune. (p. 1063)

The grandiosity of Manuele's end-of-the-world fantasies — his insistence on a complete breakdown of the self–world relationship — recalls Freud's idea of the profound connection between narcissism and paranoia.[20] Disintegrating cities and collapsing skies reflect anxieties about human mortality and man-made apocalypse, but they also function as bleak, delusional visions of grandeur and omnipotence: masturbatory fantasies. Deprived of all human connections, the self becomes the sole representative of mankind, a final and absolute personification of life, whose death necessarily coincides with complete nothingness.

> Cosi mi finsi, in una 'visione', che la spiaggia oscillasse. Un immenso maremoto scuoteva i fondi del mare singhiozzante e l'arenile e la scogliera. I due prossimi faraglioni si scontravano percuotendosi come due lottatori di pietra. E intanto la piccola luna bianca s'ingrandiva fino alla misura di un sole, prendendo il colore infuocato del solo meridiano. Non era più luna, ma sole; e il suo fuoco incendiava tutto il territorio, scagliandone la sostanza, come da un vulcano, in una volata di faville. Nella lotta, i faraglioni crollavano all'indietro, uno sull'altro. E il primo si levava in una vampa gigantesca e acuta: a questo culmine della mia 'visione', io mi masturbai. (p. 1125)

Set against a background of massive political disappointment, *Aracoeli* oscillates between two opposite and equally disturbing intuitions: a nihilistic sense of directionlessness and profound despair, and the paranoid suspicion that apparently arbitrary phenomena may in truth be part of a sinister, hidden design. Manuele's profound fascination with the absolute evil of bourgeois Fascism — 'la mia famosa INIMICIZIA' (p. 1112) — blurs the boundaries between personal and universal history, and treats society as a single, terrifying conspiracy: 'dai campi di sterminio alle guerre imperialistiche, ai genocidii, alle torture poliziesche, all'assassinio del Che Guevara, ai golpe sudamericani, alle manovre della CIA' (p. 112). Paranoia and the belief in invisible interconnectedness provoke horror, but they are also a source of narcissistic gratification and, paradoxically, of some reassurance.[21] In the violently unjust world of Morante's novel, Manuele's feelings of guilt and his fear of persecution ultimately appear like a desperate defence against meaninglessness. Once paranoid suspicion is ruled out, nihilism remains as the only legitimate response to a profound anguish, which floods into all areas of life.

And yet *Aracoeli* does not end on a note of nihilistic despair. Against the tragic force of existential disappointment — and against its counterpart, the narcissistic *reductio ad unum* of paranoia — Morante sketches a different, less heroic vision of subjectivity. Nostalgia and loss are omnipresent in Morante's novel, but they are often mediated by a melancholic and playful gaze on mortality, by a self-knowledge that is not unduly dismayed by death. In one of the novel's most striking passages, Manuele recalls a childhood fascination with appearances: a belief that the entire cosmos might in truth be a vast game of mirrors, endlessly duplicating an original world, whose existence can only be assumed. The deeper meaning of this fantasy, as Manuele points out, lies in its implications for selfhood and subjectivity; like the sky above us, the transitory shape of our mortal existence is merely a reflection of an original, higher world of forms:

> Io, da ragazzo, certe notti, ero in dubbio sulla reale esistenza delle tante miriadi di stelle che ci appaiono in cielo. Secondo me, forse esisteva solo un'unica stella creata in principio: e moltiplicata all'infinito, per i nostri sguardi terrestri, da un gioco di specchi illusorio. Di quella mia cosmogonia infantile, mi si dà, oggi, una variante autobiografica: dove questa esistenza mia presente in realtà non sarebbe che l'ultimo di una serie di riflessi ingannevoli. L'unica vera mia esistenza starebbe alla sorgente, di là dagli innumerevoli specchi deformanti che me ne contraffanno la figura, come succede nelle fiere suburbane. (p. 1213)

At first glance, Manuele's Neo-Platonic childhood cosmogony seems to affirm the necessity of a single, universal model of human behaviour. At a closer reading, however, it becomes clear that what actually matters to Manuele is not the realm of transcendental forms, but its contingent counterpart, the liberating play of reflections and doubles: 'Può darsi che quell'altra mia biografia sia soltanto immaginaria, un riflesso effimero di questa, ma anche è possibile che questa odierna, invece, sia solo un riflesso dell'altra: la vera. Si dànno, nel campo della luce, simili giochi di specchi' (pp. 1212–13). Inauthenticity — the experience of a precarious and essentially divided self — is not perceived as an obstacle to ethical and political expression, but as a source of liberation and a necessary basis for the invention of new subjectivities. As Manuele's obsession with ugliness shows, the awareness of human transience may culminate in a self-lacerating masochism, in the expectation of a lifetime of grief and guilt. In the final pages of the novel, however, agony gives way to a stoic serenity and a dark and lucid maturity:

> Pare facile, conoscere perché si piange. Ma in realtà, chi volesse, potendo, esaminare il 'seme del pianto' (o di simili moti 'manifesti') si perderebbe — io temo — in un'analisi oscura e confusa, negata a ogni formula chimica. Perché piange Cristo a Getsemani? E Achille, dopo il furto della schiava? E la bambina, che vorebbe un vestito nuovo? E l'amante tradito? E l'assassino? Ogni risposta a tali domande sarebbe — anche se verace — sempre insufficiente e approssimativa. E dunque, è solo per un gioco ozioso che io qui mi provo a scomporre nei suoi elementi il seme di quel mio pianto. (p. 1452)

In Manuele's deliberately idiosyncratic catalogue, suffering and pain appear as unavoidable pressures of nature, inexplicable but not particularly daunting. Mourning still dominates the atmosphere of the novel, but it now appears as a comic acknowledgement — rather than a tragic affirmation — of human finitude. As Simon Critchley points out, paraphrasing Freud: 'Humour has the same formal structure as depression [. . .]. The subject looks at itself like an abject object [but] instead of weeping bitter tears, it laughs at itself and finds consolation therein'.[22] Nothing, it seems, could be more unlike Manuele's earlier, tragic hubris — the hyperbolic and deeply narcissistic world-view of paranoia — than this modest inclination towards self-irony. Even Manuele's perception of death — the mysterious site of his most profound hopes of heroic redemption — is ultimately transformed by this new self-awareness. At the end of the novel, nostalgia and grief appear as transient experiences, parts of a never-ending game of mirrors. Authenticity does not originate from our cultural conventions of mourning, but from the unavoidable forces that precede such conventions: from the suffering that no living creature can escape. What brings tears of compassion to Manuele's eyes is the meaningless, 'natural' life of a nameless dog, and the memory of the 'natural' death of another dog, his childhood companion Balletto, who remains curiously absent from the novel.[23] In Manuele's memory, the two animals blur and their difference becomes insignificant when compared to their shared, inevitable suffering. Death, whatever form it takes, ultimately appears as of a piece with life, thanks to the laconic charm of a writer, who once remarked to Cesare Garboli: 'Sia ben chiaro, che in ogni modo so già cosa fare, quando morirò. Troverete in una busta un biglietto dove ci sarà scritto "Torno subito"'.[24]

Notes to Chapter 4

1. Søren Kierkegaard, *Philosophical Fragments*, trans. by Edna H. Hong and Howard V. Hong (Princeton: Princeton University Press, 1985), p. 8.
2. Elsa Morante, *Pro o contro la bomba atomica e altri scritti*, ed. by Cesare Garboli (Milan: Adelphi, 1987), p. 55.
3. Morante, *Pro o contro la bomba atomica*, p. 56.
4. Elsa Morante, *Aracoeli*, in *Opere*, ed. by Carlo Cecchi and Cesare Garboli, 2 vols (Milan: Mondadori, 1988–90), II (1990), pp. 1039–454 (p. 1047). Further references to this edition will be given after quotations in the text.
5. Marina Warner, *No Go the Bogeyman: Scaring, Lulling and Making Mock* (London: Chatto and Windus, 1998), p. 198.
6. Kaja Silverman, *The Acoustic Mirror: The Female Voice in Psychoanalysis and Cinema* (Bloomington: Indiana University Press, 1988), pp. 76–78.
7. Adam Phillips, *The Beast in the Nursery* (London: Faber and Faber, 1998), pp. 45–47.
8. The incompleteness of Manuele's linguistic regression is also reflected in the description of his grandparents: 'La Doppia Statua era *parlante*, invero, soprattutto dal lato della Nonna, poiché il Nonno si atteneva, in casa, a uno stile taciturno, esprimendo la sua temibile eloquenza principalmente con diversi moti facciali (dell'arcata sopraccigliare e dell'orbita, degli angoli delle labbra e anche del naso)'. (*Aracoeli*, p. 1400; author's italics)
9. See Sara Fortuna and Manuele Gragnolati, '"Attaccando al suo capezzolo le mie labbra ingorde": corpo, linguaggio e soggettività da Dante ad *Aracoeli* di Elsa Morante', *Nuova Corrente*, 55 (2008), 85–123, and especially their reference to Hélène Cixous, *'Coming to Writing' and Other Essays*, trans. by Deborah Jenson, introductory essay by Susan Rubin Suleiman (Cambridge, MA and London: Harvard University Press, 1991).
10. See Mary Jacobus's illuminating discussion of the maternal body and of Freud's concept of 'screen memory' in Mary Jacobus, *First Things: The Maternal Imaginary in Literature, Art, and Psychoanalysis* (New York and London: Routledge, 1995), ch. 1.

11. For a classical expression of this view, see Frank Kermode, *The Sense of an Ending* (Oxford: Oxford University Press, 1967); Barbara Herrnstein Smith, *Poetic Closure* (Chicago: University of Chicago Press, 1968).
12. The mysterious meaninglessness of Aracoeli's death recalls Julia Kristeva's reflections on *chora* as a site of pre-cognitive, pre-verbal drives: 'The semiotic *chora* is no more than the place where the subject is both generated and negated, the place where his unity succumbs before the process of charges and stases that produce him' (Julia Kristeva, *Revolution in Poetic Language*, excerpted in *The Kristeva Reader*, ed. by Toril Moi [London: Blackwell, 1986], p. 94). For a detailed analysis of the Kristevan concept of *chora* in relation to *Aracoeli*, see Fortuna and Gragnolati, ' "Attaccando al suo capezzolo [. . .]" ', and their Chapter 2 in this volume.
13. Elsa Morante, *La Storia* (Turin: Einaudi, 1974), cover-text.
14. Bruno Pischedda, *La grande sera del mondo: romanzi apocalittici nell'Italia del benessere* (Turin: Nino Aragno, 2004).
15. 'Ma, in verità, la parodia [di Elsa Morante] non solo non coincide con la finzione, ma ne costituisce l'opposto simmetrico. Poiché la parodia non mette in dubbio, come la finzione, la realtà del suo oggetto — questo è anzi, così insopportabilmente reale, che si tratta, appunto, di tenerlo a distanza.' (Giorgio Agamben, *Profanazioni* [Rome: Nottetempo, 2005], p. 52)
16. Morante, *Pro o contro la bomba atomica*, p. 99.
17. Morante's deeply pessimistic understanding of bourgeois language — not a socially and historically circumscribed object but a transhistorical force — sets *Aracoeli* apart from her earlier novels. As Lucia Re points out in an important feminist reading of *La Storia*, it is possible to view Useppe's language and behaviour as a 'poetic' alternative to the increasing regimentation of social and political life: 'a sort of oasis, albeit precarious and of all-too brief duration — tucked away secretly within the main discursive body of patriarchy and of the symbolic'. In *Aracoeli*, by contrast, there is no such recognizable figure of positive diversity. See Lucia Re, 'Utopian Longing and the Constraints of Racial and Sexual Difference in Elsa Morante's *La Storia*', *Italica*, 70.3 (Autumn 1993), 361–75 (p. 369).
18. See Louis Sass, *Madness and Modernism: Insanity in the Light of Modern Art, Literature and Thought* (New York: Basic Books, 1992).
19. Nelson Victoria, *The Secret Life of Puppets* (Cambridge, MA and London: Harvard University Press, 2001), p. 110.
20. See David Bell, *Paranoia* (London: Icon Books, 2002).
21. 'In paranoia, the primary function of the enemy is to provide a definition of the real that makes paranoia necessary. We must then begin to suspect the paranoid structure itself as a device by which consciousness maintains the polarity of self and nonself, thus preserving the concept of identity.' (Leo Bersani, *The Culture of Redemption* [Cambridge, MA: Harvard University Press, 1990], p. 189)
22. Simon Critchley, *Infinitely Demanding: Ethics of Commitment, Politics of Resistance* (London: Verso, 2007), p. 81.
23. 'Si dà il caso, infatti, che il quell'istante medesimo si trovasse a passare sotto i miei occhi un cane di nessuno, scompagnato e scondizolante, che fatalmente doveva rievocarmi una rara stagione di amicizia, piuttosto recente e già perduta. E da qui mi si propone una prima, immediata risposta: io piansi, per la memoria del mio cane Balletto.' (*Aracoeli*, p. 1452)
24. Cesare Garboli, *Il gioco segreto: Nove immagini di Elsa Morante* (Milan: Adelphi, 1995), p. 152.

PART II

Psychoanalysis

CHAPTER 5

'The Lover of a Hybrid': Memory and Fantasy in *Aracoeli*

Christoph F. E. Holzhey

Elsa Morante's *Aracoeli* is a novel that disturbs on many different levels. Its narrator Manuele indicates at the beginning that he is engaged in a 'guerra disperata' against his mother Aracoeli, and that his journey to her Andalusian origins is 'un'ultima, sballata terapia per guarire di lei' by digging around her roots, 'frugare nelle sue radici'.[1] What Manuele digs up is not only Aracoeli's past, but also his own, and from his account of the memories, fantasies, and dreams of his childhood and adolescence, mother and son emerge as equally troubled, torn, and disturbed figures. This disturbance on the level of characters is reflected in the novel's aesthetics and imparted to the reader in a way that goes beyond empathic identification. The fragmented novel jumps discontinuously between the time of the 43-year-old narrator and different parts of his life, blurring distinctions and thereby creating seemingly irresolvable tensions between past and present, reality and fantasy. Drawing attention to its own unreliability, the narrative poses its readers the frustrating challenge of sorting and ordering its elements into a coherent story. The novel can appear so disturbing and bleak on the level of both content and aesthetic form that one may wonder how it can be read other than as the desperate document of a disturbed and self-destructive writer, as it has indeed often been read.[2]

Manuele's suggestion that he seeks a cure from Aracoeli through his work of remembering and narration provides a possible answer, especially since his therapeutic attempt is arguably at least partially successful. Halfway through the book, Manuele's memories become ordered in a continuous, chronological fashion, starting with the three phases of life in the Quartieri Alti: 'l'Epoca delle Sorelle' (*Aracoeli*, p. 1265), followed by Aracoeli's second pregnancy and the aftermath of her daughter's death, continuing with Manuele's move to his grandparents, and ending with the final visit to his father. Towards the end, the novel seems to come to a conclusion, picking up many loose ends, telling the fate of the different characters, and, most importantly, leading Manuele to a sort of reconciliation with both mother and father.

However, I would like to suggest that this sense of closure only contributes to what is perhaps the most disturbing dimension of the novel, namely the ubiquity of tensions that are all the more unsettling as they are deployed in a manner that demonstrates their powerful potential and does not leave the reader indifferent. In my reading, the novel not only questions the possibility that Manuele successfully completes his cure, and indicates that the sense of closure at the end of the narrative constitutes the eerie calm before a new storm. It also questions whether such a completion would even be desirable. What the novel proposes instead, and demonstrates through its aesthetic performance, is the constitutive and therefore inescapable role of tensions and paradoxes of desire and pleasure for Manuele's subjectivity and, by extension, also for the novel's vitality.[3]

Although the impression may dominate at the end of reading the novel that Manuele has made progress through the work of remembering during his curative journey, the scattered memories of the book's first half cannot be completely forgotten and need to be integrated into the more ordered and cohesive narrative of the book's second half. What transpires then is that the work of memory stops just before a decisive and particularly dangerous phase in Manuele's life. The book ends with the scene of the final encounter with the drunken father when Manuele is thirteen years old, which must be close to the beginning of his so-called 'mystical crisis'. It is left unclear what this phase is and what precisely precipitated it, and the novel only circles around it, repeatedly referring to it as an important temporal reference point: in the section '*Ciao Pennati*', the narrator refers to an episode that he situates in time by saying that it happened during the war — 'dunque non avevo più di dodici anni' — and in a period 'ancora distante dalla mia successiva *crisi mistica*' (*Aracoeli*, pp. 1146–47); in the partisan scene of the same period, but recounted much later, he was 'ancora immaturo per la mia "crisi mistica" e per i "suicidii", che mi aspettavano di lí a poco' (p. 1215), while at a much earlier point in the novel he says that 'con lo scoppio della pubertà, intorno ai quindici anni [. . .] ebbe fine la mia *epoca mistica*, e con essa quella dei miei *suicidii*' (p. 1127). One can only speculate on what is being left out, and while the suicidal-mystical phase may well have to do with the prophecy that Manuele would be 'morto d'amore prima dei quindici anni di età' (p. 1065), it seems to function like a black hole or an empty centre constitutive for both the narrative and Manuele's subjectivity. This is precisely why the scattered allusions pointing all to the time narrated at the very end of the novel — the encounter with the father and his death a year later — indicate that the sense of closure that Manuele's narrative seems to achieve is precarious and only temporary, dependent upon not extending his memory work to the mystical crisis.

Dangerous as this crisis may have been, there are also indications that Manuele's return to it would have a great potential that is not only to be feared, but may also be more desirable than the cure he envisages. In the opening pages, as he is on his flight to Spain, Manuele notes 'certi fervori mistici' rising to his awareness 'come un risucchio' from his adolescence when he let himself be tempted 'dal suicidio, come da una spedizione rischiosa alla volta di chi sa quali paradisi: tanto più esotici e invidiati perché impossibili' (*Aracoeli*, p. 1061). Similarly ambiguous is the brief comment upon the end of his mystical-suicidal phase:

> Per me la morte, in realtà, era un'altra paura ambigua, come la vita e anche peggio. Non c'erano alternative di speranza. E i miei minisuicidii (tutti fallimentari) erano stati, in realtà, delle tragicommedie, dove la fuga nel cielo

> forse mi serviva da pretesto, mentre la mia vera speranza era di smuovere — straziandomi con le mie stesse mani — l'indifferenza totale della terra. (p. 1127)

While this passage begins with bleak hopelessness, it opens up possibilities of hope through an interpretation from another perspective marked as truer by the expression 'in realtà', namely that of tragicomedy. This reinterpretation invites being extended further to ask what it may mean to read *Aracoeli* not as a suicidal parody of Morante's earlier work, but as a tragicomedy that takes Manuele's memories as 'pretext', while the real hope is to stir the 'total indifference of earth'. What interests me here are not technical questions about the genre, but the indication in the term 'tragicomedy' of a complex combination of pleasure and pain, which has the potential to transmute disturbing experiences into paradoxical forms of pleasure and may be linked, as it is through the context of Manuele's statement, to sexuality.[4]

In the already quoted passage at the beginning of his journey, Manuele in fact wonders whether trying to find Aracoeli is not just a pretext, 'preteso' (*Aracoeli*, p. 1065). Of course, the therapeutic aim that Manuele envisages for this trip is quite the opposite to stirring indifference. It consists rather in becoming indifferent to his mother, 'frugare nelle sue radici finché s'inaridiscano sotto le mie mani, poiché di estirparle non sono capace' (p. 1065). However, what is indeed absurd ('sballata') about his therapy, in a rather precise tragicomic sense, is that it achieves the opposite of what it proclaims to seek: Manuele's journey reanimates his past and brings it to new life. Or, to stay with the image: far from drying it up, his trip waters his past and even fertilizes it. This is not to say that Manuele or the novel fail, but rather that success must be defined in terms not of achieving peaceful closure by integrating the past into a dry, indifferent order, but of unearthing a different, no doubt troubling, but also vitalizing, alternative. For if Manuele does not manage to pull up Aracoeli's roots, it is because they are also his, an inseparable part of his very subjectivity, which seems entirely constituted upon tension, ambivalence, and contradictory desires.

Even before his mother died, Manuele had tried to free himself from her — most visibly by throwing away the amulet she offered to him as protection against the prophecy that he would die of love before reaching the age of fifteen. He recognizes the paradox of this involuntary gesture, through which he hands himself over to the prescribed death of love — of love precisely for Aracoeli and a death that would precisely reunite him with his dying mother. He asks himself: 'quale gioco era questo, di ripudiare una femmina infame, nell'atto stesso in cui, come un martire, le si getta ai piedi la propria vita?' (*Aracoeli*, p. 1066).

Manuele's gesture may appear illogical and irrational, and he himself says that he was cheating against himself, but he also notes that the game has not changed until his adult present. Indeed, there also seems to be a strong consistency in Manuele's actions, sentiments, and fantasies, pointing perhaps to a different kind of logic, beyond binary oppositions and the principle of non-contradiction. His mother often appears to him split into good and bad mother: 'corro dietro alla mia fedele madre-ragazza, e alla sua icona musicante, ricacciando come un'intrusa quell'altra Aracoeli fatta donna, che in realtà mi ha lasciato laidamente orfano ancor prima d'esser morta' (*Aracoeli*, p. 1066). He tries to forget and repress this second mother, but:

> Per quanto io voglia ricacciarla, essa non mi risparmia le sue visitazioni: dove spesso si appaia con la prima Aracoeli, pari a una sua sosia sfigurata. L'una Aracoeli mi ruba l'altra; e si trasmutano e si raddoppiano e si sdoppiano l'una nell'altra. (p. 1067)

Not only does a clean, logical division not hold and the two Aracoelis keep merging in his dreams, fantasies, and memories, but he also recognizes that this is precisely how he loves her: 'E io le amo entrambe: non come uno conteso fra due amori, ma come l'amante di un ibrido, di cui, nell'orgasmo, non riconosce le specie, né capisce le trame' (p. 1067).[5] This passage points to a rather specific model of tension: Manuele contrasts his experience to a tension between two loves, that is, to a tension between two clearly distinct, intelligible, but mutually contradictory entities. What he loves, one might say, is tension itself, the tension in a hybrid that defies recognition and understanding, a tension that is already falsified by applying the clear distinctions of a rational order. Such a hybrid can only be offered to affective and intellectual experience through a narrative of constant transformation, duplication, and substitution, and it can only be approximated and circumscribed through rational language by invoking a wide range of competing theories and interpretations.

The account that the novel gives of Manuele's childhood resonates so well with psychoanalytic theories of infant development that it is hard to resist identifying the peculiar logic of hybrid tension with a pre-oedipal, imaginary, or semiotic phase preceding the entry to the symbolic order of language.[6] The novel marks this transition in terms of the shift from his mother's tongue — Spanish — to the linguistically more complex Italian of his father, and the four-year-old's move from his birthplace Totetaco to the Quartieri Alti, where he is banished from his mother's bedroom (p. 1208) and gets his curls cropped in a rite which was to celebrate both his promotion to manhood and the legitimate establishment of his family, and which he remembers as a 'sacrificio cruento' (p. 1204). Emblematic for this transition to the perhaps all-too clearly oedipal and castrating symbolic order is the elevator notice greeting Manuele in the new house of the Quartieri Alti and introducing him both to reading and the laws and distinctions of the social order (pp. 1070–71).[7] Before then, in Totetaco, Manuele had no sense of rigid distinctions or of the logical challenges to comprehend, for instance, the Trinity. As he writes in retrospect:

> Per me fra l'unità e i suoi multipli non esistevano confini precisi, così come ancora l'io non si distingueva chiaramente dal tu e dall'altro, né i sessi uno dall'altro. Per tutto il tempo di Totetaco, io non ebbi nozione di essere maschio, ossia uno che mai poteva diventare donna come Aracoeli. (p. 1186)

At the same time as providing textbook examples for the imaginary, pre-symbolic, or pre-oedipal phase of child development — including repeated invocations of the mirror-stage (e.g. p.1049 and p. 1172) — Manuele also keeps suspending the memories of his early childhood by questioning their reliability and providing conflicting explanations.[8] Although this is consistent with psychoanalytic theories, it also makes the truth value of the memories and hence also the validity of the explanations proposed appear undecidable in the novel.

The novel not only frequently thematizes the difficulty of distinguishing between different levels of subjective and objective reality and fantasy,[9] but also indicates that this difficulty may be considered as its poetic principle of narration. The protagonist ponders, for instance:

> Saranno i sogni a plagiare la veglia, o il contrario? È questo enigma che mi porta, raccontandomi, a confondere l'una con gli altri. E per sistemarli debitamente nei loro posti, io devo forzarmi a una maniera pedantesca, all'uso di un pazzo che mima la ragione (p. 1303).

This reflection is occasioned by a series of feverish dreams following and repeating Manuele's transgression of crawling into Aracoeli's bed and suckling her breast as a grown child (shortly after his sister's death). The text resonates here with the paradigmatic case that Freud invokes especially in his 'Three Essays on Sexuality' (1905) to link fantasy to both memory and the emergence of infantile sexuality. Being weaned from the breast, the child remembers satisfaction and re-experiences it in a hallucinatory fashion. At this moment, when the object of a vital function — to receive nourishment by drinking milk — is given up or lost, infant sexuality comes into being by leaning onto vital instincts and breaking away from them in the presence of fantasy.[10]

Jean Laplanche and Jean-Bertrand Pontalis have repeatedly drawn attention to this model of 'leaning' or 'propping' in order to highlight the role of fantasy for the emergence of sexuality in a specifically psychoanalytic sense as irreducible to a biological order of vital functions, needs, or instincts.[11] I would like to propose using their work to read the whole novel through a variation of the diagnosis that in the central scene of the 'Trial' Manuele makes of himself, namely that he is affected by 'confusioni patologiche della fantasia e della memoria' (*Aracoeli*, p. 1180). This passage, which will require considerable commentary, proceeds by contrasting the function of memory in Manuele with the normal operation in healthy people, where it constitutes a specific vital function, namely that of being 'maestra di vita' (p. 1180). Rather than speaking of a 'pathological' confusion, my main thesis may be formulated as saying that Manuele's memory leans away from its vital function and becomes thoroughly sexualized, making the whole narrative less of a description than an actualization or even fulfilment of (his) sexuality.

This is not to say that it is all simply made up — although on some level it is, as Manuele is himself a fictional character — and that one should not also take his memories and reflections seriously, but rather that they are also supported by fantasy and sexuality, which lean on the vital order of the novel's fictional reality and also provide a common ground from which to affect the readers of the novel. The most one can say is that the role of fantasy raises suspicions about the reality of the remembered events. This holds in particular for memories of bliss, joy, and fulfilment, such as the memory of Totetaco and — going also beyond the novel's fictional reality — of a pre-oedipal state of non-differentiation. However, whereas the large majority of Manuele's memories seems to be painful and therefore at first sight more credible, I would like to argue that they, too — as well as the tortuous movement of his thoughts, theories, and self-reflections — actualize sexuality in Freud's general sense and that this is what constitutes their aesthetic value for the novel.

The context for Manuele's diagnosis of his pathological confusions is a reflection upon the origin of memory. While sexuality plays no dominant role here, the reflection itself is conflicted and rather contorted, and pertains precisely to the characterization of Totetaco as a state before or beyond the oedipal order of identity, differentiation, and sexual difference that I quoted above and that appears shortly later in the text. Manuele begins his reflection with the rhetorical question: 'Chi può dire dove e quando la macchina dei ricordi inizia il proprio lavoro?' (*Aracoeli*, p. 1177), and juxtaposes the common notion that an infant's memory begins empty like a blank sheet with the possibility that it carries imprints of a previous existence that continue to have an effect 'simili a una lente aberrante, nelle nuove apparenze quotidiane offerte alla sua rètina' (p. 1177). At first, 'il suo campo s'inonda di forme e colori favolosi' that gradually pale until 'la memoria adulta (comunemente, almeno) provvede a dissipare fino all'ultima ombra di quel primario spettro luminoso' (p. 1177). Rather than directly pursuing this extravagant line of thought, Manuele proceeds to recount how his memory of Totetaco faded after he left the place for good and any reference to it was taboo in his family. At the time of narrating, he professes to have doubts 'dell'esistenza reale di Totetaco [. . .]. Forse, la mia prima Aracoeli dello specchio e di Totetaco non è esistita mai' (p. 1178). At the same time as confirming the narrative of fading and suppressed memories, Manuele thereby also suspends it and questions the validity of his early memories, especially the psychoanalytically relevant ones pertaining to his relation to his mother and himself.

This pattern is repeated as Manuele shifts to reporting what he was told about the place where he spent the first four years of his life. Having described the location, external appearance, interior, and surroundings of their house, he immediately questions the veracity of his description:

> Tale, o poco diversa, mi si presenta, coi suoi dintorni, la casa di Totetaco, se qui ne tento una ricostruzione logica. Ma si tratta, invero, di una ricostruzione forzosa, ossia fabbricata dalla mia ragione 'reale', senza nessun aiuto della mia memoria. Se getto uno scandaglio nella mia memoria, fino a toccarne l'intimo fondo, ne riporto alla luce un tutt'altro Totetaco: tanto veritiero e lampante che tuttora, mentre ne parlo, io rimango incerto e diviso fra i due. E denuncio così (non per la prima volta) la mia natura scissa, che spesso invalida la mia testimonianza perfino al giudizio mio proprio. (pp. 1179–80)

With no ground to trust or privilege either, Manuele keeps reason and memory equally in suspense and remains torn between two alternatives. He proceeds to exemplify the 'split nature' that he highlights here as a general characteristic of his subjectivity by transcribing one of the many internal debates in which he takes the position of several speakers to discuss dilemmas or questions such as what Totetaco was really like.

Manuele maintains that he is 'precipuamente l'imputato' but he also personifies the other positions in these 'psicodrammi' that all come to mean, basically, a trial, 'un processo' (*Aracoeli*, p. 1180). In the case at hand, Manuele is thus not only the accused who insists on having memories going back to his birth and perhaps even before, but he also impersonates the prosecution, which argues that the 'individuo qui esposto alla nostra osservazione è un tipico soggetto psicopatico e mitomane, affetto da confusioni patologiche della fantasia e della memoria' (p. 1180) as well as the defence, which argues in particular that '[e]ffettivamente, può sembrare a volte che le memorie siano prodotte dalla fantasia; mentre in realtà sempre la fantasia è prodotta dalle memorie' (p. 1186). The hearing is suspended when the accused concedes that he does not know whether his memories are reliable. A kind of understanding is thereby reached between the different positions, which however leaves everything open: the accused insists that his memories from earliest childhood in Totetaco are not retroactive inventions of his imaginations, but reflect what he has seen with his own eyes. At the same time, as he cannot vouch for the reliability of his memories, he also confirms in essence the prosecutor's diagnosis. Yet, the trial ultimately also intensifies the confusions of memory and imagination, which the prosecution considers responsible for the accused's illness.

As the distinction by the defence indicates, imagination or fantasy — the Italian word is 'fantasia' throughout — may relate to memory on several levels. When the prosecution points to the accused's 'ricordi (presunti) fino alle sue età primissime [. . .] a cominciare dal momento della nascita' (*Aracoeli*, p. 1181), it suggests that they do not correspond to an experience in early childhood but were imagined/invented at a later point. The accused cannot possibly remember Totetaco as a forest, for instance, given that there is no evidence that Rome was surrounded by forests at that time. Notwithstanding the defence's assertions, the production of memories through the imagination remains a strong possibility, for instance, when the accused claims that he has 'una memoria certa' of his birth and recalls hearing Aracoeli cry 'niña! niña!' (p. 1181).

When the prosecution maintains, by contrast, that for normal individuals 'la funzione della memoria vera e propria ha inizio [. . .] con l'età della ragione', it also implies an earlier form of memory and provides an explanation for the confusion of memory and imagination: 'Finché le facoltà di raziocinio sono assenti, o incompiute, l'individuo umano, secondo natura, è incapace di dare alle impressioni la forma e l'ordine indispensabili alla storicità di un'esperienza' (p. 1181). Here, the claim is not that what is remembered was imagined later. Rather, the suggestion is that as the impressions on the senses were not properly subjected to reason, they do not reliably reflect any objective reality, but rather have the character of imagination or fantasy. It is thus quite plausible, for instance, that when the accused marvels about the constantly changing light and colours of Totetaco, explains that the house revolves like a carousel, and relates this to the earth's rotation that Aracoeli taught him, he remembers what he has experienced at the time and thereby confirms that his powers of ratiocination were not complete enough.

At the same time, the accused's memories acquire their imaginative or fantastic character precisely through the attempt to integrate his perceptions with what he is learning from Aracoeli. They thereby indicate that the production of fantasies by memories is not only a possibility, but an inevitable component of the development of reason. Reason always comes too early or too late, as it were: it requires reliable memory to operate and develop, but memory requires reason in order to have a reliable form and order. A confusion of imagination and memory therefore seems inescapable and the only way out would be to start anew once 'the age of reason' is reached, that is, to begin with a new, empty slate of 'memoria vera e propria' and repress previous impressions and memories. While this is what the prosecutor seems to suggest happens in normal, healthy people, it is evidently not the case for the accused.

On yet a different level, one might observe that all remembering always involves the imagination in so far as it brings past perceptions or experiences again to consciousness. Conversely, also all constructions — even 'rational' ones — arguably involve imagination also in the sense of invention, as Manuele indicates when he considers the 'logical reconstruction' that presents ('presenta') the Totetaco house to him as a forced reconstruction, 'una ricostruzione forzosa' (*Aracoeli*, p. 1179). This holds also for the prosecutor's account of early memory and reason: the idea of a sharp onset of reason and of a fresh beginning of memory uncontaminated by the imagination can be considered as much a fantasy of origin as everything that Manuele produces to answer the question 'where and when the memory machine begins its work'.

Finally, one should not forget that the 'psicodrammi', in which Manuele takes on all different positions and which all come to mean a trial, are in their entirety products of Manuele's imagination. One could call them fantasies of 'A Man is Being Tried' in view of Freud's essay 'A Child is Being Beaten' (1919), where subject and object, activity and passivity, as well as sexual difference are likewise undetermined and can appear in different permutations.[12] In this context, it is significant that in the imagined trial, Manuele also impersonates both the audience, which takes the case to fall 'nel comune schema edipico', and the defence responding that this particular case does not fit 'nei soliti schemi d'obbligo' (*Aracoeli*, p. 1181). This brief interjection indicates not only that Manuele's internal psychodrama includes psychoanalytic discourse, but also invites reading it in relation to psychoanalytic debates on the Oedipus complex, its relation to the pre-oedipal, and the origin of sexuality and fantasy.

That the Oedipus complex is quickly dismissed in the trial and not mentioned again in the novel does not necessarily mean that the protagonist does not fit its structure. It is hardly surprising, for instance, that it is invoked from the outside by the audience and not pursued by the prosecution, given that the latter is completely inside the oedipal trial fantasy and represents its central element, the father — not the empirical father, of course, who is finally exposed to all his pathetic (but finally also endearing) weakness at the end of the novel, but the symbolic father defined by his symbolic function, his absence: 'lo sposo di Aracoeli, non certo il padre della mia carne' (*Aracoeli*, p. 1269), the father believing in 'l'onore militare, e la Patria coi suoi simboli sommi' (p. 1084) who adopted for himself the king of Italy as father, or ultimately Manuele's God, (temporarily) conceived of as 'un Domicilio incorporeo [. . .]. Un'astratta Paternità' (p. 1216). In *Aracoeli* — and in particular in Manuele's trial — the oedipal content is arguably so evident and all-encompassing that it can hardly be articulated from within. It is in many ways more manifest than in 'A Child is Being Beaten', where Freud seeks to establish the importance of the Oedipus complex in an analysis involving the reconstruction of different phases of the surprisingly frequent beating fantasy and the repeated use of the grammar of reversal, inversion, and substitution that he had identified in 'Instincts and their Vicissitudes' (1915).[13] Nevertheless, in both cases there is much to be said for the view of the defence that the 'pre-established pattern' of the Oedipus complex does not fit, or more precisely, that it fits, but is besides the point and fails to address the central concerns — not only of the subjects involved, but also of *Aracoeli* and even of Freud's psychoanalysis.[14]

In Laplanche's detailed commentary of 'A Child is Being Beaten', the central issue of Freud's essay is thus not the Oedipus complex but the character of sexuality at the point of its emergence. An important subtext for Freud's essay is indeed the question of primary masochism, that is, the question of whether masochism or sadism is to be regarded as the more fundamental characteristic of sexuality. Freud repeatedly seems to be pushed towards the notion of primary masochism, but he will accept it only a year later after introducing the death drive in 'Beyond the Pleasure Principle' (1920). Whereas 'A Child is Being Beaten' therefore still insists on the primacy of sadism, and considers the reconstructed masochistic fantasy of 'I am being beaten by my father' to be the result of sadistic tendencies turning against the self, Laplanche argues that primary masochism is already contained in this essay.

Laplanche's argument hinges to a great extent on a precise definition of sexuality: going back to the model of 'leaning' or 'propping', he argues that sexuality in its proper psychoanalytic, non-biological sense only emerges with a turning of (aggressive) activity against the self through fantasy: 'For sexuality, it is the reflexive [. . .] moment that is constitutive: the moment of a turning back towards self, an "autoeroticism" in which the object has been replaced by a fantasy, by an object *reflected* within the subject'.[15] The object must here be taken in a very general sense that may include not only vital functions, but even the oedipal relation.[16] Whereas the Oedipus complex is therefore only incidental, what is specific, in Laplanche's elaboration of the model of leaning is the 'privileged character of masochism in human sexuality'.[17] This claim is not limited to the analysis of 'A Child is Being Beaten', but affirms an essentially masochistic origin of all human sexuality. The point at stake is not so much the content of the fantasy — such as being beaten — but that the act of fantasizing itself constitutes a self-aggression: 'To fantasize aggression is to turn it round upon oneself, to aggress oneself: such is the moment of autoerotism, in which the indissoluble bond between fantasy as such, sexuality, and the unconscious is confirmed'.[18]

What I should like to emphasize here is the enigmatic nature of pleasure that is implied when Laplanche links the self-aggression in the act of fantasizing to masochism.[19] This pleasure can be experienced, but it cannot be integrated into an order of reason in which pleasure and pain — the unpleasure of passivity, being intruded, being beaten or being tried — are conceived of as mutually exclusive. If confusions between experienced impressions and rationally acceptable memories are therefore to be expected, their actualization in Manuele's consciousness and in the text replicates the paradoxical pleasure at the origin of sexuality and thereby also both disturbs and seduces the reader.

Laplanche does not focus on the question of pleasure, nor on the somatic conditions for the emergence of sexuality. His emphasis lies rather on establishing that neither sexuality nor fantasy emerges in a simple, spontaneous manner from some coherent natural, biological order. Whereas the model of leaning tends to highlight the child's activity — its active production of fantasies — Laplanche therefore invokes, and increasingly stresses, a seemingly alternative theory for the origin of sexuality that highlights the child's passivity with respect to the external world and considers sexuality to be 'implanted in the child from the parental universe: from its structures, meanings, and fantasies'.[20] In order to explore how this alternative theory for the origin of sexuality, which is a generalized theory of seduction (*Verführung*), may relate to the confusion of memory and fantasy in *Aracoeli*, I would like to go back to Laplanche and Pontalis's booklet 'Fantasy and the Origins of Sexuality' from 1964. Before doing so, however, I should like to clarify that rather than being contradictory, the two theories of sexuality are ultimately to be regarded as complementary: it is the breaking in of the adult world that occasions the child's fantasizing activity, which constitutes sexuality through a turning back towards the self. While the emergence of sexuality and fantasy is therefore not spontaneous, but induced from the outside, I would argue that the paradoxical, masochistic form of pleasure that I highlighted above provides the somatic condition for the possibility of being seduced into sexuality.

In their re-reading of Freud, Laplanche and Pontalis highlight the secondary role that the Oedipus complex plays for a long time in Freud's theorization, contrasting it to his preoccupation with fantasies, their origins, and relationship to sexuality and reality. As the French title 'Fantasme originaire — Fantasmes des origines — Origines du fantasmes' indicates more clearly, the text circles around some of the same questions as *Aracoeli*. In particular, it relates to Manuele's question about where and when the 'memory machine' begins its work and his different conjectures that necessarily blur the boundaries between memory and imagination in the different senses that I have indicated. In fact, the 'fantasies of origin' in the title seem to refer not only to Freud's discovery of original or primal fantasies, but also to Freud's own fantasies of the origins of fantasies.

In their postscript, the authors indicate that their intention was to try to restore to Freud's thought 'its exigencies, its repressions and returns, its ambiguities, perhaps its "naïveties"'.[21] As an example for the latter they mention Freud's 'phylogenetic hypothesis' that seeks to trace the origin of primal fantasies, which constitute the '"store of unconscious fantasies [. . .] probably of all human beings"', to '"real occurrences in the primaeval times of the human family"'.[22] This hypothesis appears no less 'naïve' than Manuele's suggestion that an infant is born with memories of a previous existence. At the same time, it may be read as an instance of the return of the seduction theory of 1895–97 that Freud quickly abandoned without entirely giving up some of its fundamental intuitions, such as the irreducibility of psychic reality to pure imagination,[23] the intuition of a 'pre-subjective structure',[24] and especially the two-stage theory of trauma that links the psychic efficacy of perceptions to something always already anterior.

Very briefly, psychic trauma involves two moments or scenes, neither of which is in itself traumatic. In the first moment, the seduction scene, the child is subjected to a sexual approach, but this incidence does not lead to a sexual reaction and has sexual connotations only from an external, adult point of view. The second scene happens after sexual maturation and is entirely innocuous except that it leads to a retroactive understanding of the first scene and to a corresponding 'deferred action', whereby the subject now reacts for the first time to the initial event lying far in the past.[25] The important point is that the first, external event 'has become an inner event, an inner "foreign body", which now breaks out from within the subject'.[26] As the subject's usual, outward-directed defence mechanisms fail for such an internal attack, the deferred action is particularly powerful and liable to pathogenic repression.

In his *New Foundations for Psychoanalysis*, Laplanche takes this temporal aspect to generalize the seduction theory. It is no longer necessary that the infant is without sexuality — which soon became one of the arguments against the seduction theory — but rather that there is 'a moment of maturation that allows the subject to react in two ways to an initial experience or to the memory of that experience'. This differential in possible reaction appears as a sufficient condition that 'memory itself, and not the new scene, [. . .] functions as a source of traumatic or auto-traumatic energy'.[27] Laplanche furthermore generalizes the theory by arguing that seduction need not involve abuse, or even unavoidable physical contact with the child, but is already given by the child's encounter with an adult world, in particular with adult language. In this theory, the child is ultimately seduced by 'enigmatic signifiers', 'verbal, non-verbal and even behavioural signifiers which are pregnant with unconscious sexual significations'.[28]

There are many examples of such enigmatic signifiers and their operation in *Aracoeli*, most overtly perhaps the word 'whore', which Manuele hears from a street-boy close to the villa where he was looking for Aracoeli after her final disappearance. 'Alla sua spiegazione, io lo rimirai tonto e incantato, come un povero barbaro forestiero dinanzi a un oracolo di Apollo delfico: poiché nella mia lingua la voce *puttane* non esisteva ancora' (*Aracoeli*, p. 1392). Zaira's explanation of the word remains vague, and when his neighbour, whom he meets on his last escape to the villa, tells him: 'Peccato che sei bruttino [. . .] Non potrai fare il mestiere di tua madre' (p. 1396), he still does not understand fully: 'Quest'ultimo accenno trascorse in incognito, come una figura velata, sulla mia piccola mente tarda'. However, Manuele hints at the fatal effect of full understanding when he tells in retrospect that 'già, invece, l'attacco iniziale: *sei bruttino*, mi avevo colpito in mezzo al petto' and caused a 'strappo fatale' that moves him a little later to throw away the protective amulet. It is only after her death, when he hears the word from a high school student, that he suddenly understands:

> E all'istante avvampai nel viso, come un ruffiano smascherato. È stato in quel punto che, alfine, la sostanza infamante — se non proprio il significato esatto — della famosa parola, mi s'è rivelato in pieno, quasi al suggerimento di uno spettro. Finché era viva, nessun indizio o discorso era bastato a farmi intendere che Aracoeli era il nostro disonore. (p. 1419)

While the text establishes no causal connections at this point — and simply proceeds by highlighting Manuele's feeling of complete abandonment and his gloomy face, which knows only two expressions, 'miserabile' and 'sinistra' — the further context, to which I will return, resonates with a model of melancholia resulting from a complete repression of Aracoeli.

The classic example of traumatic seduction is of course the primal scene, of which *Aracoeli* provides a textbook account. After retelling scenes from the last summer with Aracoeli — recalling in particular her changed voice, with a tone that is now mingled with a slimy and dirty paste rather than '*intriso di miele e di saliva*' and remains recorded in his body 'come un'altra voce mia di me stesso' (pp. 1340–41) — Manuele also remembers a scene of seeing and especially hearing his parents having sex in some service room. He writes in retrospect:

> E fra le tragiche vibrazioni del *ballo angelico* che rapiva mio padre e mia madre a pochi passi da me — qualcuna dev'essere caduta prigioniera nei miei labirinti: per aggirarvisi, spersa, fino all'ultimo silenzio. Io credo, in realtà, che proprio allora il mio cervello registrò per la prima volta quel fatale RITMO affannoso che in futuro doveva tornare per sempre a battere il mio sangue con la sua frusta convulsa e sterile. Lo registrò — senza darsene spiegazione — e là súbito se ne dimenticò (secondo la legge di tutta la mia fanciullezza riguardo al sesso e ai suoi strumenti). Ma poi da adulto, sotto alle mie fustigazioni suicide io sempre ho risentito l'eco di una reminiscenza originaria. (p. 1342)

Again, the reality of such sexually explicit scenes is not necessary in Laplanche's generalization of the seduction theory, which ultimately has as its crucial element 'a highly specific inadequacy of languages. The language of the child is not adequate to that of the adult'.[29] The child's immersion into a necessarily enigmatic adult world and language is sufficient to explain the origin of sexuality in its peculiar, traumatic sense liable first to forgetting and then to repression as soon as it is reactivated through a later event and its significance is understood.[30] In view of the quoted passage one should perhaps say that it is only more properly understood, as something enigmatic remains about the tragic vibrations and rhythm of his parent's 'ballo angelico' given that its echoes keep persisting and also play a role in the tragicomic mini-suicides of his mystic crisis. I would like to suggest that this enigmatic remainder may be related not only to the masochistic origin of sexuality, but also, via Laplanche's generalized theory of seduction through inadequate languages, to the trial scene with its diagnosis of pathological confusions of memory.

As discussed above, the 'confusioni patologiche della fantasia e della memoria' (*Aracoeli*, p. 1180) that the prosecutor identifies in Manuele can be seen as the necessary result of reason always coming too early or too late for a proper ordering and understanding of early impressions. Observing the same temporality of deferment and retroaction, one might expect early forms of memory to have quite generally a traumatizing potential — unless, of course, they are fully forgotten as the prosecutor posits it for healthy individuals. The prosecutor confirms that the accused suffers from his memories not unlike the traumatized when he contrasts the accused's pathological confusions with the normal operation of memory in healthy people, where it is 'maestra di vita' (p. 1180). At the same time, the trial focuses on epistemological questions of early memories rather than on a readily recognizable sexual content. It would seem that if Manuele suffers from his memories, it is not that he retroactively understands their sexual meaning to which he can no longer react adequately, but rather that he retroactively fails to understand his memories as he cannot integrate them into the order of matured reason.

What this suggests is that the two-stage seduction model of trauma should be combined with Freud's later, complementary model of trauma in 'Beyond the Pleasure Principle' where primary masochism is finally acknowledged.[31] Here, the focus is not on how trauma comes about — which might also be due to shell shock, for instance — but rather on the compulsive repetition of traumatic experiences in fantasy until they can be properly bound or symbolized. If Laplanche argues with Freud that sexuality (in a common, genital sense) is a privileged site of trauma, because 'sexuality alone is available for that action in two phases [. . .] of "too early" and "too late"',[32] the same may well be said about reason and the symbolic faculty of ordering and understanding. In this view, the memories of early non-differentiated impressions infused with fantasies of pre-oedipal sexuality would not be pathogenic *per se*, nor are they simply pushed back by social taboos.[33] Instead, they become traumatic only with the belated onset of the order of reason within which they appear disturbingly enigmatic and can only be repressed and/or compulsively repeated beyond the pleasure principle.

When the adult Manuele has almost reached his destination, his mother's birthplace El Almendral, he has a vision of Aracoeli in which he tells her that everything scares him, above all the idea of having sinned, especially in his intellect: 'L'intelligenza si dà per capire. E a me si è data, ma io non capisco niente. E non ho mai capito e non capirò mai niente' (p. 1428). Aracoeli's striking laconic half-Spanish answer is: 'Ma, niño mio chiquito, non c'è niente da capire'. Whereas Manuele understands all too quickly that this encounter was his own alcohol-induced invention and continues with the search of his origins, and whereas a certain Freudian reading might be content with identifying an oedipal structure of feelings of guilt, invoked here through the fear of having sinned, the suggestion seems very much to the point that there is nothing to be understood in the pre-oedipal/pre-rational impressions he remembers or fantasizes. This realization may not help in stopping their traumatic effect and compulsive repetition, but it allows for a different interpretation of Manuele's narrative. What I would like to indicate here is that, on the one hand, an order of reason is required for something to be enigmatic. It is therefore the insistence on understanding where there is nothing to be understood that produces the enigmas seducing the child and triggering an ultimately masochistic activity of fantasy. On the other hand, the paradoxical pleasure of sexuality in its masochistic origin can be understood as the material or somatic condition for the possibility of being seduced. In this view, the paradoxical pleasure at the origin of sexuality is precisely what Manuele keeps recovering and reanimating in his memories and fantasies, as well as in his reflections and multiple, often contradictory explanations.

Manuele's retelling of his belated understanding of the long-enigmatic word 'whore' (*Aracoeli*, p. 1419, see above) falls in the middle of a series of conjectures about his relationship to Aracoeli. If the novel and this section started with Manuele's love for his mother as a hybrid — not torn between loving the 'madre-ragazza' of Totetaco and 'Aracoeli fatta donna' at the Quartieri Alti, 'ma come l'amante di un ibrido, di cui, nell'orgasmo, non riconosce le specie, né capisce le trame' (p. 1067) — Manuele suggests towards the end of the book that it was actually he who defaced Aracoeli into a loathsome, shameless and raving woman in order to defend himself against her death (p. 1418). This strategy, which displaces all ambiguity or hybridity in Aracoeli onto himself, worked in so far as he ended up forgetting not only the ugly counterfeit double, but also the beautiful Aracoelis (p. 1421). However, Manuele only manages to repress Aracoeli, who keeps returning, presenting herself 'in incognito, innominata o camuffata, sotto diversi titoli, sessi, età. Perfino i miei più effimeri incontri serali [. . .] potevano essere incarnazioni di Aracoeli' (p. 1422). The novel not only invokes here a model of repression and the return of the repressed,[34] but could also be read with Freud's model of melancholia in mind. Having left Aracoeli unmourned, the adult Manuele indeed appears stuck in a melancholic state full of self-aggression, which can be read as a result of having identified with Aracoeli and of his aggression towards her.[35] While his suggestion that it was he who defaced her and called on witnesses to stone her — 'ero io l'ordinatore della strage, io l'esecutore volontario' (p. 1418) — confirms this reading, his subsequent suggestion that the cleverness of defacing her was actually her idea — 'Quella era una TUA furbizia: eri tu, che ti sfiguravi per difendermi dal contagio funebre' (p. 1421) — only seems to highlight her disambiguation into an idealized self-sacrificing good mother.

A little earlier, by contrast, Manuele suggests that Aracoeli remains immortal for him not because he or she created a repulsive Aracoeli pushing the real, well-known, and beloved Aracoeli into repression, but on the contrary because of her incomprehensible hybridity, which disappeared before Manuele could assimilate it:

> È stata la tua misteriosa ambiguità, Aracoeli, che mi ti ha resa immortale; [. . .] La tua morte tempestiva, nell'amputarmi di te, ha sbarrato la mia crescita, affinché la mia-tua invenzione bambina si serbasse immune eternamente della ragione. Solo una morte prematura può escludere i corpi adorati dai sordidi sepolcreti della norma e salvare la verità dell'assurdo contro i falsi della logica. [. . .] La tua terribile ambiguità — tua buiezza e imbroglio, tuo scandalo tuo splendore — mi accompagnerà, giocando, al traguardo del vuoto. Che tu sia benedetta, mamita, per il tuo alibi. (p. 1404)

The logic and structure, in particular the temporal structure, of the eternal attachment to Aracoeli seems here to be less that of a melancholic loss than that of a traumatizing prematurity that leads to eternal repetition because the ambiguous mother cannot be assimilated or bound into the order of reason. Seen in this light, her subsequently invoked self-sacrificing self-defacement would then rather appear as a manifestation of her 'terribile ambiguità' that cruelly makes herself immune to Manuele's reason and thereby immortally traumatic. Although Manuele's affirmation of Aracoeli's traumatizing ambiguity — 'che tu sia benedetta' — seems excessive in this passage, perhaps also ironic or sarcastic, and certainly does not prove to be stable, it can also be taken seriously as a possibility. Manuele's exclamation thus points not to sadistic tendencies against an already constituted object, which have turned masochistic through identification, as Freud's model of melancholia would have it,[36] nor to a simply compulsive repetition beyond pleasure. Instead, it resonates well with Manuele's reflections on the origin of memory and my reading of it in terms of Laplanche's theory of the emergence of infantile, pre-oedipal sexuality through both seduction and propping. '[L]a mia-tua invenzione bambina': enigmatic adult signifiers and fantasies break in at the same point as the child's fantasies break out and make sexuality lean on and away from vital functions. The privileged masochistic character of sexuality at the point of its emergence is actualized in Manuele's memories, fantasies, and tortuous movement of thought and ultimately animates the whole novel, providing a disturbing seduction also for the reader. It provokes precisely the kind of 'aumento di vitalità' that Morante's essay on the novel declares as the defining characteristic of true works of art, making them revolutionary in contrast to the false art preferred by reactionaries, which provokes nothing but the welcomed sleep of reason:

> Il fatto è che una vera opera d'arte [. . .] è sempre rivoluzionaria: giacché provoca un aumenta di vitalità, appunto. Per questo tutti i reazionari d'ogni partito preferiscono l'arte falsa, la quale non provoca altro che il benvenuto sonno della ragione; e in certi casi, magari potrà essere brava fino a provocare un collasso. L'apparizione, nel mondo, di una nuova verità poetica, è sempre inquietante, e sempre, nei suoi effetti sovversiva: giacché il suo intervento significa sempre, in qualche modo, un rinnovamento del mondo reale. Essa disturba, dunque, tutti coloro che vorrebbero, finalmente, fissare il mondo dentro un proprio schema definitivo, foss'anche a costo di anchilosare la vita.[37]

Against the falsifications of logic, the dream of reason, and a normalizing cure, *Aracoeli* deploys all kinds of memories, fantasies, and conflicting models of interpretation as pretexts to produce the kind of vitalizing tensions and paradoxical pleasures through which Manuele's tragicomic mini-suicides seek to stir the 'total indifference of earth', 'l'indifferenza totale della terra' (p. 1172).

Notes to Chapter 5

1. Elsa Morante, *Aracoeli*, in Opere, ed. by Carlo Cecchi and Cesare Garboli, 2 vols (Milan: Mondadori, 1988–1990), II (1990), pp. 1039–1454 (p. 1065). Further references to this edition will be given after quotations in the text.
2. See Sara Fortuna and Manuele Gragnolati, '"Attaccando al suo capezzolo le mie labbra ingorde": corpo, linguaggio e soggettività da Dante ad *Aracoeli* di Elsa Morante', *Nuova Corrente*, 55 (2008), 85–123, and Chapter 1 to this volume.
3. In resisting a fully teleological, liberating reading of the novel, my argument agrees in many ways with Sharon Wood's essay on Morante's first two novels, 'The Bewitched Mirror: Imagination and Narration in Elsa Morante', *The Modern Language Review*, 86.2 (April 1991), 310–21. While I agree that memory and narration are not 'triumphant' and evolve in a circular, rather than linear time, I interpret them not as tragic and suffering (p. 319), but as instrumental for a vitalizing recuperation of paradoxical forms of aesthetic pleasure.
4. Manuele suggests somewhat ambiguously that with the onset of puberty his mini-suicides through self-cutting are replaced by masturbation ending with visions of 'furiosa devastazione', 'un grido pervenivo all'orgasmo', and a convulsion 'la quale (come pure il grido) più che al piacere somigliava a un attacco di mal caduco' (*Aracoeli*, p. 1126).
5. On the construction of Aracoeli as a mother combining opposite characteristics, see Vittorio Lingiardi's '*Scene madri*: Psychoanalytic Visions from *Aracoeli* to *Volver*', Chapter 6 in this volume.

6. For the importance of the pre-oedipal for the construction of the main characters in *La Storia*, see Lucia Re, 'Utopian Longing and the Constraints of Racial and Sexual Difference in Elsa Morante's La Storia', *Italica*, 70.3 (Autumn 1993), 361–75.
7. Cf. Fortuna and Gragnolati, Chapter 2, in this volume.
8. On the importance of androgyny for the novel and Morante's ambivalent relationship to psychoanalytic theories, see Hanna Serkowska, 'The Maternal Boy: Manuele, or the Last Portrait of Morante's Androgyny', in *Under Arturo's Star: The Cultural Legacies of Elsa Morante*, ed. by Stefania Lucamante and Sharon Wood (West Lafayette, IN: Purdue University Press, 2006), pp. 157–87.
9. Acknowledging, for instance, that in common opinion 'i nostri ricordi non possono risalire più indietro del secondo o terzo anno di età', he claims to remember seeing himself suckling his mother's breast in a mirror at a much earlier time. He wonders: 'Può darsi che questo sia uno dei miei ricordi apocrifi? Nel suo lavoro continuo la macchina inquieta del mio cervello è capace di fabbricarmi delle ricostruzioni visionarie [. . .]. Succede, a ogni modo, che certi ricordi apocrifi dopo mi si scoprono più veri del vero' (*Aracoeli*, pp. 1049–50). See also Manuele's reflection in the context of the partisan scene: 'Certo nel mio passato, più di una volta, io devo essermi abbeverato — senza saperlo — in qualche affluente nascosto del fiume Oblio [. . .]. Non si dà, infatti, riapprodo dall'Oblio se non attraverso il suo gemello, la Restituzione. È in quest'altro fiume che si ribevono le memorie perdute; ma come accertarsi che le sue acque non siano drogate, e inquinate da presagi o seduzioni, fabulazioni o inganni?' (pp. 1246–47).
10. Sigmund Freud, 'Three Essays on the Theory of Sexuality', in *The Standard Edition of the Complete Psychological Works of Sigmund Freud*, ed. by James Strachey, 24 vols (London: Vintage, 2001), VII, 125–245, here especially pp. 179–83.
11. Laplanche and Pontalis problematize the pseudoscientific term 'anaclisis' usually used in English translations for Freud's term 'Anlehnung'. Cf. the entries 'Anaclitique' and 'Étayage' in Laplanche and Pontalis's *Vocabulaire de la psychanalyse* (Paris: Presses universitaires de France, 1967), pp. 23 and 148–50, and Laplanche's *Life and Death in Psychoanalysis*, trans. by Jeffrey Mehlman (Baltimore: Johns Hopkins University Press, 1976, repr. 1993), p. 16.
12. Sigmund Freud, 'A Child is Being Beaten', in *The Standard Edition*, XVII, 175–204.
13. Freud, 'Instincts and their Vicissitudes', in *The Standard Edition*, XIV, 109–40. Cf. Laplanche, *Life and Death*, who considers Freud's essay to be a 'veritable clinical confirmation of "Instincts and Their Vicissitudes"' (p. 97).
14. For an analysis of *Aracoeli*'s ambiguous relationship to psychoanalytical theories, feminism, and a symbolic order with traditional, patriarchal stereotypes, which the novel both affirms and subverts in a complex manner, see Adalgisa Giorgio, 'Nature vs Culture: Repression, Rebellion and Madness in Elsa Morante's *Aracoeli*', *MLN*, 109.1, Italian Issue (January 1994), 93–116.
15. Laplanche, *Life and Death*, p. 88.
16. Cf.: 'newly formed sexuality seems able to take as its point of departure *absolute* [sic] *anything*: the vital functions, to be sure, but also, ultimately, the 'oedipal' relation itself in its entirety' (Laplanche, *Life and Death*, p. 101).
17. Laplanche, *Life and Death*, p. 102.
18. Laplanche, *Life and Death*, p. 102.
19. For an analysis emphasizing the shattering, masochistic pleasure of sexuality and its role in aesthetics, see Leo Bersani, *The Freudian Body: Psychoanalysis and Art* (New York: Columbia University Press, 1986).
20. Laplanche, *Life and Death*, p. 48. Cf. also: Laplanche, *New Foundations for Psychoanalysis*, trans. by David Macey (Oxford: Basil Blackwell, 1989), p. 145.
21. Jean Laplanche and Jean-Bertrand Pontalis, 'Fantasy and the Origins of Sexuality' (1964), in *Formations of Fantasy*, ed. by Victor Burgin, James Donald, and Cora Kaplan (London and New York: Routledge, 1989), pp. 5–34 (p. 28).
22. Laplanche and Pontalis, 'Fantasy and Origins', p. 17, quoting Freud's 'A Case of Paranoia Running Counter to the Psychoanalytic Theory of the Disease'.
23. Laplanche and Pontalis, 'Fantasy and Origins', p. 8.
24. Laplanche and Pontalis, 'Fantasy and Origins', p. 14.
25. The Freudian term for 'deferred action' is 'Nachträglichkeit'; Laplanche and Pontalis emphasize

its importance and specificity in the entry 'Après-Coup' of their *Vocabulaire de la Psychanalyse*, pp. 33–36.
26. Laplanche and Pontalis, 'Fantasy and Origins', p. 10.
27. Laplanche, *New Foundations*, p. 112.
28. Laplanche, *New Foundations*, p. 126.
29. Laplanche, *New Foundations*, p. 130.
30. Manuele's 'avventura di spiaggia' — his first, timid encounter with a girl at the age of sixteen, which is interrupted by a young man taking his place — thus ends with a repetition of the primal scene that Manuele comments upon in retrospect as follows: 'La mia memoria si rifiutava di riconoscere quel terribile ritmo oscillante, che pure, da un'ora antica della mia fanciullezza, non aveva mai più cessato di battere nei depositi oscuri della mia sorte' (*Aracoeli*, p. 1124). Two years later, by contrast, in his second, disastrous encounter with a woman, he conceives of the 'assurdo disegno di recitare [. . .] l'azione erotica rituale: a cominciare dal "ballo angelico" nel suo ossessivo, terribile ritmo, fino al culmine urlato' (p. 1144).
31. Freud, 'Beyond the Pleasure Principle', in *The Standard Edition*, XVIII, 1–64 (p. 55).
32. Laplanche, *Life and Death*, p. 43.
33. Cf. Manuele's suggestion that he became unsure of the first Aracoeli of Totetaco because 'la parola stessa *Tote-Taco* [. . .] era tabù' in the Quartieri Alti (p. 1178).
34. Cf.: 'Accade, per leggi naturali, che certe esperienze fuori di misura, consumate da un io troppo bambino, poi si rigettano dallo stesso bambino in crescita, come le larve dei trapassati dalle tribù selvagge. E così le mie diverse Aracoeli s'erano date a una latitanza che pareva eterna; ma era invece, a quanto sembra, un loro gioco a nascondersi. Dopo, esse dovevano più volte affacciarsi di ritorno [. . .]' (*Aracoeli*, pp. 1421–22).
35. For Freud, this is 'the key to the clinical picture [of melancholia]: we perceive that the self-reproaches are reproaches against a loved object which have been shifted away from it on to the patient's own ego' (Freud, 'Mourning and Melancholia', in *The Standard Edition*, XIV, 236–60 [p. 248]).
36. Cf.: 'The self-tormenting in melancholia, which is without doubt enjoyable, signifies [. . .] a satisfaction of trends of sadism and hate which relate to an object, and which have been turned round upon the subject's own self.' (Freud, 'Mourning and Melancholia', p. 251)
37. Elsa Morante, *Pro o contro la bomba atomica e altri scritti*, in *Opere*, II, 1455–1574 (p. 1519).

CHAPTER 6

Scene madri: Psychoanalytic Visions from *Aracoeli* to *Volver*

Vittorio Lingiardi

Deeply touched by the poster of this conference, a black and fuchsia picture showing Morante and Pasolini together, the heroes of my adolescence, I remember I was not yet twenty-two when *Aracoeli* was published. It was the era of the psychoanalytic misconception, both Catholic and Communist at once, which led Pasolini to write this prayer in *Poesia in forma di rosa*:

> È difficile dire con parole di figlio
> ciò a cui nel cuore ben poco assomiglio.
> Tu sei la sola al mondo che sa, del mio cuore,
> ciò che è stato sempre, prima d'ogni altro amore.
> Per questo devo dirti ciò ch'è orrendo conoscere:
> è dentro la tua grazia che nasce la mia angoscia.
> Sei insostituibile. Per questo è dannata
> alla solitudine la vita che mi hai data.
> [. . .]
> Ti supplico, ah, ti supplico: non voler morire.
> Sono qui, solo, con te, in un futuro aprile. . .[1]

The same error makes the unhappy Manuele say in *Aracoeli*:

> Fra i vari, possibili beni, di cui la gente è ghiotta, io, per tutto il mio tempo, domandavo quest'unico: d'essere amato. Ma presto mi fu chiaro ch'io non posso piacere a nessuno, come non piaccio a me stesso; eppure non sapevo rinunciare alla mia ostinata illusione — o pretesa; mentre la mia domanda assillante ormai si legava inesorabilmente, per me, al tema della colpa e della vergogna. Ho rinunciato, alla fine, a ogni domanda; ma la colpa e la vergogna perdurano. Addirittura, anzi, io direi che formano la sostanza stessa del mio protoplasma, e disegnano la mia forma visibile, che mi denuncia al mondo. Così, quando mi succede di trovarmi fra una folla, io mi sento l'oggetto designato per un linciaggio. Il giudizio innumerevole del Collettivo punta le sue pupille omicide addosso al mio corpo.
>   Dopo i miei due fallimenti non ho più tentato amori di donne. Col mio trasferimento a Milano ebbero inizio i miei altri infelici amori. [. . .] Da loro non potevo aspettarmi amore, né l'ultima, desiata piaga. La massima grazia che potevano essi concedermi, era di lasciarsi succhiare da me. A pagamento. Loro,

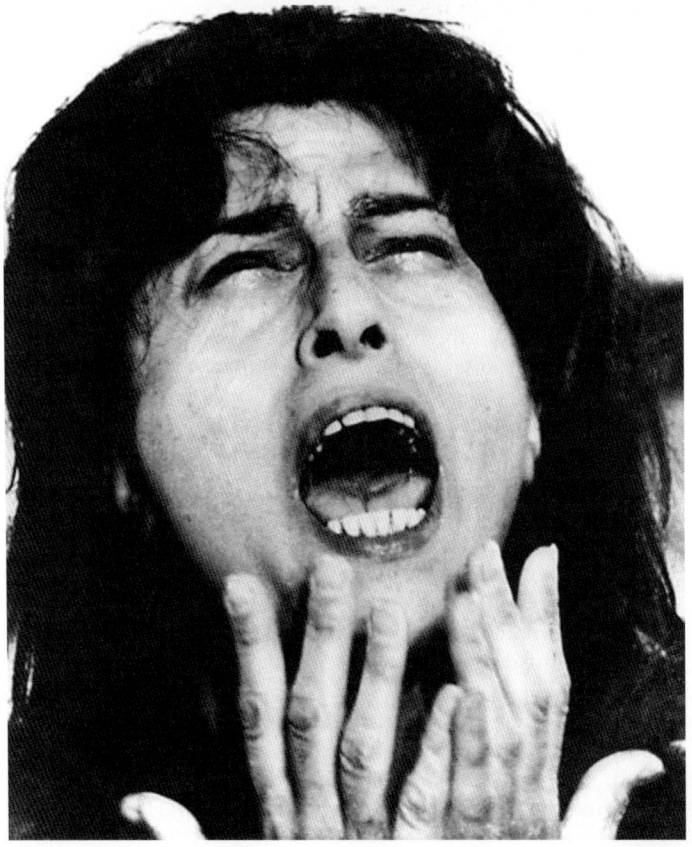

Fig. 1. Susanna Colussi in *Il Vangelo secondo Matteo* (Pasolini, 1964)
Fig. 2: Anna Magnani in *Mamma Rosa* (Pasolini, 1962)

FIG. 3. Maria Callas in *Medea* (Pasolini, 1969)

simili a statue regali. Io, come fossero santi, in ginocchio ai loro piedi. E la mia pupilla al berli, si velava, nello sguardo adorante e assonnato che ha l'infante allattato dalla madre.[2]

These are the components of *Aracoeli*, mother and son locked together in the archetypal dyad of love and sacrifice, which in Pasolini's *Vangelo* becomes the run and fall of the mother, played by Susanna Colussi (Pasolini's own mother), confronting the sacrifice of her son (Figure 1).[3]

But while Pasolini's Mother is a knot of life and death, who gives birth to the guilt and necessity of her homosexual Son 'to account of the wild pain of being men' ('rispondere | del selvaggio dolore di essere uomini'),[4] Elsa Morante's Aracoeli is much more complex than other Great Mediterranean Mothers staged by Pasolini — Magnani Mothers, Callas Mothers (Figures 2 and 3) — being far removed, almost out of biological necessity, from the classical imagery, both Greek and Christian, so dear to Pasolini.

Even if its personification splits every archetype and crystallizes its libidic tension at one extreme, it still remains bipolar in itself, a mix of positive and negative, numinous power and *mysterium fascinosum et tremendum*. This is why Jung says that love 'may summon forth unsuspected powers in the soul for which we had better be prepared'.[5] Hence the Jungian interest in the *coniunctio oppositorum*, where opposite polarities strive to achieve balance in a state of psychic tension.

Stories and tales usually show the two faces of archetype separately and alternatively (e.g. the Queen of the Night in the *Magic Flute*). This is the same phenomenon that helps us to endure the ambivalence of motherly affection, and it is well known that traumatized children organize their defence mechanisms around dissociation and splitting.[6]

The representation of the traumatizing parent is split in two — an idealized side and a persecutory side — and the child cannot use them simultaneously. This splitting can be explained as an effort to preserve a positive image of a parent capable of caring, a figure to which the child can cling, while excluding the negative figure of a violent or careless parent. The need for an attachment figure who can provide care and protection is so strong that the child who is rejected or neglected tends to blame his/her own 'unworthiness', rather than the caregiver's inadequacy:

> A) Allora lei disse piano, come un bacio nell'orecchio: 'Manuelito! Manuelito!' E portando le mie due mani sulle proprie guance, e premendole con le sue palme, mi domandò, con una voce piccola e forastica, tintinnante come un vetro frantumato:
>
> 'Sei sempre il mio niño? sei sempre il niño mio?'
>
> La mia risposta era là pronta, ma lei brusca la scansò, liberandosi le guance dalle mie mani, nell'atto di chi si strappa una benda. E proferì con un'altra voce, indurita, piatta e sconciata come da un'operazione feroce di restauro:
>
> 'E invece, io non sono più la tua mamita'. (*Aracoeli*, p. 1377)

> B) D'un tratto un sussulto, così brusco da somigliare a una percossa, mi staccò da mia madre; e i miei occhi, subitamente sbarrati, s'incontrarono coi suoi, che dilatavano le pupille fissandomi in un orrore impietrito, come si vedessero davanti un brutto animale: 'Che fai qua, tu?!' mi disse aspra, 'vattene subito via di qua'. Né saprei dire se sono stato io stesso, o lei, a buttarmi giù dal letto. La intravidi che raddrizzandosi in fretta si ricopriva il petto con la camicia; mentre già fuggivo alla traversata del corridoio, verso un pozzo di luce meridiana, terribile e accecante. Mi ritrovavo in camera mia, sbattuto in terra da un accesso di singulti convulsi e asciutti, che non risolvendosi in lagrime si rappresero in una febbre [. . .]. Così non saprei se fu vero o illusorio il tocco di una manina fresca e magra che mi lisciava la faccia lebbrosa; né se sia stata un fantasma la piccola figura di Aracoeli, che accosto al mio capezzale mi diceva, in un rimprovero dolce quanto un bacetto: 'tontillo! tontillo!'. (*Aracoeli*, pp. 1301–02)

> C) So, invece, di sicuro, che il breve evento della mattina generò una flora onirica, alquanto maligna, nel seguito delle mie notti. Lo scenario variava, ma la luce era sempre uno stesso velame azzurrastro, senza colore di tempo; e sempre io vi svolgevo la parte di escluso, o ributtato, o scacciato, o intoccabile. Sto fuori da una porta altissima, ferrea, di cui, troppo piccolo, non arrivo alla serratura. Né possiedo, del resto, nessuna chiave adatta: la sola di cui dispongo è minuscola e informe come una pallina di mollica. Inservibile. — Carponi avanzo in uno stretto corridoio cilindrico, pari a un budello, ma in realtà

è la pancia di un serpente, il quale m'ha inghiottito vivo. Nessuno doveva accorgersene, difatti, ch'io ero un topo; e dunque è stato meglio per me venire mangiato dal serpente, senza ritorno. (*Aracoeli*, p. 1302)

A firm sense of attachment is crucial in order to provide the child with a 'secure basis' for exploring the parent's mind. In this way, he/she not only gets to know the mind of the Other, but also has the opportunity to find him/herself in it, because the parent strives, in his/her turn, to understand and comprehend his/her child's mental states.[7] Thus, the child discovers in the Other an image of him/herself as an intentional being, with personal wishes and beliefs. This self-representation found in the Other is then internalized, and is pivotal in the development of the Self. Therefore, the most appropriate formulation for a model of the Self's birth does not seem to be the Cartesian 'cogito, ergo sum', but rather 'Someone thinks of me as someone who thinks, and therefore I exist as a thinker'.[8]

Apparently, *Aracoeli*'s 'power of disturbance' contains and transcends the binary rule of defensive splitting: Aracoeli's 'maternal love' appears *always and simultaneously* in its contaminating polytheism, which is much more unsettling and disturbing.[9] Aracoeli is not just one of the many deities of a Pantheon, but the 'whole' personification of all its Mothers, a unique face wearing all masks at the same time — Medusa, Medea, the Madonna.

> Aracoeli: passeggiatrice incantevole e multiforme [. . .]. Per piacermi, si travestecon tutti i costumi convenzionali [. . .]. Pastora. Idalga. Santa. Meretrice. Morta. Immortale. Vittima. Tiranna. Bambola. Dea. Schiava. Madre. Figlia. Ballerina (*Aracoeli*, p. 1194)

> E corro dietro alla mia fedele madre-ragazza, e alla sua icona musicante, ricacciando come un'intrusa quell'altra Aracoeli fatta donna, che in realtà mi ha lasciato laidamente orfano ancor prima d'esser morta. Io cerco oggi di nascondere a me stesso che questa seconda Aracoeli è anch'essa mia madre, la stessa che mi aveva portato nell'utero; e che lei pure sta insediata in ogni mio tempo, schernendo la mia ridicola pretesa di ricostruirmi, di là da lei, un nido normale. Per quanto io voglia ricacciarla, essa non mi risparmia le sue visitazioni: dove spesso si appaia con la prima Aracoeli, pari a una sua sosia sfigurata. L'una Aracoeli mi ruba l'altra; e si trasmutano e si raddoppiano e si sdoppiano l'una nell'altra.
> E io le amo entrambe: non come uno conteso fra due amori, ma come l'amante di un ibrido, di cui, nell'orgasmo, non riconosce le specie, né capisce le trame. (*Aracoeli*, pp. 1066–67)

It is difficult to find a mythological character that can be compared with Aracoeli. Maybe the Triple Hecate, so dear to Medea, goddess of the dead and deity of night, ghosts, and witchcraft. Maybe Aphrodite, in her triplicate guise of uranian, oceanic, and chthonic Goddess — who is chaste, fertile, and dissolute. Maybe Demeter, the wandering and suffering one, mother of Kore. Maybe Kali, dark mother of Time. Or, once again, an esoteric hybrid, like Hecate Aphrodisia, or an epiphany of the double Artemis who kills the beasts, but also protects them, embodying the whole lunar cycle, from Hecate to Selene, from the deadly moon with supernatural powers to the full and benevolent moon.

The gap between Pasolini and Morante implies the experience of being a daughter rather than a son, but also the passage from a Catholic to a pagan perspective (Pasolini tries to get rid of Catholicism through the idealization of a primitive world, while Aracoeli is barbarian from the start). In this sense, Morante's paganism prefigures Almodóvar's mixing of genders: his is a postmodern theogony, while hers is more mythical and creatural ('codice favoloso', 'paese di Totecaco'):

> La mattina, a Totetaco (dopo che l'Arcangelo San Gabriel aveva spalancato con la spada il sipario della luce) io venivo svegliato dalla voce ridente di Aracoeli che mi solleticava sotto il mento dicendo: Mamola mamola mamola! Poi, mandavamo insieme un bacio verso il quadro della Macarena, e ciò bastava a contentare Dio fino alla preghiera serale. Questa consisteva tutta in due parole: "Deo gratias" (perché Aracoeli non aveva pazienza per le recitazioni troppo lunghe) alle quali facevamo seguire il nostro solito frettoloso bacetto sulle punte delle dita. E il nostro unico bacio, secondo le spiegazioni di Aracoeli, toccava a tre persone (Jesus, il padre e la madre) che in realtà ne erano una: Dio. Difatti Dio era Jesus, ma era anche il padre di Jesus, e anche sua madre. Dio era un bambinetto, e al tempo stesso una gransignora in abiti di gala, e anche un uomo barbuto incoronato di spine (le stesse riconoscibili, al buio, in forma di stelle). Simili fenomeni sacri non urtavano nessuna mia logica, e il dogma della trinità non mi tornava astruso. Per me fra l'unità e i suoi multipli non esistevano confini precisi, così come ancora l'io non si distingueva chiaramente dal tu e dall'altro, né i sessi uno dall'altro. Per tutto il tempo di Totetaco, io non ebbi nozione di essere maschio, ossia uno che mai poteva diventare donna come Aracoeli. (*Aracoeli*, p. 1186)

Manuele's theogony is of the psychedelic and transgender kind, as we can see in this passage where Morante describes his dissociative state — half clinically and half forensically:

> I. 'Avevamo un giardino, con fiori non comuni, assai più grandi dei soliti. Le margherite erano grandi come girasoli, e al sole infatti nella forma facevano da specchio e ne ricevevano anche il nome: fiorisol. C'erano poi, si capisce, anche i fioriluna, i fioricometa... Gran parte dei fiori, invero, si formavano a imitazione degli astri. Ma nemmeno mancavano i fioriconchiglia, i fioripaloma, i fioridrago... Bisogna dire che esisteva una parentela stretta fra tutte le cose: tutte apparentate dalla luce'.
>
> I. 'Anche la notte era colorata. Le stelle avevano infiniti, diversi colori, oltre all'oro e all'argento. Anche figure: ci si riconosceva la corona di spine di Dio. E i gioielli, i merletti di Nostra Signora. [. . .] E si sentiva un fruscio profumato di sete, di velluti: erano gli scialli e le sottane delle Semprevergini'.
>
> D. 'Conviene rammentare che la madre del Soggetto era andalusa [. . .]. È possibile che in quella madre andalusa sopravvivessero delle teofanie ancestrali d'Arabia e d'Africa. Nel suo cattolicesimo elementare, tornavano rituali barbari e favole pagane'.
>
> I. 'Quali favole? Le Semprevergini non erano favole, ma verità documentate, visto che a casa nostra ne avevamo le fotografie. Ce n'erano di piccole, formato cartolina, e una appesa sul letto — grande al vero — a colori. Questa portava in capo, sotto una corona pesante, una cuffia di balze e ricami stupendi che le scendeva a mantiglia fino sulle spalle. Le sue guance erano floride e rosse, da parer truccate, e i suoi cigli così lunghi da sembrare finti; ma i suoi grandi occhi a mandorla sapevano di tristezza, e ne scendevano lagrime grosse e dure

come ciòttoli. Questa Signora si chiamava Macarena, e in casa nostra era di famiglia. Essa rimediava a tutto, bastava pregarla; e certo capiva tutte le lingue, però meglio di tutte lo spagnolo, poiché proveniva da Siviglia. Per ogni diverso evento, essa richiedeva una preghiera speciale. Una valeva contro la febbre e il singhiozzo, una contro le punture di vespa, una contro i tuoni: e lei tutte le esaudiva. Ricordo che una volta, mentre imparavo a camminare, cascai per terra ferendomi al ginocchio. Era una brutta ferita, vasta, sanguinante. Però Aracoeli bisbigliò a Nostra Signora Macarena la preghiera delle cadute, e poi mi diede, sul ginocchio, appena una leccatina con la lingua. Immediatamente allora si vide passare sul ginocchio una piccola nebbia, e in un attimo il ginocchio ritornò liscio e intatto: guarito'. (*Aracoeli*, pp. 1183–85)

As infant researchers have shown, the relationship between the baby and the caregiver is most destabilizing when it fails to establish an intermediate position between adhesion and detachment, as when mother and son cannot create, as Louis Sander would say, a 'competent system'.[10] The concepts of 'mirroring' and 'emotional regulation' are based on the importance of an adequate relationship of *sameness* and *difference* between the caregiver's and the baby's feelings. Actually, if the caregiver 'reflects' the baby's feelings too faithfully, the baby will not learn to elaborate them enough. On the other hand, if the 'mirrored' feelings are too different from the baby's feelings, they might become unrecognizable, making it very hard for him/her to develop a mentalizing stance.

A friend of mine, a recent mother, sent me this e-mail:

> Dear Vittorio, I'm writing in a brief pause after a bad night with A. He caught a bad cold, was scared, his eyes full of tears — now he sleeps. After the worst was over, at 4 AM we found ourselves wrapped in blankets, all his toys around us. A. was still feverish and probably understood how tired and in a bad mood I was, so he tried to entertain me: listen how many words I know: mamma, papa, mae (sea), maau (cat), ball, azie (thank you), gnogna (grandma), papaga (parrot) . . . look how many friends I got: pupino-pupazzo-bambino, big nose (the rhino), platypu, wau wau (the two dogs), the little mouse with a sombrero, the black raven . . . I'm glad he's already learned 'mare' (sea), even if he hasn't seen it yet, but I have showed it to him in pictures, and I must have pronounced it with such enthusiasm that he immediately got it . . . — after all, it's an easy word.

In this account (A. is eighteen months old), a concise e-mail example of a *competent system*, we can somehow grasp what 'intersubjectivity' means in today's psychoanalysis: the son as a subject relating to the mother (who is another subject and is perceived as such), the tension implied in the mutual recognition of two subjects, the ensuing satisfaction, the advent of a *thirdness* as a place fit for a new relationship.[11] Unlike Manuele in *Aracoeli*, 'Esto niño chiquito <u>tiene</u> cuna'.

Quoting again from Morante's novel:

> Con le sue prime nenie di culla (che furono, in realtà, il primo linguaggio umano da me udito) essa accompagna invariabilmente [. . .] l'atto di porgermi il petto o di dondolarmi. È proprio la sua tenera voce di gola, intrisa di saliva, che mi ricanta all'orecchio quelle sue canzoncine di paese. Essa le mischia con certe piccole voci di affetto e risatine scherzanti. E in queste, sembra che la sua lingua si sciolga a tenermi un discorso. [. . .] Non ne intendo, però, nessuna frase. Ne colgo solo i suoni, che piovono su di me dalla sua bocca ridarella come un tubare dall'alto. E allora d'un tratto mi attraversa una sensazione

> orribile: quasi che in questo incomprensibile balbettio lei mi significasse un avvertimento che non riesce ad articolare. Questa non è più la mia solita 'rimembranza apocrifa'; ma forse è l'anamnesi postuma di un male senza nome, che continua a minarmi da quando sono nato. Così, ho creduto di capire perché adesso, mentre mi avvicino alla vecchiaia, lei si ostina a riapparirmi nell'atto di tenere me infante fra le braccia: allo stesso modo, fra le sue braccia, essa vuole riportarmi finalmente al suo proprio nido, come l'aria porta il seme che vuole interrarsi. (*Aracoeli*, pp. 1051–52)

Manuele's often-mentioned distorted vision and his problems in locating himself in time and space — his being sucked into a continuous 'present-past' without future — may also depend on the absence of this intermediate space of 'thirdness': 'Esto niño chiquito *no tiene* cuna' (p. 1047).

Having or not having had a *cuna*, a place for containment and secure attachment, the centre of an emerging Self, an inner space where thoughts and affections are shaped: this is the main subject of contemporary psychoanalytic literature about trauma. And it was a few years after reading *Aracoeli* and after my mother's death that I turned to psychoanalysis myself, and I probably did it to get rid of my inner representations of Aracoeli's wild, furious, adoring, symbiotic, mysteric faces. I found that there were other 'choices' besides Freud's oedipal mother and Jung's Terrible Mother: Winnicott's good enough mother, Bowlby's secure base, Sander's maternal rhythm, Benjamin's mothers-not-just-mothers. The punning title of Jessica Benjamin's 1995 beautiful book *Like Subjects, Love Objects* hints at the intra-psychic/interpersonal link and at the tension between difference and sameness (*like subjects* = 'similar subjects' but also = 'in the guise of subjects').[12]

How different is the first of the 'sorti indelebili' that the 'sarto immortale' sewed in Manuel's flesh:

> MAI PIU' TU SARAI
> UN OGGETTO D'AMORE
> MAI PER NESSUNO MAI
> MAI TU SARAI UN OGGETTO
> D'AMORE. (*Aracoeli*, p. 1094)

Considering the intersubjective capacity developed after the baby's first year of life, Daniel Stern emphasizes the importance of negotiation and the sharing of meanings.[13] In this process, it is not clear if the word exists 'outside' and is given by the caregiver to the baby, or if it is the baby who discovers it, or if it is simply found or taken when the baby has already formed a concept or a feeling related to it. In short, it is a word that is given and discovered at the same time (and I think something of the sort happens also in good psychoanalytic sessions).

The e-mail of my friend — a woman and a baby *teaching each other* the words they love — sums up the very idea of mother I discovered with amazement and admiration when I read Jessica Benjamin's early papers. At the beginning of the 1990s, she interwove feminism, intersubjectivity, and gender, and taught something new — the rhythm of mutual recognition — to psychoanalysts, many of whom had only been able, until then, to see mothers as schizophrenogenic women or as devoted extensions, instruments at the baby's disposal.

Once again, Aracoeli's 'power of disturbance' consists in her 'being' all these perspectives at the same time, deforming and collapsing them in the black hole of motherhood. Such deformation is due mostly to the overpowering nature of biology but also to the childish ferocity of her narcissism. But it is also connected with her tragic awareness — the same that we find in *Il mondo salvato dai ragazzini*[14] — that the death of childhood is caused by the acquisition of a clearer view: 'Io lo so, quando cominciai a piacerle di meno: fu quando, per la prima volta, mi vennero messi gli occhiali' (*Aracoeli*, p. 1254).

Glasses are the orthoptic instrument which prints on the face of a child the shadow of his future as an adult.

Like Almodóvar's characters, Aracoeli is surreal and magically real, but she is never really *able to play* (at least in the Winnicottean sense of 'transitional space', 'presentation of the world', etc.). Men are absent in *Aracoeli*, as they are absent in *The Women* (Cukor, 1939), and in *Todo sobre mi madre* (Almodóvar, 1999).[15] In *Todo sobre mi madre* — whose title recalls Mankiewicz's *All about Eve*[16] — two women, Manuela and Sister Rosa, are also mothers. Their children have the same father, Lola, who in the meantime has changed sex. Their stories are intertwined with the motherly passion of theatrical actress Huma Rojo for a young misfit junkie girl. Almodóvar said that for him the most touching scene is when the main character Manuela, who has recently lost her only son Esteban, hands Lola, the transexual father of her son, the baby he has begotten with the nun. A woman hands a baby to someone who is supposed to be its normal father, but who has breasts — and he/she squeezes the baby between his/her fake breasts. The meaning of affects and a 'desperate vitality' are stronger than the absurdity of this scene.[17] Manuela is the core of the movie — a woman and a mother ruling over destinies. She has abandoned the man who gave her a child; she wants to track him down to hand him another woman's child.

Morante's creatural queerness, in the novel *La Storia* (1974), furnishes young Useppe with a second mother, a dog. Almodóvar's cultural queerness entrusts Lola, a transexual with AIDS, with the impossible mission of a male motherhood. A crucial dedication appears in *Todo sobre mi madre*'s end credits:

> To Bette Davis, Gena Rowlands and Romy Schneider. To all actresses who have played actresses, to all women who act, to all men who act and become women, to all people who want to be mothers, to my mother.

Motherhood as metaphor of literature, and of theatre. 'The patio of my infancy' as Almodóvar has it: 'To me, three or four women talking mean the origin of life, and also the origin of fiction and narration'.

The plot of *Volver* is well known: Raimunda is a hard worker who copes with a rude and alcoholic husband and takes care of their adolescent daughter.[18] Her sister Soledad is divorced from her husband and works as an unlicensed hairdresser. The two sisters lost both parents some years before, in one of the many fires caused by the 'solano' wind always sweeping their native land: La Mancha. This is where their mother's older sister, aunt Paula, lives. Paula has been behaving strangely for some time, talking of her sister Irene as if she were still alive. The neighbours also swear they have seen Irene's ghost wandering around Paula's home. When Paula

Fig. 4. Carmen Maura and Penelope Cruz in *Volver* (Almodóvar, 2006)

dies, strange things start happening: someone returns, someone disappears — and Raimunda's and Soledad's lives change profoundly. *Volver* is the story of a mother who has disappeared and is believed to be dead, but is still inexplicably present, as in one of those folk legends about spirits who come back to life to settle unfinished business or to ask for forgiveness — restless souls that cannot find peace.

Soledad will be the first to perceive her mother's presence: 'There is still mom's odour . . .'. This reminds us of a passage from *Aracoeli*:

> Non so come gli scienziati spieghino l'esistenza, dentro la nostra materia corporale, di questi altri organi di senso occulti, senza corpo visibile, e segregati dagli oggetti; ma pure capaci di udire, di vedere e di ogni sensazione della natura, e anche di altre. Si direbbero forniti di antenne e scandagli. Agiscono in una zona esclusa dallo spazio, però di movimento illimitato. E là in quella zona si avvera (almeno finché noi viviamo) la resurrezione carnale dei morti. (pp. 1047–48)

Soledad smells the ancient smell of memories that linger in every room, in every dress, in every warm wafer — all remnants of a painful past. Unlike Raimunda, she is ready for a regressive trip to childhood memories: she will be the one to take their mother into her house and to sleep in mommy's bed like when she was a child. We can say that *Volver* starts where *Aracoeli* ends.

The word 'mother' seems to haunt Morante. In *Aracoeli* it occurs almost two hundred times, and even appears in the first sentence. With a method that may seem deliberate but certainly is not, it also appears on the first page of *Menzogna e sortilegio*, *L'isola di Arturo*, and *La Storia*: 'One need not be a chamber to be haunted', as Emily Dickinson would say.[19]

From Elsa Morante's diaries, 1938:

> Da qualche notte non sogno; o meglio faccio sogni spezzati, confusi. Ieri notte, dopo quella orribile veglia nervosa, sognai mia sorella che faceva i compiti (questo ritorna spesso, ora) e passava in rivista certe cartoline colorate

raffiguranti quadri sacri celebri. Vedevo le Madonne, i blu e i rossi cupi. Mio fratello maggiore (anche la prepotenza di costui ritorna spesso in queste notti) voleva impedirglielo. (La stanza era buia, in un chiarore notturno). Io ero nuda. A un certo punto per dispetto egli mi sospinse così nuda dinanzi alla vetrata aperta. Questa vetrata dava su una vasta pianura, la casa era quasi su un picco, al di sopra. Ma lontanissimo, oltre la pianura, in cima a un'altura sorgeva una casa di forma gotica o araba. Malgrado l'enorme distanza, vedevo benissimo gli abitanti di quella casa osservarmi, così nuda, con chiari gesti di disapprovazione. [. . .] Più tardi, ed ero semisveglia, si accostò a me chino sulla mia testa il pallore di mia madre. Non posso chiamare altrimenti quel viso d'ombra, con pochi capelli scendenti e bianchi. Ma era consolante, dolcissimo. Più che vederlo, lo sentivo, e me ne venne subito un terrore cosciente. 'Se viene da me così, e se la sento così, — pensai — vuol dire che è morta'. Più volte, da quando lessi che spesso nel momento della morte si apparisce alle persone care, nell'infanzia e nell'adolescenza ho avuto questa paura. Stanotte ho sognato la sua stanchezza. Io, o mia sorella, seduta a un tavolino facevo il compito, e c'era vicino mia madre, col viso stanco di certe volte, la carne pesta e bianchissima, violacea sulle guance, gli occhi azzurri smorti e un po' febbrili, i capelli grigi, corti in disordine, le labbra pallide.[20]

Melodrama is the main divide between Morante's and Almodóvar's language. Morante's polytheism is archaic, Almodóvar's polytheism is postmodern. Behind Almodóvar we can see Hollywood, Truman Capote and Tennessee Williams, Buñuel and Mankiewicz, Bergman and Woody Allen. It is a mix of Mediterranean and American history, with a touch of Jewish humour: mothers descending on imperial elevators (Mankiewicz, *Suddenly, Last Summer*, 1959), talking from the clouds (Allen, *New York Stories*, 1989), rushing on motorcycles (Almodóvar, *Mujeres al borde de un ataque de nervios*, 1988);[21] and also Northern, Bergmanian mothers, metaphysical and intangible (Bergman, *Cries and whispers*, 1972).[22]

An Italian movie, *Respiro* (in the English version, *Respiro: Grazia's Island*), directed by Emanuele Crialese (2002), catches something of the whole female universe stretching from Morante to Almodóvar — the Alma-Coeli who holds together the miracle and the damnation of motherhood, through Valeria Golino's extraordinary performance — a mother who is at once radiant and furious, childish, and funereal.[23] And there is another Italian movie that I would like to mention in this homage to Aracoeli's cinematic epiphanies: *Un'ora sola ti vorrei*, by Alina Marazzi (2002).[24] Based on the notebooks, letters, and clinical charts of her mother, who committed suicide when Alina was seven years old, it is an *après-coup* mourning, a surrender to the cruelty of loss, and also of course a creative reparation of maternal harm.

Since 'nothing in the world ever embraces us so completely as the mother', as Jung says, 'when the neurotic complains that the world does not understand him, he is telling us in a word that he wants his mother'.[25] This is also true in the case of Manuele's posthumous curse against Aracoeli:

E diamoci qua stasera, la malanotte. Malanotte a te Aracoeli, che hai ricevuto il seme di me come una grazia, e l'hai covato nel tuo calduccio ventre come un tesoro, e poi ti sei sgravata di me con gioia per consegnarmi, nudo, ai tuoi sicari. Dalla concezione al parto all'allattamento alla piccola scuola dei passi e dell'alfabeto, tu non facesti altro che tendere e incrociare su di me — tendere

> e incrociare — i fili della tua macchinazione criminosa. Era meglio se tu mi abortivi, o mi soffocavi con le tue mani alla nascita, piuttosto che nutrirmi e crescermi col tuo amore infido, come una bestiola allevata per il macello. In realtà, mentre mi sorridevi coi tuoi occhi innamorati, tu ammiccavi ai tuoi mandanti. E intanto il filtro stregato che tu impastavi giorno e notte nella mia carne, era proprio questo: il tuo falso eccessivo amore, a cui mi rendesti assuefatto, come a un vizio incurabile. Se tu avessi imparato le scienze positive dell'anima, potresti almeno riconoscere i tuoi crimini materni. Si tratta, ormai, di nozioni elementari; ma il tuo cervello incapace non fu accessibile mai, per sua natura, a nessuna scienza. (*Aracoeli*, p. 1163)

On the edge of death's edge, the cry of separation and loss is bound to resonate forever. Its echo is so violent that in *Todo sobre mi madre* Almodóvar has to leave it off the screen and assign it to a voice-over.

> Ma la tua morte cresce ogni giorno.
> E in questa piena che monta io cado e mi riavvento
> in corsa dirotta, per un segno,
> un punto nella tua direzione.[26]

Almodóvarian vitalism demands that Esteban's heart be transplanted and donated. On the other hand, Morante surrenders to oblivion, to a 'memory decline': 'Ma quando la memoria è masticata dalle sabbie | anche la pulsazione del dolore è troncata'.[27]

The heartbreaking *Addio* from *Il mondo salvato dai ragazzini* celebrates the end of every possible childhood: our childhood and our children's — those we had and those we didn't have and those we lost. Furthermore, it marks the social end of a generation and of an anthropology — the same end that will first drive Pasolini to create the *Trilogy of Life* and then to abjure it: 'O pudore di un'infanzia uccisa, | Perdonami questa indecenza di sopravvivere'.[28]

Volver begins in a cemetery. *Aracoeli* begins with the desertion of a cemetery: 'Sono passati trentasei anni da quando mia madre fu sepolta nel cimitero di Campo Verano, a Roma (mia città natale). Io non sono mai stato là dentro a visitarla' (p. 1043). In *Volver*'s cemetery, hard-working women chatter while dusting the graves of their beloved ones. They are the living, who take care of the departed. They talk with the dead, with themselves, with their own history, with their own mistakes. Like ghosts, Almodóvar's women don't want to abandon the places where they were happy and unhappy, where everything started and where they will keep coming back in dreams, wishes, and nightmares.

We must learn to tell about our mother, about her history of life and death, if we want to be able to tell about ourselves. The architect Antoni Gaudì, another great Spaniard, said that 'originalidad es *volver* al origen'. The Spanish verb *volver* means both 'turning' and 'returning'. Turning to behold the past means accepting the return of the mother after her death. Telling about it, telling about her, is the only chance to repair, and maybe reconstruct, an inner object that will keep transforming us forever.

Aracoeli and *Volver* plunge us deep into the well of memory and our relationship with the maternal imago, that is, down into an obstinate, irreducible, and hardly merciful past that never ends. Returning means surviving, and withstanding the pain of a mother who dies, falls ill, or goes mad while you're still a child. One could imagine that the words of the song *Volver*, written by Carlos Gardel in 1961 — the very words Irene had taught Raimunda when her niece was still a child — were already there, ready and waiting for Almodóvar and his movie: 'Tengo miedo del encuentro con el pasado que vuelve a enfrentarse con mi vida. [. . .] Sentir que es un soplo la vida que veinte años no es nada que febril la mirada errante en las sombras te busca y te nombra'.

Notes to Chapter 6

1. 'Supplica a mia madre', in *Poesia in forma di rosa* (1964), in Pier Paolo Pasolini, *Tutte le poesie*, ed. by Walter Siti (Milan: Mondadori, 2003), p. 1102.
2. Elsa Morante, *Aracoeli*, in *Opere*, ed. by Carlo Cecchi and Cesare Garboli, 2 vols (Milan: Mondadori, 1988–90), II (1990), pp. 1039–1454 (pp. 1054–55, 1158). Further references to this edition will be given after quotations in the text.
3. *Il Vangelo secondo Matteo* [*The Gospel According to St Matthew*]. Dir. Pier Paolo Pasolini. Arco Film. 1964.
4. Pasolini, 'La ballata delle madri', in *Poesia in forma di rosa*, p. 1084.
5. Carl G. Jung, 'On the Psychology of the Unconscious', in *The Collected Works of C. G. Jung*, ed. by Herbert Read and others, trans. by R. F. C. Hull, 20 vols (London: Routledge & K. Paul, 1953–79), VII (1966), p. 103.
6. Philip M. Bromberg, *Standing in the Spaces: Essays on Clinical Process, Trauma, and Dissociation* (Hillsdale, NJ: The Analytic Press, 1998); Peter Fonagy, 'Attachment and Borderline Personality Disorder', *Journal of the American Psychoanalytic Association*, 48.4 (2000), 1129–46.
7. John Bowlby, *A Secure Base* (London: Basic Books, 1988).
8. Peter Fonagy, Mary Target, Gyorgy Gergely, and Elliot L. Jurist, *Affect Regulation, Mentalization and the Development of Self* (New York: Other Press, 2005).
9. Vittorio Lingiardi, 'Dreaming Gender: Restoration and Transformation', *Studies in Gender and Sexuality*, 8.4 (2007), 313–31.
10. Louis W. Sander, 'The event-structure of regulation in the neonate-caregiver system as a biological background for early organization of psychic structure', in *Frontiers in Self Psychology: Progress in Self Psychology*, III, ed. by Arnold Goldberg (Hillsdale, NJ: The Analytic Press, 1988), pp. 64–77; id., 'Thinking Differently: Principles of Process in Living Systems and the Specificity of Being Known', *Psychoanalytic Dialogues*, 12.1 (2002), 11–42.
11. See also Jessica Benjamin, 'The Rhythm of Recognition: Comments on the Work of Louis Sander', *Psychoanalytic Dialogues*, 12.1 (2002), 43–54.
12. Jessica Benjamin, *Like Subjects, Love Objects: Essays on Recognition and Sexual Difference* (New Haven: Yale University Press, 1995).
13. Daniel N. Stern, *The Interpersonal World of the Infant* (New York: Basic Books, 1985); id., *The Motherhood Constellation: A Unified View of Parent–Infant Psychotherapy* (New York: Basic Books, 1995).
14. Elsa Morante, *Il mondo salvato dai ragazzini e altri poemi* (1968), in *Opere*, II, 3–253.
15. *The Women*. Dir. George Cukor. Metro-Goldwyn-Mayer (MGM). 1939; *Todo sobre mi madre*. Dir. Pedro Almodóvar. El Deseo S.A. 1999.
16. *All About Eve*. Dir. Joseph L. Mankiewicz. 20th Century Fox. 1950.
17. Pasolini, *Il Vangelo*, 1964.
18. *Volver*. Dir. Pedro Almodóvar. Canal + España. 2006.
19. Emily Dickinson, '*The Complete Poems of Emily Dickinson*, ed. by T. H. Johnson (Boston: Little Brown & Co., 1960), no. 670.
20. Elsa Morante, *Lettere ad Antonio [Diario 1938]*, in *Opere*, II, 1594–95.
21. *Suddenly, Last Summer*. Dir. Joseph L. Mankiewicz. Horizon Pictures (II). 1959; *New York Stories*. Dir. Woody Allen, Francis Ford Coppola and Martin Scorsese. Touchstone Pictures. 1989; *Mujeres al borde de un ataque de nervios*. Dir. Pedro Almodóvar. El Deseo S.A. 1988.
22. *Cries and whispers*. Dir. Ingmar Bergman. Cinematograph AB. 1972.

23. *Respiro*. Dir. Emanuele Crialese. Eurimages. 2002.
24. *Un'ora sola ti vorrei*. Dir. Alina Marazzi. Bartlebyfilm. 2002.
25. Carl G. Jung, 'Symbols of Transformation', in *The Collected Works of C. G. Jung*, v (1956), p. 682.
26. Elsa Morante, *Addio*, in *Il mondo salvato dai ragazzini e altri poemi* (Turin: Einaudi, 1968), p. 8.
27. Morante, *Addio*, p. 22.
28. Morante, *Addio*, p. 8.

CHAPTER 7

Baubo — Another and Additional Name of Aracoeli: Morante's Queer Feminism

Astrid Deuber-Mankowsky

Names

Names play a multi-faceted and constitutive role in the complex cross-referential structure of the text in Elsa Morante's last novel *Aracoeli*. The names of the novel's characters are tropes rather than proper names, transitional points in which heterogeneous stories converge from diverse temporal and topographical directions and are directed and dispersed in new directions. The characters move within the areas of conflict of these stories and yet struggle to both escape and comply with the ambiguity of their names.

The allegorization of names causes a peculiar split in both the text and the characters. The names uncover an independent existence which opens up a labyrinth of meaning, which in turn prevents the characters from assuming an identity and the novel from developing meaning and a closed unity. This applies not only to the protagonist Aracoeli, who gives the title to the novel, but also to all other characters. In particular, it applies to the first-person narrator and child of Aracoeli, Manuele, who is also referred to as *Manuel*, *Manolito*, and *Manuelito* in the Spanish versions of the name. The narrative threads which condense in the name Emanuele/Manuele are counter-striving, that is, they run in different directions and through their heterogeneity subvert the abjections which, as Judith Butler has vividly shown, are constitutive of the subject and the formation of (sexual) identities.[1]

Morante's text brings these abjections to the surface. At one stage, in a peculiar and isolated irruption of the writing self into the intradiegetic perspective of the first-person narrator, Morante calls the novel 'il mio povero ultimo romanzo andaluso', 'una fabbrica d'ombre equivoche, per trastullo dei miei giorni vani'.[2] This applies to the novel no less than to its characters, yet at the same time it is an opus of language which displays an endless array of nuances. The novel is an exploration of the boundaries set by an unfathomable reality, which for Morante is always an equivalent to 'life', to the desire for knowledge and the search for meaning.[3] The strength and power of Morante's novel lie precisely in the consistent recourse to the ambiguous and the abysmal.

Manuele alias Vittorio Emanuele Maria

As the novel says, at his father's wish Manuele had been entered into the Roman register of births in 1932 as Vittorio Emanuele Maria in honour of Italy's King Vittorio Emanuele III of Savoy. This entry into the register of births is the starting point of a concatenation of stories and meanings connected to the name of the king and to the father's wish, which is itself projected in the name. In the early 1930s the King of Italy hardly retained any political power: he had delegated command of the armed forces to Mussolini and was no longer a powerful figure. The figure of the father is similarly powerless: unlike the precocious and perceptive Manuele, the prodigy, he is not endued with sensitivity for language and imagination and knows only one expression to articulate the unchanging love for his wife Aracoeli: 'Amore mio. Amore mio, Amore mio' (*Aracoeli*, p. 1340).

The first-person narrator recalls that the father and son's common, exclusive love for Aracoeli generated feelings not of rivalry but of gratitude. The 'Oedipus-scheme', as the text says, is not adequately suited to grasp the story of this triangle. In fact, it does not fit into any prefabricated scheme. To the question of how the case could be described the advocate replies: 'Eterno amore' (*Aracoeli*, p. 1182).

The writing self Manuele belongs neither to the female nor to the male sex; one lover, who claims to be 'un frocetto comune', an ordinary little gay guy, rejects him, with the reproach: 'Non sei nemmeno una vera checca, sei un maschio fallito, un rottame di classe fuori servizio, buono per il Museo dei Fasci defunti' (*Aracoeli*, p. 1096). Indeed, at a certain point in the novel, when describing his non-oedipal relationship with his father, Manuele classes himself as part of the 'razza triste' which has never known 'la vera tragedia della gelosia' and lapses into a state of 'ammirazione disperata' instead of envying the rival (p. 1207). He considers himself relegated to those liminal areas of life which could be described, in the terms of Judith Butler, as the 'domain of abject beings'.[4]

As Butler argues, the domain of abject beings designates 'those 'unlivable' and 'uninhabitable' zones of social life which are nevertheless densely populated by those who do not enjoy the status of the subject, but whose living under the sign of the 'unlivable' is required to circumscribe the domain of the subject'.[5] On the one hand, Manuele's life is considered to be lived under the sign of the 'unlivable'. On the other hand, the formulation of the 'razza triste' of which Manuele considers himself part suggests counting him as one of those, as Butler further claims, who rejected the melancholic abjections required for the development of '*gender* identification', i.e. the identification with *one* gender.[6]

In her book *The Psychic Life of Power* Butler analyses heterosexual gender affiliation as a 'kind of melancholy', and also as 'one of the effects of melancholy'.[7] Departing from Freud's essay 'Mourning and Melancholia', she reads Freud's 'Three Essays on the Theory of Sexuality', in which Freud explains the psychic development which leads to the adoption of male or alternatively female gender identification. At its root are 'the effects of a laborious and uncertain accomplishment', which 'are established in part through prohibitions which *demand the loss* of certain sexual attachments, and demand as well that those losses *not* be avowed, and *not* be grieved'.[8] Butler consequently calls the heterosexual gender the 'melancholic gender'. It is formed not only through implementing the prohibition of incest but, prior to that, 'by enforcing the prohibition on homosexuality'.[9] If, as Freud's theses suggest, the adoption of masculinity and femininity are implemented through an always tenuous heterosexuality then, as Judith Butler argues, we might understand 'the force of this accomplishment as mandating the abandonment of homosexual attachments or, perhaps more trenchantly, *preempting* the possibility of homosexual attachment, a foreclosure of possibility which produces a domain of homosexuality understood as unlivable passion and ungrievable loss'.[10]

Manuele's character initially seems to get very close to this homophobic construction. In fact, 'unlivable passion' is one of his central and determining characteristics. We would even have to accuse the novel of indiscriminately, candidly re-enacting Butler's thesis of homosexuality if, as suggested by the literary scholar Walter Siti, we interpret the character of Manuele as a portrait of Pasolini. According to Siti this was Morante's way of interpreting death and getting over Pasolini's death, with whom Morante had had a long, intimate, and at the same time complicated relationship.[11] As Siti maintains, 'one would almost be tempted to say that Morante carried out an experiment in Zola's sense of the term: what would it have been like to be a *niñomadrero* homosexual who loathed his own body just as she did at that time'.[12] Siti hints at the fact that Morante was suffering from an indefinable illness when writing the novel. However, I would argue that the illness and the insurmountable alienation of the body are not, as Siti's interpretation suggests, dealt with in the character of Manuele, but in that of Aracoeli, in particular in whom 'si svolgeva una qualche azione subdola e creda, a cui la tua materia si assuefaceva servilmente', as we read in the text (*Aracoeli*, p. 1332).[13] Our own body, as Morante further comments on this power, is 'straniero a noi stessi quanto gli ammassi stellari o i fondi vulcanici. Nessun dialogo possibile. Nessun alfabeto comune' (p. 1352). This 'power' can only be inadequately described by the illness which sets in after the untimely death of her small, eagerly desired daughter — who dies just a few weeks after her birth. It transforms the beautiful, young, adorable, and life-affirming Aracoeli into an erratic, nymphomaniac, transgressive, and extraordinary woman who eventually leaves her husband and son in order to spend the last months preceding her death in a brothel.

Siti points out that Pasolini was killed on the beach of Ostia on 2 November 1975 — the same date on which, in the novel, Manuele encounters Aracoeli's spirit in the Andalusian desert. He interprets this as further confirmation of his argument that Manuele should be considered a literary portrait of Pasolini. However, contrary to Siti's interpretation, it seems to me that it is not a reunion between Manuele and Aracoeli that occurs on that day in the Andalusian desert and Manuele does not return to 'the maternal womb'.[14] What happens is rather to be seen as a separation from the dead. As it says in the novel after the — perhaps only fictitious — encounter with Aracoeli: 'E questo è l'addio' (*Aracoeli*, p. 1428). Aracoeli's spirit consequently dissolves into nothing. Manuele, for his part, returns to the living and while passing through Aracoeli's village remembers his very first Spanish word, *perro*, which means 'dog' and at the same time is a symbol for melancholy. In his mother's village he starts speaking to an elderly man in Spanish. As the novel says:

'anch'io mi faccio forte, con lui, di tutto il mio spagnolo' (p. 1430). The search for Aracoeli, the process of memory, the transposition of ambivalent feelings into linguistic images, the encounter and farewell in the desert of El Almendral all open the barred access to his first language, the language of the mother.[15]

Manuele is a member of the 'razza triste', but there is also a degree of melancholy in him. It manifests itself in the abjection of the scandalous, sinister, and frivolous Aracoeli, who defies the desire for idealization and rejects her formerly much beloved 'niño', making him 'laidamente orfano ancor prima d'esser morta' (*Aracoeli*, p. 1066). As Morante describes Manuele's denial of reality, 'a costo di calunniarti e maledirti e rinnegarti, io non ho MAI voluto riconoscere la denunciata impossibile miseria del tuo ultimo segreto' (p. 1404). The young boy is unable to acknowledge Aracoeli's 'terribile ambiguità' and to mourn her sudden death; what follows precisely accords with the story told in Freud's 1917 essay on 'Mourning and Melancholia' about the formation and the effect of melancholy: 'The relationship with the object [. . .] is complicated by the conflict of ambivalence. Thus in melancholia a series of individual battles for the object begins, in which love and hatred struggle with one another, one to free the libido from the object, the other to maintain the existing libido position against the onslaught'.[16] This battle persists until the struggle for the object is exchanged for the conflict in the ego which, as Freud claims, is similar in effect to a painful wound.[17] Life only returns to Manuele when he is assailed by Aracoeli's voice thirty-six years after her death (*Aracoeli*, p. 13). He follows the call of her voice, which triggers a synaesthesic perception of the physical presence of a young and beautiful Aracoeli. He decides to look for Aracoeli in her village in Andalusia and starts remembering the happiest and most painful time of his life. Aracoeli's call also triggers the process of writing and the creation of the novel. The writing process is directed against death and melancholy, while at the same time it is steeped in death and melancholy.

For the son '*paternità*', *fatherhood*, which appears in italics in the text, assumes a meaning equivalent to *absence*, which is also set in italics in the text (*Aracoeli*, p. 1269). In this way the child reacts to the father's aversion to his own fatherhood; perhaps, as the first-person narrator conjectures, this is because his father had been brought up by an austere and unloved father himself and had always desired a paternal figure, whom he ultimately found in Victor Emanuel III, the King of Italy. Manuele enters this story when his name was first inserted into the register of births, and soon starts to worship his father with a religious, almost cult-like reverence and in accordance with Aracoeli's 'fede adorante', her venerating belief in her husband: he turns his father into the father his own father would have desired. He himself says: 'non sono mai stato figlio di un padre' (p. 1270).

As Manuele continues the description of his relationship with his father: 'la sua razza era differente dalla nostra' (*Aracoeli*, p. 1270) — by 'nostra' he is referring to himself and his mother. Between his body and that of his father — a uniformed Comandante of the Italian navy who was away on business most of the time — 'si era stesa (e si infittiva con la mia crescita) una nebbia confusa: pari a quella, appunto che vela ai mortali le apparizioni sfavillanti dei Superni' (p. 1270). By turning to the 'Superni', celestials, a new narrative thread interferes with the relationship between Manuele and his father. According to this narrative the masculinity embodied by the father is seen to reach back to Roman imperialism, thus revealing a concept of humanity as divided into demigods and non-humans. Therefore, in the next sentence Morante compares the indistinct fog which separated Manuele from his father's body with the fog which blinded the eyes of the Aztecs when the whites entered their territory for the first time. Morante underlines the association of white masculinity with the abjection which makes up the very concept itself by allowing Manuele, for whom his father represents the 'paradigm' of 'VIRILITÀ' [MASCULINITY], to write the sentence: 'già fino da allora, a me provocava un senso di separazione forzosa: come a un piccolo Giudeo del Primo Secolo la persona di un Romano' (p. 1270).

In the genealogy of the King of Fascist Italy the Comandante is traced back to the figure of the Roman posing as demigod. At the same time, Manuele, who considers himself as a member of the corrupt, 'sad race', also identifies with the figure of the Jew displaced into exile. In the line-up of the narrative threads connected to the name Vittorio Emanuele III, the King of Fascist Italy, and the desire for the father which is inscribed in these names, Morante discovers the violence which constitutes this MASCULINITY in capital letters. We only have to call to mind Sarah Kofman's interpretation of Robert Antelm's *The Human Race* in order to grasp the dimension of this violence during National Socialism: as Kofman argues, the deported felt perpetually called into question as a species because those who purportedly belonged to a higher, divine species had the intention of gradually merging them into the animal species by providing worse 'living' conditions than those of animals.[18]

The last addition to the name, Maria, which is dedicated to the Virgin Mother, has its origin in Aracoeli's wish. This wish opens a new chain of stories which lead to Andalusia, to the domain and the narrative realm of the mother-lover and the girl Aracoeli. Aracoeli agrees to the name Emanuele all the more because its Spanish version is Manuel, which in turn is the name of her beloved younger brother who has remained in her birthplace in Andalusia. The discovery of the equivalence between Emanuele and Manuel made her blush from joy. Manuel the uncle and beloved brother, who as a boy had fought with the partisans and had been killed by Franco's troops, is far more than a namesake for Manuele the nephew, who knows his uncle only from his mother's stories. Manuel is his hero, his better ego, his love. The idea of Manuel turns into a substitute of love for Aracoeli when Manuele, the son, can no longer love Aracoeli. As the first-person narrator comments, Aracoeli's appearance in the form of her brother is natural as their mother had always asserted that sister and brother had always been alike as two peas in a pod (*Aracoeli*, pp. 1330–31). And from now on, as Morante writes, for me 'le due seduzioni di Aracoeli e di Manuel mi si fusero in una: il "paradiso" di Manuel filtrava attraverso gli aloni varianti di Aracoeli' (p. 1331). At that point not only Manuel but also Aracoeli had died.

The two seductions of Aracoeli and Manuel not only transgress the law of the family — the incest taboo and the prohibition on homosexuality — but also the boundary between life and death.

Baubo

How can we analyse the novel *Aracoeli* without on the one hand losing ourselves in the labyrinth of meaning of the text and on the other missing out on the complexity of this baroque writing? I will attempt to do precisely this by taking a detour, adding a further name to Aracoeli's many names, which Manuele refers to as 'costumi convenzionali che sempre fanno sognare gli imberbi': 'Pastora. Idalga. Santa. Meretrice. Morta. Immortale. Vittima. Tiranna. Bambola. Dea. Schiava. Madre. Figlia. Ballerina' (*Aracoeli*, p. 1194). This additional name is *Baubo*. I thereby refer to Nietzsche, in whose philosophy of affirmation the name *Baubo* stands for truth and life. In the preface to *The Gay Science* Nietzsche advocates an enlightened service to images, the worship of appearance, and a philosophy of surfaces. He associates this plea with a warning about the will to truth, which is shameless and indecent, because, as Nietzsche comments on his warning with an ironic undertone: 'Perhaps truth is a woman who has reasons for not letting us see her reasons? Perhaps her name is — to speak Greek — Baubo?'.[19]

Baubo is the name of the female creature, demon, nurse, and also Thracian, i.e. barbarian and uneducated slave, who put an end to Demeter's mourning for the loss of her daughter Persephone. Persephone had been abducted by Hades and taken to the underworld. Baubo is said to have amused the goddess of grain and fertility by pulling up her skirt and uncovering her vulva in an obscene manner. Baubo comforted Demeter by reminding her of the meaning of fertility and the power of bearing new life. Baubo is the Greek word for vulva and furthermore, as George Devereux has pointed out, it is associated with *baubon*, which means 'Godemiché' or dildo but has only been applied to dildos used by women. Devereux further underlines that the artificial phallus which is according to myth used by Dionysus to simulate homosexual coitus would never have been called a *baubon*.[20] This peculiar ambivalence of meaning associated with the name Baubo is further enhanced by the fact that in some sources and illustrations the head and the arm of Iacchus protruded from Baubo's vulva. Iacchus is a further name for Bacchus or Dionysus.[21]

According to Kofman, Nietzsche's designation of truth with the name Baubo is to be interpreted as the demand to affirm the power of agonal ambiguity while at the same time accepting the absence of a deeper meaning.[22] Baubo functions as an apotropaism which is meant to prevent the philosopher from idealism and the downfall into melancholy. What reasons does Nietzsche have for calling truth a woman who has reasons for not letting us see her reasons ('Gründe') and calling her Baubo? These reasons lie not only in the fact that truth is in truth unfounded. Baubo's reasons for veiling her *Gründe* are at the same time directed at a cause, inasmuch they protect the philosopher from himself and from the will to truth. As Nietzsche writes on a further occasion, this will is 'a hidden will to death'.[23] In this way the will to truth turns into a symptom for the melancholy abjection of the world as it is: gratuitous and abysmal, deceptive and senseless. To put it sharply, Baubo protects the philosopher from the will to truth and also to some extent from the confrontation with truth.

One could say that Baubo's message is the very same message that Aracoeli delivers to a grown-up Manuele during their farewell in the desert of El Almendral: 'Dovunque, ho peccato', as Manuele puts it, 'nelle intenzioni e nei fini e negli atti ma peggio di tutto nell'intelligenza. L'intelligenza si dà per capire. E a me si è data, ma io non capisco niente. E non ho mai capito e non capirò mai niente'. Aracoeli's answer, in accordance with Nietzsche, is that 'Ma, niño mio chiquito, non c'è niente da capire' (*Aracoeli*, p. 1428).

Aracoeli is not only just as obscene, abysmal, erratic, and resistive as Baubo, she is not only of a confusing hermaphrodeity, barbaric, and not befitting her rank — her rough origins, as it says in the novel, are a 'scheletro in un armadio' in Manuele's father's family (p. 1068). Aracoeli is not only desperate about the death of her daughter, just like Demeter who is comforted by Baubo. At the same time Aracoeli is also the figure in which Morante gives expression to the agonal ambivalence, the abysmal, the seductive power and the indifference in terms of which life responds to the search for meaning, explanations, and reasons. One could also say, with reference to Nietzsche: Aracoeli is another name for life.

Aracoeli

Aracoeli — unlike Baubo — is not a Greek name, but a female name common in Spain, and at the same time a name from Christian liturgy which means 'celestial altar' and refers back to the cult of the Roman goddess Juno Moneta.[24] Her sexual excesses do not appear as a sign of power and fertility but as scandal and illness. Her eagerly desired daughter '*Encarnación*', called *Carina* within the family (pp. 1275), dies shortly after birth and is not brought back to her.[25] Aracoeli herself is immortal only as an erratic spirit and demon.

When traits of Baubo appear in Aracoeli, these are distorted by the haggish figure which Baubo has assumed through Christianity. In the character of Aracoeli the traits of the Greek Baubo, who stands for the fertility of life, and the Christian Baubo, who is rejected as a witch and a sow, eclipse one another, as unmediated as picture puzzles.[26] Baubo appears in the first part of Goethe's *Faust* riding on a sow, as the leader of all witches:

> VOICE: Our ancient Baubo rides alone
> with a mother sow beneath her buttocks.
> CHORUS: We like to cheer when cheers are due!
> Let Lady Baubo lead the crew.
> With mother on a strapping swine
> The other hags will stay in line.[27]

My thesis is that Morante's queer feminism consists of the fact that in the constellation of Aracoeli and Manuele — who is not accidentally called *el niño*, which also means Christ Child — she superimposes the appearance of the Virgin Mary and her child with the image of the obscene Baubo from whose vulva protrudes the head and the hand of Iacchus/Bacchus. 'Conviene rammentare', as it says in the text at some point, 'che la madre del soggetto era andalusa. [. . .] È possibile che in quella madre andalusa sopravvivessero delle teofanie ancestrali d'Arabia e d'Africa. Nel suo cattolicesimo elementare tornavano rituali barbari e favole pagane' (*Aracoeli*, p. 1185).

The battle of these different traditions and meanings is also a battle for the meaning of life and death. This is shown particularly well in the figure of Baubo, who in the Greek myth is able to comfort and amuse Demeter, the goddess of fertility and grain, while in the Christian adaptation she transforms into a demonic witch and the avatar of death.

From the point of view of this queer feminism the scene in which Aracoeli sends Manuele to the ice-cream vendor in order to masturbate in front of a church's facade during his short absence appears as a strong scene of resistance:

> Stava sempre là, in quel vano sgombro del marciapiede, pari a una mendicante, ma s'era adesso accovacciata e raccolta, le mani affondate nel grembo. E s'era data a un febbrile moto oscillante che accompagnava con un dondolio meccanico della testa, come assorta in un'estasi ottusa, mentre i suoi occhi si tenevano fissi alla facciata della chiesa in uno stupore torbido, avverso e quasi vendicativo'. (*Aracoeli*, p. 1387)

Here Aracoeli is like a rejected Baubo in 1941 Rome.

Aracoeli then enters the church with Manuele, whilst remaining uncovered like a heretic (*Aracoeli*, p. 1378): 'e sguardava in direzione dell'altare con la protervia di una gatta che si arruffa contro un cane immenso' (p. 1380). If we consider the meaning applied to the cat in Pasolini and Morante's cosmos of meaning — Pasolini had compared Morante to a cat and she used the term to describe herself — the sovereignty and precision of Morante's play with names and meaning is further emphasized. Aracoeli, instead of assuming the role of celestial altar, herself likens her glance to the audacity of a cat starting a fight with a dog, the synonym of melancholy. Under this gaze the church is transformed from a 'dipendenza [. . .] del paradiso', into a 'deposito provvisorio della morte' (p. 1389). For a short moment the affirmation of life returns to Aracoeli alias Baubo in all its ambivalence.

The name Aracoeli, which seemed 'natural' to Manuele in the first years of living with Aracoeli, is remembered by the adolescent as a 'segno di diversità, un titolo unico: in cui mia madre rimane separata e rinchiusa, come dentro una cornice tortile e massiccia, dipinta d'oro' (*Aracoeli*, p. 1048). This golden frame in his memory transforms into the frame of a baroque mirror which reflects the 'primissima visione' of Manuele's self (p. 1049). The golden frame was an heirloom of his paternal family. It remains unclear throughout the novel whether this is a memory or an illusion, and whether Aracoeli's voice is real or fictitious. The novel as a whole is a unique baroque struggle for meaning, a rebellion against the noise and at the same time a reflection on the boundaries of the meaningful side of language. As Manuele puts it in a scene set in the Andalusian desert: 'Non è possibile che una simile quantità di materia sia solo una valanga di rifiuti, senza un brandello — almeno — di significato. Forse, una sua possibile parola di vita eterna mi è stata qua trasmessa a mia insaputa, per via subliminale, e mi si spiegherà a suo tempo?' (p. 1202).

Aracoeli refuses to give the answer which Manuele searches for in her. Through the text's proliferation of meanings she is liberated from the frame and leaves Manuele with the doubt as to whether she is worthy of her name or whether she is just making fun of him.[28] She laughs at him, plays hide-and-seek as in her early days in Totetaco (*Aracoeli*, p. 1193), confuses his search for reasons with her 'blink and buzz', and pits the exchangeability of signs against the search for truth.

The Sting of the Giant Wasp

After his encounter with Aracoeli, Manuele is left behind on his own, with the memory of his first, maternal language. The short conversation with the old man in El Almendral, Aracoeli's village, ends with Manuele asking him whether he had ever heard of the Muñoz Muñoz family — Aracoeli's family name. The answer is: 'Qui in giro tutta la gente porta questo cognome' (*Aracoeli*, p. 1430).

The novel ends with the description of the last encounter with the father and leads to a most 'queer' happy ending. When young Manuele returns to Rome after the end of the war, he finds his parents' home empty. He finds out from his paternal aunt that his father had deserted from the royal fleet and subsequently had to go into hiding. As his aunt explains with her cheeks blazing red with embarrassment and shame, the king had not behaved in an honourable way, and this had been the final blow for his father. She sends Manuele to see his father who is now living in one of the few bombed quarters of Rome near the cemetery Campo Verano where Aracoeli had been buried. Manuele finds his father in a desolate, degrading state. He is wearing an old dressing gown and is in an untended state, drunken and foul-smelling. Manuele feels aversion and disgust. No real conversation takes place, the father says goodbye with the words 'Ci rivedremo presto?', and Manuele flees through the war-ridden quarter to a cafe where he buys a sweet bun and starts crying.

His weeping turns into a brilliant ending, a substitute for the explanation denied by Aracoeli. In the last pages of the novel the first-person narrator again departs on a search, and this time it is the search for the reason behind his tears. He finds this in his memory in a 'trafittura acutissima, quale di un pungiglione di vespa gigante che dal collo mi penetrasse fino in fondo alla gola' (*Aracoeli*, p. 1453). This unequivocal erotic fantasy finally leads to the conclusion that Manuele was weeping with love. And not with love for Aracoeli, but with love for his father, Eugenio Ottone Amedeo.

This sting of the giant wasp which penetrated his neck through to his throat occurs once more — one year later, when Manuele receives the news of his father's death. Back then he had not understood the call of the double signal. Only now, after his journey to the Andalusian desert, does he recognize the 'piccola belva sanguinaria' as a messenger of his father who in this way tries to make him realize the 'motivo innominato' of his tears: love. It is obviously a love which has left the ideal of the norm of heterosexuality behind, and which is not channelled through the prohibition on homosexual relations. Not only is it directed at the father, who has lost the denomination of MASCULINITY, deserted from the royal fleet, lapsed into alcoholism, and lives in a doss-house in a run-down quarter near the bombed cemetery. Manuele can grasp the message only after regaining access to his first language: Aracoeli's language. In this language, as was quite natural in the early period Manuele spent with Aracoeli in Totetaco, there is no gender divide. At that time, as it says in the novel, Manuele does not know 'di essere maschio, ossia uno che mai poteva diventare donna come Aracoeli' (*Aracoeli*, p. 1186). The violent sting of the giant wasp annihilates this 'knowledge' and thus at the same time proves to be a sign from Aracoeli.

Translated by Katrin Wehling-Giorgi

Notes to Chapter 7

1. See Judith Butler, *Gender Trouble: Feminism and the Subversion of Identity* (New York: Routledge, 1990).
2. Elsa Morante, *Aracoeli*, in *Opere*, ed. by Carlo Cecchi and Cesare Garboli, 2 vols (Milan: Mondadori, 1988–90), II (1990), pp. 1039–1454 (p. 1200). Further references to this edition will be given after quotations in the text.
3. See Filippo La Porta, 'The "Dragon of Unreality" against the "Dream of a Thing": On Morante and Pasolini', in *Under Arturo's Star: The Cultural Legacies of Elsa Morante*, ed. by Stefania Lucamante and Sharon Wood (West Lafayette, IN: Purdue University Press, 2006), pp. 290–309.
4. Judith Butler, *Bodies That Matter: On The Discursive Limits of 'Sex'* (New York and London: Routledge, 1993), p. 3.
5. Butler, *Bodies That Matter*, p. 3.
6. Judith Butler, 'Melancholy Gender — Refused Identification', in *The Psychic Life of Power: Theories of Subjection* (Stanford: Stanford University Press, 1997), pp. 132–50.
7. Butler, 'Melancholy Gender', p. 132.
8. Butler, 'Melancholy Gender', p. 135. Butler is here referring to all the dead who have died from AIDS.
9. Butler, 'Melancholy Gender', p. 135.
10. Butler, *The Psychic Life of Power*, p. 135.
11. See Walter Siti, 'Elsa Morante and Pier Paolo Pasolini', in *Under Arturo's Star*, pp. 268–89.
12. Siti, p. 286.
13. See also: *Aracoeli*, p. 1352.
14. Siti, p. 286.
15. See Sara Fortuna and Manuele Gragnolati's essay, Chapter 2, in this volume.
16. Sigmund Freud, 'Mourning and Melancholia', in *On Murder, Mourning and Melancholia*, trans. by Shaun Whiteside (London: Penguin, 2005), pp. 203–18 (p. 216); German original, 'Trauer und Melancholie', in Sigmund Freud, *Gesammelte Werke*, X (Frankfurt a.M.: Suhrkamp, 1999), pp. 428–46 (p. 444).
17. Freud, 'Mourning and Melancholia', p. 218.
18. Sarah Kofman, *Paroles suffoquées* (Paris: Galilée, 1987), pp. 65–66.
19. Friedrich Nietzsche, *Die fröhliche Wissenschaft*, in *Kritische Studienausgabe*, ed. by Giorgio Colli and Mazzino Montanari, 15 vols (Berlin; New York: de Gruyter, 1988), III, 352. The translation is mine. See also Francesca Cadel's essay in this volume (Chapter 10).
20. George Devereux, *Baubo: die mytische Vulva*, trans. by Eva Moldenhauer (Frankfurt a.M.: Syndikat, 1981), p. 71.
21. Devereux, *Baubo*, p. 33.
22. Sarah Kofman, *Nietzsche et la scène philosophique* (Paris: Union Générale d'Éditions, 1979), p. 2.
23. Nietzsche, *Die fröhliche Wissenschaft*, p. 576; my translation.
24. In Rome there is a famous church called Santa Maria in Aracoeli. From the fourth century BC in its place there stood a temple of Juno in which it is said that the Coming of Christ was prophesied to Emperor Augustus. The emperor had asked the prophetess Sybil whether someone grander than him would be born. The following midday a golden circle appeared around the sun in the centre of which the most beautiful Virgin stood on an altar, with a child on her lap. Augustus consequently ordered the erection of a celestial altar in the temple of Juno. Today this temple is located in the Chapel of Saint Helena, the mother of Emperor Constantine, who is

buried here. It is interesting that since AD 286 the Roman mint was located next to the temple of Juno. The vicinity of the mint and the temple is the reason why the name 'Moneta', which is Juno's sobriquet, was first applied to the mint and then transferred to the coins themselves. Moneta means the 'Warner'/'she who warns'. Juno was not only in charge of everything pertaining to femininity, but she was also the patron of the city of Rome. To date the church Santa Maria in Aracoeli remains the church of the Roman people.

25. If it had been a boy, Aracoeli would have called him 'NOBODY' (p. 1276).
26. Devereux explains the connection between the sow and Baubo by pointing out that the Corinthian word for vulva — 'Choiros' — also meant pig; see Devereux, p. 36.
27. Johann Wolfgang von Goethe, 'Walpurgis Night', in *Faust: Part I*, trans. by Peter Salm (New York: Bantam Books, 1985), p. 271.
28. Manuele dreams of the sentences '*Non è degna di questo nome!*' and '*La signora si diverte!*' (p. 1410). However Aracoeli, who is hardly literate, only signs her farewell letter with the first four letters of her name: 'ARAC' (p. 1384).

Intermezzo

CHAPTER 8

Staging the Passion of Aracoeli

Agnese Grieco

How can I discuss a play which has already been done, without my considerations appearing to be mere justifications in hindsight for the artistic choices made? Moreover, how to talk about it to a potential audience, most of whom have not seen 'La Passione di Aracoeli'? And again: shouldn't a play be enough in itself? ('Of course it should'!) These are a few examples of the doubts that I had when I set about writing this.

I would therefore like to invite anyone who might read these brief notes to see them as a short travel diary. The themes and visions that guided me are evidence of a specific path of interpretation and 'cross contamination' of genres. Perhaps that is what makes them interesting.

Towards a Voice-led Theatre

When literature and theatre meet, we are immediately faced with questions on theory and aesthetics, which are interesting from the perspective of both these forms of artistic expression.

Indeed, the interaction between the stage — I use stage in the broadest, most generic sense of the term (anywhere can become a stage if necessary) — actors, audience, and literary text opens up a wide array of possibilities leading to the creation and later performance of 'works' that can vary considerably.

These range from the typical stage adaptation of a literary text, right up to the equally traditional dramatic reading of the chosen text — which may be abridged to a lesser or greater extent — via the 'staged reading' or *mise en espace*. The terms allude to various open forms of dramatic adaptation, with varying degrees of faithfulness to the original work, to a performance in the usual sense of the word.

In the case of a classic 'theatrical adaptation' of a literary text, we generally focus on the theatrical potential, or intrinsic theatrical quality, already found in the original work — mainly speaking in terms of the physiognomy of the characters, the structure of their interactions, dialogues, and key dramatic moments. Once this theatrical quality has been identified and defined, the text needs to be developed as far as possible into a fully staged form. So the dramaturgical challenge here is to translate one genre into another. This means respecting and at the same time betraying the original text, within a framework of accepted conventions. It should, however, be remembered that modern and contemporary theatrical writing and practice have shown how 'real theatre' can be based on literature, creating more or less conventional plays, without necessarily having to accept and reproduce the conventions of classical dramatic literature. In such cases novels are not 'dramatized' for the stage; instead, a different dramaturgical reworking of the text is chosen. What is more, authors such as Samuel Beckett or Heiner Müller have carried out plenty of experiments in their alternative work for the theatre.

A traditional 'dramatic reading', on the other hand, would seem to place itself on the opposite yet complementary side of a theatrical adaptation of a literary work. This option appears to be deliberately anti-theatrical. In a 'simple' reading, the actor's voice tends to mingle with that of the writer. It evokes the author and with him, his supreme position, the artistry of narrative, thus bringing out the special quality of the literary genre. To some extent, the actor/reader then plays with a sort of 'spectator's inner voice' — the spectator in turn being a potential reader — in a special monological dimension. Indeed, the actor is not required to interpret a character, but instead a subject/object: a text, together with its author. For example, the actor will give different voices to the various characters in the work of literature, but will always take care to maintain that core of stylistic unity and textual identity which bears out the legitimacy of his task. The reader/actor mustn't 'do too much', and veer dangerously towards theatre. Much in the same way as a concert musician, the actor performs the text for the audience. Moreover, the musicality of the text — if you will forgive my deliberately vague wording — is often one of the crucial elements on which an actor will base his or her reading.

The purpose of this short introduction is to contextualize my dramatic work based on Elsa Morante's *Aracoeli* and the subsequent staged reading of it intended for two actors and a mezzo-soprano, performed at the Berlin Institute for Cultural Inquiry on 11 April 2008. Indeed, the staged experiment is placed in what I call the middle space between the idea of a full translation of the literary genre into the theatrical genre, and the overt monological faithfulness to the literary genre. In other words, the performance balances on the ridge between minimal and maximal theatricality. An underlying question immediately arises in this middle space, which we could formulate in very general terms as: *How* does a text *speak*? And, *who is speaking* in the text? The question reaches beyond the obvious answer, being: the author and/or the various characters. It becomes: *how to listen to* a text if we want to *give it a voice*. By this I mean giving a voice to the text beyond the obvious narrative structure, without accepting classical dramatic conventions. In this space of tension between text, listening, and reproduction, multiple interpretations, aesthetic choices and subjective sensibilities run into each other. And this is true for any given text.

I like to call this meeting between literature and theatrical perspective a *dramaturgy of the voice and of listening*. This dimension relates to the specific context of the theatre in a subtle, complex way: not only in terms of subtraction — given that a staged event is not yet 'real theatre' — but also in the name of freedom of experimentation. And I believe that here once again, the theatrical event displays its protean nature, the richness of its communicative potential.

The music of Aracoeli

When I began working on *Aracoeli* I could see how it would be a difficult task to work through and present this novel by Morante to the audience. It is a text of a Lucretian nature and an Indian vision, denser than ever, rich in contradictions, in questions that are asked and left unanswered; rich in secret passages towards 'areas of meaning' that are unexplored and difficult to explore. It is an 'exorbitant' book that is deliberately anti-illuminist and, if anything, informed by the crushing gaze of the baroque. In my opinion *Aracoeli* places Elsa Morante on the same level as the modern female mystics. By this I mean on the level of the female thinkers of paradox. And it is precisely paradox that seems to me to be one of the key characteristics of this novel. Alongside the more political one of scandal.

Paradox, scandal, Christology. The deep Spanish connections woven into this novel seemed to lead me towards the 'burning bones' (the miracle) and the 'agonic faith' described by the philosopher Miguel de Unamuno. *Mystery, faith, rite and linguistic/ geographic dislocation* (Italy/Spain).

Without a certain amount of faith and subjective passion, I felt it would be difficult if not impossible to tackle this dramaturgical work. Faith in Morante's language, in her plastic, evocative strength. Passion for the abysses of the story told.

In this light (or perhaps darkness), I immediately saw that the presence and function of music would be crucial for the staged work. It could expand upon and interpret that which Manuele, the main character in the novel, tells us about the songs his mother taught him when he was a child. However, this is not music in the sense of a reconstruction or reproduction of the material that Morante describes in some detail (popular Spanish lullabies, which I could have philologically reconstructed and used directly), but in the sense of a subterranean constancy. A sort of basso continuo that is consubstantial to Aracoeli, a foreigner in the Italian land and language.

My idea was to give a female human singing voice the task of underlining some of the profound tensions in Morante's text. Again, there was a paradoxical dimension: the singer, present on stage throughout, could/should have 'been and not been' Aracoeli. It was up to the audience to decide on each separate occasion. She could be given the (artistic) power to evoke the novel's character in flesh and blood; but certainly not the power to interpret the novel in the classic sense. Indeed, Lisa Nathan was called upon to give life to the shadow of Aracoeli, to her past, to the world of visions/hallucinations which her son describes in the novel. However, if at any point in the evening the 'character of Aracoeli' were to appear theatrically, it would have happened thanks to *her*; i.e. through the dramatic voice and movements of a singer. She herself was estranged, a spectator of the story told by the actors.

In order to underline the distance from an illustrative, literal intention, I therefore decided with the singer to create a musical selection for this *mise en espace* that brought together ancient, 'lost' Spanish melodies (including some Sephardic melodies, to pick up on the Jewish undercurrents in Morante's novel), wedding and funeral songs, a playful popular lullaby, and even a reworking of a song taken from a Pedro Almodóvar film. What convinced me to include the latter were above all the lyrics, which talk about the pain connected with erotic passion, and the compulsive, insatiable desire for satisfaction. A musical prologue to the nymphomania eventually confessed to by the mother, the song melts into a lament similar to sobbing.

Combinations of different languages. The *mise en espace* of *Aracoeli* was staged in Berlin, in German. Hence the inclusion of Spanish songs underlined the otherness of the character Aracoeli, even more so than it would have if the performance had been in Italian (the language in which the novel was written).

Such effects are not at all uncommon when it comes to working with several languages on stage. All the more so if we take into account the impact of the actor's performance, which hinges each time upon the actor's own language, highlighting its specific colouring and qualities. While the German translation of Morante's text managed to retain her style of long sentences perfectly, I felt that it lost a little of its colourfulness, its painterly quality, and its elusive playfulness. Instead it took on a solid, architectural nature — whether more classical or baroque I couldn't say. The German text became less sensual and perhaps lost some of the subtle, anarchic ironies of the original, but moved confidently forward in terms of its theoretical construct, making the musical caesura all the more profound.

The shades of the voices were balanced thus: the voices of actors Frank Arnold and Anne Tismer, both with a high, clear, similar register, alongside the tones of a dramatic mezzo-soprano.

In parallel to the musical pathway, two themes guided me in my dramaturgical work on 'Aracoeli' when it came to choosing the passages of text and then staging them. The first concerns the identity of the narrative voice. This is a key question for a theatrical work. The second concerns the figure of passion as a container of opposite needs. This theme is deliberately reflected by the title chosen for the staged reading: 'La Passione di Aracoeli' [The Passion of Aracoeli].

Aracoeli or the Double Tongue

Who is speaking in *Aracoeli* the novel? Taken literally, the question is a pointless one. For *Aracoeli* is a novel built around the perspective of one narrative voice, namely Manuele's, making it a monologue-novel. A man recounts his own past story, while at the same time remarking on what is happening to him in the present. So is it a text for one actor alone?

My theatrical experiment with *Aracoeli* began with the idea of working with two actors, with two voices: one female and one male. Two voices, to narrate a trinity: Manuele/Aracoeli/Elsa Morante.

The idea was to shift from a male monologue, written by a woman, to an *androgynous* text. In other words, an androgynous voice split into male and female. In this stage transcription, gender boundaries did not necessarily need to be respected — and in fact the same can be said of the novel. From a formal point of view, I thought of the shift from the 'novel' to a 'spoken text' in which there would be a constant intermingling of pure dramatic dialogue, description, and confession, the perspective of memory and the solidity of the present. This would happen in an unbroken flow of dialogue which was not, however, a true dialogue. The mingling/confusion/coexistence of genders and identities, as much as points in time and narrative perspectives, also seemed to me to be a constant motif running throughout the novel. Unfortunately, or perhaps fortunately, it is not a logical motif; it is not frozen in a fixed style, but is always ambiguous, precarious, threatened by doubt. Moreover, in *Aracoeli* Elsa Morante never gives the reader that (albeit fleeting) inner serenity that may come from an awareness of possessing knowledge through reading — even if it were simply a really reliable true story. On the contrary, in *Aracoeli* nothing is certain; not even the doctor's diagnosis which is supposed to resolve the mystery of the 'wretched lady's' illness. Everything escapes, and again it does not escape memory, or narrative, but explanation — even for those who have 'faithfully' experienced the events, as Manuele complains again and again.

As I was saying, right from the beginning the hypothesis behind my work was to think of *Aracoeli* as a sort of continuous flow of two voices, real/unreal; although in the context of the novel, this contrast seems of little importance. The voice of an abandoned son, a sort of living cadaver, as he sees himself; and that of a dead mother, evoked from within and magically present in the son's consciousness. It is therefore something different, more tangible, than a 'mere' ghost of the mind and soul to be spoken to in an 'inner monologue'. Let us recall the dead mother who returns, alive, well and mischievous, even hiding under the bed, in Pedro Almodóvar's film *Volver* — which Vittorio Lingiardi spoke about during the conference. A powerful exorcism is at work in *Aracoeli*. In flesh and in words. Turning to the theological/philosophical ether, we might mention the mystery of transubstantiation, or the mysteries of of the Holy Trinity — into which, as Elsa Morante tells us, Manuelito was quickly and successfully initiated as a child. But this is not just about those mysteries.

A premise. The text classically offers us a Freudian 'manifest scene': the reconstruction of the facts, of the earthly vicissitudes of Aracoeli Muñoz Muñoz, the 'remarkable story' of a woman with an unhappy fate, desperately loved by a son and a husband, together with the interpretation which she attempts to give her son: an interpretative storyline, contradictory, full of enigmas, almost oracular, sometimes stuttering owing to the insecurity and loneliness of the narrator. This posthumous 'interpretation' should conceal the Secret of the Mother and at the same time the Logos of the Son should germinate within it. This is the last mystery of their 'great love', no longer of this earth.

So far, there seems to be nothing radically different from a passionate narrative or account from memory. In order for *Aracoeli* to appear a 'two voice' text, we need to take a step further, venturing into the pages of the novel. I believe that the duality of the voices, the successful double alchemy, does not depend only on Elsa Morante's remarkable literary talent; it also touches upon something quite deliberate. The Aracoeli/Manuele pair (within the Morante trinity), a real, haunted hybrid, has its so-called genetic roots in the theory of knowledge with which Morante presents us in her novel. A theory of knowledge which is deliberately not rational, but not necessarily immediately irrational.

When reflecting upon the scant concrete information that the child had about his mother's biographical and geographical origins, the narrative voice forewarns us from the beginning:

> Da parte sua, poi, mia madre stessa, fino dai tempi della nostra intimità esclusiva, mi aveva lasciato nella mia ignoranza. Forse, del resto, essa sentiva che anch'io, come lei di me, inconsapevolmente di lei sapevo tutto. La sua storia mi era stata trasmessa, fino da quando io le crescevo nell'utero, attraverso il messaggio cifrato che aveva trasmesso dalla sua pelle alla mia il colore moreno. E sarebbe stato, dunque, vano tentare una traduzione terrestre di quanto io portavo, congenito dentro di me, già stampato nel proprio codice favoloso.[1]

Manuele *knows* everything about his mother. This conveyed knowledge is also a productive imprinting, an immanent creative code with the potential to 'continue growing and changing' in the fusion with the other, and even later, in the physical cellular detachment. It seems that any duality of subject and object is purposefully negated in *Aracoeli*. In the process of knowledge, there is no wax tablet on which things are stamped; on the contrary, the counter-rational model evoked refers to a continuity of the fabric, or fabrics; it enjoins the appropriation/activation/repetition of a code that has been transmitted. This is why nothing in the world could truly invalidate or 'belie' the maternal narrative of Aracoeli's son. This is why nothing could be further from Elsa Morante's novel than the 'modern' literary device of describing the same event from different perspectives. For example, how Aracoeli would have told her own story is a question that simply doesn't arise in this case. Listening to her son, we are forced to think that in some way we are also listening to Aracoeli. It is she herself, seductive and fearsome, who continues to speak through him: a forlorn child in a wretched body, he is now the tongue of her and of himself, as he always has been. Ever since the days of *Totetaco*. Indeed, even after his mother's physical death, despite everything, Manuele continues — and how could he do otherwise? — to 'know and bear everything within him'. He just has to reactivate that original, founding closeness of the cells, of the pulsing of the womb, of the 'blood'. This reactivation consists in his memory, his writing, and his story. The actors' task is to make it sensitive. And at the end of the novel, Aracoeli does indeed appear — initially from a vast distance. The alibi — life — which opens into nothing:

> È stata la tua misteriosa ambiguità, Aracoeli, che ti ha resa immortale; e non per caso, forse, quel tetro agosto della mia 'villeggiatura' — che preparava il mio passaggio all'età della ragione — è stato il punto scelto per la tua morte. La tua morte tempestiva, nell'amputarmi di te, ha sbarrato la mia crescita, affinché la mia-tua invenzione bambina si serbasse immune eternamente dalla ragione. Solo una morte prematura può escludere i corpi adorati dai sordidi sepolcri della norma e salvare la verità dell'assurdo contro i falsi della logica. A costo di calunniarti e maledirti e rinnegarti io non ho MAI voluto riconoscere la denunciata impossibile miseria del tuo ultimo segreto. E così ti ringrazio per il nostro intrigo puerile. La tua terribile ambiguità — tua buiezza e imbroglio, tuo scandalo, tuo splendore — mi accompagnerà, giocando, nel vuoto. Che tu sia benedetta, mamita, per il tuo alibi. (*Aracoeli*, p. 1404)

Credo quia absurdum. The gap between natural aphasic and 'natured' speaker, the ciphered code, the biological image, are all constant themes, even obsessions in *Aracoeli*. The 'conceiving flesh' has no say, but is an ambiguous substratum there to be interpreted. Manuele is inhabited by Aracoeli, just as once upon a time he lived inside her. Aracoeli's premature death preserves her, in her son's eyes, from prosaic old age, and its dulling pace. It saves her, hampering the growth of her son.

The Passion of Aracoeli

In our (Christian) collective religious and allegorical imagination, passion summons up a journey through stations of pain. So in the title, I intended to hint at the similarities between Aracoeli's story and the model of the Passio Christi, the icon of every human pain suffered by men and for men. *Aracoeli martyr, Aracoeli scandal, Aracoeli salvific. Aracoeli divine.* In her son's words, Aracoeli in any case has the right to an aura of divinity. Starting with her perfect — sometimes even sickly — adherence to the Marian iconography of a virginal 'Madonna of the Milk'; right through her appearance, again in her son's words, akin to a pagan statue with empty eyes, shell-encrusted and covered in seaweed, a sacred/natural artefact thrown up by the waves; right up to her more popular function as a special interlocutor of angels and Macarenas.

However, passion dominates in Aracoeli, in its profane sense too: erotic suffering, with all the weight of the grandiosity, aggressiveness, and destruction that it brings with it. Aracoeli suffers in her body of love, is hurt in that body, in that flesh which harbours desire and the conception of life. From Loving Kidnapped Virgin, Magnificent Mother, Lady of the Starry Sky, little Muñoz Muñoz will fall into the *demimonde* of bourgeois prostitution; she is illuminated or obscured — that is debatable — by her feverish nymphomania.

Aracoeli is a text in which meanings are dramatically overturned. This happens with the cruelty of a geometrical syllogism. Morante magnifies maternity and the carnal union of mother and child, and then deftly destroys it. In the same way, passion, as a path of stations of pain and of greatness, does not result in any sort of transfiguration in the novel — and much less in (Christian) redemption. Perhaps in dissolution, annulment (playing a little with 'Indian' words).

We know that the first station of the *Passion of Aracoeli* is joyful. The idyll of Monte Sacro is a sort of Prologue or Joyful Sanctuary, which will later be overturned and turned inside out like a bleeding glove.

Loaded with Christian motifs and, especially at the beginning, with images inspired by the cult of Mary, Morante's text makes full use of the holy, blessed imagery of shining maternity. However, Morante shows not just the splendid triumph, but also the dark martyrdom of a mother. The *same* mother. A martyrdom in the flesh. As from flesh we are born. Always through the son's eyes, we are forced to observe how the 'holy body' of Aracoeli becomes obscene, a refuge for desire, shameless, vulgar, bestial, corrupted, like Dante's leopard, the animal with the speckled skin, the foul-smelling lust. While the modesty of that woman, a child-mother, filled her son with adoration, the feline arching of Aracoeli's back in the throes of desire scares him terribly. The mother turns into a beast. The hand with which she revealed (and concealed) her turgid breast, warm with milk, from her son's view now becomes the hand which desperately stimulates the clitoris. The repeated, jolting movements, the scandal, the loneliness and the new hallucinations. No longer a magical world of Macarenas and Ladies, but Fish Men, Camel Women; no lullaby but the low rhythm of coitus, which the child interiorizes as a tribal dance.

In my opinion, if we are talking about mothers in *Aracoeli*, at this point it is Leopardi's Mother Nature — and Lucretius also comes to mind. The hidden, omnipotent Great Mother (but perhaps omnipotence is a term that's still too close to human thought) which deep down pulls the threads of the story together.

Even the Virgin Mary, 'armed with a sword', placed above the cradle to protect Manuele's dead baby sister Carina, did not manage to fulfil the task she had been set. She failed, poor folk image, overloaded with colours, bows, ex-votos, and prayers. She had to bend her head before that other, more powerful Lady. It is Mother Nature whom Else Morante faces up to in Aracoeli with her head held high, or even with the violence of blasphemy. This is not the sunny, seaside nature of *L'Isola di Arturo*, generous with her free, majestic gifts. In that case Nature was identical to the son, Arturo as a boy; androgynous, strong, and cocksure like Arturo, innocent, ready for adventure. A *Nature natured* with trees and stars, enjoyable. A Nature that has by now entered the realm of form, beauty, meaning, and aesthetics, even with her wild mane of waves and pine thickets. Instead, Nature in *Aracoeli* appears not like the landscape which welcomes and enhances, the frame for a story; but rather like Living Matter, multiform Proteus, Aristotelian *hule* which drags it own fathomless mystery with it, the nothing/everything of life and death. Omnipotent Mother Nature, a chemical sanctuary rich in ravines and caves. Just as the mother's body was to the son, and the mother's to the mother and vice versa, the son's body to her, his mother, and to himself. Two strangers joined together.

Manuele, the son and narrator, is no philosopher. He operates through images. Illuminations, perhaps. Morante is even less of a philosopher, in the traditional sense. On the contrary, she sets out to attack Reason head on.

Let us begin again: what happens when Nature is flesh, body? Corruption and death are never far off. It doesn't take much for the beloved landscape, the face and body of the Mother to suddenly change in the eyes of the son. After the death of her newborn baby girl:

> Aracoeli [. . .] si aggirava per le stanze avvolta in coperte e scialli, perché dovunque sentiva freddo. Camminava storta, come una mezza cieca [. . .]. Dalle orbite, brutalmente cerchiati, i globi degli occhi le sporgevano inerti, così sbiaditi da parere coperti di polvere. La faccia, da tonda, le si era fatta quasi triangolare, rassomigliando al muso di una bestiola selvatica. Ogni scampanellata o voce estranea la metteva in allarme, spingendola a lasciare la poltrona dove se ne stava rintanata; e, nello spostarsi incassava la testa fra le spalle, come fosse inseguita in una caccia. (*Aracoeli*, p. 1299)

But it's not so much in the exterior, it is *inside* Aracoeli that Nature wove her cloth and her deceit.[2] Given the events which have taken place, a profound psychological disturbance would not be so 'out of the ordinary', and would not necessarily herald other misfortunes. But evil is at work in the depths of the flesh; at the first unexpected haemorrhage Aracoeli, as conscious and precise as the best diagnostician, places that evil in her abdomen and her head, in her womb and in her soul. Not only that: for Manuele the witness, this degradation of the body marks the beginning of the disintegration in the novel; the true painful detachment between meaning and object, matter and sense. A division which was totally foreign to the happy motherhood at *Totetaco*, and Manuele's attachment to his mother. Here begins the true painful mystery and the need to interpret the symptoms. Everything becomes complicated. For the son, the truth withdraws into the ravines, into the dreams perhaps, and the hallucinations.

In actual fact, it was not Carina's birth which affected Aracoeli — a happy, socially accepted bride at last — but the first operation by the 'labour surgeons' with their knives in her belly:

> E in una suggestione indovina, io credetti di scoprire il segreto che mi veniva nascosto. Ossia: la sera della sua partenza, mia madre non era andata alla villa, come volevano farmi credere; ma a quella clinica speciale delle donne, dove già — secondo certe mie subdole apprensioni di allora — l'avevano tagliata coi coltelli per il parto, a subirvi di nuovo, forse, altre ferite inconcepibili. (*Aracoeli*, p. 1313)

Inconceivable wounds, to treat a haemorrhage? Besides, Manuele had already had a vision. A not insignificant detail is that this happened after his Mother harshly drove him away while he again tried to drink from her breast, which perhaps still held some sweet drop that had not been taken by his now dead baby sister:

> Di continuo mi appariva Aracoeli, anzi non proprio lei, ma l'oscuro suo corpo di carne, quale una caverna di stupendi misteri e di tenebre cruente. Là dentro germinavano occhi, mani e capelli, vi abitavano pupi e reginelle prigioniere, ne sgorgavano latte zuccherino e sangue. . . Era un focolaio di morbi? Era una magione di Dio? forse, come un serpe, vi si torceva la morte? (p. 1310)

The Nature which appears in *Aracoeli* is *female*, deep down and in the chemical mystery of the generative power of her womb. It is here that Morante 'takes the bull by the horns'. She magnifies and destroys, she extols, she ruins, but perhaps she also tries to reach another shore.

A deep impression remains, or at least it remained with me during and after the work on the text and later with the actors: Aracoeli, this female/mother/martyr/torturer, plunged into the darkest abysses of the flesh and biology, represents — just as much as Manuele does — a 'resistance fighter', an outsider. Her experience, in her son's words, signals a desperate way out — once again, a paradox — from the repetition of the life cycle, which wants only itself. Like Hamlet in Horatio's words: This notable and woeful tale must be told.

Notes to Chapter 8

1. Elsa Morante, *Aracoeli*, in *Opere*, ed. by Carlo Cecchi and Cesare Garboli, 2 vols (Milan: Mondadori, 1988–90), II (1990), pp. 1039–1454 (p. 1041). Further references to this edition will be given after quotations in the text.
2. Cf. In this context, see also the last novella of Thomas Mann, *Die Betrogene* (*The Deceived*). Nature plays with the body and the soul of the heroine, and her hidden illness (cancer) appears to her to be a fruit of a late love.

PART III
❖
Elsa e gli altri

CHAPTER 9

Aracoeli and Gadda's *La cognizione del dolore*: Disturbed Sons, Disturbing Mothers

Giuseppe Stellardi

Why mention Gadda in relation to Elsa Morante? What can *Aracoeli* and *La cognizione del dolore* possibly have in common?

The external chronology and the socio-historical context of the two works, for one thing, set them apart: Morante's last novel was published in 1982, whereas Gadda's first one appeared initially in instalments between 1938 and 1941.[1] A forty-year gap (with a world war and the end of a dictatorship in between) may not be a decisive factor in itself, but it certainly signals at the very least a significant historical divide, suggesting the likelihood of an accompanying, profound mutation of perspectives (political, literary, or other).

More significant is the stylistic difference. Whereas Gadda, with the baroque polyphony and '(pre-)postmodern'[2] parodic folds characteristic of his language, is seen as a daring literary innovator, Morante seems to embrace a more traditional approach to narrative writing.[3] Also, *La cognizione* is narrated in the past and in the third person by an extra-diegetic, anonymous, omniscient narrator, whereas *Aracoeli* is a long monologue in the present time (with extensive flashbacks) by the protagonist, Manuele.

Furthermore, the setting is fictional in Gadda (an imaginary South American country, closely resembling the author's native Brianza, in a time that — without explicit mention of it — seems to correspond to the 'ventennio'), mostly real in Morante (Rome, Milan, Spain, over a time-span ranging from the Italian Fascist era to the death of the Spanish dictator, Francisco Franco). However, if the setting is openly imaginary in Gadda and essentially realistic in Morante, the effect of both characterization and narrative setup is such that *La cognizione* sounds scrupulously truthful, whereas *Aracoeli* — projecting on the page the probably distorted subjective vision of its narrator-protagonist — emanates an aura of uncertainty. For this aspect at least, the novel belongs to the literary model whose archetypes (within the Italian twentieth-century tradition) can be found in Svevo's *La coscienza di Zeno*, or the Pirandello of *Uno, nessuno e centomila*. The 'unreliable narrator' is a crucial component of this literary model and Manuele, with his tendency to dwell in the past and uncommon disposition to dream, re-proposes the mind-structure of a Zeno Cosini.[4]

Ultimately, the two novels 'feel' different when we read them. Despite this, however, a strong, obvious parallel unites them: they both tell the story of a single male character, whose life and destiny seem to have been profoundly and permanently affected by events taking place during infancy and childhood, and in particular by the influence of a powerful and (in very different ways) disturbing maternal figure.

Let's take a look at the two protagonists. They show at first sight considerable differences, particularly in social standing and psychological characterization: whereas Manuele is almost an outcast, very close to the margins of society by virtue of his ill-defined professional position, lack of significant social relations, weak character and degrading sexual habits, Gonzalo leads an unimpeachable life of bourgeois respectability and apparent fulfilment, surrounded in his villa by the fearful deference of servants and peasants, as well as of his old mother.

Nevertheless, there are striking, if superficial similarities. For instance, the age of the two protagonists: Manuele is forty-three years old at the time of his journey to Spain, almost exactly Gadda's age when (following his mother's death in 1936) he started writing *La cognizione*. Considering that the novel's hero is most certainly an autobiographical projection, we can safely assume that forty-three is, approximately, Gonzalo's age, too. But age is not the only thing they have in common. Their background is similar: both are the offspring of respectable bourgeois families. And similar also is their state of secret malaise: Gonzalo, too — like Manuele — is undergoing a profound personal crisis that has no obvious causes or possible cure, and which Gadda's narrating voice felicitously names 'il male oscuro':

> di cui le storie e le leggi e le universe discipline delle gran cattedre persistono a dover ignorare la causa, i modi: e lo si porta dentro di sé per tutto il fulgurato scoscendere d'una vita, più greve ogni giorno, immedicato. (*La cognizione*, p. 690)[5]

So, Gonzalo and Manuele are two clear examples of male, middle-aged, bourgeois disadaptation, of that syndrome of discontent that finds its origin in the passionate, youthful, pre-romantic, suicidal heroes of Goethe and Foscolo, and then — through subtle transformations, and primarily relentless extenuation — turns itself into the literary expression of the curse of modern society: the inexplicable unhappiness of contemporary man. Love is at the root of Werther/Ortis's as well as Gonzalo/Manuele's fate. But a complete reversal has taken place in the course of this process: whereas Werther and Ortis, young and full of life, nobly commit suicide out of unrequited love, our two heroes' sufferings, albeit still related to the central issue of love (as we shall see), have become altogether less heroic, noble, or even simply understandable. Precisely for that reason, they come to symbolize the dark side of the triumphant modern world. They are the incomprehensible side-effect of the incessant progress of civilization. But is it merely a negligible sub-product, or the symptom of a fatal and universal fault, the secret time-bomb that will in the end annihilate the entire species?[6]

Be it as it may, introspective self-centredness is one of the symptoms of this elusive illness. Manuele and Gonzalo show a similar detachment from their surrounding environment, and in particular a lack of engagement with the political issues of the time, and more generally a lack of participation in collective dynamics — beyond of course what is unavoidable. Their desperate solitude is quite poignantly described, in terms most of the time devoid of any attempt at ennobling heroicization.

Not only do Gonzalo and Manuele have a problem in common, they also both seem to trace it back to the very early stages of their life, and more precisely to the figure of the mother. Each mother is seen as crucially connected with (if not responsible for) the son's misery. But, here again, a significant divergence manifests itself.

In *La cognizione*, the mother is mentioned only as *la signora*, or *la madre*, or *la mamma*. She unmistakably corresponds, to a large extent, to the real-life person of Adele Lehr, Gadda's own mother. *La signora* is described as an elderly, sweet lady, sharing with a son on the verge of middle age a simple but dignified existence in her villa in the countryside, making friends with peasants, doing good deeds, and preserving the memory of her husband and of her (other) son, both long dead. But, in the same way as the apparently idyllic life he leads is in fact an intolerable hell to Gonzalo, so too does the superficially saintly image of the mother hide an altogether more disturbing truth (for him, at least). She is indeed remembered by Gonzalo, in her previous and now remote incarnation as a young mother, as 'una belva': a sadistic educator, who eagerly introjected and ruthlessly implemented all dogmas of bourgeois education and behaviour. The protagonist's recollection of his childhood is that of a painful and senseless mortification at the hands of his educators: his teachers, his father, but primarily his mother, to whom he ascribes in large part the responsibility for his 'illness'.[7]

The opposite applies to Manuele. He remembers his infancy and early childhood as a time of bliss, marked by a state of total fusion with the person of his loving mother, young and beautiful Aracoeli. This exclusive, self-contained, and perfectly fulfilling relationship is progressively affected and ultimately destroyed by a sequence of events, narrated by Manuele in long flashbacks interspersed into the present-time narrative: the removal of the mother–son dyad from 'Totetaco' (the secluded, secret haven in the Montemario quarter of Rome where the two are initially confined by bourgeois conventions) to the apartment in the Quartieri Alti, where their induction into respectable society can take place; the second pregnancy of Aracoeli, leading to the birth of a little sister, who will die almost immediately; the tragic descent of Aracoeli into madness and nymphomania, accompanied by her incomprehensible (for him) rejection of her son, Manuele; and finally her departure and, later, her death.

The two mothers are antithetic, and this is evident even in their ethnic and geographic provenance. Adele Lehr (Gadda's real mother, truthfully portrayed under the guise of Gonzalo's mother) was of Germanic origins, and inclinations.[8] A teacher by profession, she was well-educated and perfectly at ease in polite society. Aracoeli is Spanish by nationality, and Mediterranean in temperament; thoroughly uneducated and blissfully ignorant, she has considerable difficulties in learning Italian, as well as in obeying (and, first of all, understanding) the dictates of bourgeois behaviour.

The difference between the two mothers is dramatically accentuated when it comes to their relationship with their respective sons, and in particular to their pedagogical demeanour: if Aracoeli is ultimately unable (also in her educational methods) to abide by the rules of middle-class decorum, and at first swamps Manuele in unbounded maternal love (only to subject him subsequently to a traumatic rejection), *la signora* instead seems to have internalized the strictest demands of the paternal-symbolic order and, in the pursuit of an almost inhuman pedagogical ideal, deprives young Gonzalo of any sign of real affection. As a result, in the early part of his life Manuele is drowned in love, whereas Gonzalo is starved of it.

But, once again, it might be said that the effect on the two men is structurally similar: an emotional imbalance in the mother–son relationship in the early years leads to disastrous consequences later on, and essentially to an inability to live a 'normal' relational life. It is important to pay attention, however, to significant differences in those 'consequences', particularly at the level of the psychological makeup of the characters; if Manuele's behaviour seems essentially marked by masochistic traits (highlighted especially in his often degrading relationships with his male lovers), in Gonzalo's case there are obvious sadistic connotations (emerging in daydreams hinging on the extermination of unwelcome visitors, or in moments of uncontrollable rage,[9] resulting in outrageous rants, or the destruction of symbolically significant objects, such as his father's portrait, or a watch received in gift from his mother).

A further point worth mentioning, if only *en passant*, concerns the marginality of both fathers: one, Gonzalo's, is long dead, nor does he seem to hold or to have held a very important place in his heart (whereas the memory of his brother, killed in war, is both sacred and painful, being connected with a bundle of inextricable sentiments, including remorse and jealousy); the other, Manuele's father, during the child's early years is most of the time absent on duties connected with his position in the Italian navy, and in his brief visits much more interested in Aracoeli than in his son, who in exchange feels for him no more than distant respect. This respect turns later to disgust when, after the end of the war, Manuele visits him (now, after Aracoeli's death, no more than a human wreck); until, in the end, Manuele undergoes the sudden revelation of a different sentiment for him (more on this later).

Returning to the sons, I would like to suggest that the main dissimilarity between Manuele and Gonzalo (who, as we have seen, both embody the same, unhappy aspect of the human condition in the modern world) concerns their respective relationships to love. Both suffer from a form of mutilation, with long-lasting consequences; but if for Manuele the syndrome is that of a *loss* of love, in Gonzalo's case it is more appropriate to talk of an originary *lack* of love. What might seem at first sight a subtle distinction reveals itself instead as a crucial difference.

Manuele's curse is that (as he knows full well) he will never be loved *again* in the boundless, unrestrained manner Aracoeli loved him in the first years of his life.[10] The *loss* of love (after extreme overabundance of it) is naturally a very heavy burden to bear.

Gonzalo's fate, however, is even worse: he's never been loved in the first place, he never had (or at any rate can't remember having, but it amounts to the same thing) the gratuitous and immeasurable affection of a loving mother.[11] As a result of this primary *lack* of love, Gonzalo's syndrome is more complex, and his case receives an altogether darker complexion, as we shall see.

The whole problem affecting our two heroes, therefore, revolves around what I should like to describe as the *remembrance of love*: although in both cases the diagnosis is one of insufficient love, Manuele distinctly remembers being loved, and this recollection is the fulcrum of his life; Gonzalo doesn't, and for him, too, this is the central truth of his existence. What follows is the inevitable consequence of this simple but momentous premise.

Aracoeli is the story of Manuele's attempt to return to his mother, to find her again, and — with her — the immensity of the love he remembers having bound the two of them. It doesn't matter that for a time he had rejected and even forgotten about Aracoeli; in the end he abandons whatever little he has (home, job, relations), the minuscule securities of his senseless life, to set his course again towards his sole true star. He then embarks on a private anabasis, which geographically and spiritually takes him back to Aracoeli in the disembodied shape in which, alone, she can now be found, at the topographical locus of her origins.

Gonzalo has nowhere to return to. In his vain attempts to get to the root of his problems, he comes to identify his mother (who, as already mentioned, has no name in the book: compare this to the place Aracoeli, and her name, occupy in Morante's novel, and in Manuele's language) as the ultimate source of his unhappiness, so that the physical attack perpetrated (probably by thieves) against her in the final chapter has the unmistakable signs of a materialization of the son's (more or less unconscious) matricidal desires.

It is interesting that neither Manuele nor Gonzalo (unlike their distant ancestors, young Werther and Jacopo Ortis) wish to take leave of their own unhappy existence; they expect (obscurely, and mistakenly) to recover the fullness of their life, one by re-conjoining himself with Aracoeli, the other (semi-consciously) by ridding himself once and for all of his mother. Neither can succeed: summoning a ghost from the depths of the past cannot possibly result in the reconstitution of a relationship that was bodily and physical as much as spiritual; on the other hand, the 'killing' of the mother will only add further bleakness to Gonzalo's existence.[12]

Before going any further, I shall at this point introduce a consideration that may seem far removed from the matter at hand, and from the ideological makeup of both works, and authors. It has to do with the definition of Christianity; there are of course many possible definitions, but there is one that has (as shall be seen) a direct relevance to the present discussion. It goes like this: Christianity is the remembrance of the love of God. That's all. In its simplicity, this is a truly enlightening phrase.[13] I take it as meaning that the joy and hope of Christian life (for those who believe in the Christian message, of course) does not have its origin and justification within the human being, in anything that one does or doesn't, but in God, and cannot therefore be affected by anything that happens to the human being. It also means that, no matter what depth of depravation and dejection one should fall into, the certainty of having been loved once, to the extent of having been brought into life, for no reason other than love, should always remain as the North Star of salvation for all men. The undivided and unconditional love of God, that preceded and exceeds all sins, loss, and despair, is what gave life to the entire universe and to all human beings, of course, not just Christians. But the Christian is the one who preserves the recollection of the love of God, and draws from it the very meaning of his life, as well as the ability to love not only God, but also others, in return for the love gratuitously received.[14]

Now, am I suggesting that Morante and Gadda are Christian writers? Before replying too hastily with a resounding no, we should at least mention the Christological qualities and air of holiness pertaining to the little Usé, the co-protagonist of Morante's *La Storia*. And we should also remember that the title of *La cognizione del dolore* was translated into English as *Acquainted with Grief*, again with an obvious biblical and evangelical reference.[15]

However, I readily concede that it would be difficult to find in either *Aracoeli* or *La cognizione del dolore* any specific evidence of religious belief on the part of the two protagonists, and I am not in the least attempting to demonstrate that Elsa Morante and Carlo Emilio Gadda are Christians. But the metaphorical possibilities offered by this truly unlikely interpretative angle are quite illuminating and deserve to be pursued.

Ultimately, at least by virtue of the definition provided above, the answer to the question must be no for Gadda, given the absence in his work (and certainly in Gonzalo) of that essential Christian quality that is charity, or love; for Morante the surprising answer could be yes, provided one doesn't think of Christianity as a church, that is, a social institution, or a codified set of rites and rules, but rather as a manifestation of the fundamental disposition of the human being to remember love, and to love in return.

But let us return now to earth. Within the immanent, non-religious dimension, only one human experience resembles (in the collective imaginary) the relationship that Christians, according to the definition given above, believe to exist between their creator and themselves; it is, of course, that of maternity. A mother, in giving birth, replicates the act of creation, and her love for her child is comparable to that of God for his creatures, in that it is truly gratuitous and uncalculating. It is also absolute and unconditional, in that it doesn't depend on any requirements being fulfilled, other than the existence of her child. (I should stress that I am far from implying that this is a correct, factual, and universally true interpretation of the phenomenon of maternal love; it is, instead, a cultural stereotype that happens to chime with one of the fundamental attributes of the Christian God. I add that it is by no means necessary to assume that maternal, 'Aracoelian' love is a diminished copy of divine love: we are free to believe instead that Christian love, and the entire edifice of Christianity, is but a projection and amplification of a common idealization of maternal love. None of this affects the powerful metaphorical impact of those ideas.)

It is no surprise, therefore, that Aracoeli for Manuele is God. Blocked in his emotional and ideological development by the trauma of his mother's illness, rejection, and death, and prevented at some level from accessing the symbolic realm, he hasn't truly moved on, and still re-enacts (or at least seeks), especially in his sexual relationships, the total, adoring dependency that was his normal and satisfying state of being in the presence of Aracoeli. Now that she is gone, Manuele tries to establish with her a link, a bind that can only be described as religious: Aracoeli occupies the space of the divine in her son's life.

This resolves, among other things, what I perceive as a little riddle, which doesn't seem to have a proper solution in the text itself. Why does Manuele not accept a perfectly plausible medical, positivistic explanation of his mother's illness?[16] It may be that, in his resentment at having been so unjustly rejected by his mother, he doesn't want to let her off so easily. Also, he promptly detects aunt Monda's ulterior motives ('Certo, il suo era un pretesto inventato per salvaguardare l'onore della famiglia' (*Aracoeli*, p. 1441)), and so is inevitably suspicious of the 'logical' explanation that, at the same time as having scientific validity, also saves the family's face. But the primary reason for his refusal may be another one: perhaps he rejects the 'charitable' explanation because it diminishes Aracoeli's divinity. The divine is not questionable. Manuele can hate Aracoeli, can even try to forget her for a time, but he can't accept seeing her lowered to the station of a common mortal. Also, as a divine being she needs no justification, nor does she need to explain her own behaviour; no matter how hurtful, incomprehensible, and unacceptable her conduct towards Manuele is, it is still better for him to take it as the expression of an impenetrable, superior will, rather than the manifestation of human illness and decay.

Gonzalo's world is truly devoid of any God, and of any love. With no recollection of ever having been loved by a God, or by a mother, the *hidalgo*[17] is condemned to a loveless life. Any attempt to penetrate his carapace of suspicion and cynicism is systematically rebuked by him.[18] Lacking the experience (or the memory) of the only form of love that triggers the ability to love, he not only is unlovable, but also — which is much worse — is fundamentally incapable of love. I should stress again that what truly matters is that he doesn't *remember* having been loved in that (or any other) way. The lack of boundless maternal love — a truly disastrous mutilation for a human being — could perhaps be compensated, if Gonzalo could believe in God: but he clearly can't.

By contrast, having been loved in that boundless manner, and remembering it all too well, Manuele will forever suffer withdrawal symptoms, but at the same time is forever enabled to love back (in his own pathetic and unsatisfactory way), even knowing that he will never be loved again. The last sentence of *Aracoeli* is emblematic: 'ma certi individui sono più inclini a piangere d'amore, che di morte' (p. 1454). In a communal destiny of loss, love is Manuele's saving grace.

The basic definition of the two characters can also be connected with this fundamental configuration. Gonzalo's only possible relationship to the divine/maternal is violence, rage, and blasphemy.[19] Manuele's disposition towards the only manifestation of the divine he knows and loves, Aracoeli, is prayer; which again shows the profoundly religious nature of his relationship to her.

The attribute of the divine, be it the Christian God or its parallel, Aracoeli, is a power of salvation. The circulation of love set in motion at the moment of creation/birth is not easily stopped, although of course it is within the possibilities of human free will to do so. This is why Manuele is and remains capable of love.

Manuele's ability to love, and its full significance, is revealed (albeit somewhat enigmatically) at the end of the novel, when he suddenly discovers that the acute emotion he had felt after his last encounter with his father (by then the pathetic and utterly unlovable figure of a chronic alcoholic) was nothing other than love. The (unjustified and illogical) love of his father is the seal of Aracoeli's final gift: Manuele will not be loved again, but he will forever be able to love. Such is the (secretly) salvific sense of Morante's last and bleakest book.

Gonzalo's destiny is only superficially similar, but is in fact much darker. Disconnected from a primordial source of unqualified love, his world is as poisoned and rotten as that of Hamlet, prince of Denmark.[20] Like Hamlet, he is condemned to a spasmodic pursuit of truth against all false pretences of society and family, but in so doing he can only resort do destruction and, ultimately, is doomed to self-destruction. This is what the insistent Gaddian *leitmotiv* of matricide suggests: the aggression against the mother is the equivalent of the revolt against God and his creation. Although it may be conducted in the name of justice and truth, it is the gesture of Satan, it denies life itself, and cannot possibly lead to salvation. The crusade against mendacious appearances, ultimately, does not justify the assault against life itself: nothing does.

And this does not simply pertain to the realm of literary fiction; for Gadda, too, literature is the battlefield of truth and justice:

> Nella mia vita di 'umiliato e offeso' la narrazione mi è apparsa, talvolta, lo strumento che mi avrebbe consentito di ristabilire la 'mia' verità, il 'mio' modo di vedere, cioè: lo strumento della rivendicazione contro gli oltraggi del destino e de' suoi umani proietti: lo strumento, in assoluto, del riscatto e della vendetta.[21]

But the war is lost in advance.

Manuele doesn't pursue truth, he doesn't have to. He simply follows Aracoeli, and this is an enterprise of love, because love is a bond with a person, not the subservience to a concept; and in the end he finds her again (albeit in a hallucinatory fashion). To her he confesses his sins:

> Dovunque, ho peccato. Nelle intenzioni e nei fini e negli atti ma peggio di tutto nell'intelligenza. L'intelligenza si dà per capire. E a me si è data, ma io non capisco niente. E non ho mai capito e non capirò mai niente. (*Aracoeli*, p. 1428)

But Aracoeli absolves him, at the same time revealing the ultimate truth: 'Ma, niño mio chiquito, non c'è niente da capire'. Manuele can be spared Gonzalo's pointless and loveless search for justice and truth, and will be saved through love.

There is therefore a positive conclusion to Aracoeli: positive, but not *pro*positive, in that it doesn't entail a project, a concept, an analysis, or a solution, even less a plan or a strategy. It simply states the pointless immortality of love, which never has its reason in *something* (the specific reasons and needs of a specific subject), but rather in (the love received from or given to) *someone* else. Love is then an infinite transfer of force, an infinite postponement of hope, through which salvation, if not achieved, can at least infinitely be deferred, and expected.

All of this is also reflected at the level of stylistic and linguistic differences between the two novels. In Gadda we witness a perennial tension, seldom resolved in some state of equilibrium; this condition has been abundantly described by critics (and sometimes by Gadda himself) as the *baroque* quality of his language, constantly propelling it, through alternating centrifugal and centripetal forces, beyond stasis or balance, beyond itself. It is also, possibly, what prevents Gadda from resolving any of his major works into some sort of satisfyingly linear conclusion. His writing shifts between stylistic extremes (from lyrical verticality to paratactical accumulation, from pathos to bathos, from philosophical sequentiality to irrational associations), in an ongoing and incurable spasm of both the mind and the heart.

Morante's novel, instead, despite the bleakness of the story and of Manuele's prospects in life, conveys some sort of stoical serenity. True, Manuele doesn't have much to look forward to in his future, but his universe, albeit in turmoil, is firmly rooted, and so is his language, and so is Morante's novel. The work is solidly organized and properly (if enigmatically) concluded. Gadda's protagonist, instead, despite (or perhaps precisely because of) his obsessive search for truth, is ultimately and fatally disorientated, and so is the narrative that conveys Gonzalo's tale.

It is significant that both novels can be seen as being organized around forms of travel. Manuele moves in space towards his mother's origins, in time towards his own past, and in spirit towards Aracoeli; and — with the proviso that neither he nor we can be certain of the veracity of what we are told — all these movements reach their goal. So, both he and the novel he inhabits contradict the bleakness of his life, of its content, by charting a meaningful universe. In *La cognizione* we (the reader) move progressively towards Gonzalo, through the tales of the villagers and then the doctor's visit to his patient, in his villa, on his bed; but we don't reach *him*, never getting to the bottom of his truth. Gonzalo himself is in a state of constant but disordered, impatient motion, never happy where he is, always picking up his small suitcase, to go to work, certainly, but also to escape from his village, his villa, his mother, himself. His universe (and that of the novel) is chaotic; nothing in it makes sense or has a real direction.

In conclusion, Gadda and Morante are perhaps the two Italian authors who, after Dante, have approached the theme of love in the most striking way; both have steered clear of romantic stereotypes and attempted to recover, in their own respective literary worlds, a more primordial dimension of the most fundamental binding force in human experience. In doing so, they have struck an original, sincere, and profoundly touching chord that sets them apart from most contemporary writers.

Although both novels deal with the same problem, they ultimately point in opposite directions: if Gonzalo, in his Hamletic pursuit of truth and justice, seems destined to a nihilistic rejection of life (symbolized by the mother) and ultimately to self-destruction, Manuele's indelible memories of Aracoeli's boundless love seem to provide a path to some sort of salvation, providing him with an incomprehensible but indestructible potential for human empathy.

I have briefly shown that the divide separating Gonzalo from Manuele is also reflected structurally, linguistically, and stylistically: whereas *La cognizione* constantly and in all sorts of ways oscillates between implosion and explosion (silence and logorrhoea, lyricism and the baroque), *Aracoeli* is clearly dominated by an anamnestic (in both the philosophical and medical meaning), linear-circular, and almost Dantesque orientation, 'saving' the text from the destiny of internal incompleteness and infinite displacement that affects most of Gadda's narrative writing. Certainly, Manuele's last encounter with Aracoeli is not the same as Dante's vision of God; but, in a world, like that of Morante, without God, this is perhaps as far as man can go in the direction of the divine.

Notes to Chapter 9

1. Then complete in 1963, with a second, augmented edition in 1970. Carlo Emilio Gadda, *La cognizione del dolore*, in *Romanzi e racconti*, ed. by Raffaella Rodondi, Guido Lucchini, and Emilio Manzotti, 2 vols (Milan: Garzanti, 1990), I, 571–772; Elsa Morante, *Aracoeli*, 1st edn (Turin: Einaudi, 1982), quoted from *Opere*, ed. by Carlo Cecchi and Cesare Garboli, 2 vols (Milan: Mondadori, 1988–90), II (1990), pp. 1039–1454. Further references to these editions will be given after quotations in the text.
2. There is considerable debate concerning the classification of this author in terms of the modern/postmodern distinction. I have contributed to it in 'L'alba della *Cognizione*: Gadda postmoderno?', in *Disharmony Established: Festschrift for Gian Carlo Roscioni*, Proceedings of the first EJGS international conference, Edinburgh, 10–11 April 2003, ed. by Emilio Manzotti and Federica G. Pedriali, *Electronic Journal of Gadda Studies* [henceforward *EJGS*], 4.3 (2004) <http://www.arts.ed.ac.uk/italian/gadda/Pages/journal/supp3atti1/articles/stellaconf1/articles/stellaconf1.php> [accessed 14 September 2008]). Now revised in Giuseppe Stellardi, *Gadda: miseria e grandezza della letteratura* (Florence: Franco Cesati, 2006).
3. This does not exclude the validity of an entirely different critical approach to the two authors: in Gadda it is possible to identify a profound streak of conservatism (not only in politics, but also in his literary allegiances), whilst in Morante's work one can readily perceive traits of great originality, as some other contributions in this same volume show.
4. Manuele is aware of the unreliability of his own 'testimony'; see for instance the imaginary dialogue between *l'Accusa* and *l'Imputato*: 'A. "[. . .] Ritiene, in definitiva, il Soggetto, che le sue memorie siano ATTENDIBILI?" | I.: "Purtroppo, io non lo so"' (*Aracoeli*, p. 1186).
5. 'Il male oscuro' will later become the title not only of a successful novel by Giuseppe Berto (1964, turned into a movie in 1990), but also of a famous song by Lelio Luttazzi ('il male oscuro, il male oscuro, quello che fa picchiar la testa contro il muro'), showing how Gadda's phrase struck a durable chord in the collective imaginary of Italian society.
6. We are reminded, once more, of *La coscienza di Zeno*, and precisely of its last page, evoking (with its 'prophecy' of a final explosion) exactly this catastrophic scenario.
7. There are also other causes for his unhappiness; the traumas related to the war and to the death of his brother are specifically mentioned. It goes without saying that the causal system so identified never achieves the status of a positive, scientific explanation: it remains confined to the role of a subjective and perhaps arbitrary reconstruction. The anonymous narrating voice, however, does not dismiss the 'reality' of Gonzalo's ailments, inviting the reader to 'consider everything', and suggesting the existence of remote origins, directly linked to the mother, for his condition:

    'Ma tutto, tutto, è bene che si soppesi. Il figlio pareva aver dimenticato al di là d'ogni immagine lo strazio di quegli anni, la incenerita giovinezza. Il suo rancore veniva da una lontananza più tetra, come se fra lui e la mamma ci fosse qualcosa di irreparabile, di più atroce d'ogni guerra: e d'ogni spaventosa morte.' (*La cognizione*, p. 691)

    And later on, following the exposition of one of Gonzalo's moment of 'madness': 'Ma nulla accade senza ragione. Un mero arbitrio della iniquità è a stento pensabile in un animo non crudele'; and the narrator hypothesises 'che vi fosse una ragione o una causa, o più ragioni o più cause, forse, ignote agli umani, irreparabili, perché l'animo dello hidalgo andasse così privo di ogni gioia' (*La cognizione*, p. 712).
8. Gonzalo himself is described as *germanico*, and this trait is connected explicitly to his mother's blood:

'Per parte materna [. . .] veniva di sangue barbaro, germanico e unno, oltreché langobardo; [. . .]. Germanico era in certe maníe d'ordine e di silenzio, e nell'odio della carta unta, dei gusci d'ovo, e dell'indugiare sulla porta coi convenevoli. In certo rovello interno a voler risalire il deflusso delle significazioni e delle cause, in certo disdegno della superficie-vernice, in certa lentezza e opacità del giudizio [. . .]. Germanica, soprattutto, certa pedanteria piú tenace del verme solitario, e per lui disastrosa, tanto dal barbiere che dallo stampatore.' (*La cognizione*, p. 606).

9. 'Impotente rabbia era in lui, nel figlio: dàtole un pretesto, subito si liberava in parole, tumultuando, vane e turpi: in efferate minacce. Come urlo di demente dal fondo di un carcere' (*La cognizione*, p. 688).

10. 'MAI PIÚ TU SARAI | UN OGGETTO D'AMORE | MAI PER NESSUNO MAI | MAI TU SARAI UN OGGETTO | D'AMORE' (*Aracoeli*, p. 1094).

11. In Gonzalo's mind, it isn't necessarily the case that *la signora* was utterly incapable of maternal love; what makes things even more painful for him is that he believes she loved her *other* son (his dead brother) a lot more than him, whom for some mysterious reason she saw as 'defective': 'la prova difettiva di natura' (*La cognizione*, p. 678).

12. Gonzalo, of course, doesn't kill his mother, but the theme of matricide is obsessively present from the early phases of Gadda's literary career, and the threat itself is clearly uttered by Gonzalo in a moment of desperate rage: 'Se ti trovo ancora nel braco dei maiali, scannerò te e loro' (*La cognizione*, p. 737). But he also knows that the removal of the mother will not heal his wounds: see the dialogue with the doctor, during which Gonzalo recounts his obscure dream-premonition of the death of the mother, leading to his own complete freedom, but also to further misery, 'nella casa vuotata delle anime' (*La cognizione*, p. 633).

13. The current pontiff, Pope Benedict XVI, has insisted repeatedly on this theme. As the then Cardinal Joseph Ratzinger, he wrote: 'Christianity is this remembrance of the look of love that the Lord directs to man, this look that preserves the fullness of his truth and the ultimate guarantee of his dignity' (*Christianity and the Crisis of Cultures* (San Francisco: Ignatius Press, 2006), p. 71).

14. Which means that our ability to love will never be as full as that of God, who loved us unconditionally, and not in return for love already received.

15. 'He was despised and rejected by men; a man of sorrows, and acquainted with grief' (Isaiah 53. 3; *The New Oxford Annotated Bible* (Oxford: Oxford University Press, 1973)).

16. Such a justification of Aracoeli's intolerable behaviour is charitably offered by aunt Monda: 'Adesso che sei grande', proferí, 'tu devi saperlo. La tua mamma si è sempre comportata da Signora! da vera Signora! E quella sua condotta. . . strana degli ultimi tempi era un sintomo. . . una conseguenza della sua malattia. Sono effetti che si verificano, in certi casi. Me l'ha spiegato un Professore: uno specialista esimio!' (*Aracoeli*, p. 1441) But Manuele doesn't accept the explanation: 'Io mi scontorsi sulla sedia. Non ho creduto a questa nuova storia della vecchia Raimonda' (*Aracoeli*, p. 1441).

17. One of the aliases used to refer to Gonzalo in the novel; others are *il marchese*, or simply *il figlio*.

18. We see such advances attempted (clumsily) by the Doctor, and (fearfully) by the mother herself. But nothing can get through Gonzalo's disdain for what he considers vain and deceitful appearances ('bugie meritorie, grasse', *La cognizione*, p. 632).

19. See my 'La violenza in Gadda', *EJGS*, 6 (2007) <www.arts.ed.ac.uk/italian/gadda/Pages/journal/issue6/articles/stellarviol06.php> [accessed 14 September 2008].

20. 'Something is rotten in the state of Denmark'. For a summary of the significance of Hamlet's figure for Gadda, and the presence of a fundamental Hamletic structure in *La cognizione del dolore*, see my 'Amleto', *EJGS*, 3.1 (2008) <http://www.arts.ed.ac.uk/italian/gadda/Pages/resources/walks/pge/amletostellardi.php> [accessed 14 September 2008].

21. Carlo Emilio Gadda, 'Intervista al microfono', in *I viaggi la morte*, in *Saggi giornali favole e altri scritti*, ed. by Liliana Orlando, Clelia Martignoni, and Dante Isella, 2 vols (Milan: Garzanti, 1991), I, 503.

CHAPTER 10

Politics and Sexuality in Pasolini's *Petrolio*

Francesca Cadel

Pasolini's *Petrolio* is a complex, problematic text, an *opera aperta*, according to Eco's definition: a literary work understood as an open, internally dynamic, and psychologically engaged field of meaning.[1]

In his posthumous unfinished novel, Pasolini intended to share the *summa* of his knowledge with his readers — his intellectual and biopolitical legacy — in the form of a contemporary narrative, inclusive of many different genres (from autobiography to the essay) and media (from film documentary[2] to radio and TV interviews). I quote from Pasolini's 1973 Project Note:

> La ricostruzione si vale dunque dei vari manoscritti conservati [. . .] ma anche dell'apporto di altri materiali [. . .] un enorme quantitativo di documenti storici che hanno attinenza coi fatti del libro: specialmente per quel che riguarda la politica e, ancor più la storia dell'ENI [. . .]. L'autore dell'edizione critica 'riassumerà' quindi, sulla base di tali documenti — in uno stile piano, oggettivo, grigio, ecc. — lunghi brani di storia generale, per legare tra loro i 'frammenti' dell'opera ricostruita [. . .]. Il carattere frammentario dell'insieme del libro, fa sì, per esempio che certi 'pezzi narrativi' siano in sè perfetti, ma non si possa capire, per esempio, se si tratta di fatti reali, di sogni o di congetture fatte da qualche personaggio.[3]

My essay focuses on the Mattei Affair and the selected/fragmented path I've been following in my close reading, which is connected to a chapter in my book project, *Italian Cultural Landscapes in Post-Fascist Italy: Umberto Saba, Pier Paolo Pasolini and Elsa Morante*.

Pasolini's *Petrolio* and Morante's *Aracoeli* can be read assuming that a deep posthumous dialogue exists between these two texts, like the dialogue between Morante's *Il mondo salvato dai ragazzini* and *La Storia* — both quoted in *Petrolio* — and despite the significant differences between the two authors.[4] As Franco Fortini alluded and Walter Siti documented, Morante and Pasolini's work implies their reciprocal role as mentors and friends throughout the decades and up to a certain point, specifically in their representation of the mutational process — involving both politics and sexuality — taking place in Italy in the 1960s and early 1970s.[5] These were the years in which a strategy of tension between Italy's Red and Black entities became constitutive of politics and society. *Petrolio* represents this phase within a key symbolism indicative of both politics and sexuality: 'il misto' [the mixed], a symbolism also used by Morante in *Aracoeli*.

Enrico Mattei (1906–62) was a quintessential post-Fascist historical figure and the leading actor of the reconversion (against the governmental directives he had received actually to dismantle it) of the formerly Fascist oil state company (AGIP) into a new and reinvigorated organism, the national Fund Trust ENI, Ente Nazionale Idrocarburi.

Mattei was killed in a suspect plane crash on 27 October 1962, the same year he had refused to accept the conditions of one of the 'Seven Sisters' — an expression used to refer to the major multinational oil companies — who had asked him to stop dealing directly with the oil producing governments, making contracts at a 50 per cent rate of sharing with the countries (Russia, China, Iran, Egypt, among others) where oil had been found.

ENI is at the very heart of *Petrolio*'s structure as a novel, since its protagonist — 'l'uomo diviso' (a man divided) named after the author's father: Carlo — is in fact an ENI engineer and (as Mattei was) a left-wing Christian Democrat. Carlo is actually involved in Mattei's murder — and the reader is given this essential information from the very beginning of *Petrolio*'s posthumous edition, in one of the many numbered proposal notes (dated FORTE, 8 September 1973) from which the novel's plot is structured, entitled 'First, *initiatory* journey (Argonauts)':

> A questo punto proprio come uomo di sinistra viene scelto (è una contropartita per avere poi ciò che egli vuole) per una operazione di destra, estrema destra: la complicità in un delitto (l'uccisione di Mattei datata alla fine degli Anni Cinquanta?) che lo mette in contatto con la CIA e con la mafia. Ma egli vive tutto questo come in un sogno. Da complice ideale, non capisce e non vede niente. La manovra delittuosa avviene nella pensione SICILIA, a Torino. (*Petrolio*, p. 5)

Carlo's position within 'real power' and after Mattei's death is strategic. Pasolini takes care of making this point clear from the very beginning of his novel, in what he calls his 'prefatory folly':

> Quando arrivarono gli Anni Sessanta, egli era pronto a viverli. Era anzi quello il suo momento. Fu quello il momento in cui divenne [un cattolico di sinistra]: e questo gli consentì da una parte di differenziarsi o distinguersi dal potere, e, nel tempo stesso, attraverso il suo lavoro specifico e specialistico in quella punta tecnicamente avanzata che era l'ENI anche dopo la morte di Mattei, di inserirsi quasi con spavalderia (mai ostentata) nello 'spazio' dove si trova il potere reale. (*Petrolio*, p. 33)

The entire *Mattei affair* (1962), initially dated to the end of the 1950s, then moved forward chronologically to the late 1960s, is central to the very structure of *Petrolio*, as we can read in Pasolini's successive notes 20–30 (dated 16 October 1974), also named *Storia del problema del petrolio e retroscena/LAMPI SULL'ENI*, where Mattei's successor, Eugenio Cefis — Aldo Troya in the novel — is about to be made new president of ENI:

> In questo preciso momento storico (IL BLOCCO POLITICO) Troya (!) sta per essere fatto presidente dell'ENI: e ciò implica la soppressione del suo predecessore (caso Mattei, cronologicamente spostato in avanti). Egli con la

cricca politica ha bisogno di anticomunismo ('68): *bombe attribuite ai fascisti*. (*Petrolio*, pp. 117–18)

Eugenio Cefis became Mattei's powerful successor and finally moved ENI towards a new multinational identity: in 1971 he became president of the new society called MONTEDISON, progressively extending his financial powers up to controlling both national media and secret services between 1971 and 1974. Pasolini had been very sensitive to this fusion from its very beginning, as attested in an ironic footnote, in his poem *L'enigma di Pio XII*, published in *Trasumanar e organizzar* (1971).[6]

As we can read in the Meridiani-Mondadori annotated second edition of *Petrolio*, edited by Walter Siti and Silvia De Laude, Pasolini became interested in the role of Eugenio Cefis, after reading a speech he gave at the National Military Academy in Modena (23 February 1972). The speech had been published in the psychoanalytic journal directed by Elvio Fachinelli (*L'erba voglio*, n. 6, 1972) and it is filed within *Petrolio*'s manuscript. However it is not included in the novel, despite the intent to do so, expressed in Pasolini's notes 20–30, attributing the same watershed structural value to Cefis' speeches and to the two episodes in which Carlo (gendered female) is having sex with twenty boys:

> **inserire i discorsi di Cefis: i quali servono a dividere in due parti il romanzo in modo perfettamente simmetrico e esplicito (un po' come i due episodi dei venti ragazzi, ecc.) (*Petrolio*, p. 118)

In this speech the new Montedison president described the upcoming horizons of multinational finance and the twilight of national economies: this is indeed *Petrolio*'s global cultural landscape. Another fundamental source of Pasolini's interest in Cefis was a book he received from the same Fachinelli: Giorgio Steimetz's *Questo è Cefis, l'altra faccia dell'onorato presidente*.[7]

In *Petrolio*, Pasolini is extremely detailed in his descriptions and understanding of the passage from a national to a multinational ENI-Montedison; he explicitly calls his readers' attention towards this mutational process within the power structure of ENI, as well as towards the key role played by the character named Aldo Troya — Eugenio Cefis — in the novel:

> Ora, se l'ENI era un'azienda, era anche un 'topos' del potere [. . .]. C'era stato in quegli anni [. . .] un oscuro spostarsi di pedine in un settore importante per un organismo di potere, statale e insieme non statale com'era l'ENI: il settore della stampa [. . .]. Su questo punto vorrei richiamare l'attenzione del lettore: infatti Aldo Troja, vicepresidente dell'ENI, è destinato a diventare uno dei personaggi chiave della nostra storia. (Appunto 20, p. 90)

Beginning with note 22 — *Il cosiddetto impero dei Troya: lui, Troya* — Troya/Cefis is described carefully, both physically and psychologically, as a character defined by the mixed elements of his nature and politics: '*il misto*'. He's a figure without any weakness, but the reader knows from the very first lines of his portrait, that he's guilty: 'La prima cosa che colpisce di lui è il sorriso [. . .] è decisamente un sorriso colpevole' (*Petrolio*, p. 94). Troya/Cefis is indeed treated as the key character (*guilty*) in a classic detective story, and Pasolini is explicit about this point:

> Il linguaggio con cui egli si esprimeva era la sua attività; perciò io, per interpretarlo, dovrei essere un mercialista oltre che un detective. Mi sono arrangiato, ed ecco cosa sono venuto a sapere. (*Petrolio*, p. 96)

An interesting part of Troya/Cefis's biography is his Friulian roots (he was born in Sacile) and his participation in the anti-Fascist Resistance, in a mixed group (not communist), linked to De Gasperi and the Republicans, active in Lombardia from 1943 to 1945. This allows Pasolini to indulge his writing with many autobiographical aspects. His beloved Friulian landscapes are described in their most realistic details, as well as in their linguistic specificities: from peripheral Sacile, where Venetian is spoken, to the central Cividale del Friuli — 'la Firenze del Friuli' — at the heart of the most authentic Friulian/Ladin region, where the purest Friulian is spoken. These are indeed extremely interesting pages, where autobiography is used in a twisted direction and produces an effect of estrangement in the reader, aware of all these implications, telling that something else is at stake here. This is true specifically with regard to the theme of Resistance and its connection to Pasolini's own traumatic memories: the death of his brother Guido (who joined the Osoppo Brigade), killed in the Friulian Alps, at Porzus, in what is still considered one of the bloodiest pages in the internal conflict that arose in Northern Italy between the Garibaldi Brigade (Communist) and the Osoppo Brigade (linked to De Gasperi and the Republicans).

In *Petrolio*, the theme of Italian Resistance is always used realistically, never ideologically or romantically: that is to say, Pasolini specifies his characters' past links with the anti-Fascist Resistance only to show their realistic connection with the constitution of a new state power after the Second World War. He insists on this structural pattern within Italian executives' careers (the necessity of an anti-Fascist Resistance pedigree in order to get to power) and he often specifies the casual elements involved in it, as in the case of the Chief of Police in Turin.[8]

In this sense Pasolini builds a powerful rationalization and understanding of his personal biographic trauma: the bare fact that he had chosen not to join his brother Guido, staying instead in Casarsa writing poems and making love not war, and the fact that Guido died and Pier Paolo survived. In a way *Petrolio* analyses the deepest implications of Pasolini's survival of his brother for thirty restless years, testifying to his own personal resistance to state power in post-Fascist Italy, both as an intellectual and as a homosexual artist: 'con le armi della poesia'. In this sense this quote from the description of the two Carlos's 'depths of themselves', is extremely significant:

> In altre parole, intimità, commozione e solennità erano vissute dai due Carli nel profondo [. . .]; mentre in superficie, o, per dir meglio, in pratica, erano ignorate [. . .]. La sua [di Carlo secondo] libertà sessuale non era in fondo che l'affermazione, iterata mille volte, di un diritto contro una repressività incartapecorita [. . .]. [In questa] [. . .] testarda, infantile e in fondo umile riaffermazione del proprio diritto a commettere [un'infrazione] sessuale, non c'era in fondo che un po' di anarchia e molto idillio. (*Petrolio*, p. 184)

What leads us back to the element of '*misto*', so structural to *Petrolio*'s representation of politics and sexuality, is that the character of Troya/Cefis is imagined to be a member of the same group of partisans in which Mattei/Bonocore was the leader: both Mattei and Cefis were indeed Christian Democrats with a past in the anti-Fascist resistance.

Troya/Cefis, the key character of the detective story involved in this novel and the architect of Mattei/Bonocore's elimination, is described by Pasolini as an invincible pragmatist, a successful example of accumulation and expansion, with no real ambition (ambition was indeed Mattei/Bonocore's weak side) except to represent with his actions the championship of a specific — and mixed — post-Fascist reality:

> Troya emigrato a Milano nel 1943 [. . .]. Partecipò [. . .] alla Resistenza (questo, come vedremo, costituisce lo *scandalo*). C'era una formazione mista degasperiana e repubblicana (il *misto* cominciò subito, come si vede), che lottava sui monti della Brianza. Il capo di questa formazione partigiana era l'attuale presidente dell'Eni, Ernesto Bonocore [. . .]. La cosa che vorrei sottolineare è la seguente: Troya nella formazione partigiana era *secondo*. E la cosa pareva gli si addicesse magnificamente fin da allora. Non vorrei mitizzare: ma Troya non ci teneva a primeggiare per primeggiare. Era qualcosa di più che ambizioso [. . .]. In qualità di 'secondo' (vicecomandante o vicepresidente) la sua tendenza ascetica a 'realizzare' si attuava molto meglio. [. . .] Egli non avanzava, accumulava. Non saliva, si espandeva. Sarebbe troppo lungo, e per me, poi, impossibile, seguire tutta la lenta storia (due decenni) di questa accumulazione e di questa espansione. (*Petrolio*, pp. 96–97)

Indeed these pages are fundamental in order to understand the mixed nature of the events Pasolini is discussing in his novel and the deeply traumatic origins of the new Italian Republic (the First Republic 1948–94, as it is now called by historians). Troya/Cefis helps us understand the reasons for the development of that colonial 'sviluppo senza progresso' Pasolini was constantly addressing as the major failure of the anti-Fascist Resistance, which meant bitter disillusion for an entire generation. At the end of one of his most important articles, originally published in *Corriere della Sera* on 18 February 1975, with the title 'Il vuoto di potere in Italia', at the time known as *L'articolo delle lucciole* (the article of fireflies), Pasolini wrote: 'Ad ogni modo, quanto a me (se ciò ha qualche interesse per il lettore) sia chiaro: io, ancorché multinazionale, darei l'intera Montedison per una lucciola'.

In a sense *Aracoeli*'s bitter representation of 1968 Italian intellectuals, ready to change their minds, and join the centre-right wing parties to finally get to power (and TV) — as is the case of the Marxist-Leninist young master, lecturing Manuel on gender, class, and sexuality — is deeply linked to Pasolini's complex understanding of post-Fascist reality.[9] In this sense, with *Aracoeli*, Morante rejects her initial empathy and enthusiasm for the youth movements of 1968 (*Il mondo salvato dai ragazzini*), embracing Pasolini's perspective and his conflictual relationship with Italian students since his poem *Il P.C.I. ai giovani* (1968). After his death Morante seems to refer to Pasolini through her own poetics, accepting his critique of her *radical chic* revolutionary attitudes. From the very first pages of her last novel,[10] which starts on the very day Pasolini was killed, between 1 and 2 November 1975, Morante overcomes the significant differences that opposed her idyllic vision of 1968 revolutionaries to Pasolini's resilient defence of institutions.[11]

As for the myth of 'Resistenza' — so powerfully deconstructed in *Petrolio* — an estranged, ambiguously anamorphic representation of Italian partisans can be found in *Aracoeli*.[12] In a long passage devoted to the traumatic partisan trial Manuele experienced as a child in the autumn of 1944, we can read a poetic enunciation, which is also meant to be a parodic definition. It is uttered by one of the two sadistic 'Chiefs', or rather 'fake partisans' Manuele had the misfortune to encounter while he was wandering about the Piedmont hills, in the same regions where Pavese's and Calvino's narrators, Corrado and Pin, had been represented as witnesses:[13]

> 'Noi non siamo soggetti da guerriglia
> siamo rampolli d'ottima famiglia
> io visconte lui conte
> e non andiamo al fronte.
> Lui alienato io alienista
> e dunque c'intendiamo a prima vista
> e insieme ci aggiustiamo
> per l'amore cristiano.
> Niente paura! Male non facciamo!
> non siamo TIGRI ma TROIE siamo!'
> (*Aracoeli*, pp. 1243–44)

The adult Manuele would finally read his 'comical "partisan" venture' — and his bitter disillusion — as a 'memory gap':

> Certo nel mio passato, più di una volta, io devo essermi abbeverato — senza saperlo — in qualche affluente nascosto del fiume Oblio [. . .]. E forse quella mia febbre autunnale del 1944 fu uno di tali emissari invisibili. È un fatto che, da allora, soltanto oggi mi è tornata alla memoria la mia comica impresa 'partigiana' [. . .]. Nel punto stesso che vedevo questa scena, io me n'ero subito dimenticato. Come allo scoppio di una bolla, al suo posto subentrava un 'vuoto di memoria'. (*Aracoeli*, pp. 1246–47)

It seems to me that — besides all issues of memory, identity, and self-representation in this novel — a 'memory gap' is indeed the category Morante applied to Italy's Fascist and post-Fascist twentieth-century history, as represented in *Aracoeli*'s complex time images.

Getting back to *Petrolio*, it is important to notice, that despite all metamorphosis involved in the book: — of gender and politics, history and anthropology, landscapes and tradition — this is a novel about the obsession of identity, and this very fact is related by the author to a metaliterary element: the end of the novel (often called the poem by Pasolini):

> Questo poema non è un poema sulla dissociazione [. . .]. Al contrario, questo poema è il poema dell'ossessione dell'identità e, insieme, della sua frantumazione. La dissociazione è ordine, L'ossessione dell'identità e la sua frantumazione è disordine. (*Petrolio*, p. 181)

Here Pasolini is confessing to his reader the problems he envisaged while trying to keep his poem/novel readable, which — he admits — is not the case with *Petrolio*:

> Il motivo della dissociazione altro dunque non è che la regola narrativa che assicura limitatezza e leggibilità a questo poema; il quale, a causa dell'altro

> motivo, più vero, dell'ossessione dell'identità e della sua frantumazione, sarebbe per sua natura illimitato e illeggibile. (*Petrolio*, p. 181)

That is to say that male or female, Carlo primo or number 1, instead of Carlo secondo or number 2 — his bourgeois or lumpenproletarian manifestations — all this should not really matter to the reader, I mean at the deepest level: of trying to make order, understanding dissociations, to keep on using Pasolini's terms. What does matter is instead the understanding of Pasolini's *obsession with identity* (hence disorder and fragmentation) as the dominant element in the novel, and the very reason of its internally dynamic and psychologically engaged field of meaning. In *Petrolio* the normative process is understood and represented through this very contradiction, and in opposition to the paternal order — that seems instead to be alluded to as salvific at the end of *Aracoeli*.

Let's make a little step backward, and read once more the important Note 4, where Pasolini asks 'What is a novel?'. He begins his answer with this statement: 'Carlo è il nome di mio padre' (*Petrolio*, p. 29). From this crucial choice (as it was crucial that Pasolini dedicated his 1942 *Poesie a Casarsa* to his father), the entire novel develops its search for the 'machinic composition of totalitarian powers', therefore its 'micro-political struggle for the liberation of desire', and identity.[14] That is to say that the 'machinic assemblage' (Guattari) of totalitarian power needs to be constantly individuated, dismantled, and dismembered: this is the essence of resistance in Pasolini's terms. He's extremely clear about this strategy, from the very beginning of *Petrolio*, where Pasolini's essentially schizophrenic representation of identity is represented as a liberating force:

> Come mio padre mai avrebbe accettato di spaccarsi in due, capace di ammazzare — come ammazzavano i fascisti — per difendere la sua unità — così egli [Carlo], *al contrario, non avrebbe mai accettato di fingere di essere uno se in realtà era [spaccato in due]. Avrebbe potuto anche lasciarsi ammazzare pur di essere coerente con questa realtà.* (*Petrolio*, p. 30, my emphasis)

I'd like to get now towards a conclusion, using an example where the themes of politics and sexuality are specifically addressed.

Towards the end of the *Visione*,[15] where Pasolini's entire experience and understanding of reality (and comodification) have declined to a hellish level, Carlo experiences the vortex of an ascent (in the chariot of the Gods): he gets to a point where the entire city of Rome is described within an anthropomorphized and gendered symbolism:

> Carlo [osservò] che tutte le cupole, rivestite di nuovi materiali, avevano assunto l'aspetto inequivocabile di seni, coi loro capezzoli anatomicamente perfetti, a 'trompe l'oeil'. Tutte le piazze erano state modificate [. . .] in modo da far loro prendere la forma di enormi fiche. Infine, tutti i campanili [. . .] erano stati trasformati in una serie di cazzi di tutte le dimensioni. (*Petrolio*, p. 382)

Finally, Pasolini seems to suggest a cinematographic crane shot from above, which happens indeed to refer (oxymoronically) to the final images of Rossellini's 1945 *Open City*: his final glance on children, Rome, and the Catholic Church, as a symbol of hope after Nazism and Fascism in that movie. At the end of the Vision,

Pasolini's Carlo sees instead the symbol of Nazism — the swastika[16] — as the symbol of the city of Rome in the 1960s, that is to say the obligation to conform to a superimposed social and economic model:

> Quando il carro fu al suo zenit, sul Centro, e si fermò, tutto l'insieme della Città poté essere abbracciato con un solo sguardo: la sua forma era quella — anch'essa inequivocabile — di un'immensa Croce Uncinata (*Petrolio*, p. 382)

Though reaching this point of the Vision, Carlo did not reach its final meaning, and the reader is told to be very careful at this point (note 74, *Last Flash of the Vision*), since there will be a mystical moment which will include liberating laughter.

Carlo is walking towards the limits of hell, marked by clear borders, which are finally reached. After a walk in his neighbourhood, the Quadraro, one of the poor slums in 1970s Rome, long before Cinecittà, which appears on the skyline, Carlo has his last vision, the last image of it:

> Fu appunto passando attraverso quello slargo, poco prima della sua casa [. . .] che a Carlo apparve — staccata — l'ultima Scena della sua Visione [. . .]. Al posto di quelle case apparve un enorme Tabernacolo [. . .]. In questo Tabernacolo — le cui forme del resto erano assai imprecise e si sfacevano nel cielo scintillante — era contenuto un grande simulacro [. . .] alto tre volte almeno un uomo di statura normale. [. . .] un mostro muliebre [il taglio della vulva coincideva col taglio del mento] [. . .]. Questo mostro muliebre [. . .] reggeva con la mano destra, un lungo bastone, della sua stessa altezza: e questo bastone era senza possibilità di dubbio, un lungo e nodoso membro virile. (*Petrolio*, pp. 384–85)[17]

With this sudden apparition we move forward, towards the real implications of Carlo's — and Pasolini's — infernal/parodic visions, which are expressed by an inscription located at the feet of the image: 'HO ERETTO QUESTA STATUA PER RIDERE' (pp. 385–86). This inscription brings us back to Elsa Morante, and the dialogue between the two authors, since it is a specific quote from Morante's 1968 *Il mondo salvato dai ragazzini*,[18] as well as from *La Storia*:

> 'È uno scherzo
>   uno scherzo
>   tutto uno scherzo!' [. . .]
>   Il silenzio in realtà era parlante! anzi, era fatto di voci [. . .]. Però dentro ci si distinguevano chi sa come, una per una, tutte le frasi e i discorsi, a migliaia, e a migliaia di migliaia: e le canzonette, e i belati, e il mare, e le sirene d'allarme, e gli spari, e le tossi, e i motori, e i convogli per Auschwitz, e i grilli, e le bombe dirompenti, e il grugnito minimo dell'animaluccio senza coda . . . e 'che me lo dài un bacetto, a Usè?'. . .[19]

In Pasolini's *Petrolio*, the game with reality — as it is — is accepted with all its final consequences, and despite all delusional moments, despite death and Fascism. In his unfinished last novel, devoted to the essence of totalitarian power and the state — its massacres and silent mysteries — Pasolini imagined the possibility of a radical liberation, a mystical act which will be 'un atto risolutore, vitale, pienamente positivo e orgiastico: esso ristabilirà la serenità della vita e la ripresa del corso della storia' (p. 387). In this sense the use of the rite of *anasyrma* in *Petrolio* is indicative of a liberating — and hilarious — force, within social order, and the role of both politics and sexuality:

> A quanto pare, tutta la storia umana non fa altro che ripeterci una cosa: *è solo ciò che è stato*. E infatti Carlo, spogliandosi, vide *che gli stava succedendo ciò che gli era già successo*. Compiendo veloce l'*anasyrma* ecco che nello [. . .] specchio del cesso, che lo aveva già specchiato da studente, anziché Polyhymnia rivide Polyhymnos, o se si vuole, Baubo anziche Baubon. Polyhymnia o Polyhymnos, Baubo o Baubon la cosa non cambia poi molto, per la verità. È causa di riso — magari sacro — e con riferimenti funebri — sia per il bambino che per la divinità cosmica [. . .]. Ciò non toglie che fu con profonda emozione che Carlo — nel vecchio specchio del cesso — vide che il suo torace era un magro torace senza seni, e, toltisi — appunto secondo il rito dell *anasyrma*, senza però che nel suo caso specifico nessuno ridesse — i calzoni e le mutande, vide che di nuovo gli penzolava in fondo alla pancia, sotto i radi peli, il vecchio pene. (*Petrolio*, pp. 504–05)

Anasyrma — as it is discussed in Alain Delaniou's book on Shiva and Dionysus — is the sacred act of lifting up one's skirt in order to show the genitals.[20] It is used in connection with shamanism and religious rituals in several different cultures: it represents the liberating power of the androgynous and bisexual nature of human beings, linking all ages from early childhood to death. It refers to the mystery of life, time, and death, as quintessential to eroticism, laughter, and the sacred. This is also probably a topic Pasolini and Morante — who was a savant more than anybody else in a men's club — might have discussed together, and who knows who had learnt from whom. What is important and matters here is that *Petrolio* attests to an endless engagement with reality: against any suicidal drive. Pasolini — like his character Carlo — 'Avrebbe potuto anche lasciarsi ammazzare pur di essere coerente con questa realtà', but this is another story.

Notes to Chapter 10

1. The bibliography on *Petrolio* is extremely rich. I'd like to mention two major conferences held in Italy: the first, organized and edited by Carla Benedetti and Maria Antonietta Grignani in 1993 at the University of Pavia (Collegio Ghisleri): *A partire da Petrolio: Pasolini interroga la letteratura*, ed. by Carla Benedetti and Maria Antonietta Grignani (Ravenna: Longo, 1995); the second, organized in 2005 by Marco Antonio Bazzocchi and Circolo Arcigay Il Cassero in Bologna: *Progetto Petrolio: una giornata di studi sul romanzo incompiuto di Pier Paolo Pasolini*, ed. by Paolo Salerno (Bologna: CLUEB, 2006).
2. Specifically Bernardo Bertolucci's 1967 documentary 'La via del petrolio', commissioned by ENI-Montedison between 1966 and 1967, recently restaured by ENI and Cineteca Nazionale.
3. Pier Paolo Pasolini, *Petrolio* (Turin: Einaudi, 1992), pp. 3–4. All my quotations in Italian are from this edition; available in English as Pier Paolo Pasolini, *Petrolio*, trans. by Ann Goldstein (New York: Pantheon, 1997).
4. Elsa Morante, *Aracoeli* (Turin: Einaudi, 1982); *Il mondo salvato dai ragazzini e altri poemi* (Turin: Einaudi, 1968); *La Storia*, (Turin: Einaudi, 1974); now all in: Elsa Morante, *Opere*, ed. by Carlo Cecchi and Cesare Garboli, 2 vols (Milan: Mondadori, 1988–90).
5. See Franco Fortini, *Attraverso Pasolini* (Turin: Einaudi, 1993), p. 240: 'Sono sempre più persuaso che tutto l'ultimo Pasolini vada letto come una sorta di dialogo con la Morante'. On Pasolini and Morante, see Walter Siti, 'Elsa Morante nell'opera di Pier Paolo Pasolini', in *Vent'anni dopo 'La Storia': Omaggio a Elsa Morante*, ed. by Concetta D'Angeli and Giacomo Magrini, Atti del Convegno (Pisa, 24–26 gennaio 1994), *Studi novecenteschi* [Special Issue], 47–48 (June–December 1994), 131–48, reprinted in English translation in *Under Arturo's Star: The Cultural Legacies of Elsa Morante*, ed. by Stefania Lucamante and Sharon Wood (West Lafayette, IN: Purdue University Press, 2006), pp. 268–89.

6. Pier Paolo Pasolini, *Trasumanar e organizzar* (Milan: Garzanti, 1971), p. 15: 'Deformo Paolo, certo, nella mia coscienza di papa, umanista, e non ne ho coscienza, perché due nature/come quella feudale e quella borghese fondendosi (2) [. . .] (2) La parola 'fusione' non aveva ancora subito la lieve alterazione semantica dovuta alla fusione tra la Edison e la Montecatini.'
7. Giorgio Steimetz, *Questo è Cefis, l'altra faccia dell'onorato presidente* (Milan: Ami, 1972). On Pasolini's interest in Eugenio Cefis, see Gianni D'Elia, *Il petrolio delle stragi* (Milan: Effgie, 2006).
8. Egli era di origine marchigiana, e per natura era da una parte incerto e nevrotico, dall'altra pacifico e privo di vere ambizioni Sennonché il caso aveva voluto che durante la Guerra si trovasse in Piemonte e lì, sempre per caso avesse partecipato alla guerra partigiana. (*Petrolio*, pp. 471–72).
9. Cf. Morante, *Aracoeli*, in *Opere*, II (1990), pp. 1039–1454 (pp. 1156–58). Further references to this edition will be given after quotations in the text.
10. Morante, *Aracoeli*, p. 1058. Here the slogans of the Italian Workerist (*Operaismo*) Movement ('È ora! È ora! | Il Potere a chi lavora!') heard by Manuele while he's leaving Milan for his mysterious journey to Spain, on 1 November 1975, are radically opposed to Manuele's sensitivity and understanding of reality.
11. Cf. Pier Paolo Pasolini, *Il mondo salvato dai ragazzini*, first published in *Paragone* (October 1968), then in Pasolini, *Trasumanar e organizzar*, pp. 31–47. Cf. p. 32: 'Si è fratelli nell'istituzione, nell'ansia della norma: | ciò è misero, è vile, ma è commovente'. In *Trasumanar e Organizzar* see also: 'Egli o tu', the poem Pasolini devoted to the memory of Bob Kennedy, and 'L'enigma di Pio XII'.
12. For a reading of Morante's *Aracoeli* through the lens of anamorphosis, see Rebecca West's essay in this volume (Chapter 3).
13. See Cesare Pavese's Corrado in *La casa in collina*, first published in *Prima che il gallo canti* (Turin: Einaudi, 1949) and Italo Calvino's Pin in *Il sentiero dei nidi di ragno* (Turin: Einaudi, 1949).
14. See Félix Guattari, 'Everybody Wants to Be a Fascist', lecture delivered in Milan for the Colloquium 'Psychoanalysis and Politics', December 1973, trans. by Susanne Fletcher, then published in Félix Guattari, *Chaosophy*, ed. by Sylvère Lotringer (New York: Semiotext[e], 1995), pp. 225–50, cf. p. 237:
    It seems to me that the constant search for this machinic composition of totalitarian powers is the indispensable corollary of a micro-political struggle for the liberation of desire. The minute you stop facing it head-on, you can abruptly oscillate from a position of revolutionary openness to a position of totalitarian foreclosure [. . .].
15. From p. 323, *Appunto* 71, 'Il Merda (Visione: paragrafo primo)', to *Appunto* 74, 'Ultimo sprazzo della Visione', pp. 383–85.
16. It is interesting to notice that this image might have been inspired by Elsa Morante's *La Storia*, p. 61: 'Su San Pietro, al posto della croce cristiana, avrebbero messo la croce uncinata'.
17. This is indeed an old image Pasolini kept in his own closet, with his various unpublished manuscripts: cf. Pier Paolo Pasolini, *Amado mio, preceduto da Atti impuri* (Milan: Garzanti, 1982), originally written in the 1940s, pp. 147–48:
    Sai Desi [. . .] quei porci di S.: un giorno a casa loro stavano malignando sul mio conto [. . .]. Ma io, amici, non ho il senso del buco, dissi entrando tra lo spavento generale, siete in errore [. . .]. Ridevo: non ho il senso del buco, a tre anni cominciò il famoso ciclo di sogni in cui mi trovavo dentro un cunicolo scavato in un monte: era spaventoso. A tredici anni (ma ahimè si trattava solo di residui diurni) cominciai a sognare di donne, il buco non l'avevano: il loro ventre era di pietra [. . .]. Amici [. . .] immaginatemi col battente di una porta in mano, i gangheri bene in vista [. . .] voi che fareste? Infilereste il c. . . della porta nella f. . . dei gangheri; invece io niente affatto, resterei col battente in mano, e magari me lo lascerei cadere sui piedi.
18. Morante, *Il mondo salvato dai ragazzini*, p. 151: 'TUTTO QUESTO | IN SOSTANZA E VERITÀ | NON È NIENT'ALTRO | CHE UN GIOCO'.
19. Morante, *La Storia*, pp. 510–11.
20. See Alain Daniélou, *Gods of Love and Ecstasy: The Traditions of Shiva and Dionysus* (Rochester: Inner Traditions, 1992). Original text in French available as: *Shiva et Dionysos: Religion de Nature*

et d'Eros (Paris: Fayard, 1979). Pasolini was extremely interested in anthropology and the history of religions since his youth: he knew Franz Cumont's work, specifically his studies on the Mithraic mysteries, as attested since his first book of Friulian poems, *Poesie a Casarsa* (see the poem *David*).

CHAPTER 11

Between Italy and Spain: The Tragedy of History and the Salvific Power of Love in Elsa Morante and María Zambrano

Elisa Martínez Garrido

The mother is the central core of Morante's work from the beginning. From *Le bellissime avventure di Caterì dalla trecciolina* (1942) to *Aracoeli* (1982), an often narcissistic and symbiotic motherly love is the force that sinks the deranged subject into sadomasochistic relationships and is the driving force behind the author's writing.

Elsa Morante's writing stems from a lack of love from the original mother and a loss related to her own frustrated maternity.[1] This is why the texts of Elsa Morante revolve in an obsessive way around an ambiguous, contradictory duality and a disassociated maternal relationship. The mother is the primal and wild force of nature and origins, the absolute good, but simultaneously, as its antagonistic opposite, the mother is for Elsa Morante the most important figure of any tragic force, of *hybris*, and of destruction and death. While Elsa Morante's literary journeys are centred on the mother, at the same time, in many cases, the damnation or rescue of the male protagonists depends on the possibility of their encounter with the father. For instance, it is not fortuitous that both Arturo, the protagonist of *L'isola di Arturo* (1957), and Manuele, the protagonist of *Aracoeli* (1982), must confront their father, or the man who represents him, in the end.

However, with respect to Morante's previous novels, *Aracoeli* represents a turning point in the concept of beatific motherly love. While in previous works the positive and negative realities of motherhood were disassociated in two different female characters, in Morante's last novel they are mixed in a single character: Aracoeli is neither Nunziatella of *L'isola di Arturo* nor Ida of *La Storia* (1974); Aracoeli follows Nunziatella at the beginning but, in a second phase, she becomes the heiress of the romantic passion of Anna, the mother of Elisa in *Menzogna e sortilegio* (1948), in an even more perverse and devastating way.

The duplicity and dichotomy of the main character is a high point of the 1982 novel.[2] Duplicity and antagonism are important hermeneutic characteristics for the final understanding of this work. However, it is also important to point out that it is not only Aracoeli's character that is based on this dichotomy; this internal feature is also found in most of the others, such as Manuele's father, Eugenio, and his aunt Monda.

Many of Elsa Morante's novels are founded semantically and rhetorically on the dichotomy of a character split between opposite traits, and stage a perpetual chain of circumstances that is not ruled by the principle of non-contradiction. This is for instance why *oxymoron* is the key rhetorical figure of *Aracoeli*:[3] a wounding contradiction represents itself in the *parodic* tragedy (tragicomedy) of its characters and, simultaneously, points to an oblique way to salvation and reconciliation.[4]

We can say that, in a way, *Aracoeli* tells the agonizing passage of characters posited on the threshold or border of an epoch, a history, or a new psychology. The text speaks of the existential and historical agony associated with the passage from a heroic, beatific, solar, and diurnal reality to its opposite: an anti-heroic, orphic, malignant, nocturnal, and telluric reality. Moreover, on the existential passage of Morante's broken characters and their internal contradictions is superimposed a forced voyage between two worlds, between here and there, even the beyond.

In this way, the threshold, the border, or the boundary allows for a duality of vision, a double *mirare* in continuous contradiction, reconciled only at the end. *Aracoeli* confronts two opposing worlds, Italy and Spain, in a spatial and geographic framework — the parental and maternal worlds respectively. Spain, more specifically Andalusia, always represented for Elsa Morante the epitome of the mythic, uncontaminated land, the essential south. Andalusia belongs to the same mythical ancestral realm as Sicily and the Amalfi coastline, which are the locations of her previous works. But, for Morante, Andalusia is without doubt the nearest European version of the exoticism and archaism of India and Africa. The southern worlds are metaphoric variants of the wild, primitive innocence of a world in an uncontaminated natural state.

Elsa Morante's 'Gypsy and Moorish Andalusia' represents, in *Aracoeli*, the prototype of an ancient land, the charmed and fabulous genre of legends and popular songs.[5] Andalusia is, for the writer, a magic land still not soiled by the vertiginous and devastating rhythms of history and progress. It is worthwhile to point out that the setting of Morante's last novel is Almeria, the wildest and most remote province of Spain. Furthermore, Morante places the action in a small hamlet of the *Sierra de los Filabres*, in the mountains, in an obscure locality lost among white slates, arid hills, and prickly pears: El Almendral.

When visited by Elsa Morante in the 1960s and 1970s, this remote hamlet, like the Cabo de Gata, Las Negras, or La Isleta del Moro, was, no doubt, a *finis terrae*.[6] Almeria is still today, in a sense, a frontier land, a meeting point between both Orient and Occident and between Europe and Africa.[7] The historical, cultural, and human problems related to borders and frontiers are not only associated with the geographic separation of Spain and Italy. They are also present in the text in the parental space, inside Italy. In this case, it is a boundary or interface between the inner and the outer worlds: Rome and the Puglie contrast with Piedmont and Milan, marking political, cultural, and key geographic divisions during the inner voyage and maturation of the character.

Rome is the end of Manuele's return journey from Piedmont after he flees from school. In the novel, Rome is also the political boundary between the two Italies, both in the text and in the real world, from 1943 onwards, during the Italian Civil War (*Aracoeli*, pp. 1215–17). For Manuele, Rome is also a space related to the mother: both the Rome of Totetaco (Monte Sacro) and the Rome of Quartieri Alti are marked by the figure of Aracoeli. The Puglie, referred to in the novel through Daniele, colour the southern aspects of Rome, thanks to this most pure and innocent character (pp. 1314–24). Piedmont — the rigid space of Manuele's grandparents — and Milan — the cold and inhospitable Northern city of Manuele's adult life — appear in the novel as the opposites of Rome and the Puglie on the one side, and of Almeria and El Almendral on the other (pp. 1422–26).

Milan is the geographical and metaphorical starting point of Manuele's voyage towards Spain, which was still under Franco's rule in 1975. For Manuele, and probably for the writer, Milan represents the epitome of the old industrial, alienated, and foreign city (*Aracoeli*, pp. 1044–46). The descent from Milan to Almeria conveys a clear journey across the border, one that creates a duality of two confronting worlds. Therefore, Manuele's return journey to his origins, which leads to his particular *anabasis*, is marked by a disassociated vision. Milan is the industrial North, the city of business and money, whereas Almeria clearly represents the opposite: nature, fantasy, and love.

While it is true that the end of *Aracoeli* is ambiguous and open to several hermeneutic possibilities, in my interpretation Manuele's *anabasis* probably has no return.[8] There is no explicit allusion to Manuele's 'last journey', that is, to his death, nor to his life after the visit to El Almendral and his encounter with the ghostly voice of Aracoeli. In any case, thanks to his journey to the Spanish South, Manuele finds an unconscious reconciliation with himself and his father.[9]

Borders and History

Returning to the idea of borders, we must stress that the ones erected in the novel are not only spatial but also temporal. The historical time frame in which the story is set relates to a series of temporal limits which mark the beginning and the end of an epoch for Spain: the rise of Fascism with the Spanish Civil War, declared on 18 July 1936, and the death of Franco on 20 November 1975.

Between July 1936 and April 1939, a rehearsal of the approaching Second World War took place in Spain. This second conflict initiated the fight in Europe against Nazism and Fascism. At that moment, Aracoeli travels to Italy, after her marriage following her kidnapping (according to an ancient southern Spanish tradition),[10] and, after the years in Totetaco, she lives with Eugenio and his family, who are loyal to the Crown and to the regime of Mussolini. Simultaneously, Manuel Muñoz Muñoz, Aracoeli's brother, dies in Spain for his anti-Fascist and communist ideals.

In contrast, Manuele's return to Spain begins shortly before 20 November 1975.[11] When he starts his journey towards Almeria, Francisco Franco's death occurs, and with it the last European dictatorship ends; consequently, a new social model is born in Spain. The end of Fascism is followed by an advanced democracy, which Elsa

Morante presents as the first glimpse of our present-day consumer society with its advanced technology and devastating progress.

Consequently, between his birth and his journey to El Almendral, the character of Manuele goes through some of the critical moments of the history of Europe and some of the deep cultural and anthropological transformations of contemporary society: the defeat of the Spanish Republic, the Italian Civil War in Piedmont, the liberation of Italy by the American troops, the fall of Fascism, the arrival of democracy, the industrialization of northern Italy, and the associated increase of wealth (*Aracoeli*, pp. 1436–46).

During his journey to the Spanish South, Manuele also experiences Franco's death, the beginning of the transition to democracy, the arrival of tourism, and the spiritual decline of Almeria, which is fully devoted to the business of spaghetti-western movies (p. 1426). A new mass society has started the corruption of the wild paradise of the remote Andalusian south. In a way *Aracoeli* is an allegory of the Western crisis between 1936 and 1975, and the existential complexity of a broken, disassociated, dispersed human being can be considered as a metaphor for the inner conflict of contemporary humankind.[12]

In *Aracoeli* this dual, antagonistic reality marks the tragic behaviour of the female protagonist, who evolves from being the sacred symbol of beatific motherhood, as when her image as a nursing *Madonna* is framed in the mirror in a sort of 'Quattrocento' painting (p. 1049), to the (also sacred) representation of a terrifying sexuality, as she became a nymphomaniac and a prostitute, a slave of an evil which is not only sexual, but located both in the mind and in the belly.[13]

Aracoeli's evil starts with her second pregnancy,[14] but her degradation deepens after the death of her little daughter Encarnación-Carina (*Aracoeli*, p. 1294), which almost coincides with that of her brother Manuel (pp. 1280, 1288, 1329–30). The announcement of this death to Manuele, told in a darkly humorous vein, emphasizes the novel's tragicomedy. After the death of Carina — a double of herself —, after the death of her brother (pp. 1330–31) — another double of Aracoeli because of their astonishing physical likeness —, and after Aracoeli has endured the process of 'domestication' inflicted by aunt Monda, the female protagonist undergoes a dramatic change (p. 1343): no longer a Madonna, but a prostitute, a sort of female demon, the embodiment of evil par excellence.

But why this antagonistic metamorphosis? This is, no doubt, the hermeneutic key to the ultimate understanding of the novel. The morbid transformation of Aracoeli, which stems from a personal loss and illness, becomes a symbol for the evils of history and the agony and death which invaded Europe during the Second World War. The evil that shakes Europe during the time of Aracoeli's life makes her a sort of sacrificial victim: the blood flowing down her vagina just after the death of Carina, as well as the blood soaking the bandages on her head when she is in the hospital for the removal of a brain tumour just before her death, are clear symbols of her sacrifice.[15]

In this sense it is possible to analyse Aracoeli's *definitive transgression*, when she refuses the help of God inside a church. The protagonist feels herself unfairly damaged, as she has been physically and psychologically invaded by evil. After this transgression, Aracoeli decides to go to the Quinta and to become a prostitute (pp. 1379, 1380, 1388, 1391, 1392).

Elsa Morante and María Zambrano: Towards a Spiritual Reflection of Evil and Agony in Europe

This idea of Aracoeli's sacrifice and the mystical reflections on the European tragedy are similar to those of other female thinkers such as Simone Weil and María Zambrano.[16]

It is well documented that the character of Aracoeli was inspired by the personal tragedy of Araceli, the sister of the Spanish thinker.[17] Moreover, as María Zambrano met Elsa Morante during her exile in Rome in the 1950s, it is possible to relate their respective reflections on evil and agony in Europe.

The Andalusian thinker, a pilgrim and an exile, a tireless traveller in search for truth beyond many borders, wrote her work *La agonía de Europa* during her first period of exile in America.[18] This text is built on a tragic journey through the cultural and spiritual crisis of the contemporary Western world. María Zambrano was particularly interested in the central core of this crisis, because, in her opinion, only after facing evil could salvation be found.

Like Elsa Morante, Simone Weil, and Hannah Arendt, María Zambrano thought, following St Augustine, that salvation is possible only by proceeding from the individual to the multitude.[19] It should not be forgotten that María Zambrano repeated her quests in search of truth during the great Spanish and European periods of crisis; at that time the images of the road and journeys are more vivid, because when one travels, one can be more aware of the cruel metamorphosis of place and of periods of agony.

This reflection, elaborated in the 1940s as a consequence of the tragedy in Europe, is the basis of Zambrano's magisterial work *El Hombre y lo divino*, written in Rome and published in Mexico City in 1955 by Fondo de Cultura Económica. In this work piety and love open the door to the *other* and form the core of the mystic thoughts of the philosopher. This is the existential and thematic core that allows a correlation between Zambrano and Morante, who from this point of view can be considered as mystical thinkers.[20] *La agonía de Europa* is a book dedicated to María Zambrano's mother, Araceli, who lived the tragic war years in France with her second daughter, María's sister who, as we know, was also named Araceli.[21]

From the collection of Zambrano's essays that form *La agonía de Europa*, I would like now to concentrate on the piece entitled *El corazón*, included in the third part of the book, *La esperanza de Europa*, where one finds an explicit reference to St Augustine. The Spanish thinker considered, following the African bishop, that only the heart, love, and the feelings that come from the soul could illuminate the Western darkness. The proud disillusionment of this dark reasoning is at the root of European agony and its violence. Hope will return to Europe after a return to the truth of the heart:

> El corazón se encuentra en confusión y dispersión siempre; cuando nos damos cuenta que lo tenemos es que está en otro que se ha enajenado. Pero esta

dispersión y esta obscuridad-'abotargado mi corazón'-piden claridad y unidad. Y sólo al hallar la verdad, enamorándose de ella, la alcanza. 'El hombre superior utiliza su corazón como un espejo', dice el *Tao Te-king*. El corazón limpio y reunido ha dejado de ser un estorbo para ser un medio, un medio de encontrar y poseer la verdad, reflejándola.

Pero San Agustín no revela el corazón para hacer de él un espejo sino algo más activo. Es el amor el que va a conferir la unidad, el tener la verdad enamorándose de ella.[22]

[The Heart is always confused and dispersed: when we realize we've got one it is because it is estranged from another. But this dispersion and darkness of 'my swollen and drowsy heart' needs clarity and unity. And only when we find the truth and fall in love with it do we reach it. 'The superior man uses his heart like a mirror' says the *Tao Te-ching*. In this way a clean and reunited heart stops being an impediment and becomes a means for finding and possessing the truth. Yet St Augustine does not reveal the heart to make it a mirror, but something rather more active. It is love that grants unity and has the truth falling in love with it.][23]

Coming back from *La agonía de Europa* to *Aracoeli* and pausing for a moment to consider the goal of Manuele's journey to southern, almost African, lands, one finds an echo of María Zambrano's words. The meeting with the heart and love is the ultimate goal of Manuele's travel to El Almendral. In this obscure hamlet of the desert of Almería, the protagonist had the revelation of the saviour and truth: love, more specifically the love for his father. This revelation opens a whole range of hermeneutic possibilities.[24]

This is shown clearly by the dialogue between Manuele and Aracoeli's ghost in El Almendral:

'Volevo dirti che tutto mi fa paura'.
 'E piú di tutto, che?'
 'Aver peccato'.
 'Tu! E dove hai peccato tu povero niño?!'
 'Dovunque ho peccato. Nelle intenzioni e nei fini e negli atti, ma peggio di tutto nell'intelligenza. L'intelligenza si da per capire. E a me si è data, ma io non capisco niente. E non ho mai capito niente, e non capirò mai niente'.
 'Ma niño mio chiquito non c'è niente da capire'
 La sento che manda un riso, tenero. E questo è l'addio. (*Aracoeli*, pp. 1427–28)

These lines give rise again to the question: why does Aracoeli tell Manuele that there is nothing to understand? Why is life a comedy as Carlo Davide says to Useppe in the *1947* chapter of *La Storia*?[25] My hypothesis is that, following Zambrano, there is nothing to understand with the mind because the only possibility of hope for the protagonist is to be led by the heart.

The only way out, therefore, the revelation of the ultimate truth, as Elsa Morante says using Umberto Saba's verses, is related to piety, love, and forgiveness.[26] Indeed, *Aracoeli* ends with the words *amare* and *amore*.[27] Through love, Manuele is able to return to a state of unity, in the precise magical space where the love story between Aracoeli and Eugenio took place. As is said in the novel:

> Eravamo integri, prima della Genesi; [. . .] Gli dei non sono maciullati dalla macchina dei sensi. Sono integri. Passato presente e futuro — tenebre e luce — morte e vita — i multipli e gli addendi — i diversi e i contrari — per loro sono tutti uno. Forse il nostro traguardo è QUELLO. (*Aracoeli*, p. 1289)

In *Aracoeli* love, heart and 'knowledge about the soul' allow Manuele to overcome the limits, borders, and exile.[28]

As María Zambrano says, exiles are blessed because their search, their path, will lead to the truth; a similar process happens to Manuele. The protagonist of *Aracoeli* finds his own resurrection (the love of his father) after crossing the borders of time and space in his journey to the kingdom of death.[29]

The union between father and son, mediated by the mother, opens *Aracoeli* to a positive interpretation. This interpretation, based on the reconciliation of opposites, is worked out by means of the mythical archetype of the triad.[30] In the novel, the tragic and Dionysiac Aracoeli, a victim of the evil of history, becomes the loving bridge between son and father. Her sacrifice and death allow for a positive and hopeful end.[31] The evil of history and the evil of life open, then, a new way to the continuity of life in spite of pain and misery.[32]

In conclusion, Manuele is transformed into a pious subject, integrated in the vital potentialities that overcome death thanks to his love for his father narrated at the end of the work.[33] In *Aracoeli*, with the revelation of love and the fortifying crying of the protagonist, the unity of trinity will be achieved; the closing of the sacred circle that is perpetuated in the mythical unconsciousness is the principle of life, beyond time and death.[34] As María Zambrano said: 'La caridad es la salida de la tragedia' [charity is the way out from tragedy].[35]

Notes to Chapter 11

1. Elio Gioanola, 'Elsa Morante e la storia', in *Elsa Morante. La voce di una scrittrice e di un'intellettuale rivolta al secolo XXI*, ed. by Elisa Martínez Garrido (Madrid: Universidad Complutense de Madrid, 2003), pp. 71–83 (pp. 78–79), and Cesare Garboli, *Il gioco segreto: Nove immagini di Elsa Morante* (Milan: Adelphi, 2005), p. 106.
2. Concetta D'Angeli, in *Leggere Elsa Morante: 'Aracoeli', 'La Storia' e 'il mondo salvato dai ragazzini'* (Rome: Carocci, 2003), p. 71, points out that dichotomy is a key concept for understanding Elsa Morante's work. For the Italian critic, duplicity is reserved only for the female protagonist, Aracoeli. Yet, in my opinion, duplicity is a common trait present in any character in the novel.
3. *Oxymoron* is one of the recurring figures in mystical language (D'Angeli, *Leggere Elsa Morante*, pp. 68–69; Elisa Martínez Garrido, 'Bestiario, allegoria e parola ne *La Storia* di Elsa Morante: Un'altra via al sacro', in *Elsa Morante: La voce di una scrittrice*, ed. by Martínez Garrido, pp. 85–107 (p. 98); Giovanni Pozzi, *Alternatim* (Milan: Adelphi, 1996), pp. 17–44).
4. *Parody* and *parodic* are words repeated constantly and obsessively in Elsa Morante's work from *L'isola di Arturo* onwards, where *Parodia* is a name of Arturo's father. In *Aracoeli* its complexity is even greater. Thanks to Morante's reflection about dissociation and dichotomy, *parodia* becomes the central core of this text (D'Angeli, *Leggere Elsa Morante*, pp. 32–39; Sara Fortuna and Manuele Gragnolati, '"Attaccando al suo capezzolo le mie labbra ingorde": corpo, linguaggio e soggettività da Dante ad Aracoeli di Elsa Morante', *Nuova Corrente*, 55 [2008], pp. 85–123 [pp. 94–95]). But, at the end of the novel, this parodic vision is eliminated by *caritas* and love.
5. The Andalusian identity is a combination of Gypsy (Oriental) and Moorish (Arabic) culture. The syntagm 'Gypsy and Moorish Andalusia' corresponds to a very popular Spanish song composed by Isaac Albéniz in his work *Suite Iberia*.

6. Elsa Morante made two journeys to Spain, in 1962 and in 1976. During the first one, in December 1962, almost one year after her visit to India, she stayed for Christmas with her friend Allen Midgette. During her second visit to Andalusia, in 1976, also at Christmas time, she visited El Almendral with Carlo Cecchi. This second occasion was probably the partial inspiration for her last novel (See *Cronologia* in Elsa Morante, *Opere*, ed. by Carlo Cecchi and Cesare Garboli, 2 vols (Milan: Mondadori, 1988–90), I (1988), pp. lxxvi and lxxxvi).
7. Elsa Morante, *Aracoeli*, in *Opere*, II (1990), pp. 1039–1454 (p. 1089). Further references to this edition will be given after quotations in the text.
8. The adult Manuele remembers his imaginary suicides during his adolescence. For the protagonist, suicide is a destiny. This is the reason why Manuele identifies himself with the dead *guerrillero* of ETA after his arrival in Madrid (*Aracoeli*, pp. 1056–57). On the other hand, death could have been, for the young Manuele, a sweet and welcoming way out after the loss of his mother and his dog Balletto (pp. 1215–17). This is deemed the only available possibility of a return to early childhood, to the world of affection until his journey to El Almendral. The hypothetical suicide of Manuele has also been suggested by Concetta D'Angeli (*Leggere Elsa Morante*, p. 18). We must not forget that the protagonist doesn't want to return to Milan, so it is probable that he decides to remain in Andalusia. This definitive stay in Almeria could be interpreted in a suicidal key. Remember that Manuele says at the beginning of his journey: '*Ma tu, mamita, aiutami. Come fanno le gatte con i loro piccoli nati mali, tu rimangiami. Accogli la mia deformità nella tua voragine pietosa*' (*Aracoeli*, p. 1174).
9. One should remember that death can be soothing even without religious connotations: if Manuele eventually dies in El Almendral, after the admission of his love for his father, this could be a serene death.
10. We must remember that the novel uses the word *rapimento*: 'È certo che mia madre non aveva mai veduto Almeria prima del suo *rapimento*' (p. 1091, italics in the original). This fact can demonstrate that Elsa Morante probably knew this ancestral Andalusian habit, still present today in North African countries. Aracoeli married Eugenio in church in the presence of God before the *rapimento* and before their journey to Italy (ibid.). Obviously, it is possible to consider it as an illegal marriage.
11. Manuele was also born on 4 November. Yet the date of his birthday is not clear. In one passage of *Aracoeli* the text gives the date of 4 November 1938 (p. 1057) and in another one says 4 November 1936 (p. 1069). Probably, Elsa Morante did not control this question in a precise way. The illegal marriage between Aracoeli and Eugenio also took place in November, on 1 November 1931 to be precise, All Saints' Day (p. 1091). It is important also to remark that the Spanish Republic was established in April 1931, with Manuel Azaña as prime minister. At the same time, in D'Angeli's opinion, thanks to the coincidence between the date when Manuele's journey to Almeria starts and the date of Pasolini's death, also 1 November, it is possible to establish a clear relationship between the protagonist of *Aracoeli* and Pasolini (D'Angeli, *Leggere Elsa Morante*, pp. 19–26).
12. As we know, Elsa Morante transfers herself more easily into the masculine characters than into the female ones. The writer admits this point in relation to Arturo (see Alba Andreini, 'La Morante e il diario: autoritratto di donna e di scrittrice', in *Elsa Morante: La voce di una scrittrice*, ed. by Martínez Garrido, pp. 9–22 (p. 12) and Marco Bardini, *Morante Elsa. Italiana. Di professione, poeta* (Pisa: Nistri-Lischi, 1999), p. 55). This is the reason why Manuele shares most of the existential worries of the writer. Through Manuele's character Elsa Morante expresses her deep historical and individual disappointment. At the same time, she confesses her more vivid hope: love.
13. See *Aracoeli*, pp. 1308, 1309, 1332, 1333, 1335, 1371, 1377, 1411, 1415, 1417.
14. My point of view is slightly different from Adalgisa Giorgio's book, *Writing Mothers and Daughters: Renegotiating the Mother in Western European Narratives by Women* (Oxford and New York: Berghahn Books, 2002), pp. 17, 18, 23. It is true that Aracoeli is very happy during her second pregnancy, but her health deteriorates during this period in parallel with the progress of her previous 'domestication' under the influence of aunt Monda (*Aracoeli*, pp. 1134–35).
15. Blood is present in *Aracoeli* in most of the passages dealing with the illness of the protagonist (pp. 1308, 1309, 1415, 1417). Before her death, Aracoeli pronounces the same word: 'E dal movimento

del suo fiato più che da un vero suono, s'intese che diceva: "sangre. . .sangre. . ."' (p. 1417). The presence of *sangre* is related to the idea of sacrifice; see also D'Angeli, *Leggere Elsa Morante*, p. 62.

16. For an in-depth look into the common points between Elsa Morante and Simone Weil, see Claude Cazalé Bérard in this volume (Chapter 13) and Concetta D'Angeli, 'Due donne appassionate: Elsa Morante e Simone Weil', in *Elsa Morante: La voce di una scrittrice*, ed. by Martínez Garrido, pp. 61–70.
17. Araceli, the sister of María Zambrano, suffered from severe nervous breakdowns after the violent death of her husband, Manuel Núñez, arrested and tortured by the Gestapo in France. Later on he was handed to Franco's police, who shot him (See José Luis Abellán, *María Zambrano: Una pensadora de nuestro tiempo* (Barcelona: Anthropos. Huellas de los saberes de la historia, 2006), pp. 53–59). According to Juan Carlos Marset (*El exilio andaluz en México*, Catálogo de la Feria Internacional del Libro de Guadalajara, ed. by Junta de Andalucía (Sevilla: Renacimiento, 2006), pp. 109–52), the name of María Zambrano's brother-in-law was Manuel Muñoz, the same as the uncle of Manuele; clearly, a new thread in the relationship between Elsa Morante and María Zambrano. It is also true that most family names in Gergal and in El Almendral are composed by the redoubling of the same *apellido* (family name). This fact has been corroborated for me by the Mayor of Gergal, Leonor Membibres.
18. The book was published in Puerto Rico in 1945.
19. Hannah Arendt wrote her thesis about love in Saint Augustine in 1929: *Der Liebesbegriff bei Augustin: Versuch einer philosophischen Interpretation*. In 1936 the work was translated into English by E. B. Ashton as *Love and Saint Augustine*. For the German thinker, as for Elsa Morante, Simone Weil, and María Zambrano, love is the centre of existence, and is more powerful than Aristotelian and Cartesian thought. Through Augustine, María Zambrano, like the other three intellectuals, delivered a strong blow to Western philosophy.
20. I use the term 'mystic' in the sense of Michel Hulin, *Mística salvaje* (Madrid: Siruela, 2007) and Jesús Moreno Sanz, *Ciencia de la compasión: Escritos sobre el Islam, el lenguaje místico y la fe brahamánica* (Madrid: Trotta, 1999); that is, as a cognitive and emotional attitude that assumes a perpetual dialogue with the *other*, not only in the usual sense of a theological experience. In this same way, see 'El trato con lo Divino: la piedad', one of the most important chapters of María Zambrano's *El Hombre y lo divino* (Madrid: Fondo de Cultura Económica, 1993), pp. 214–15.
21. María Zambrano, *La agonía de Europa* (Madrid: Siruela, 2000).
22. Zambrano, *La agonía de Europa*, p. 78
23. The translation is mine. Bear in mind that Maria Zambrano's prose is poetic, open and free and offers diverse possibilities for interpretation.
24. Although most of the critics have considered the novel as a *fallimento* (D'Angeli, *Leggere Elsa Morante*, p. 28 and Garboli, *Il gioco segreto*, p. 96), in my opinion, the fact that *Aracoeli* ends with *ti amo*, said by Manuele to the memory of his father, permits a reconciliation with the figure of Eugenio and with himself. I consider that Manuele is saved, even if he dies in El Almendral, because he makes explicit his love for his father. Manuele supersedes his initial marginality and dissociation, always present at the core of the novel, thanks to love.
25. Morante, *La Storia*, in *Opere*, II, 255–1036 (p. 874).
26. Elsa Morante, *Pro o contro la bomba atomica e altri scritti*, in *Opere*, II, 1455–1574 (p. 1491).
27. It is interesting to remember that Manuele says: 'fino dalla mia nascita, paternità significava assenza', 'non sono mai stato figlio di un padre' (p. 1235). Trying to fulfil his emptiness, Manuele travels to El Almendral. In the lands of Almeria, the protagonist realizes his love for his father. This is the real reason why Manuele must return to the magical and fantastic scenario of his origins.
28. *Hacia un saber sobre el alma* [*Towards a Knowledge About the Soul*] is the title of a very famous book by María Zambrano published in Madrid by Alianza Editorial in 1987; the first edition was published in Puerto Rico in 1940.
29. See Fortuna and Gragnolati, pp. 89 and 111.
30. We cannot discuss in detail the whole of the unconscious problematic about the archetype of the triad and the later Christian evolution of trinity. Carl Jung, in his famous *La simbología del espíritu* [*Spirit's Symbology*] (México: Fondo de Cultura Económica, 1981), pp. 290–99, deals with

this problem in clarifying pages. Here we would like to point out the great importance of the feminine and maternal element inside the triad or Trinitarian union. Without doubt, Aracoeli will bring Manuele to a *vita nuova* as Beatrice did with Dante. Aracoeli is the necessary mediator that allows the fusion of the contraries in the path to the search for the spiritual union between father and son, thanks to her sacrifice. In this sense, see the reflection of Rosario Scrimieri about the *Vita nuova* in a Jungian key, in *Despertar el alma: Estudio junguiano sobre la 'Vita nuova'* (Madrid: Ediciones La Discreta, 2005). It is well known that Dante is a very important author for the whole work of Elsa Morante (see Fortuna and Gragnolati in this volume, Chapter 2). In this way, it is possible to suppose that the spiritual achievements of the great medieval writer can also be traced in *Aracoeli*. Manuele finds a *vita nuova* in the union with the spirit of his father after pain and desolation in his personal *anabasis*, by the intercession of a beatific maternity. Indeed, Manuele's journey is determined by God: 'Anda, niño, anda que Dios te lo manda' (*Aracoeli*, pp. 1046 and 1086); a voyage dictated, then, by the enthusiasm, in an etymological sense (*enthusiasmòs*, holy invitation), as the text says (p. 1046). On the other hand, trinity is a word repeated frequently in the work, and the Trinitarian union is a very familiar issue for Manuele:

> E il nostro unico bacio, secondo le spiegazioni di Aracoeli, toccava a tre persone (Jesus, il padre e la madre) che in realtà ne erano una: Dio. Difatti Dio era Jesus, ma era anche il padre de Jesus, e anche sua madre. Dio era un bambinetto, e al tempo stesso una gransignora in abiti di gala, e anche un buon barbuto incoronato di spine (le stesse riconoscibili al buio, in forme di stelle). Simili fenomeni sacri non urtavano nessuna mia logica, e il dogma della trinità non mi tornava astruso. (p. 1186)

31. In this sense the name of the female protagonist, Aracoeli, reaches its most remarkable and deepest meaning. She, the mother of Manuele, represents the celestial altar (*aracoeli*) because, thanks to her, the father and son can attain unity. For more information about the name Aracoeli, see D'Angeli, *Leggere Elsa Morante*, p. 74.
32. In this way, the evil, the most devastating sexuality, illness, and death can be transcended thanks to the Trinitarian union with the help of the maternal figure. That is, as stated by Maria Luisa Von Franz in her work *La passion de Perpétue*: 'la Trinité, prenant le pas sur la quaternité en tant que symbole natural de la totalité, comporte une signification suprême et salvatrice' (cited in Scrimieri, p. 244).
33. It is worth remembering that Manuele sees a stray dog fleeing full of terror from human abuses, before he meets his mother's ghost. In this scene, the protagonist makes explicit his pity for the animal, deeper than the one he feels towards the human beings (*Aracoeli*, p. 1428).
34. The archetype of the circle, present in most of the spiritual expressions, symbolizes the transcending of time and death, and the Trinitarian union. This is also the meaning that we can find in Dante's *Paradiso*, where the circle represents the mystery of the unity and trinity of God (*Pd* XXXIII: 138, in Andrea Mariani, 'cerchio', in *Enciclopedia Dantesca*, ed. by Umberto Bosco, 2nd rev. edn, 6 vols (Rome: Enciclopedia d'Italia, 1984), I, 919–20). The return to the origin and the union between father and son, thanks to the mother, is an evident expression of 'eternal return'. In reference to the archetype of the circle see the passage where Manuele describes the 'indalo', which is even drawn in the text of the novel, as well as the importance of the cross in this work (*Aracoeli*, pp. 1088, 1120, 1124).
35. María Zambrano, *Hacia un saber sobre el alma* (Madrid: Alianza Editorial, 1987), p. 141. The translation is mine.

PART IV

❖

Religion

CHAPTER 12

The Womb of Dreams: Cabbalistic Themes and Images in Elsa Morante's *Aracoeli*

Sergio Parussa

In 1963, as part of her collection of short stories *Lo scialle andaluso* [*The Andalusian Shawl*], Elsa Morante published a brief work of juvenile prose entitled 'Il ladro dei lumi' ['The Thief of Lights'].[1] The story is told by a first-person narrator who remembers herself as a child living in the Jewish ghetto of an unspecified city at an unspecified time in history. At night, when her parents and older sister go out, the girl stays home to keep her old grandmother company and observes the life of the ghetto unfolding below the house windows. Across the street from the house is a brothel. At its end is the Temple. Behind the stained glass of the Temple's windows the girl sees the reddening glow of the lamps that the guardian Jusvin lights every night for the dead.

One night, though, the girl observes a different scene. When Jusvin enters the Temple, the lamps die out one by one; when the guardian walks out, the Temple is shrouded in darkness. Later she learns from her mother that Jusvin, being poor, steals oil from the lamps to save money and feed his six children. The girl is told to keep quiet since God will punish the theft. Soon the guardian falls ill and rapidly dies. His illness and death are, in the girl's eyes, the signs of divine punishment, as well as of God's inscrutable justice.

During the same summer another fact intervenes to trouble the girl's conscience. One day, while she is walking back home, she loses a lottery ticket that she has bought for her father. As Jusvin fears God for his theft, the girl fears her father for losing the lottery ticket. 'Pensavo di non tornare piú a casa, di uscire dal Ghetto, di uscire dalla città e di morire. Nel pensiero chiamavo mio padre, in quell'ora, col soprannome che gli dava la gente: *il gobbetto*'.[2]

At about the same time Morante was writing of the little hunchback in 'The Thief of Lights', Walter Benjamin dedicated one section of his childhood memoir to the same imaginary creature. In Morante's story and in Benjamin's memoir, whenever the child fears that something goes awry, is broken or lost, a little hunchback appears.[3] Although the two texts are different in content and style, their reference to the figure of the little hunchback suggests an intellectual kinship. In both texts the little hunchback points to a common intellectual horizon in which the understanding of contemporary history is filtered through an intertwining of past and future, ancient mysticism and modern psychology, dream and prophecy. In his anomalous, contracted form, the little hunchback hints at a common idea of loss and of time: at something that was lost and forgotten, not only in the past but also in the future.

On the one hand the little hunchback is a creative personification of ancestral childhood fears (of 'terrori primordiali' as Morante wrote in an editorial footnote to her story):[4] he is akin to the bogeyman, an archetypal figure of children's imagination in turn-of-the-century Europe. His physical imperfection mirrors the child's sense of physical and moral inadequacy: in Benjamin his smallness hints at the child's uncertainty about his own body and actions; in Morante his curved posture evokes the weight of the father, both the divine and the human, as well as the difficulty in understanding how to distinguish between good and evil; and ultimately, in both, it speaks of the working of justice and of the shaping of the child's consciousness.

On the other hand, the little hunchback's hump, his deformity, may allude to the shape that things take when they cannot develop fully, when they are forgotten and fall into oblivion. If his presence may refer to the child's fear of wrongdoing, his lack of plenitude, and ultimately his vanishing, may allude to a lost future and to the failure of history. Begun in Italy, in 1932, *Berlin Childhood around 1900* was revised by Benjamin until 1938. Less than two years later, in an attempt to escape from the Nazis, Benjamin fled from Paris and died in Port Bou, at the border with Spain. 'The Thief of Lights' was written in 1935, the first in a series of terrible years for Italian Jews.[5] In October of that year the Italian army invaded Ethiopia, starting a war that set the stage for the implementation of racial politics in Italy. The year 1935 also marks the beginning of an anti-Semitic campaign in Italian newspapers that would culminate in 1938 with the promulgation of the racial laws. Morante's mother was Jewish, and after 8 September 1943, she and Moravia left Rome, in flight from the Nazis, and went into hiding in Fondi, a village near Latina. There, she began to conceive her novel *La Storia* whose plot is constructed around the main character's fear that the authorities may discover her secret, that the Fascists and Nazis may find out that she is Jewish. Perhaps the girl's fears in 'The Thief of Lights' are, like those in *La Storia*, echoes of fearful historical times; they mirror the circle that, little by little, was closing in on Jews like the walls of a ghetto.

'The Thief of Lights', however, also hints at a spiritual depth that, I would argue, comes to the surface again in Morante's last novel, *Aracoeli* (1982). In 'The Thief of Lights' the narrator is not fully certain whether the girl in the story is really herself as a child. 'Sebbene io non abbia ancora vissuto un numero d'anni sufficiente per poterlo credere,' she says at the very beginning, 'sono quasi certa di essere stata io, quella ragazzina'.[6] 'Quella ragazzina fui io', she adds at the end of the story, 'o forse mia madre, o forse la madre di mia madre'.[7] Here one can think of Morante's personal taste for maternal descent; or one can see an indirect reference to Jewish law according to which Jewish status derives from one's mother; or one can foresee Manuele's uterine ancestry in *Aracoeli* — his claim of the right to return to the mother's womb. 'Io sono morta e rinata,' says the narrator at the end of 'The Thief of Lights', 'e ad ogni nascita si inizia un nuovo processo incerto'.[8] If she is dead and reborn, is her voice merely the voice of a girl? Could it be that her voice is also the voice of the soul, which transcends time and history; which is born and reborn and continually returns to the physical world in different bodies? And finally can all this be read as an echo of *Gilgul Neshamot*, the principle in Jewish Cabbala that describes the cycle of life of the souls and their reincarnation in different bodies? 'Chi può dire', writes Morante in *Aracoeli*,

> dove e quando la macchina dei ricordi inizia il proprio lavoro? In genere si suppone che, al momento della nascita, la nostra memoria sia un foglio bianco; però non è escluso che, invece, ogni nuovo nato porti in sé la stampa di chi sa quali soggiorni anteriori [. . .].[9]

Like the girl in 'The Thief of Lights', Manuele in *Aracoeli* wonders if he bears in himself the imprint of a previous existence. Perhaps the narrative texture of these two stories, which open and close Morante's career, is woven with deeper spiritual meanings that allude to images, notions, and symbols of Jewish Cabbala.[10] In this article I would like to suggest a reading of some of these images and to explore how they may help to reveal that a secret texture of hope lies behind Manuele's seemingly desperate journey.

★ ★ ★

Aracoeli tells the story of a 43-year-old Italian man who travels to Andalusia in search of his mother's birthplace. Despite its simplicity, the plot of the novel contains, like an allegory, several levels of meaning. First of all, the novel tells of Manuele's historical journey towards southern Spain — a journey which is described in great detail and with precise spatial and temporal references: the main character of the novel begins his journey on 30 October 1975, only few days before the death of the Spanish dictator Franco; the stops of his journey are named one by one — Roma, Milano, Madrid, Almeria, Gergal, El Almendral — in a sequence that, by going from big cities, to smaller towns to a village, describes a movement through a series of ever smaller concentric circles. Secondly, there is the oedipal journey of an adult son in search of his mother's lost love. Finally, I would argue, there is the spiritual journey of a soul that would like to find, or find again, a new and different body.

The journey to Aracoeli, however, is not a *nóstos* in classical style. It is not the story of a hero's homecoming whose journey back home breaches the fracture that kept him away from his land for years. No healing awaits Manuele at the end of his journey; rather, a painful and deep recognition lies ahead for him. He sees himself as 'un finto Ulisse di terra' (*Aracoeli*, p. 1201). At the same time the journey to Aracoeli is not a *quest* in the style of chivalric poetry. It is not a search for a person or object that may magically help to heal wounds, to resolve contradictions. When Manuele arrives at El Almendral, he realizes that Aracoeli's birthplace is nothing more than a deserted old village where everybody shares the same surname. Manuele is not pushed by 'la [. . .] febbre pulsante (come, nella fola dei Cavalieri, l'invisibile cinto d'oro)' (p. 1220) towards a heroic deed. Manuele's journey is a search of a different nature. Morante writes:

> A volte [. . .] nei vivi prende a battere una pulsione disperata, che li stimola a cercare i loro morti non solo nel tempo, ma nello spazio. C'è chi li insegue all'indietro nel passato e chi si protende al miraggio di raggiungerli in un futuro ultimo; [. . .] In quest'autunno nebbioso [. . ..] io non vedo altro che un binario storto, lungo il quale il solito me stesso, sempre solo e sempre piú vecchio, séguita a portarsi su e giú, come un pendolare ubriaco. (*Aracoeli*, pp. 1043–44)

Manuele's search for Aracoeli is neither a journey towards a past that peacefully seals the circle of time, nor a journey towards a future that solves contradictions; it is rather a wavering path running along a twisted track, back and forth, here and there, up and down, from heaven to earth, from earth to heaven: it is a blind and visionary coming and going in which times intertwine, past becomes future and future becomes past, in which memories become mysterious and unspeakable like prophetic dreams and dreams take on the concrete and truthful character of memories. Perhaps the journey to Aracoeli is a journey with a messianic taste: it is a search for a reunion with the mother whose conclusion, which is constantly expected and announced, is constantly displaced, neither towards the past, nor towards the future, but towards a time in which past and future will meet, in which the soul will find, or will find again, her authentic body.[11] 'Lì', says Manuele, '[Aracoeli] sarà pronta a riconoscermi all'arrivo. Il corpo di cui mi vergogno mi cascherà di dosso come un travestimento da commedia' (p. 1193).

It is precisely in this perspective that *Aracoeli*'s imagery recalls themes and symbols of Jewish Cabbala. Instead of the traditional opposition between real and ideal, finite and infinite time, limited and unlimited space, mortal body and immortal soul, in Cabbala there is an interdependence between higher and lower worlds, in which the body remains forever in tension with the soul, in which the soul travels up and down in cycles of regeneration and in new bodies. In this light, the search for Aracoeli becomes not so much the story of a fallacious body in search of an authentic soul in the past or future, as the uncertain travel of a disoriented soul that sets out in search of her true body.

Certainly, while reading Morante's novel, one has the impression that the character of Aracoeli combines pagan, Jewish, Islamic, and Christian memories. Aracoeli is sometimes described as an Andalusian girl, sometimes as a gypsy; sometimes she shows the forced diligence of a little Jewish zealot bent over the Talmud and the Torah (p. 1263), or the joy of the Queen of Sheba listening to the Song of Songs recited by King Solomon (p. 1268); sometimes she is compared to a veiled Arab girl (p. 1406), sometimes to a Catholic woman devoted to the cult of the Saints. Perhaps, in her, as well as in the choice of Andalusia as the geographical background for the novel, Morante alludes to a land where Jews, Muslims, and Christians lived peacefully and where their cultures long flourished together; and perhaps the fact that Manuele's journey takes place during Franco's slow death is also a way of hinting at the end of that dark political season that had begun hundreds of years earlier, in 1492, with the expulsion of Jews and Muslims from Spain: an event that marked the end of peaceful cohabitation between different cultures, as well as the beginning of the Jewish Diaspora of Europe. And it may be no accident that the *Zohar*, the *Book of Splendour*, one of the most important texts of Jewish Cabbala, first appeared in thirteenth-century Spain. Manuele's maternal star is to be found in the land where that star was darkened, but also where it had shone the most brightly.

In the rest of my article I will discuss *Aracoeli*'s consonances with Jewish Cabbala by focusing on some specific images and symbols, namely the Dream, the Garden of Eden, the Tree of Life, and the Luminous Darkness.

Dream

Dreams are central narrative tools both in Cabbala and in *Aracoeli*. According to the *Zohar*, while the body is asleep, dreams carry the soul on a journey that crosses the borders that separate worlds. It is mostly through dreams, during sleep, says the *Zohar*, that the soul undertakes her spiritual journey in search of her truth. Similarly, in *Aracoeli*, the vehicles of Manuele's journey are not so much his active memories, as all the activities of the mind that are beneath consciousness, such as impressions, emotions, sensations, and dreams that seize him during his moments of sleep. Manuele suffers from the 'vizio morboso del sonno' (p. 1045), from bouts of dozing, from a sort of 'narcosis' (p. 1061) that opens up for him the doors of the irrational, the gates of the 'theater of dreaming' (p. 1175): grandiose and fascinating flights of the imagination, but also descents into delirium and deceit, '[. . .] Questo viaggio assurdo in Andalusia [. . .] non è forse altro che un fantasma onirico della mia accidia: mentre in realtà il mio corpo dorme, istupidito dagli ipnotici, in una qualche mia cameraccia d'affitto a Milano' (p. 1115). While his body is sleeping in Milan, his soul is travelling to Andalusia. 'Ci sono dunque dei sensi particolari al sogno? (Al di là di quelli fisici?)' wonders Morante in her 1938 journal of dreams.[12] Next to the five bodily senses, there may be others that are specific to the act of dreaming and that give access to a mysterious, non-rational form of knowledge: 'Stanotte, vera fantasmagoria di sogni. In una sola notte ho viaggiato per molti luoghi, ho cambiato case e paesi, ho vissuto miracoli e guerre'.[13]

The soul's journey through dreams, however, is uncertain. According to the *Zohar*, it is hard for the soul to understand the nature of dreams. Some dreams are trustworthy; some are deceitful. The dreams of the righteous come from the world of truth, those of the wicked come from the world of deceit. The latter come from demons, the former from the Archangel Gabriel. As a child, Manuele sleeps the sleep of the just and, in the morning, when Aracoeli's pleasant voice wakes him up, the Archangel Gabriel '[. . .] spalanc[a] con la spada il sipario di luce' (p. 1186). As an adult, however, he often falls asleep and becomes prey to 'deliri [. . .] futili e tetri' (p. 1045), and struggles to distinguish between trustworthy dreams and deceitful images.[14]

However, in Cabbala, this division between good and bad dreams, between absolute truth on the one hand, and complete falsehood on the other, is not as clear-cut as it seems. As a matter of fact, every dream may contain a grain of truth about past, present, and future. Similarly, in his sleep, Manuele dreams and remembers, remembers and dreams as if he were no longer able, or no longer willing, to distinguish between objective memories and subjective dreams, as if he believed that all his memories, or pseudo-memories, as he himself calls them (p. 1049), may reveal themselves to be truer than truth:

> Può darsi che questo sia uno dei miei ricordi apocrifi? Nel suo lavoro continuo, la macchina inquieta del mio cervello è capace di fabbricarmi delle ricostruzioni visionarie — a volte remote e fittizie come morgane, e a volte prossime e possessive, al punto che io m'incarno in loro. Succede, a ogni modo, che certi ricordi apocrifi dopo mi si scoprono piú veri del vero. (*Aracoeli*, pp. 1049–50)

For Manuele, an impression may perhaps be a trustworthy dream, a dream may contain a vision, a vision may hint at a prophecy.[15] When he is accused of suffering from 'confusioni patologiche della fantasia e della memoria' (p. 1180), he retorts to his accuser by saying: 'Effettivamente, può sembrare a volte che le memorie siano prodotte dalla fantasia; mentre in realtà sempre la fantasia è prodotta dalle memorie' (p. 1186). Let me now analyse one of these dream-memories.

Moses' Basket and the Vision of the Indian Maiden

Manuele's first stop in Andalusia is Gergal, the city 'già battut[a] certo dai passi di Aracoeli' (p. 1213). As soon as Manuele arrives near Gergal, the novel changes pace. Its usually long-winded, elaborated sentences make way for a series of short, simple phrases. The syntax is broken; the usage of words seems to allude to deeper symbolism: 'La corriera si arresta. È l'arrivo. Infossata in una larga buca al di sotto della strada, Gergal mi si mostra súbito tutta intera' (p. 1212). Only two of the travellers on the bus, get off at Gergal. They are an old man and an old woman of peasant appearance, whose birdlike features remind Manuele of Semitic profiles. The two old Semites are carrying together, by its two handles, a basket covered with a cloth: perhaps an allusion to the basket in which the little Moses, in Exodus 2. 3, was abandoned to the waters of the river Nile. Few pages earlier, Manuele had described himself as an orphan, a mongrel, or a puppy abandoned by his family on the side of a road: 'Il mio stato era proprio quello di un animale bastardo, che appena cucciolo portarono via dal suo covo, dentro un sacco, scaricandolo, per disfarsene, sul margine di una carraia' (p. 1047).

Like Moses, or a mongrel, or a puppy, Manuele imagines himself as a child who has been abandoned and rescued; but, unlike Moses, Manuele has not been 'pulled out of the waters' — as the etymology of Moses' name seems to suggest[16] — for a new life; but, as he himself says, has been torn from the waters of the uterus for a life that has no miracles to offer (p. 1173). Unlike Moses, he has no gifts — he is neither a political leader, nor a prophet of divine revelations; but ironically he is a dreamer of faulty dreams, a near- and far-sighted visionary, and an antiphrastic prophet who can prophecy only his own plight.

As a matter of fact, while walking towards Gergal, Manuele has a visual experience that, by definition, is a minor and deceitful form of vision: he experiences a déjà-vu. The route down to Gergal is familiar to him as though he had set out in this direction once before, 'preceduto da questi due vecchi' (p. 1212). The term déjà-vu is defined by scientists neither as a 'vision', nor as an act of 'precognition', nor as a 'prophecy'; they rather describe it as an anomaly of memory: it is the impression of recalling to memory as real an experience which is actually illusory. In this novel, however, we are not in the realm of logos and science. We are, instead, in a universe where subjective counts as much as objective, and dreams count as much as memories. As a matter of fact, Manuele keeps returning to his déjà-vu as if he believed that even deceiving memories, even faint images which have risen from the depth of his consciousness, may contain a grain of truth about himself:

> Ma quando e dove, dunque — io mi chiedo ancora — m'è già accaduto di trovarmi al medesimo passo, dietro ai due vecchi dalla faccia semita? Mi trastullo all'idea che tale sciarada adombri una qualche indicazione plausibile sul vero Mestesso: così come un frammento geroglifico, riaffiorato da un centimetro di sabbia, porta alla scoperta di una reggia. (pp. 1213–14)

In psychoanalysis the fragment of a dream may reveal a truth about the life of the psyche in a primitive state of consciousness; in Cabbala it may hint at the life of the soul in a past body. Here déjà-vu may provide some plausible hints about Manuele's true self. Linked to this vision, from the depths of his recollections, another dream-memory rises: a shadow that flashed before his eyes years before, in the smoke of a drugged cigarette. It is the vision of a beautiful Indian maiden in which Manuele recognizes himself. Led by a couple of black hawks, the girl, with a merry, almost dancing step, descends towards her grave: a pyre whose flames turn her into a Phoenix. The vision is nothing more than a phantasm under the effect of hashish, an ephemeral reflection seen on the glass of a window; but it strikes Manuele as a small epiphany, a parable that may refer to the true hidden theme of his life. It makes him doubt whether this double is just an imagination, a reflection of his present body descending towards Gergal, or, instead, whether the contrary is true and his present body is a reflection of the Indian maiden descending towards her grave, and hers is his true self. Is the girl's beautiful body a memory or a dream, does she represent the past or the future, is she a symbol of loss or of hope? Is this a memory of the way humans were before the expulsion from the Garden of Eden or is this a prefiguration of the way we will be after the end of times?[17]

The Garden of Eden

Morante's novel could also be described as the story of an individual who is in search of a lost Eden, which, for him, coincides with his early childhood memories as well as with his mother's birthplace, with Totetaco and El Almendral.

> Non so dove né quando, ho imparato che nella lingua spagnola *almendral* significa mandorleto. E a questo nome, un giardino arboreo, dai fruttini cerulei con dolci semi candidi, m'accoglie per un istante nel suo grembo luminoso. (p. 1086)

The *almendra*, of course, is a biblical tree and, as such, here is a clear metaphor for the Garden of Eden and for the maternal womb as lost paradise.

Moreover the almond also evokes a sensory experience. What is remembered of the Garden of Eden is also its taste, its perfume, and its texture. 'Sapevo, di là da ogni dubbio, che esso non mi proveniva dalla ragione, ma da una nostalgia dei sensi' (p. 1047). It is therefore not reason, but instinct that put Manuele on Aracoeli's trail: it is the sound of his mother's voice, the smell of her skin, her physical presence that compels him to travel to Andalusia:

> La tentazione del viaggio mi aveva invaso recentemente con la voce stessa di mia madre. Non è stata una trascrizione astratta della memoria [. . .] ma proprio la voce fisica di lei, col suo sapore tenero di gola e di saliva. [. . .] Non so come gli scienziati spieghino l'esistenza, dentro la nostra materia corporale, di questi altri organi di senso occulti, senza corpo visibile, e segregati dagli oggetti; ma pure capaci di udire, di vedere e di ogni sensazione della natura, e anche di altre. (p. 1048)

It is not the scientists, but the Cabbalists who explain how our memories of the earthly paradise are inscribed not only within our souls, but also within our bodies, not only in our minds in the form of abstract memories, but also in our senses in the form of physical memories. The profound wisdom of *Hokhmah* — one of the ten emanations of the Cabbalistic Tree of Life — cannot be known consciously, only absorbed. In the words of Isaac the Blind, one of the earliest Cabbalists, 'the inner, subtle essences can be contemplated only by *sucking*, not by knowing'.[18]

In this perspective, the *Zohar* describes our life as a series of attempts at recasting our origins by returning to the Garden of Eden, by rediscovering it as a place from which both our souls and our bodies emanate. Manuele, of course, is not a believer. For him the word 'god' is nothing more than a portion of a nursery-rhyme, the song of his first steps:

> Anda niños anda
> que Dios te lo manda.
> [. . .]
>
> Da tempo questo Dios da filastrocca, e con esso il Theòs dei Testamenti, e Dio, Dieu, God e Gott e gli altri loro sinonimi con tutte le loro corti e le loro Vergini, per me non sono altro che *notte e nebbia*. Ma assurdamente, tuttora, in me persiste l'ultimo miraggio di un quache paradiso. (p. 1086; emphasis is mine)

Perhaps it is not by chance that Morante chose the expression 'night and fog' to describe Manuele's atheism. *Nuit et brouillard* (*Night and Fog*) is the title of a 1955 documentary film on the Nazi concentration camps, directed by Alain Resnais for the tenth anniversary of the liberation of France. The title of the documentary makes a direct reference to the '*Nacht und Nebel Erlass*' [Night and Fog Decree] — a law promulgated by Hitler on 7 December 1941 that established new guidelines for the treatment of civilians arrested in the occupied countries for offences against the Reich and its armed forces. This new policy resulted in the kidnapping and disappearance of many political activists throughout Nazi Germany's occupied territories. Once deported to Germany these prisoners simply ceased to exist for their relatives and friends; no information had to be given as to their fate: they all had to vanish without a trace, into 'Nacht und Nebel', 'night and fog'. Hitler did not invent this expression, but borrowed it from Wagner's opera *Das Rheingold* (1869), in which the dwarf Alberich changes into a column of smoke and disappears while singing: 'Nacht und Nebel, niemand gleich' [Night and fog, no longer anyone]. The character of Alberich in Wagner's opera has been interpreted as an embodiment of anti-Semitic stereotypes. In this perspective the choice of the expression on Hitler's part would also contain a sinister allusion to Nazi anti-Semitism and to the night and fog of Auschwitz in which European Jews vanished. In Resnais's documentary the title explicitly takes on this meaning when the film's narrator observes that during the train ride to the concentration camp 'death makes its first choice. [. . .] A second one is made upon arrival in the night and fog'.[19] Here the title becomes a direct metaphor for the concentration camps in which every meaning becomes invisible and is lost as in a dark and foggy night.

Is the use of the expression 'night and fog' on Morante's part a conscious, direct reference to the Shoah? Or is it one of those occasions when the writer's subconscious reasons make their way through her writing? Morante had already used this same expression in her 1974 novel *History*, when she makes reference to the atrocities committed by the Italian Fascists and the Nazi soldiers in January 1944, in occupied Italy: '*January*. In the cities of occupied Italy, and chiefly in Rome, the police set up special units, which employ professional sadists, German and Italian, with license to arrest, torture, and kill, at their whim, according to the Hitler system of *notte e nebbia*'.[20] It is clear from this passage that, eight years before *Aracoeli*, Morante knew that, apart from its metaphorical use, the expression *night and fog* referred to precise historical facts. However one wants to read these references, in *Aracoeli* Manuele's atheism is linked to the fate of Jews in twentieth-century Europe, to the Shoah, and the Shoah becomes the tunnel at the end of which there is no more faith. The reference is all the more significant since it is part of the driving metaphor of the novel, that of vision. Thus, night and fog do not simply distort sight, but rather end any possibility of vision.

Nonetheless, within Manuele, a dream-memory of a possible paradise absurdly remains. 'Ma', he says, 'assurdamente, tuttora, in me persiste l'ultimo miraggio di un qualche paradiso' (p. 1086).[21]

The Tree of Life

Morante tackles this paradox on page 199 of *Aracoeli*, where she makes direct reference to the biblical Tree of Knowledge and the Cabbalistic Tree of Life, and reflects upon their possible meanings. While looking at a postcard sent by Uncle Manuel before his death, Manuele imagines him riding a gigantic bull and wonders whatever happened to the wholeness of humans before they were expelled from Eden. Perhaps, he continues, there is a radiant other world from which Manuel can come back to deny his own death. Perhaps nothing is ever completely lost, because nothing is ever completely mortal. If it is so, he concludes, then everything depends on perception: the world as it appears to us is nothing more than a deception produced by our senses, which are mutilated after the fall from Eden. Perhaps, then, the expulsion of Adam and Eve from the Garden of Eden hides an ambiguous and provocative game: eating the fruit of the tree of knowledge was liberating because the same gates that closed off the Garden of Eden opened the countless gardens of the worlds where the secret fruit of the other tree, the Tree of Life, is hidden (*Aracoeli*, p. 1289).

What Morante is doing here seems very similar to what the Cabbalists do: they both base their narratives on the myth of the Garden of Eden by positing it as true. According to the Cabbalists, the Garden of Eden and the nature of life in it are lost to us. They are obscured by our inheritance, the Tree of Knowledge, and by our senses. Yet the Cabbalists find ways to recover this lost past utilizing the other tree of the garden, the Tree of Life. The Tree of Life is a graphic representation of the process by which the universe came into existence. It consists of ten branches, ten holy emanations called *sefirot*, which represent the stages along which the energy of creation — turned into matter when the universe came into being — may retrace its step back to its original source; and the human soul can be reunited with God. In a similar way Morante writes in *Aracoeli* that humans, in their journey along the Tree of Life, may be able to find the secret fruit that will make them whole again:

> si può supporre che davvero un qualche minimo germe o spora della vegetazione sterminata sia l'occulto portatore della nostra metamorfosi definitiva. [. . .] Il nascondiglio del 'frutto' segreto si potrebbe anche cercare, forse, in altri regni della natura. Potrebbe essere una pietra, un'ala d'insetto, una cenere d'ossa. (p. 1290)

The fragile and confused condition of humans, wrote the sixteenth-century Jewish Cabbalist Isaac Luria, will end only with the advent of the Messiah. Till then the soul, because of its sensorial limitations, will not be capable of returning to its divine origin and will have to wander through the bodies of humans, and also through the bodies of inanimate things, like woods, rivers, and stones. Then invisible things will be seen, incomprehensible ones will be understood, what is lost will be restored, what is divided will be united again: left and right, feminine and masculine, darkness and light (p. 1289). '"Che le tenebre diventino tenebre luminose | e la luce diventi luce tenebrosa"' (p. 1290), concludes Morante with a quote that echoes the *Zoharic* theme of the luminous darkness.

Luminous Darkness

The image of luminous darkness is a central concept in the *Zohar*. The Zoharic commentary on Genesis 1. 1 begins with a reference to the paradoxical conjunction of light and darkness: 'At the head of the potency of the King, | He engraved engravings in luster on high. | *A spark of impenetrable darkness* flashed | within the concealed of the concealed | from the head of infinity'.[22] Light and darkness are already contained within one another at the moment of creation.

In this perspective, for the *Zohar*, to see the light through darkness is the ultimate form of perfection. The most complete spiritual pattern is the one that incorporates evil as well as good since divine unity depends on the containment of evil in good. It follows, therefore, that one can see the light only through darkness, one achieves holiness through contact with the unholy and by means of that contact the unholy is transformed and contained in the holy: it is a descent for the sake of ascent.[23]

Manuele's journey is also described as a *descent* along a chromatic stairway (*Aracoeli*, p. 1247). As the soul goes down the Tree of Life in her uncertain journey back to the divine creative energy, so Manuele goes down the steps of his chromatic stairway hoping to find a way out from his present body. To every step of the stairway, as to every stage in the Tree of Life, corresponds a colour, a sound, an access to a different level of consciousness. Step after step, Manuele descends along this stairway trying to reach the lowest step and the ineffable treasure of his extreme body; but his stairway is 'storta, zoppa e lunatica' (p. 1247) and in the end he finds himself at the top of the steps again, trapped like an expatriate in his ordinary, everyday body, still battered by iridescences, haloes, and precarious visions.

Among the various schools that had an influence upon the *Zohar*, notes Eliot Wolfson in *Luminal Darkness*, one particular 'gnostic' school posited the existence of a demonic realm parallel the realm of the divine. According to these Cabbalists,

> as there are ten holy emanations (*sefirot*), so there are ten 'emanations of the left'. [. . .] The 'emanations of the left' have their origin in and are sustained by the left side of the divine realm itself. That is to say, therefore, that the demonic has a root within the divine.[24]

The path along the Tree of Life is one in which opposites mingle, in which unholy and holy, left and right, light and darkness, mix with each other, in which — as in Morante's story 'The Thief of Lights' — the brothel and the Temple happen to be on the same street, or — as in *Aracoeli* — the sacred childhood garden of Totetaco encounters the profane garden of the *Quinta*.[25]

The Masculine and the Feminine Principles

In mystical terms, the containment of the demonic left within the divine right is also an essential component of the unification of the feminine with the masculine aspect of the divine.[26] At the end of Manuele's journey, there is a similar promise: once he is reunited with his mother there won't be a distinction between boy and girl, male and female because *there* the feminine and the masculine will merge: '[Aracoeli] sarà pronta a riconoscermi all'arrivo. [. . .] Uguali lei e io, tornati coetanei. Bambino? bambina? Certi dati, là, non hanno corso. Maschio o femmina non significa niente. Là, non si cresce' (p. 1193).[27]

Although the human condition in the Garden of Eden is lost, both Cabbala and *Aracoeli* seem to conceive the possibility of a new subject which will have a larger consciousness, closer to the one humans had in Eden; a subject that will originate from a union between masculine and feminine.

Literary critics have often noted that the opposition between masculine and feminine principles, paternal and maternal realms, are at the core of Morante's literary imagery. Both *Arturo*'s Procida and *Aracoeli*'s Andalusia are landscapes peopled, on the one hand, with distant and unreachable fathers and, on the other, with engaging and available mothers. In *Aracoeli* the opposition of masculine and feminine is pushed to such extremes to become the very root of the disharmony of the world. On the one hand, there is the watery, colourful, enchanted world of Aracoeli, the '*mother star*', on the other, there is the distant, military world of the Admiral, 'un reame virile e paterno, negato alle madri: stella altrui, proprietà e sacrario dei padri', closed even to Manuele's desire (p. 1327).[28] Interestingly, in drawing this opposition between masculine and feminine principles, Morante seems to join other twentieth-century writers in making a connection between the feminine principle and Judaism; and she does so not only through the figure of the mother, but also through that of the son. Twice in the novel the narrator refers to virility as a quality that has something to do with the ancient Romans and imagines himself as a little Jew separated from it: 'e la VIRILITÀ adulta, già fino da allora, a me provocava un senso di separazione forzosa: come a un piccolo Giudeo del Primo Secolo la persona di un Romano' (p. 1270).

In recent interpretations of the Cabbala, scholars have argued that a fundamental distinction between the rationalistic and the mystical strain of Judaism, as exemplified by the *Zohar*, is the belief that God is a complex and dynamic entity, which has both a male and a female dimension. The conjunction of these two aspects of God would maintain the harmony of the universe. Conversely, their separation and opposition would be at the root of the disharmony of the world. In this perspective the ideal human would be the reconstitution of the male androgyne;[29] and the way for this reconstitution would be a journey of union with the mother, meant as the *Shekinah*, the female divine principle, the presence of God among humans. 'The Kabbalah', writes David Rosenberg,

> reveals that sex is messianic, future-oriented, and that it is a yearning for unity and for the body of the mother. The messianic desire for the end of time is equal to returning to the mother's body — the body of the *Shekinah*, formerly taboo like our mother's [. . .] but now through her we can be reborn into the messianic age and out of exile, a place beyond time where the cosmos is in balance and we are not any more in danger.[30]

According to Rosenberg's interpretation, in Cabbala, returning to the *Shekinah* also means to make oneself to be born again, both in retrospect and in the future. Isn't this also *Aracoeli*'s journey?

In his recent book *Eros and Cabbala*, Moshe Idel has warned about excessive simplifications in the study of as complex a subject as medieval Jewish Cabbala. He wonders, for instance, to what extent it was possible, in some forms of Cabbala, to transfer the ideal of divine androgyneity to human androgyneity.[31] He also expresses doubts when diverse Cabbalistic literatures are described to be consonant to psychological and philosophical modern systems.[32] What I am proposing in this article is certainly not to shed new light on medieval Jewish Cabbala by finding consonances between medieval mysticism and modern literature. My aim is rather to show how, in a modern literary text, the use of old Cabbalistic themes and images may provide a writer with a fresh language to describe a reality as mysterious and ungraspable as the modern one. When old concepts and images are used in contexts that are distant and different from the ones in which those concepts and images were conceived, their historical accuracy may be *betrayed*. However, in this re-use, they encounter new meanings: they come back to life in the present by becoming different. Old notions carry with them echoes of the past, traces of their history, vestiges of an ancient meaning or of old usages. They carry a vision of the world that is distant and different from the current one, but that, precisely by virtue of that distance, of that historical depth, can speak beyond the speaker's, the storyteller's, and the writer's intentions and generate new meanings, new life in the present: both for those distant and different concepts as well as for the present text that hosts them. By telling Manuele's story, by framing it within a narrative horizon that doesn't take into account historical accuracy, but freely combines medieval mysticism with modern psychology, *Aracoeli* infuses new life in old images and concepts and a renewed faith in the acts of writing and of storytelling. It gives new possibilities both to the past in the present and to the present seen through the lens of that past; or, as Manuele would say, it may give new life to an old self by draping it in a new garment, to an ancient soul in a new body.

Literary critics have often referred to *Aracoeli*'s obscure, pessimistic, self-destructive legacy. Nonetheless, within *Aracoeli*'s dense symbolism, within its thick web of intertextual references, within its use of Cabbalistic themes and images there may be a way of looking at the world which hints at a hope: at the possibility that, in undertaking a journey towards a historical, psychological, and spiritual mother, towards a womb of dreams, even a bespectacled and disoriented soul can find its way home.

Notes to Chapter 12

1. Morante's short story can be read in Italian in Elsa Morante, *Opere*, ed. by Carlo Cecchi and Cesare Garboli, 2 vols (Milan: Mondadori, 1988–90), I (1988), pp. 1409–14. For the title of this article, I am indebted to David Rosenberg, *Dreams of Being Eaten Alive: The Literary Core of the Kabbalah* (New York: Harmony Books, 2000). Besides Rosenberg's essay my discussion of Cabbalistic concepts is based mostly on Giulio Busi, *I simboli del pensiero ebraico: Lessico ragionato in settanta voci* (Turin: Einaudi, 1999); Moshe Idel, *Kabbalah and Eros* (New Haven and London: Yale University Press, 2005); *Zohar: Annotated and Explained*, ed. and trans. by Daniel C. Matt (Woodstock, VT: Skylight Publishing, 2002) and *The Zohar*, ed. and trans. by Daniel Matt (Stanford, CA: Stanford University Press, 2004); Gershom Scholem, *Major Trends in Jewish Mysticism*, with a foreword by Robert Alter (New York: Schocken Books, 1995); *The Wisdom of the Zohar: An Anthology of Texts,* ed. by Isaiah Tishby and trans. by David Goldstein, 3 vols (Oxford University Press: Oxford, 1989); Elliot R. Wolfson, *Luminal Darkness: Imaginal Gleanings from Zoharic Literature* (Oxford: Oneworld, 2007).
2. Morante, 'Il ladro dei lumi', p. 1413. Italics in the original.
3. Walter Benjamin, *Berlin Childhood around 1900*, trans. by Howard Eiland (Cambridge, MA: Belknap Press of Harvard University Press, 2006), pp. 120–22.
4. Morante, 'Il ladro dei lumi', p. 1579.
5. 'The Thief of Lights' is, to my knowledge, the first short story by Morante that openly deals with a Jewish theme. It may not be entirely by chance that, although written in 1935, 'The Thief of Lights' was not included in Morante's first collection of short stories, *Il gioco segreto* [*The Secret Game*], published in 1941, but only in her second collection, *Lo scialle andaluso* [*The Andalusian Shawl*], published in 1963. Other Italian writers published works that dealt with Jewish themes at about the same time: Giorgio Bassani's *The Garden of the Finzi-Contini* was published in 1962 and Natalia Ginzburg's *The Things We Used to Say* in 1963. All these books were published shortly after the Eichmann trial, when the Shoah started to become part of the collective historical consciousness in Italy.
6. Morante, 'Il ladro dei lumi', p. 1409.
7. Morante, 'Il ladro dei lumi', p. 1414.
8. Morante, 'Il ladro dei lumi', p. 1414.
9. Elsa Morante, *Aracoeli*, in *Opere*, ed. by Carlo Cecchi and Cesare Garboli, 2 vols (Milan: Mondadori, 1988–90), II (1990), p. 1177. Further references to this edition of *Aracoeli* will be given after quotations in the text.
10. The word 'Cabbala' appears three times in *Aracoeli* (pp. 1166, 1236) with the meaning of 'deceit'.
11. Here are just some examples of the expressions used by Morante's narrator to express his profound disaffection with his body, as well as his desire to regenerate himself into a new body by means of a journey in search of the mother: 'il solito me stesso' (p. 1044), '[il] mio corpo disorientato' (p. 1047), '[il] mio protoplasma', 'la mia forma visibile, che mi denuncia al mondo'

(p. 1054), as well as 'una carne splendente' (p. 1116), '[il] mio corpo reale' (p. 1170), 'l'unico e vero Sestesso' (p. 1171), 'il tesoro indicibile del mio corpo estremo' (p. 1248).
12. Elsa Morante, *Diario 1938*, ed. by Alda Andreini (Turin: Einaudi, 2005), p. 6. I take this opportunity to thank Marco Formisano for calling my attention to this work by Morante.
13. Morante, *Diario 1938*, p. 27.
14. Manuele struggles to see what surrounds him since his senses are limited: he is near- and far-sighted, he wears glasses whose thick lenses both weaken and heighten his sight: 'nella direzione del mio futuro, io non vedo altro che un binario storto' (*Aracoeli*, p. 1044), 'Vedo (o credo di vedere)' (p. 1212), 'la mia vista balorda che li trasfigura' (p. 1054), 'Fui sempre miope — e astigmatico — fino da ragazzino, e con l'età adulta, da qualche anno, mi è sopravvenuta in aggiunta la presbiopia' (p. 1060), 'le mie pupille annebbiate dal sopore' (p. 1062).
15. 'There are many levels in the mystery of dreams,' wrote Rabbi Eleazar of Worms in a commentary to the *Zohar*, 'and they are all part of the mystery of Wisdom. Come and see. Dream is one level, and vision is one level, and prophecy is one level, and they are all levels one above the other'. See Tishby, *The Wisdom of the Zohar*, p. 121. These levels, however, are all interdependent since in the *Zohar* the worlds of above are not separated from the worlds of below. Since it is said in the *Talmud* that a dream is a sixtieth part of prophecy, sometimes dreams are described by the Cabbalists as 'visions', dreams which have a lower status than prophecy, although they are similar in nature.
16. 'And the child grew, and she brought him unto Pharaoh's daughter, and he became her son. And she called his name Moses: and she said, *Because I drew him out of the water*' (Exodus 2. 10; my emphasis). The name Moses has consonances with a verb that in Hebrew means 'to pull out of the waters'.
17. It is not by chance, then, that the symbol that ties Manuele's dreams together is the rainbow, the unmistakable sign of the divine presence. In the Bible, the rainbow is the symbol of the alliance between God and humans. As such, it foretells the presence of the *Shekhinah*, the feminine spirit of God on earth. In the *Zohar*, the colours of the rainbow indicate the redemption promised by God to humans. In *Aracoeli* rainbows seem to appear every time there is an allusion to such promise and to its fleeting, but persistent nature, every time Manuele remembers, or dreams of, an Eden-like state of physical and spiritual harmony. When, on his way to Gergal, he suddenly remembers himself as a beautiful Indian maiden, the girl appears dressed in a light and precious material, *all the colours of the rainbow*. Manuele's dream-memory culminates in the vanishing of the girl among the flames of a pyre where she is transformed into a Phoenix: a fantastic bird with feathers which are *all the colours of the rainbow*. All these rainbows are like colourful flags that signal Manuele's memories of a harmonious Garden of Eden as well as the dreams, often frustrated, of its permanence (p. 1214). Childhood memories are also associated with rainbow-like colours in the following passage: 'Ma in realtà, bastava che i piccoli tumuli male ricoperti della mia infanzia venissero un poco rimossi, e súbito ne prorompevano raggi di colori meravigliosi, che tornavano a trafiggermi con le loro terribili punte' (pp. 1135–36). The rainbow, however, that shrouds Manuele's dream-memory, the vision in which his body is always reborn and renewed like a Phoenix, vanishes as soon as another dream-memory comes to mind: 'L'iride misteriosa che mi aveva sfiorato sul passo di due vecchi semiti, giú per la discesa di Gergal, si è sperduta a questo scontro canzonatorio, senza lasciarmi traccia' (p. 1247).
18. Daniel C. Matt, *Essential Kabbalah: The Heart of Jewish Mysticism* (San Francisco: Harper, 1995), p. 113. Emphasis is mine.
19. Richard Raskin, '*Nuit et Brouillard*' *by Alain Resnais: On the Making, Reception and Functions of a Major Documentary Film* (Aarhus: Aarhus University Press, 1987), p. 83: 'La mort fait son premier choix. [. . .] Un second est fait à l'arrivée dans le nuit et le brouillard'.
20. Elsa Morante, *La Storia*, in *Opere*, ed. by Carlo Cecchi and Cesare Garboli, 2 vols (Milan: Mondadori, 1988–90), II (1990), p. 499.
21. Here too Manuele seems to describe a dream-memory: the memory of a past that doesn't go away and the dream of a future that he is not able to grasp, it is something that is neither before, nor behind him, but is intertwined in inextricable ways with his soul. Here too Manuele's vision plays in a minor key: it is an uncertain, diminished, humbled vision. After the déjà-vu, the *fata morgana*, the reflection on the window pane, the fragile and vanishing rainbows, Manuele has a

mirage: he is prey to that optical phenomenon that creates the illusion of seeing objects that are not there. He has a vision of a reality which is postponed in time and displaced to another space: it is Aracoeli's unreachable El Almendral.

22. Cf. Matt, *Zohar: Annotated and Explained*. Emphasis is mine.
23. Wolfson, *Luminal Darkness*, p. 34: 'There is, first of all, the zoharic claim that the path of the spiritual adept is one of *descent* followed by ascent, that is, before one achieves the status of holiness one must descend into the realm of evil'. Emphasis is mine. On the notion of descent for the sake of ascent, cf. *Zohar* 1:83a and Tishby, pp. 457–58.
24. Wolfson, *Luminal Darkness*, pp. 1–2.
25. In this perspective the character of the camel-woman, who introduces Aracoeli to the world of the *Quinta*, may be interpreted as a demonic figure. In a late Jewish legend the snake appears to Eve disguised as a camel. See also Louis Ginzberg, *The Legend of the Jews*, trans. by Henrietta Szold, 4 vols (Philadelphia: The Jewish Publication Society of America, 1968), I, 71: 'Among the animals the serpent was notable. Of all of them he had the most excellent qualities, in some of which he resembled man. Like man he stood upright upon two feet, and in height he was equal to the camel'.
26. Wolfson, *Luminal Darkness*, p. 40.
27. 'Per tutto il tempo di Totetaco, io non ebbi nozione di essere maschio, ossia uno che mai poteva diventare donna come Aracoeli' (*Aracoeli*, p. 1186).
28. Conversely, the harmony of the world of Totetaco originates from the loving union of mother and father — who looks at her 'come un'anima che, alla risurrezione dei corpi, ritrova in Paradiso, insieme con la letizia celeste, anche quella carnale' (p. 1206).
29. Wolfson, *Luminal Darkness*, pp. 144–84. See also Moshe Idel, *Kabbalah and Eros* (New Haven and London: Yale University Press, 2005).
30. Rosenberg, p. 44.
31. Idel, p. 54.
32. Idel, pp. 12–15, 98–99.

CHAPTER 13

Morante and Weil: The Aporiae of History and the End of the Fairy Tale

Claude Cazalé Bérard

To retrace the entire literary production of Elsa Morante, beginning with the earliest youthful trials, allows us to grasp the central thread that unites fables, stories, essays, and novels through *Aracoeli*, which reinvents the literary genre of the *Bildungsroman*.

I would like, in fact, to confirm the hypothesis that this last novel brings to maturation the themes, figures, narrative, and metanarrative procedures which appear in the first stirrings of the author's creative *iter*, thus offering a complete vision of life and of the world which integrates the painful stages of the quest for knowledge and love, never separated in Morante's oeuvre.

I would like to restore both the work's autonomous value and its function as a completion of the poetic parabola travelled by Elsa Morante, up to the ultimate, unrenounceable, intellectual and ethical engagement.[1]

If Aracoeli reveals with a smile (who knows whether tender or mocking) to her adult, precociously aged son — arrived as he has at the terminus of the research and the voyage that have brought him finally to the empty point of origin — 'Ma, niño mio chiquito, non c'è niente da capire', aren't we perhaps allowed to ask ourselves to what degree a possibility of recognition, of love, and therefore of salvation still exists for Elsa Morante — through her ultimate and degraded alibi? In fact, there remains the unresolved alternative of the two subtitles, drafted and then discarded: 'A fable of love', or else 'A voyage of love'.[2]

I intend, therefore, to study in depth the reasons and the modality of this ultimate tragic and desperate closing speech against modernity (both bourgeois and technological), entrusted to a messenger who is lucid even in his fragility and impotence: a modernity confronted with the aporiae of History, threatened with witnessing the end of fairy tales, myths, and utopias.

My proposition is that, with her messianic and eschatological drive embodied in Davide Segre, drowning in self-destructive delirium, the author arrives — beyond the degrading end of heroes and when the hope of an Edenic return is definitively lost — at the discovery of a desert — '*la sassaia*' — that would be neither the predestined passage towards a Promised Land, nor the location of the historical adventure, of the salvific regeneration of a people, but rather the apocalyptic land of extermination, madness, death, and of the absence of an omnipotent father God: in his place one finds, instead, emptiness, the inconceivable and incommunicable mystery of a love exposed in its nudity, its uselessness, and the gratuitousness of suffering without compensation and without resurrection.

Weil and the F.P.: *Senza i conforti della religione*

Before confronting the last stage of the route, we must go back to the conceptual and poetic premises of such a decisive choice, in particular to Morante's encounter with the thought of Simone Weil.

The text most consonant with the reading of the French philosopher is surely the unfinished novel *Senza i conforti della religione*, for which the chosen theme was, as was repeatedly announced, what she calls 'il solito tema — unico, per quanto variato (e squisitamente filosofico) dei precedenti romanzi, e cioè "*il difficile rapporto fra le ragioni umane e le ragioni misteriose della realtà*"'.[3] Morante began *Senza i conforti* at the end of the 1950s and left it unfinished, probably around the time of Bill Morrow's death in 1962, while the novel's themes and characters moved into the works that postdate *Il mondo salvato dai ragazzini*, that is, *La Storia* and *Aracoeli*.[4]

Senza i conforti della religione introduces characters and situations that will later be found in *La Storia* and *Aracoeli*: Useppe (the son of an elementary school teacher), Aracoeli (a young woman from Spain who dreams of becoming a star), the Quartieri Alti and the bombing of San Lorenzo.[5] There are also signs of Morante's own spiritual crisis. A note written on an envelope and entitled '*Appunti vari per* Senza i conforti della religione' reads: 'Evoluzione nel libro sulla mia idea di Dio: Nell'infanzia lo prego anche per mie minuzie, poi lo cerco nel nostro, nel mio e suo, silenzio'.[6]

Even if these words refer to the thoughts of the character Giuseppe, they also coincide with some personal problems of the author. This crisis was surely aggravated by the tragic death of the young painter evoked in the *Addio* of the *MSR*, whom Morante loved as a lover or, more likely, as a mother, and probably also by the death of her own mother: 'L'urlo del ragazzo che precipita accecato dal male sacro [. . .] la mozza litania cristiana nel deposito | dell'ospedale, intorno alla vecchia ebrea morta | che scostò la croce con le sue manine deliranti. | SENZA I CONFORTI DELLA RELIGIONE'.[7]

Morante's tormented interest in the question of God, already present in her youthful writings (stories of paradisiacal raptures, of ecstatic flights, etc.) and in particular in the *Lettere ad Antonio* (dreams of cathedrals, feelings of guilt, anxiety of purity, impatience due to a physical and spiritual 'heaviness', etc.), becomes deeper and more dramatic in the period between the ideation of *Senza i conforti* and the *MSR*, where the name of Simone Weil appears explicitly, numbered among the F.P. The inquiry into the divine mystery continued to be more deeply explored in *La Storia* and in *Aracoeli*, in particular with the innocent requests of Useppe, with the anguished *quêtes* of Davide Segre and of Manuele, with the destiny of those minor heroes who 'carry in their eyes nothing more than a perpetual question', as Elsa wrote in a note.[8]

The essential traits that the protagonists of Morante's novels have in common are precisely the obscure and irremediable sense of guilt tied to the sense of exile from a paradisiacal condition, the insistent demand for grace, and the wait for forgiveness: these sentiments inhabit Morante, who leaves numerous literary notes, signs of consensus or of perplexity, anxious interrogations on the pages of Simone Weil, whom she read in French, with extraordinary attention and sympathy. An attentive reading of the notes demonstrates the two authors' profound thematic and argumentative convergence.[9]

As for the specific theme of the '*pesanteur*', it belongs to the broadest and most radical question in the existential and spiritual drama of the creature who aspires to free herself from the material world, from corporeal and psychic impurity, from faults, from the sins that hide from her the knowledge of good and of truth, which hold her prisoner in time, blocking her from raising herself up to God and to the eternal. We can recognize in Weil and in Morante an analogous aspiration to renounce the 'I', renounce the illusions of desire and of the imagination, counterbalanced by the choice of love as the principle of knowledge.[10]

The reflections on ethics and on poetics that Morante undertook in those same years, beginning with the essay dedicated to Umberto Saba (*Il poeta di tutta la vita*) and with the pamphlet entitled *Pro o contro la bomba atomica* (1965) — in which one can recognize the influence of Simone Weil's political thought (*Oppression et liberté*, 1955; *Écrits de Londres et dernières lettres*, 1957; *Écrits historiques et politiques*, 1960) — are inspired by this problem.[11] But it is above all in subsequent works that an anonymous, collective voice breaks through: the voice of the mad man in the *MSR* or the narrating voice in *La Storia*. The renunciation of one's own identity, individualization, and separation is dramatically put on stage in *Aracoeli*, with the vain regression '*ad uterum*', which does not permit the protagonist to escape the '*pesanteur*' (attachment, possession, dependence). Rather, this renunciation precipitates him into the 'maternal vortex' and thus makes him lose any possibility of love or salvation. This, therefore, is very far from the mystical asceticism, the Weilian 'uncreation', which obliterates the 'I' in an act of love and total dedication to God. This is the free acceptance of the void, of death, and even of God's silence, as the most extreme and definitive form of separation.[12]

The theme of the real and metaphorical 'fall', opposed to the fantastical and dreamed 'flight', is therefore central in the evolution of Morante's literary production, but even more clearly in the preparatory drafts of *Aracoeli* — as is confirmed by the intriguing project of a novel entitled *Superman. An autobiography*: the *incipit* is dated 18 September 1975, but the writing was almost immediately interrupted (after twenty-two pages). The homodiegetic protagonist presents himself as a young man with a Spanish mother, as a sort of adventurous knight who went wandering around the world but was afflicted with 'cadute nel vuoto' [blackouts] which overtook him in the process of some extreme action and from which he would awake 'senza più memoria di stato civile, né punto di partenza, né direzione', prey to an anguished sense of guilt:

> Sempre, a questi risvegli, la mia prima domanda è stata: che cosa ho fatto?! Che cosa: ossia quale male, quale infrazione, giacché in generale, prima di cadere

nel sonno, avevo scavalcato in qualche modo i confini del proibito, o m'ero inguaiato, in qualche modo.[13]

Now, the condition of suffering and alienation of this bizarre superhero (or perhaps an anti-hero?), more a victim (struck by epilepsy, drugged?) than guilty, capable of 'voli sovrumani', but paradoxically without memory of his own prodigies and of his own identity, cannot but evoke the tragic destiny of Bill Morrow, who fell from a New York skyscraper: it is no coincidence that New York, under the name of Metropolis, is in fact the city of Superman (hidden under the false identity of the journalist Clark Kent), created in 1938 by Jerry Spiegel and Joe Shuster, sons of Jewish immigrants.

Morante's choice would be surprising if we did not remember that the popular comic figure (America's favourite adventure-strip character), advocate of justice with extraordinary powers, idealistic defender of freedom and democracy so that he could appeal to the expectations of the American public, took on the mission of fighting Nazism: Goebbels, in fact, considered him a Jew. The episode published on 27 February 1940 in *Look Magazine* is notable. In it Superman tried to interrupt the Second World War by kidnapping Hitler and Stalin. We should not forget that, even in adolescence, Morante had invented a hero, an ideal male figure who found his incarnation in the 'trasvolatore oceanico', the famous Charles Lindbergh, to whom she dedicated *Lettere d'amore*, signed '*Velivola*'.[14]

But the 'blackouts' of Morante's Superman re-echo above all — here, in a vein of pitiable derision and beyond the effects of epilepsy and drug abuse evoked in *MSR* and in *La Storia* — the interior, mystic experience that Morante read about in *La pesanteur et la grâce*.

At this point the link between this project for a science fiction novel and the last works by Morante should be clear enough: even this character of an unhappy hero (perhaps 'mortally wounded') — like F.P., Useppe, Davide Segre, Manuele — can be interpreted as a disquieting Christological figure: 'Ma stavolta [. . .] ebbi il presentimento immediato di aver commesso qualcosa di irreparabile. E che quest'ultima stazione di transito per me era il chiodo di giuntura dei due pali della croce.'[15] Moreover, there is another significant coincidence: the title of the interrupted novel *Superman* was found written on the back of a paper on which was glued (perhaps in the planning of a future cover image for *Aracoeli*) the photograph of that Peruvian cross which appears transfigured in a disturbing animalistic ugliness in Manuele's surreal vision. As for Manuele, when he arrives at the end of his search for his origins, he realizes that he has arrived 'at the knot of the cross'.

The Angel of History: Memory and Clairvoyance

Amongst the subterranean currents that are produced between the writings and the personalities of the two authors, the story *Via dell'Angelo* (1937) constitutes a singular case, considering that it was written at such an early date: it is cited in the *Letters to Antonio*, with evident reference to dream experiences. The story of this *visio in somnis* — unless it is a case of supernatural apparition, which has the formal characteristics and ingredients of the fantastic, with its disturbing strangeness —

is in fact comparable to the autobiographical story of a mystical experience that Simone Weil had included at the end of the tenth *Cahier* of Marseilles entrusted in 1942 to Gustave Thibon, then published more definitively as a *Prologue* to *La connaissance surnaturelle*.[16]

It is obviously not my intention to suggest a derivation (absolutely impossible in chronological terms), but rather to underline the extraordinary consonance of the two texts in their representation of an initiation to love as a total dedication and an emptying out of the 'I', in the form of a dream or a vision, in order to open up a space for divine epiphany. Weil evokes, in this text of rare poetic intensity, not only the transposition of rites (prayer, penitence, Eucharist), situated within a frame of sentimental, romantic exaltation, but also the secret and intimacy outside the space and time of reality, the savouring of a paradisiacal happiness, the brutal exile from Eden, the consciousness of an indignity, of an insufficiency, the emptiness and silence of abandonment, and the vulnerability and uncertainty of love defrauded of presence. In *Via dell'Angelo*, which presents a more ample narrative development, richer in peripetiae, one finds the same stages of the supernatural experience (where the traits of dream and vision are deliberately confused). Therefore the texts of Weil and Morante seem linked through a complex analogy of spiritual situations and fantastic transfigurations.[17]

In those years of literary apprenticeship, Morante wrote fairy tales (*Corriere dei piccoli*) and stories for the most part inspired by ancient tradition and popular anecdotes (*I diritti della scuola*), by Hebrew and Christian legends (*Meridiano di Roma*), with a predilection for stories telling of angelic figures, whose presence is traceable in the names and toponyms ('Angelo', 'Madre Cherubina', 'Via dell'Angelo', the 'Angeli della Guardia', etc.): so Manuel in *Aracoeli* is seen as an Archangel ('Era armato da espada, e a volte mi prendeva la figura di un arcangelo, con grandi plurime ali leggere e metalliche, svarianti nei colori argento e oro').[18]

There is a true Morantian angelology that includes cats, linked by mysterious analogy and common paradisiacal origin to angels; sacred figures (Christ, Beato Angelico, Daniel and Tobias in *Aracoeli*); the Books of Sacred Scripture (Gospel and the Song of Songs in *La Storia*; the *Torah*, the *Talmud* and the Song of Songs in *Aracoeli*); the learned and popular repertory of the *exempla* used not only in the little edifying stories, but in the novels, noticeably in *La Storia* and *Aracoeli*.

But to return to our comparison, we should note the curious and completely improbable likeness of the young student of *Via dell'Angelo*, Antonia, to Simone Weil. It makes us think of that photo of Simone's still green youth, taken during the Spanish Civil War, wrapped in combat clothes too large for her slender body, with eyeglasses and smiling because of the adventurous undertaking of finding herself there, an unlikely postulant in war, strangely burdened with a rifle carried like a scapular. But the year after, in 1937, Simone Weil, as she voyages through Italy, sick, felt pressed by an irresistible force to kneel in a church in Assisi.[19] Some of the figurative and thematic elements are found again in *Aracoeli*, where they are parodied, as in the last blasphemous supplication of Aracoeli, at that point shrouded in vice, and in Manuele's gratifying childhood visions, he too who was under-grown and made ugly by glasses. For him the voice from the other side is the grotesque voice of a loudspeaker, and the epiphanies are reduced to the cruel jokes of Manuel Muñoz Muñoz, the fantastic combatant of the Spanish Civil War, or of Aracoeli, his divine girlfriend: that is to say, the only divine figures to whom he was ready to submit to the point of death, the only ones in whom he believed in his amorous madness.

Even Walter Benjamin offered Morante the arguments she needed to compare the modern novel (in general 'unformed', 'abstract', conforming to fashion and rejected by her) to the story informed by the greatest attention to real things, full of true content, which responded to an internal system of thought, to a moral engagement, to a universal vision of relationships among humans and between them and the world (*The Narrator: Considerations on the work of Nicola Leskov*). Benjamin insisted on the exemplary function that narration should maintain contrary to the individualistic and disintegratory evolution of the 'modern novel': 'L'arte del narrare volge al tramonto perché il lato epico della verità, la saggezza vien meno'.[20] The combination of Morante's concept of narration and that of Benjamin is not limited to the necessary exemplary dimension of the story; the world on the brink of catastrophe, described by Morante, is also the same as that visited by Benjamin's angel of history, the *Angelus Novus*: from *Menzogna e sortilegio* to *L'isola d'Arturo*, to *La Storia* and *Aracoeli*, we can say that History catches up with narrators and characters and forces them to turn and look backwards, with eyes widened in a stupor, with their gaze sharpened by terror. Chased out of the happy days of their childhood (as if from Paradise), torn from their mothers (or from a stepmother, as in *L'isola d'Arturo*), or else betrayed by them (*Menzogna e sortilegio*, *Lo scialle andaluso*, *Addio* in *MSR*, *Aracoeli*. . .), children or adults, they are forced to search for a meaning, to explore an often traumatic past, to try to loosen the knot of lies, to dissolve the veil of consolatory illusions. Often they find nothing but massacres and the dead while the wind of the future drags them violently towards the abyss, like an angel powerless to interrupt the inhumanity, to judge, to redeem, or to condemn. An impotent angel because his feet are hampered by deformity or by chains?[21]

Daughters of Zion: The Voices in the Song of Songs

Beyond what the combinations thus far documented can reveal to us, it is surely the poetic invention that best reveals the breadth of Simone Weil's presence in Morante's work: the recognition of the painful membership in a communal history and memory is expressed in the *Canzone degli F.P.*, through the reference to the Song of Songs associated with the moving figure of the young, unhappy philosopher-girl:

> sorelluccia inviolata
> ultima colomba dei diluvi stroncata
> bellezza del Cantico dei Cantici camuffata in quei tuoi buffi
> occhiali da scolara miope
> [. . .]
> Lo so
> Che per una ragazza partita all'ordalia della Croce,
> e approdata sola alla colpa delirante dell'esilio

> è un orrido labirinto spinato il lettuccio straniero d'ospedale
> dove il suo piccolo corpo ebreo si lascia
> alla febbre suicida
> per consumare in se stesso l'intera strage dei lager.[22]

The peculiar presence of the Song of Songs, considered as the highest and happiest celebration of human and divine love with the image of death, of the massacre of the *lager* (concentration camp), is striking. In reality, Morante sees Weil (and herself) caught between two opposing forces: faith in the salvific power of love and in a possible redemption ('l'ordalia della Croce') and the sad awareness of the desire for power and domination at work in the world; but after Auschwitz, after Hiroshima, the narrator cannot help but foresee that humanity is about to plunge into the abyss, and tries to give voice to a dream, to a utopia (*La canzone clandestina della grande opera*) invalidated though by the suspicion of unreality ('IN SOSTANZA E IN VERITÀ, TUTTO QUESTO | NON È ALTRO | CHE UN GIOCO').

For this reason, if Morante cites or rewrites, more than once, the title, verses, or stanzas of the poem, it is always within the context of tragic situations that contain the separation of lovers, in which love is tricked or overcome by death (*MSR*, *La Storia*, *Aracoeli*). It even seems that Morante is re-reading the pages of Jewish or Christian exegetical comments that traditionally interpret the Song of Songs as a story of loved shared, troubled but triumphant, between God and his people, between Christ and the soul of the believer, from a pitilessly negative point of view of betrayal and abandonment. There are in fact the variously metamorphosed allusions to the vain and hopeless search for the beloved in many verses of the *Alibi*, in the *Addio* of the *MSR*, in *La Storia* (where some stanzas are transformed in Ida's wrenching lament, when she rediscovers herself as a suffering and persecuted part of 'her people'). There are also signs of scepticism about the possibility of the consolation of faith (because of genocide): 'without the comforts of religion'? If love gives access to consciousness, this can guide us to uncover the torment, and poetry that is born from such a conscience cannot but describe its horror. Weil herself did not flee the temptation of suicide, the same temptation that touched Elsa in her youth and ended up destroying her.

Yet Simone Weil (who, in her *Lettera a un religioso*, explicitly cited the Song of Songs, amongst the books of the Old Testament that should be 'saved', that is, the books of Job, Daniel, Tobias, some of the Psalms of David, the same books that Morante cited)[23] had also celebrated love as the origin and foundation of Creation with elevated mystic and poetic inspiration. The act of God, she wrote, is 'an act of love'. And so love cannot but be the beginning and the end in the order of human creation (even if we need 'to love God... as if he did NOT exist').

Analogously, the mystery of creation serves as a background to the sacred representation of *Il mondo salvato dai ragazzini*, in *La canzone di Giuda e dello sposalizio*. Here the language of the 'nuptial chamber', attributed to the mystics and to Simone Weil, the language of the intimacy with the Spouse with God, has been interpreted by Morante from a de-sacralizing perspective.

An ancient and authoritative passage from the *Confessions* of Saint Augustine (which was one of Morante's spiritual readings) probably inaugurated, in the

Christian memorial and autobiographical tradition, the evocation of the 'nuptial language' as an encounter with the divine through the mediation of woman (Dante was the poetic transcriber of this): the intimate, profound, and serene colloquium that Augustine had with his mother, Monica, while she was dying. The moment is idyllic: mother and son, in Ostia, look out at the Tiber from the window that looks over the garden, and are overtaken by a paradisiacal vision. Augustine obtains the ultimate grace and the most extreme revelation through Monica's intercession on the threshold of her departure: the viaticum for the voyage that he must finally take alone towards God. Beatrice will not act differently towards Dante.

This mysterious 'nuptial language' reappears, precisely in the novels of Elsa Morante, as a trace of the original intimacy, of the congenital, prenatal colloquium between mother and son. It is that of Manuele with his mother Aracoeli, whose Spanish name is, in itself, a 'sign of difference'.

Manuele, in his childhood remembrance (or in his apocryphal memories) sprung out in the course of his reversed pilgrimage, evokes the paradisiacal and fusional experience of Monte Sacro (the quarter of Rome chosen for its name?), or, better, of Totetaco, according to the secret amorous language that thus united the child to the mother:

> Quel magico giardino fiorito stamane dentro la stanzuccia buia dal chiuso delle mie palpebre, intende significarmi che, in realtà, la corriera di El Almendral mi riporterà a Totetaco. [. . .] Aracoeli non [. . .] la medesima dello specchio, ma una anteriore alla mia nascita, [. . .] sarà pronta a riconoscermi all'arrivo. Il corpo di cui mi vergogno mi cascherà di dosso come un travestimento da commedia, e in me, ridendo, lei riconosce l'infante di Totetaco. Uguali lei e io, tornati coetanei. Bambino? Bambina? Certi dati, là, non hanno corso. Maschio o femmina non significa niente. Là, non si cresce. (*Aracoeli*, pp. 1192–93)

We are at the moment of the most intensive 'regressive fusion' and of the maximum ambivalence between mother and son, as we will see, which I would interpret as the cause of fatal immaturity and of a destiny inscribed from birth (p. 1056). The language of Totetaco, 'il nostro primo idioma d'amore' (p. 1065), in reality, as Manuele ends up suspecting, is only a creator of sortilege and fictions: 'le nostre 1400 giornate a Totetaco sono tutta una balera fantastica, dove il giorno e la notte ripetono i loro giri allacciandosi e rincorrendosi come in una coppia ballerina' (p. 1189); it is a language that reappears briefly, in a fragile miracle, after death has erupted into the protective familial nest: 'Spesso mi stringeva e mi baciava, vezzeggiandomi con un suo linguaggio divino, mischiato d'italiano e di spagnolo, e che non si udiva più fra noi, dai tempi di Totetaco' (p. 1334). It remains, definitively, as a dead and obsolete trace of a lost paradise, no longer reachable by an adult definitively deprived of love:

> Anzi, in proposito, io mi domando perfino se con questo viaggio, sotto il folle pretesto di ritrovare Aracoeli, io non voglia piuttosto tentare un'ultima, sballata terapia per guarire di lei. Frugare nelle sue radici finché s'inaridiscano sotto le mie mani, poiché di estirparle non sono capace. (p. 1065)

The 'nuptial language' for Elsa/Manuele, in the decadent world corrupted by bourgeois hypocrisy and dominating violence (Spanish and Italian fascism), can no longer be revelatory of eternal and universal truths, but only the pitiful consolatory instrument fabricated by a mother who is fascinatingly ambiguous, guiltily adored as a substitution for God, for the Celestial Spouse:

> È stata la tua misteriosa ambiguità, Aracoeli, che mi ti ha resa immortale; [...] A costo di calunniarti e maledirti e rinnegarti, io non ho MAI voluto riconoscere la denunciata impossibile miseria del tuo ultimo segreto. E così ti ringrazio per il nostro intrigo puerile. La tua terribile ambiguità — tua buiezza e imbroglio, tuo scandalo tuo splendore — mi accompagnerà, giocando, al traguardo del vuoto. Che tu sia benedetta, mamita, per il tuo alibi. (*Aracoeli*, p. 1404)

The 'nuptial language' would have remained, rather, pure of contaminations and of consolatory lies, according to Morante, only in its mysterious relationship with animals: those who (together with the custodial angels) are our only contact with the other side. In a fantastical evocation of the *Paradiso Terrestre* (1950), Elsa Morante claimed, in fact, to interpret the presence of animals on earth (above all that of Siamese cats) as a merciful divine concession.[24]

Yet, contrary to other young Morantian heroes (Arturo, Useppe, the child Aracoeli...), Manuele is frustrated by the brief passage of his dog Balletto, cannot even enjoy that innocent and blessed form of love, and is destined to undergo 'la piú nera infelicità terrestre: di esistere vivi dove non c'è nessuno che ci ama' (*Aracoeli*, p. 1398).

A Passion without Resurrection

With the brief story *Infanzia* (1939), full of fairy-tale grace, Morante anticipates the pauses of Edenic contemplation which will be among her happiest.[25] The little Angelo, born of woman, but through a miraculous birth (without a father? without sin?) seems to be destined (even though he is 'homely' like Manuele) for a heroic and luminous future, immune to every fault and human failing:

> Forse, simile a questa è l'infanzia degli eroi. Ma oggi nessuno è solo come Angelo, nato dalla serva allo stabilimento dei bagni, sul fiume. Non ha padre, e la serva, sempre occupata, lo depose quasi appena nato in una cuccia d'erba, sulla riva, da dove lo raccoglie soltanto all'ora del latte, e quand'è notte, all'ora di dormire. In quell'erba, Angelo cresce. Sue madrine, che egli solo conobbe, furono le grandi maghe del fiume, dagli occhi verdi aperti, dai capelli d'acqua, dalla voce sperduta. Assorte e distese, come chi dorme, fuggono lungo la corrente; ma non si dimenticano di lui. Lo difendono dalle vespe e dai capitomboli e meravigliate guardano nel libro del suo destino, pieno di parole e figure stupende. Inventano per ninnarlo indicibili canzoni, che alternano coi suoni teneri, con le smorfie che piacciono all'età sua: "povero Angelo, — dicono a volte, — come sei bruttino!" E, tutte in coro, ridono.[26]

The writer rewrites, in reality, a sort of myth (Moses, Jesus, Arjuna, Buddha), which will serve as an outline for her future novels carrying the indelible sign of a birth that takes place outside the bounds of normality, or else a secret birth, which renders the characters' childhood surrounded by mystery and prodigies: in different ways, Arturo, Useppe, Manuele are born and grow in a real or imagined fusion with the mother (at times substituted by the protective presence of a dog or of a figure resembling a guardian angel): an exclusive relationship from which the distant or absent paternal figure remains excluded. Now, if Morante draws from medieval biblical tradition many aspects of the 'paradisiacal escapes' (including artificial paradises) conceded to those characters of her poetic invention who are marked by some 'difference' (predestined name, Jewishness, epilepsy, homosexuality, etc.), she then tragically reverses the allegorical significance, the salvific message consecrated by a secular tradition. The effect of those supernatural contacts is perverted, as if a deforming lens were used which gives to most of her shadowy 'gothic' stories that 'disturbing strangeness' that came from the interruption of perturbing and threatening manifestations into the everyday reality: surreal figures, or spectral, or macabre ones (*Lo scolaro pallido*, *L'anima*, *Appuntamento*). Within the mystery, at the end, always lies coiled a threat of death.

In *La Storia*, in fact, the famous motif of the 'boy who understood the language of birds' is brought out, entwined, in the episode of Useppe and Bella's marvellous excursions in the little Tiberian 'paradise', with the equally traditional motif of innocent creatures rescued from terrestrial life to fly away into the ever after (the calf, Blitz), or else the legendary 'voyages to Paradise'. Morante forcibly introduces into the narrative development — therefore amongst the horrors of the war in the historical temporality — a magical interval, a spiral that opens onto the infinite and the eternal (a theme re-proposed in *Aracoeli*, with the legend of the 'minor Panda'): as she well knew, such momentary experiences in the *al di là* are described in hagiographic and exemplary tradition as not humanly sustainable, nor able to be assimilated in the earthly life; the contact with the supernatural that is conceded by divine grace to certain beings marked (by innocence or sanctity) allows only a 'passage' or a momentary 'return' to normal temporality, since the 'voyage' was nothing more than a foretaste, a preview of redemption (as for Augustine's mother). Morante maintains the provisory nature of such states, but without allowing the certainty of salvation to compensate for it. Another 'exemplary' episode refers more directly to *Aracoeli*, where the theme of sudden perception of another dimension beyond apparent reality returns. Manuele recounts his singular experience:

> E in quel punto il tempo si è fermato, rendendomi a un senso indicibile, unico e totale, al quale potrei dare un nome: ETERNITÀ. (È strano come l'ETERNITÀ si lasci captare piuttosto in un segmento effimero che in una continuità estesa. Ma il corpo non sostiene la prova, e torna al disordine).
> (*Aracoeli*, pp. 1292–93)

Yet it is the newborn Carina Encarnacion (it is significant that here the reference to the mystery of the Incarnation of Christ, the condition of a promise of Redemption is here, instead, lost) who untimely leaves the world (just as Antonio, Morante's older brother, has done).

The infantile trust in mystery and in Paradise — a joke of divine grace, conceded to pure souls? — illuminates Manuele's still innocent childhood, who believes that his uncle, a Spanish combatant, is a heroic defender of the Republic, admitted to Paradise in the company of that Daniel the Fearless, the biblical Daniel from whom sprung the noble and ancient race of his guardian, a member of those mysterious celestial genealogies which escape the destruction of History, and are miraculously adopted into Eternity.

Manuele asks himself, precisely what it is within the fruit of knowledge that bought us the ruinous exile from the Earthly Paradise. As an adult, he re-proposes in the form of a rhapsody those word-indications of an analogical mechanism, directly connected to Weil's reflections on time, consciousness, and the integrity of conquering a condition of immortality through purity:

> Certi casi fortuiti si caricano — con l'avanzare dell'età — di una mistica esaltata e arbitraria, che rode fuori tempo un tessuto già corroso, come fa il morbillo su un organismo adulto. Oggi, quella cartolina, recapitata postuma per via di un disservizio postale, mi si fa credere un alibi di Manuel, a noi fatto pervenire da lui stesso, di là dal suo radioso oltremondo, per darci smentita della sua morte. Un simile scherzo affettuoso gli somiglia; e lui non per niente avrebbe scelto la figura della Puerta d'Oro. [. . .] Come l'amuleto di Aracoeli, e il carrettino dei gelati, e Totetaco, e ogni minima comparsa della commedia, così la Puerta di Manuel è immortale. I nostri organi di senso, in realtà, sono delle mutilazioni. Eravamo integri, prima della Genesi; e può darsi che la cacciata dall'Eden vada intesa, nel suo senso occulto, per un gioco ambiguo e provocatorio: 'Avete mangiato il frutto *proibito*', dice la sentenza del Signore, 'ma non quello *segreto* della vita, che io, Padrone del giardino, vi tengo nascosto, perché vi renderebbe uguale agli dei'. Ora, il gioco equivoco della cacciata potrebbe insinuarsi in questo punto: in realtà, *le porte stesse che ci hanno chiuso il giardino dell'Eden, ci hanno aperto i giardini innumerevoli del mondo. E dove si nasconde, allora, il frutto segreto? di là, o di qua dalle porte?* Su questo, la sentenza è muta. Muta o cifrata? Nel secondo caso, proprio il suo silenzio ambiguo ce ne indicherebbe, forse, la chiave. 'Andatevene di qui', direbbe la sentenza rovesciata del Signore, 'in virtù del frutto proibito, siete liberi dall'Eden, e vi si aprono i campi della terra, dove si nasconde il frutto segreto. Trovatelo, e sarete uguale agli dei'. Gli dei non sono maciullati dalla macchina dei sensi. Sono integri. Passato presente e futuro — tenebre e luce — morte e vita — i multipli e gli addendi — i diversi e i contrari — per loro sono tutti uno. Forse il nostro traguardo è QUELLO. Né sarebbe lecito negare che il succo dell'integrità deificante possa scoprircisi in qualche semplice prodotto della terra. [. . .] Né si esclude poi che il Signore, nei suoi responsi, ricorra a simboli o metafore: il nascondiglio del 'frutto' segreto si potrebbe anche cercare, forse, in altri regni della terra. Potrebbe essere una pietra, un'ala d'insetto, una cenere d'ossa; o magari una parola inventata, un pensiero mai concepito da nessuno. . . Allora si vedranno le cose invisibili, e si capiranno quelle incomprese, e quelle perdute si restituiranno.
> 'Che le tenebre diventino tenebre luminose
> e la luce diventi luce tenebrosa'.
>
> (*Aracoeli*, pp. 1288–90)

Between the fabulous and the apocalyptic, Manuele's meditation leads to the Mystery hidden in words: we are close to the paradoxes of Cabbalistic thought, which are deliberately evoked out of context by Morante, with a parodic intent, in the image of Aracoeli bent over the fashion magazines that she was reading: 'Essa li esaminava con la diligenza accigliata e un poco forzosa di un piccolo zelante ebreo chino sul Talmud o sulla Torah' (p. 1263).

When Manuele finally comes to know himself, he pitilessly accuses Aracoeli of having hidden the truth from him (an echo of the reproaches made by the young suicide of *Addio* to the lover-mother-girl for having fooled him with dreams and wonders):

> Dicono che, immergendosi allo specchio dei propri occhi — con attenzione cruciale e al tempo stesso con abbandono — si arrivi a distinguere finalmente in fondo alla pupilla l'ultimo Altro, anzi l'unico e vero Sestesso, il centro di ogni esistenza e della nostra, insomma quel punto che avrebbe nome Dio. Invece, nello stagno acquoso dei miei occhi, io non ho scorto altro che la piccola ombra diluita (quasi naufraga) di quel solito niño tardivo che vegeta segregato dentro di me. Sempre il medesimo, con la sua domanda d'amore ormai scaduta e inservibile, ma ostinata fino all'indecenza. (p. 1171)

He voices with desperate violence his late realization, which is nothing but an extreme cry of love/hatred — his 'extreme fable' — for the mother for whom he sacrificed his very identity (in order to merge with his heroic brother), renouncing his own sexual difference (with reference to his mother) in an insane attempt to identify himself in her, and self-destructing in his search for the empty, inconsistent origin. Unhappy, narcissistic Manuele transgresses the Christian precept, loving his mother as himself and himself as his mother in an incestuous delirium, which sends him back always to his own image, like an infernal damnation, and which re-echoes that of Oedipus who blinds himself for his incest with another mother. Yet it also evokes the degrading ramblings of Davide Segre, whose traces it seems to follow. Left alone and forever prey to maternal spells, he ends up applying to himself the fable of the 'immortal tailor', reading into it a tremendous revelation:

> Come ogni altra favola antica, anche questa forse comunica qualcosa di vero. E in tal caso a me comunica che io, di certo, non sono un corpo miracoloso. Se avessi una sonda adatta, potrei ripescare in fondo al mio passato la data lontana di quella notte in cui fui visitato dal sarto immortale. Da allora fra le sorti indelebili della mia trama futura, ormai cucite dentro la mia carne, la prima diceva:
>
> > MAI PIÙ TU SARAI
> > UN OGGETTO D'AMORE
> > MAI PER NESSUNO MAI
> > MAI TU SARAI UN OGGETTO
> > D'AMORE.
> >   (*Aracoeli*, p. 1094)

The exercising of attention, the wait for interior illumination, the emptying of self, which are present in Weil's texts, cannot give Manuele access to divine grace, because he remains a prisoner of his own imagination, and a slave to the exclusive relationship with his mother:

> El niñomadrero. La favola mammarola è stantia, ovvio reperto da seduta psicanalitica, o tema da canzonetta edificante. C'era una volta uno specchio dove io, mirandomi, potevo innamorarmi di me stesso: erano i tuoi occhi, Aracoeli, che m'incoronavano re di bellezza nelle loro piccole pozze incantate. E questo fu il miraggio che tu mi fabbricasti all'origine, proiettandolo su tutti i miei Sahara futuri, di là dai tuoi orrori e dalla tua morte. Il tuo corpo è disciolto, senza più occhi né latte né mestruo né saliva. È rigettato dallo spazio, niente altro che un infimo delirio; mentre io sopravvivo, canuto Narciso che non crepa, sviato dalle tue morgane. (p. 1172)

The suspicion that his childhood paradise is only an illusion or a trick, instead of a promise of happiness, ultimately finds confirmation. Precisely because the paternal presence was lacking for this child, accustomed to erroneously believing himself the object of an absolute and eternal love, in his initiation into adulthood, he was impeded in his acceptance of the separation from the maternal womb — an acceptance necessary for his maturation and autonomy.[27] It is because of this that contact with the real world, beyond phantasmagoria and fairy tales maintained by child-mothers, can only be traumatic and destructive.

Does this condemnation refer back to the exile from Paradise, and entail, with the passage of time, the mortal outcome to which all are subject, except perhaps the young, 'beautiful fresh, children', who are foreign and hostile to it? Or the 'poets' who receive some compensation from posterity?

Manuele is also 'divided' and capable of speaking with many voices to himself (like Saba in 'Canto a tre voci' beloved by Morante). He is obsessed with memories and dreams, with feelings of guilt and the yearning for purity. The absence of a father has stunted his psychological development and he is marked by an irreversible sense of being different from other people. Still, he is not a poet like the beloved Saba, but only a 'pupazzo borghese disarmato e sfasciato, una sagoma da tiro a segno' (*Aracoeli*, p. 1174). He is incapable, therefore, of exorcising his fear and conquering the monsters.

Salvation is not promised to him, since he did not have as a mother Monica who guided Saint Augustine to the God of the Christians, nor a Beatrice who on the threshold of Paradise obtained Dante's penitence, with the confession and the recognition of his sins, and thus his redemption: 'pon giù il seme del piangere ed ascolta' (Purg. XXXI, 46). In fact, Morante re-evokes Dante's verse when she shows Manuele anxious to know the reason, the 'seeds of crying', of his own unrestrained bursting into tears after the last devastating encounter with Eugenio, a mysteriously absent father, in his prime splendid because of his good looks and his military prestige, now miserably impoverished, reduced to impotence and silence among the carnage of the destroyed city and the uncovered tombs. All of this signifies, in the meantime, that the mother or the beloved woman can no longer be a guide to salvation, in a definitively corrupted and decayed world, but only an unhappy cause of self-destructive regression: perhaps even Aracoeli exhumed and fled? Returned as an empty form, a fatuous shadow in her fantastical Andalusia?

Yet, in this unexpected epilogue, the reminder of Dante is not without a meaning. If Manuele understands, only after the death of his father, that his desperate tears were tears of love, it signifies that he, in that moment, was conscious of the loss of something now unreachable by fault of erroneous love ('per male obietto'?), of the self-deception of a corrupt intelligence:

> Dovunque, ho peccato. Nelle intenzioni e nei fini e negli atti ma peggio di tutto nell'intelligenza. L'intelligenza si dà per capire. E a me si è data, ma io non capisco niente. E non ho mai capito e non capirò mai niente. (*Aracoeli*, p. 1428)

Above all because of a paternity that was ignored, lost or denied, farther away still and inaccessible, chosen as a provisory compensation for a brief period of time?

> Dentro di me, a quel tempo, non appassiva ancora del tutto lo spirito naturale avventuriero. La morte era un'avventura, e la fede un'avventura (da qui, poco piú tardi, mi ridussi alla fede in Dio: non piú, certo, il Dio di Aracoeli, con le Vergini e gli Angeli della Guardia. Il mio Dio — del resto, provvisorio — fu un Domicilio incorporeo, di là dai numeri e dal Verbo e dai fenomeni. Un'astratta Paternità). (*Aracoeli*, p. 1216)

We have to ask ourselves, therefore, if the message entrusted by Morante to her novel does not far surpass the limits of a psychological drama, of a tragic familiar story.

The End of the Fairy Tale and the Aporiae of History

One theme of the novel, in reality fundamental for the comprehension of the entire problem, does not seem to have received deserved interest on the part of critics (but see now Sergio Parussa's essay in this volume): we refer to the presence of the Shoah, which at first sight should not interrupt the plot constructed around the question of young Manuele's failed initiation to maturity. We know just to what extent he is ignorant of the political events that have turned his world upside down, and how much, in the end, even his idolized uncle as a luminous hero of Spain remains a spectral image. The only spark of rebellion, typical of an unprepared and naive adolescent, precipitates him into a grotesque misadventure that has no relation to the tragic events that taint the country with blood, nor to the struggles of the partisans or the Spanish republicans of whom, furthermore, he knows nothing concrete. Manuele will live through a hallucinatory posthumous encounter with his uncle, under the sign of deconsecrated and humiliating ups and downs, which have become a metaphor for the regressive process that hurls him into the infernal maw of the maternal mystery.

But not even the aftermath of the war, and still less the years of youthful contestation, find him conscious and engaged, unlike the Morante of the *MSR*: rather he declares himself hostile and disdainful with regard to the young protesters, all assimilated, with rancour, in those young people who humiliated him and rejected his miserable and squalid pleas for love (a memory of the bitterness of the elderly Saba of the *Epigrafe*?). So it is certainly not the political question of the extermination of the Jews and of Fascism's responsibility for their persecution that is called into question in *Aracoeli*, while it is precisely this question that forms the nervous centre of the *MSR* or of *La Storia*. Rather, it is the ethical and religious question that is central to *Aracoeli*.

If the end of History is a tragic collapse of a world already condemned, after Hiroshima, to a perennial threat of atomic destruction, no less so is the end of *Aracoeli*, in spite of the child Manuele's preference for stories with happy endings. By this stage we know that heroes, like Superman, can die and that the Messiah can fail: the luminous Arturo has left for the war, Davide Segre has turned into a suicidal executioner, Manuel Muñoz Muñoz has died without glory and without redemption in spite of the 'cartolina dal Paradiso' and the promise of Christ on the cross ('Domani sarai con me in Paradiso') — all of these signs have proved bewitching and false. If it is true that the old Jew, named Shalom in Manuele's story, who had fled from Russia — a disturbing figure halfway between a hermit and a wandering Jew busy meditating on eternal truths — and hid in the snow, finally obtains baptism (unlike Simone Weil) and seems to die in peace, it is also true that he has by then become a blind and ghostly figure — perhaps like those creatures in the concentration camps stripped of their human form. Is this the cruel joke of a useless conversion that no longer grants salvation?[28]

Morante wants to denounce, with her last works — and above all with *Aracoeli* — in the most radical and atrocious manner, the absence and even the withdrawal of a God the Father, to say nothing of his impotence, thus reaching the conclusions not only of Saba ('Dopo Maidaneck.. .') and Primo Levi ('C'è Auschwitz, quindi non può esserci Dio'), but also of the ancient and enigmatic interpretation of mystic and esoteric Judaism, of Zohar and of the Cabbalah, which teaches (according to the doctrine of the *Tzimtzùm*: contraction, refolding, auto-limitation) that God withdrew from the world at the moment of Creation so that man might exist in good and in evil. This is an extreme (and heterodox) position which Simone Weil approaches (distancing herself from the Christian faith) when she affirms that our vocation is to love God as if He does not exist (since He can love nothing but Himself), and to unite ourselves with Him through our own annihilation ('Debbo amare di essere nulla'). In fact Weil seems to prefigure Manuele's destiny: 'Questo è il mistero dei misteri [. . .] Bisogna essere in un deserto perché colui che dobbiamo amare è assente. [. . .] Nulla di ciò che esiste è assolutamente degno d'amore. Bisogna quindi amare ciò che non esiste'[29].

Perhaps to the 'Eli, eli .. .' torn from a Christ abandoned by everyone and by God himself, like all of the poor sinners of this world, the only response is the one given by Aracoeli to her deluded son (deluded even in the name that is not his, emptied of its etymological significance: an 'Emmanuel' that no longer means 'God with us', but alludes to a poor derelict 'without a father') in his desperate desire to reach that which is true and eternal: 'Ma, niño mio chiquito, non c'è niente da capire' (*Aracoeli*, p. 1428).

Translated by Jessica M. Nadeau

Notes to Chapter 13

1. See Marco Bardini, 'Le confessioni di una figlia del secolo', in *Morante Elsa. Italiana. Di professione, poeta* (Pisa: Nistri-Lischi, 1999), pp. 555–616.
2. Simona Cives, 'Elsa Morante: "Senza i conforti della religione"', in *Le stanze di Elsa*, ed. by Giuliana Zagra and Simonetta Buttò (Rome: Colombo, 2006), pp. 49–65.
3. Cives, 'Elsa Morante', pp. 50–51.
4. Elsa Morante, *Il mondo salvato dai ragazzini e altri poemi* (Turin: Einaudi, 1968), henceforth *MSR*.
5. It should be noted that Aracoeli has the same first name as Maria Zambrano's sister. See Elisa Martínez Garrido, 'Bestiario, allegoria e parola ne *La Storia* di Elsa Morante: Un'altra via al sacro', in *Elsa Morante: La voce di una scrittrice e di un'intellettuale rivolta al secolo XXI*, ed. by Elisa Martínez Garrido (Madrid: Universidad Complutense de Madrid, 2003), pp. 85–107 (p. 99). See also Martínez Garrido's essay in this volume.
6. Cives, 'Elsa Morante', p. 51.
7. Elsa Morante, 'La sera domenicale', in *MSR*, p. 29.
8. Cives, 'Elsa Morante', p. 59. *La Storia*, published in 1974, immediately precedes the composition of *Aracoeli*, which probably began in 1975 (the year of Pasolini's death), led the author to visit El Almendral in 1977, and ended in 1980.
9. Concetta D'Angeli, 'Il paradiso nella storia', *Studi novecenteschi*, 21 (1994), 215–35. See also, Concetta D'Angeli, 'Due donne appassionate: Elsa Morante e Simone Weil', in *Elsa Morante:*

La voce di una scrittrice e di un'intellettuale rivolta al secolo XXI, ed. by Elisa Martínez Garrido, pp. 61–70; Bardini, 'Le confessioni di una figlia del secolo', p. 597. See also, Marco Bardini, 'Realtà ed esperienza estetica negli scritti saggistici di Elsa Morante', in *Elsa Morante: La voce di una scrittrice*, ed. by Martínez Garrido, pp. 23–36.

10. In the notes she wrote in the margins of her copy of Weil's *Cahiers*, Morante humbly admits her inability to imitate Weil's heroic asceticism ('my fault', 'have I been unfaithful?', 'I do not exist', 'are absolutely the things that I have come to believe are perennially in question' — 1961. 62–63–64).
11. Elsa Morante, *Pro o contro la bomba atomica e altri scritti*, ed. by Cesare Garboli (Milan: Adelphi, 1997).
12. Simone Weil, *L'ombra e la grazia* (Milan: Rusconi, 1985), p. 46.
13. Cives, 'Elsa Morante', p. 61.
14. Elena Porciani, *L'alibi del sogno nella scrittura giovanile di Elsa Morante* (Soveria Mannelli: Iride, 2006), pp. 197–98.
15. Cives, 'Elsa Morante', pp. 61–63.
16. Simone Weil, *Prologue à la connaissance surnaturelle*, in *Œuvres* (Paris: Gallimard, 1999), pp. 806–07.
17. Elsa Morante, *Via dell'angelo*, in *Lo scialle andaluso* (Turin: Einaudi, 1963), p. 63.
18. Elsa Morante, *Aracoeli*, in *Opere*, ed. by Carlo Cecchi and Cesare Garboli, 2 vols (Milan: Mondadori, 1988–90), II (1990), pp. 1039–1454 (p. 1216). Further references to this edition will be given after quotations in the text.
19. Simone Weil, *Prologue* 806: 'Agenouille-toi', 'Tombe à genoux', compared to: 'Prega! Figlia, Prega! Si diresse all'inginocchiatoio [...] Antonia inginocchiata', in Morante, *Via dell'Angelo*, pp. 65–67. Aracoeli will do so scandalously in the church.
20. Walter Benjamin, 'Il narratore: Considerazioni sull'opera di Nicola Leskov', in *Angelus Novus: Saggi e frammenti*, ed. by Renato Solmi (Turin: Einaudi, 1995), p. 251.
21. Fabrizio Desideri, 'Apocalissi profana: figure della verità in Walter Benjamin', in *Walter Benjamin, Angelus Novus*, pp. 309–39:

> Secondo il *Midrash ha-Ne' elam* al *Libro di Ruth*, ricordato da Gerschom Scholem in uno dei suoi studi sulla Kabbalah, a mezzanotte si leva dal paradiso il vento del Nord e una scintilla scaturisce dal fuoco di Dio (quello della potestà del Giudizio) e colpisce sotto l'ala l'Arcangelo Gabriele. In quel momento, quando il grido di Gabriele sveglia tutti i galli della terra, l'Angelo, che si annota ogni giorno le azioni degli uomini, dopo il suo 'canto del gallo' celeste, prende lettura di esse. È allora che, se non fosse paralizzato dalla deformità delle dita dei suoi piedi, 'egli arderebbe il mondo con la sua fiamma'. La tempesta che si impiglia nelle ali dell'Angelo della storia, tenendole dispiegate come vele, ricorda il vento del Nord di questo *Midrash*. L'impotenza a redimere rimanda all'incapacità di Giudizio. Non formula assoluzioni né emette condanne. Il tono accusatorio ridiviene subito quello del lamento. L'Angelo della storia è anche Angelo del lutto per l'Inumanità di cui vorrebbe condividere le sorti. (p. 338)

22. Morante, *MSR*, p. 124.
23. Simone Weil, *Lettera a un religioso* (Milan: Adelphi, 1996).
24. Elsa Morante, *Il paradiso terrestre*, in *Pro o contro. . .*, pp. 19–20.
25. Elsa Morante, *Racconti dimenticati* (Turin: Einaudi, 2002), pp. 156–60.
26. Morante, *Racconti dimenticati*, p. 156
27. See Laura Benedetti, *The Tigress in the Snow: Motherhood and Literature in Twentieth-Century Italy* (Toronto: University of Toronto Press, 2007), pp. 78–84; Benedetti says: 'According to this interpretation, each of Elsa Morante's major narrative works brought her closer to a crisis that she finally reached in *Aracoeli*; [. . .] Every attempt to recover as an adult the enchanted world of childhood is destined to be futile or even dangerous' (p. 82).
28. See, Cives, 'Elsa Morante', p. 65: Morante's autograph note:

> Note importanti per il corso del romanzo. [. . .] 2) il finale deve dare il senso della <u>fine del mondo</u>. 3) <u>Significati</u> — la discesa di Orfeo agli inferi — (Aracoeli) creatura che si vendica (inconsapevolmente) dei delitti collettivi con la propria degradazione e distruzione — decadenza e rovina della civiltà borghese — le madri e la morte — Chiusura dei cicli (nelle 4 dimensioni) — la fine del mondo — ecc.

29. Weil, *L'ombra e la grazia*, p. 117.

CHAPTER 14

Indian Traces:
Aracoeli, Pasolini's *L'odore dell'India*, and Moravia's *Un'idea dell'India*

Mimma Congedo

The starting point for this essay was the observation — shared by some scholars, including Concetta D'Angeli — that Oriental literature and philosophy are an important cultural reference for Elsa Morante's later works.[1] Another cue for the paper, related to this first one, was obviously given by the actual event of the journey to India made together by Elsa Morante, Pier Paolo Pasolini, and Alberto Moravia in 1961. Thus, there are two guiding questions to this essay: can we find any Eastern, or better any Indian trace in *Aracoeli*? And, can we identify any common themes in *Aracoeli*, *L'odore dell'India*, and *Un'idea dell'India*? Of course, these two questions overlap to a certain extent, but they can still be seen as independent of one another, and I will answer them separately, starting from the latter.

I would like to begin my analysis with the theme of the journey, which is evidently shared by the three texts under consideration. Manuele's journey in *Aracoeli* echoes various cultural and mythical models, such as Dante's journey, the Orpheus myth, Homer's *Odyssey*, or Virgil's *Aeneid*.[2] In this sense, a main interpretative category for Manuele's journey is the descent into the underworld, a connotation that is also related to the reading of his journey as a sort of psychoanalytical process, focused on the mother–child relationship.[3]

Together with these literary and psychoanalytic models, and partially overlapping with them, one can relate Manuele's journey to the *topos* of the *quête*: Manuele's search is a search for his mother, that is, for his origin, which coincides with a search for his (lost) self. In fact — before Manuele is somehow 'rejected' for the first time by Aracoeli for wearing glasses, thus revealing for the first time his ugliness to her eyes — the Edenic condition of 'Totetaco' and of the first period at the 'Quartieri Alti' corresponds to a mutual symbiosis of the mother and the child. In this *quête*, memory and time also play a key role, as the spatial journey to Spain corresponds to a temporal one, into the depths of Manuele's past.[4]

However, Aracoeli's image is extremely ambivalent in the text: if in Manuele's early childhood she shares a symbiotic union with the child, after the separation — definitely marked when she rejects Manuele from her breast — Aracoeli becomes the perennial rejecting Other, whose love and recognition the protagonist desperately tries to obtain again.

I think that Aracoeli's otherness is fundamentally related to her characterization as a 'primitive' creature; her figure is centred on a constellation of magic/irrationality/nature/darkness/body/sexuality. This primitiveness especially characterizes her both at the beginning and at the end of her evolution as a character. It is not by chance that Adalgisa Giorgio describes Aracoeli's evolution as a journey from 'Nature to Culture [. . .] and then back to Nature'.[5] However, one can affirm that such a primitiveness never abandons Aracoeli, not even during her 'cultural' phase, as Manuele himself says:

> Tu nel fondo rimanesti sempre la bifolca che eri all'origine, anche se col tempo avevi imparato a distinguere il renard argenté dal renard bleu e lo chemisier dal tailleur; e a sbattere un cocktail nei suoi vari ingredienti.[6]

In other words, Aracoeli's world seems to be related to a (logical) universe other than the civilized/bourgeois one, represented in the novel by the 'Comandante', Manuele's father, by his family and by their milieu. In this sense, Aracoeli is the *diverso par excellence*, and Manuele's nostalgia for the union with Aracoeli may also correspond to the desire for a dimension that is felt as more authentic than the civilized/bourgeois one, and obviously as totally different from it. It is exactly because it is felt as more authentic and closer to one's true being that this order generates a nostalgia and a 'journey' back to it.

For example, while travelling to El Almendral, Manuele explicitly says that he is actually going back to Totetaco, the place of his symbiotic union with Aracoeli: 'la corriera di El Almendral mi riporterà a Totetaco' (*Aracoeli*, p. 1192), even if the Aracoeli waiting there for Manuele is still a child:

> Questa Aracoeli non è la medesima dello specchio, ma una anteriore alla mia nascita, la quale tuttavia sarà pronta a riconoscermi all'arrivo. Il corpo di cui mi vergogno mi cascherà di dosso come un travestimento da commedia, e in me, ridendo, lei riconosce l'infante di Totetaco. Uguali lei e io, tornati coetanei. Bambino? Bambina? Certi dati, là, non hanno corso. Maschio o femmina non significa niente. Là, non si cresce. (p. 1193)

It is thus evident that the nostalgia for the union with Aracoeli is also a nostalgia for a logic other than the current one, a logic where categories like male and female 'non significano niente' and, most interestingly, where time and history do not exist, as 'Là, non si cresce'. This lack of a historical dimension also strongly characterizes Aracoeli as a primitive, and it is closely related to her alternative logic (for instance, she cannot even follow and understand the plot of a movie).[7] Such an alternative logic is also connected to her powerful corporeity and proximity to a sort of magic dimension:

> Si capiva che, dopo la grande conquista dell'alfabeto e dell'italiano, il suo intelletto oramai toccava una frontiera prescritta, oltre la quale, per lei, non vi sarebbe alimento, né cittadinanza. Questo, essa *lo sentiva* senza saperlo, attraverso una sua *intelligenza quasi fisica*, nascosta perfino a lei stessa, ma che oggi credo di riconoscere (quasi l'ombra stellata di notti innumerevoli) nella profondità dei suoi occhi. La sua era *un'intelligenza diversa dalla nostra*: era una

> *sostanza ombrosa, imperscrutabile e segreta, che scorreva in tutto il suo corpo*, quale un'infinita *memoria carnale* mischiata di tripudio e di malinconia. Essa la rendeva *capace* — io credo — *di avvertire*, negli spazi e nei tempi, *presenze, movimenti e meteore negate alla nostra cognizione*; ma davanti agli esercizi del pensiero astratto, si rifugiava in una zona di stupore e assenza, al *modo di un piccolo animale* a cui venga offerta in pasto una materia non commestibile. L'intelligenza misteriosa, che non aveva stanza nel suo pensiero, era una pellegrina incognita dentro di lei; così come, *fra noi, era un'estranea*. E si muoveva inconsapevole di qua dalla Storia, e dalla politica, e dai libri e dai giornali, come una nomade attendata in una terra di nessuno. (p. 1261, my emphasis)[8]

Besides the aspects that I have highlighted above, I would like to stress in this passage the parallel between Aracoeli and a small animal, a parallel that evokes her affinity with nature.[9] This use of the analogy between Aracoeli and the animal realm is not surprising, as we know that she is made of 'fibre animali' (p. 1332).[10]

In the above-mentioned long passage, it is also interesting to note that Aracoeli's 'intelligenza misteriosa' 'fra noi era un'estranea'. Of course, this 'noi' is Manuele's bourgeois familiar milieu. We know that Manuele perceives himself as a bourgeois, for instance when he says 'm'hai generato borghese' (p. 1172), and it is therefore remarkable that he explicitly recognizes Aracoeli's otherness, which marks her again as the diverse other of a civilized/bourgeois order.

This mark of diversity is associated with Aracoeli quite early in the novel, and again it involves the clash between two logical orders, the primitive/natural one and the bourgeois/cultural one, as we can read in the following passage recalling the moment when Manuele and his mother move from Totetaco and are 'portati in mezzo al mondo', that is into the civilized bourgeois milieu:

> Aracoeli. Nei primi anni della mia convivenza con lei, questo suo nome, s'intende, mi suonava del tutto naturale. Però quando, io e lei, *fummo portati in mezzo al mondo*, mi avvidi che esso la distingueva, nella città, fra le altre donne. Difatti le nostre conoscenti si chiamavano Anna, Paola o Luisa, ovvero, in qualche caso, Raimonda, Patrizia, Perla o Camilla. 'Aracoeli!' esclamavano le signore, 'che bel nome! *Che nome strano!*'. Ho imparato in seguito che in Spagna è uso comune battezzare le bambine con simili nomi, anche latini, della chiesa o della liturgia. Ma pure, via via, con l'età adulta, quel nome Aracoeli si è scritto nel mio ricordo quale un *segno di diversità*, un titolo unico: in cui mia madre rimane *separata e rinchiusa*, come dentro una cornice tortile e massiccia, dipinta d'oro. (*Aracoeli*, p. 1048, my emphasis)

Another element that makes Aracoeli totally diverse from the bourgeois order is the scandalous sexual behaviour that distinguishes her at the end of her evolution as a character. The passages on Aracoeli's sexuality are very abundant in the text, but I would like to recall one in particular, where Aracoeli's wild sexual behaviour is marked as a disorder. After describing the decay of her mother's body, Manuele says: 'e da tutta la sua materia emanava una sorta di greve disordine, che offendeva la sua grazia, quanto uno sfregio' (p. 1354).

On the one hand, such a disorder cannot be accepted by the bourgeois/civilized milieu, which — embodied in the neighbours, and later on in Manuele's grandparents — rejects Aracoeli as a prostitute. However, on the other hand, even in this case we can see that the bourgeois order manifests a desire, a fascination, a sort of nostalgia, for the diversity represented by Aracoeli.

For instance, we know that Manuele's father never rejects his wife, hiding himself in a kind of quasi-voluntary blindness to her sexual intercourse with other men. But even more than this, his love for Aracoeli — coloured by a sort of tender piety, especially when she is ill — remains someway unaltered even after her death. Also, Zia Monda — one of the main bearers of the bourgeois rules in Aracoeli's civilization process — has an unexpected reaction to Aracoeli's disorder:

> Piú strano, invece, era il suo contegno con Aracoeli: la quale non sembrava destarle indignazione e scandalo (come ci si sarebbe aspettato da lei) ma piuttosto una *trepidazione affascinata*, e quasi *un'umiltà ammirativa*. La guardava, *come un cardellino di gabbia guarderebbe i voli mai visti di una cicogna; e pareva elemosinare da lei qualche confidenza segreta* [. . .]. Perfino alla vista di certi abbigliamenti, che rinnegavano la sua scuola di decenza e signorilità, essa non si permetteva nessuna osservazione. (*Aracoeli*, p. 1368, my emphasis)

And Manuele himself, notwithstanding his contrasting and ambivalent love/hate feelings for Aracoeli, does not actually reject the 'disordered' Aracoeli, whose image he tends to merge in a hybrid with the 'sacred' one, the chaste Aracoeli of Totetaco and the first period at the Quartieri Alti: 'E io le amo entrambe: non come uno conteso fra due amori, ma come l'amante di un ibrido, di cui, nell'orgasmo, non riconosce le specie, né capisce le trame' (p. 1067).

This polarization between a rejection/disgust and a desire/piety/love for Aracoeli's otherness is a constant factor in the whole novel, but I believe that in the text the positive feeling is predominant: Aracoeli, in her diversity, is fundamentally an object of desire, piety, and love. As Adalgisa Giorgio puts it, Aracoeli's mark of diversity — her marginality, in Giorgio's words — is not connoted by Elsa Morante as a lack, but rather as an 'empowering condition, because it allows her character to resist being crushed by History'.[11]

In *Aracoeli*, the opposition between the 'natural' and the 'civilized' basically corresponds to the opposition between the peasant world and the bourgeois one, as Giovanna Rosa highlights: 'Nell'ultimo romanzo, abbandonato lo scenario deprimente della promiscuità piccolo-borghese, la Morante ha voluto mettere in scena l'incontro tra la naturalità vitale del popolo contadino e il prestigio sicuro dell'alta borghesia cittadina'.[12] Aracoeli is actually a poor Andalusian peasant, and 'il Comandante', an officer of the Italian 'Regia Marina', brings her from her uncivilized land to his civilized world.

We know that the opposition Nature/Civilization or Culture is also typical of colonial discourse, which translates such opposition as that between extra-European and European cultures, and between East and West. Furthermore, we know that the opposition Nature/Culture also forms part of this colonial discourse as a distinction between non-industrial and industrial societies, which is quite close to the peasant/bourgeois distinction.

In this colonial rhetoric, the terms of the hierarchy are very clear: the civilized/bourgeois/industrial/European/West world is superior to the natural/peasant/non-industrial/extra-European/East that results in being *Other* than the West. As

Edward Said argued, Orientalism itself creates the same opposition, summarizing complex Asian cultural formations in a few general features, in opposition to the Western ones (e.g. democracy vs. despotism).[13] In this frame, we can state that in general India appears to a Western eye as the land of mysticism, spirituality, superstition, and religion; and we can actually identify as a commonplace the opposition between a rational West and a mystic India, which is mirrored — just to give one example — in the persistent prejudice against the existence of an Indian philosophy.[14]

I believe that we can find traces of this opposition even in Pier Paolo Pasolini's *L'odore dell'India* and in Alberto Moravia's *Un'idea dell'India*. It is evident that both Pasolini and Moravia perceive India as the *diverso*, the 'Other' that Europe has to face. The description of their journey continuously plays on the opposition between a peasant India and a bourgeois Europe, between a religious India and a non-religious Europe.[15]

Furthermore, it is interesting to note that the Indian situation is often compared to that of the European Middle Ages, and Indian religion is compared to medieval Christianity or to Classical polytheism, thus implying a sort of common ground between India and Europe, which Europe has overcome — or lost — forever. What emerges from Pasolini and Moravia's texts is actually an ambivalent feeling towards the 'other' represented by India: their reactions vary from a total disgust to a tender piety, from a rejection of the Indian reality to a kind of 'nostalgia' for a dimension that Europe has lost forever. The process of westernization is alternatively seen either as a danger or as the only chance for India, and Indian culture is alternatively seen as primitive and superstitious or as a culture even more 'advanced' than the Western one. This polarization of feelings and attitudes is quite close to the one generated by Aracoeli.

It is for these reasons that I see an interesting consonance between *Aracoeli* on the one hand and Pasolini's and Moravia's texts on the other: they all stage a journey towards the *diverso*, or 'other', represented as a disturbing and puzzling dimension, which contrasts with the rational/bourgeois/European and Western order. In a way, the affinity between Aracoeli's peasant and primitive world and the extra-European one is even suggested by Morante herself, who writes that Aracoeli's 'cattolicesimo elementare' is 'abitato da figure di chiesa, leggende afro-asiatiche e statue della processione' (*Aracoeli*, p. 1089).

Of course, there are differences between the three texts. First of all, Pasolini and Moravia are describing a true journey, as they are writing — respectively — a sort of diary and a reportage, not a novel.[16] There are also some differences in the way they report their experiences of India, which sometimes also produce two different points of view on India: very briefly, one may affirm that Pasolini is more interested in the particular, while Moravia looks for a more general perspective.[17]

However, beyond such different approaches to India, one can identify a shared feeling in the two texts; as Enzo Siciliano puts it: 'La complementarietà tra Moravia e Pasolini va rintracciata nella passione che entrambi hanno per il primitivo e il barbarico culturale'.[18] The main difference I identify between Morante's connotation of the primitive in *Aracoeli*, and Moravia and Pasolini's one in *Un'idea dell'India* and *L'odore dell'India*, lies in the fact that — as already mentioned — I believe that Morante fundamentally connotes Aracoeli's diversity/otherness in a positive way, while Pasolini's and Moravia's gaze at the diversity/otherness of India is more ambiguous, and in their texts such a diversity is often seen more as a lack than as an empowering position.

In opening his work, Pasolini overwhelms the reader with his perception of India as a puzzling place of diversity, urging like a beast within himself:

> Sono le prime ore della mia presenza in India, e io *non so dominare la bestia assetata chiusa dentro di me*, come in una gabbia. [. . .] Il mare è pacifico, non dà segno di presenza. Lungo la spalletta che lo contiene, ci sono delle automobili in sosta e, vicino ad esse, *quegli esseri favolosi, senza radici, senza senso, colmi di significati dubbi e inquietanti, dotati di un fascino potente*, che sono i primi indiani di un'esperienza che vuol essere esclusiva come la mia. (*L'odore dell'India*, pp. 9–10; my emphasis)[19]

I believe that the opposition rational/irrational — which we have found in *Aracoeli* — is here concealed, as Indian people appear as 'favolosi', 'senza senso' to Pasolini's Western eye. From the beginning, Pasolini perceives India as both disturbing and fascinating, since Indians are at the same time 'colmi di significati dubbi e inquietanti' and 'dotati di un fascino potente': we have a polarization of feelings, attached to the experience of diversity, which we have also found in *Aracoeli* and which emerges from Moravia's text too.

In opening his text, Moravia is even more explicit in recognizing the otherness of India, which may either be horrid or sublime, but is always puzzling. The incipit of *Un'idea dell'India* is written as an interview, in which Moravia answers the questions asked by a hypothetical interlocutor. India immediately appears as an enigma, because it is impossible to define it: 'l'India è l'India', Moravia replies twice to his interlocutor asking 'what is India?'. Also, India can only be felt, as a silent, invisible presence: 'neppure io so veramente che cosa sia l'India. La sento, ecco tutto. Anche tu dovresti sentirla. [. . .] Dovresti sentire l'India come si sente, al buio, la presenza di qualcuno che non si vede, che tace, eppure c'è' (*Un'idea dell'India*, p. 5).

The questions go on until Moravia states: 'l'India è il contrario dell'Europa' and 'l'India è il paese della religione' (p. 6), thus implying an opposition between India and Europe on the basis of the presence or lack of religion. But then, what is religion? Moravia brings in many examples to explain this, because Indian religion is an existential condition, hard to conceive of in European terms. As Moravia himself states: 'L'India è il paese della *religione come situazione esistenziale*. Della religione senza più. Per assurdo, anche se in India non ci fossero religioni, l'India sarebbe egualmente il paese della religione' (*Un'idea dell'India*, p. 8; my emphasis). I will quote just one of the examples Moravia uses in order to give an idea of what religion is like in India. Such a passage shows the duality and ambiguity linked to Indian religion, both horrid and sublime at the same time:

> La religione è il simbolo fallico custodito nelle celle dei templi, stilizzato in forma di enorme paracarro di pietra nera, unto e lucido di olio votivo, sparso sulla punta di corolle rosse di fiori, immerso in una oscurità sinistra, promiscua, puzzolente, sordida e agghiacciante. Al tempo stesso la religione è il Budda

> gigantesco nella roccia dell'ultima grotta di Ajanta, disteso in stato di nirvana in una penombra pulita e monastica, la testa appoggiata sulla mano, il braccio disteso lungo il fianco, le palpebre abbassate, si direbbe, non tanto sugli occhi, quanto sul mondo intero che è dentro di lui. (*Un'idea dell'India*, pp. 9–10)

In a very famous passage, Pasolini also deals with Indian religion, crystallizing it in a gesture and a feature:

> Io non so bene cosa sia la religione indiana [. . .]. Però posso dire una cosa: che gli indù sono *il popolo più caro, più dolce, più mite che sia possibile conoscere. La non violenza è nelle sue radici, nella ragione stessa della sua vita.* [. . .] Basta guardare come dicono sì. Anziché annuire come noi alzando e abbassando la testa, la scuotono circa come quando noi diciamo di no: ma la differenza del gesto è tuttavia enorme. Il loro no che significa sì consiste in un far ondeggiare il capo (il loro capo bruno e ondulato con quella povera pelle nera, che è il colore più bello che possa avere una pelle) teneramente [. . .]. Viste a distanza le masse indiane si fissano nella memoria, con quel gesto di assentimento, e il sorriso infantile e radioso negli occhi che l'accompagna. La loro religione è in quel gesto. (*L'odore dell'India*, pp. 32–33; my emphasis)

This characterization of the Indian people as sweet, non-violent, and meek occurs again and again in the text, revealing quite a paternalistic attitude towards them. In fact, the prevailing feeling in Pasolini's text is a pitiful one, which seems to mitigate his horror of India: 'eravamo ormai verso la fine del nostro viaggio in India, ed eravamo mezzi dissanguati dalla pena e dalla pietà' (*L'odore dell'India*, pp. 49–50).

However, Indian religion — which strongly characterizes India — is not only made of sweetness and non-violence; Indian religion is also degenerate and someway barbarous, as is the European medieval one, and it is so far from rationality that it results in being an 'alienation' and a 'neurosis':

> È un fatto, comunque, che in India l'atmosfera è favorevole alla religiosità, come dicono anche i referti più banali. Ma a me non risulta che gli indiani siano molto occupati da seri problemi religiosi. Certe loro forme di religiosità sono coatte, tipicamente medioevali: alienazioni dovute all'orrenda situazione economica e igienica del paese, vere e proprie nevrosi mistiche, che ricordano quelle europee, appunto, del medioevo, che possono colpire individui o intere comunità. Ma più che una religiosità specifica (quella che dà i fenomeni mistici o la potenza clericale) ho osservato tra gli indiani una religiosità generica e diffusa: un prodotto medio della religione. La non violenza, insomma, la mitezza, la bontà degli indù. Essi hanno perso contatto con le fonti dirette della loro religione (che è evidentemente una religione degenerata) ma continuano a esserne dei frutti viventi. Così la loro religione, che è la più astratta e filosofica del mondo, in teoria, è ora, in realtà, una religione totalmente pratica: un modo di vivere. (*L'odore dell'India*, p. 42)

Again, dealing with Indian castes and religion, Pasolini affirms that 'Tutto in India, a osservare bene, tende a classificarsi, cioè a fissarsi degenerando' (p. 80); and again this tendency towards a classification may result in something opposite to degeneration: Indian religion may even turn out to be more than sweetness, it may be something sublime. Describing an old lady who sings during her agony, Pasolini reveals the possible opposite effects of the Indian classifying and ritualizing attitude:

> In questo caso, ripeto, la codificazione (o ritualizzazione che pone riparo alla miseria psicologica indù) aveva qualcosa di sublime. In altri casi si ha il processo esattamente contrario, si arriva cioè al sordido, all'immondo. Basta pensare per esempio l'atroce involuzione che hanno subito le misure igieniche. (Pasolini, *L'odore dell'India*, p. 83)

Like Pasolini, Moravia explicitly mentions the Middle Ages in relation to India. At the beginning of the text, imagining describing the European reality from the point of view of an Indian, he states that the Middle Ages are the only European period that is to some extent close to the Indian mentality. However, because Europe usually conceives of the Middle Ages as a barbarous age, an Indian cannot but conclude that Europe is not religious at all, thus being totally different from India:

> Non è vero che il nostro indiano ignori il medioevo; egli, anzi, lo apprezza perché, appunto, è il solo periodo storico dell'Europa che gli faccia pensare all'India. Ma egli sa pure che per la grande maggioranza degli europei il ricordo atavico del medioevo è un ricordo di ignoranza, di infelicità, di rozzezza, di arretratezza e di miseria. Nella persistenza tenace di questo pregiudizio del senso comune popolare contro il medioevo, il nostro indiano ravvisa una prova di più che in fondo l'Europa non è religiosa. E infatti la fine del medioevo gli europei la chiamano Rinascimento; secondo il punto di vista dell'India dovrebbero invece chiamarla Decadenza. (Moravia, *Un'idea dell'India*, p. 7)

Actually, the prejudice against the Middle Ages is not only a popular one, if — as we have seen — Pasolini himself uses the comparison between Indian religion and the European Middle Ages in order to highlight the degenerate side of the former. In this respect, Moravia's usage of the Middle Ages in the above passage appears to be less straightforward, but it is evident that he uses it in order to show the opposition between a religious India and a no longer religious Europe.

In another passage on religion Moravia again uses the European Middle Ages in order to explain the Indian reality. This time, however, Indian religion is described as more similar to ancient polytheism than to medieval Christianity. What Moravia now finds medieval in India is 'una povertà malata e frenetica', an expression that recalls the ferment and seething of the Indian villages and bazaars, also often compared to those of the Middle Ages. This passage on religion, which I will quote extensively as it is a central one, is one of those in which India appears to be the lost Other of Europe; the Other that Europe should recognize firstly because it bears an authentic and natural dimension once known in Europe itself, and secondly — surprisingly — because such an authentic and natural dimension is not far away from a European recent discovery, that of psychoanalysis:

> Per il viaggiatore occidentale dotato di sensibilità l'India significa due traumi: il primo è quello provocato dall'incontro con una povertà malata e frenetica, di tipo medievale, che in Occidente è scomparsa da alcuni secoli; il secondo dall'urto con la religione politeistica a fondo naturalistico anch'essa morta da secoli in Europa, e in India, invece, ancora fiorente. [. . .] Il trauma della religione è in parte ingiustificato. Il viaggiatore occidentale del 1961 non è, infatti, il viaggiatore del 1861: negli ultimi cinquant'anni è avvenuta in Occidente una rivoluzione culturale che ci permette non soltanto di comprendere meglio la religione indiana ma anche, per così dire, di metterci al suo livello, in comunicazione diretta. [. . .] Così, mentre è comprensibile che

l'abate Dubois, il quale scrisse il suo libro sull'India ai primi dell'Ottocento, condanni, senza neppure tentare di capirli, certi culti e simboli religiosi indiani, meno comprensibile è che il viaggiatore proveniente dagli Stati Uniti, dove lavorano e prosperano migliaia di dottori psicanalisti, si scandalizzi, per esempio, nel tempio di Tanjore dove quegli stessi impulsi, che la psicanalisi mette all'origine di gran parte dei nostri atti, sono espressi simbolicamente in innumerevoli ex voto naturalistici. In realtà egli dovrebbe, invece, riconoscere che tremila e più anni or sono in India ebbe luogo, sul piano religioso, la stessa operazione di recupero culturale che, sul piano scientifico, è stata mandata ad effetto, ai nostri giorni, dalla psicanalisi. Ma il trauma, forse, è dovuto anche ad un altro fatto; la natura, non più trascesa e resa umana dal cristianesimo, la natura immediata e cruda, incombente coi suoi problemi di vita e di morte non indagati razionalmente dalla scienza ma simbolizzati con terrore dalla religione, questa natura primitiva è presente nei templi induisti, come lo era probabilmente nei sacrari delle antiche religioni mediterranee, in una forma oppressiva e minacciosa. Il viaggiatore europeo, avvezzo alle chiese, entrando in questi templi ha come la sensazione di fare un salto indietro di venti secoli, in un mondo che era il suo ma che lui ha ormai dimenticato. E non rendendosi conto che, come abbiamo detto, si tratta di un mondo che negli ultimi tempi è tornato ad affiorare nella cultura moderna, prova insieme turbamento e ripugnanza. (Moravia, *Un'idea dell'India*, pp. 55–56)

In this passage we can find attached to India some key elements that are quite similar to those attached to *Aracoeli*. Indian religion is described as a constellation of nature/irrationality/sexuality and as a threatening, disturbing, and disgusting experience for a European. But, as for *Aracoeli*, we also find here a sort of admiration and nostalgia for the wisdom concealed in Indian religion: admiration, because it anticipates a cultural operation that, though 'obviously' at the 'higher rational level of science', has been fulfilled in the West only 'nowadays' by psychoanalysis; nostalgia, because Indian religion represents a world that the West 'has forgotten' and — notwithstanding the psychoanalytical revolution — cannot easily regain.

Of course, like Pasolini, in other passages Moravia does not hesitate to condemn the Indian religion for being degenerate. And even more, he indicates such degeneration as one of the causes of the poverty of India:

Il secondo motivo storico, anch'esso remoto, dell'arretratezza e miseria indiana va ricercato nelle religioni o meglio nella degenerazione superstiziosa di concezioni altrimenti profondissime quali il brahmanesimo, il buddismo e il jainismo. [. . .] la vita indiana è piena di credenze oscure e irrazionali [. . .]. Questa'immensa congerie di credenze fossili paralizza la vita indiana producendo un danno economico ingente [. . .] e ostacolando i progressi dell'educazione e della cultura. (*Un'idea dell'India*, p. 80)

As Moravia himself affirmed in an interview, he thought that India — like the whole Third World — in order to overcome its poverty should have followed the path of industrialization until the end, as the peasant culture was no more able to produce anything good; on the contrary, Pasolini thought that India and the Third World had been ruined by industrialism.[20]

L'odore dell'India shows that Pasolini actually considers India as a 'peasant country', as the author himself states, where the middle class is arising.[21] The rise of the middle class is seen as a possible danger for India. Commenting upon a trivial episode of bullying of which he and Moravia were the victims and perpetrated by a small group of young men of the middle class, Pasolini says:

> Voglia il cielo che questa non sia la strada dell'appena formata borghesia indiana. Certo, oggettivamente, il pericolo c'è. I deboli hanno una forte tendenza a diventare violenti, i fragili a diventare feroci: sarebbe terribile che un popolo di quattrocento milioni di abitanti, che in questo momento ha un così forte peso nella scena storica e nel mondo, si occidentalizzasse in questo modo meccanico e deteriore. Tutto c'è da augurare a questo popolo fuorché l'esperienza borghese, che finirebbe per diventare di tipo balcanico, spagnolo o borbonico. (*L'odore dell'India*, pp. 71–72)

Here again, as in *Aracoeli*, we find the opposition peasant/bourgeois, which in this case marks the difference between India and Europe. We perceive that in India the bourgeois order and a mechanical acceptance of industrialization are likely to become a deterioration of the peasant dimension (something which, however, has also occurred in some European realities). The peasant condition is thus indirectly presented as more authentic than the bourgeois one.

However, industrialization and westernization are likely to pervade India very slowly, as India — like Aracoeli — in her primitiveness never changes, escaping history and mutation. Crows are everywhere in India, and for Pasolini it is as if they keep saying that India is always the same: 'I gridi delle cornacchie ci seguono, più o meno fitti e disordinati, per tutta l'India. È una iterazione significativa: pare che dicano: siamo sempre qui, perché l'India è sempre così' (*L'odore dell'India*, p. 95);[22] also, the carts used by the Indian peasants are very simple, like those invented by men thousands of years ago:

> Sono carrette elementari, quelle inventate dall'uomo due o tremila anni fa: un cassone su due ruote piene, e, davanti, il bufalo che trascina paziente il vecchio peso di membra umane, scure e coperte di stracci bianchi, o del mucchio di canne. (*L'odore dell'India*, p. 96)

Moravia also speaks about the way India escapes history. A beautiful chapter of Moravia's book is entitled 'Nightmares and Mirages', a title that perfectly embodies the polarization between attraction and repulsion which India provokes in a European visitor. In this chapter Moravia discusses the strong impression of unreality that always accompanies the traveller in his wanderings around India, where unreality and illusion were actually also elaborated as fundamental philosophical concepts. The first appearance of unreality is the nightmare: the climate itself is always cruel, both in winter and in the monsoon season, the caste system is absurd, the miserable living conditions are unbelievable, and Indian architecture is monstrous.[23] But even beauty in India is connected to unreality: a beautiful Indian landscape is always vague, and quite often beautiful examples of art and architecture impress the traveller's memory as a snapshot that cannot be related to any historical context, to any concrete civilization:

> Questo miraggio è proprio in India anche delle opere degli uomini quando sono belle e in accordo con l'ambiente naturale. Niente è più irreale di certe cittadine fortificate che sorgono improvvise dalle irreali pianure indiane. [. . .]

> rimangono nella memoria piuttosto come apparizioni incantevoli di incerta origine e significato che come aspetti concreti di una civiltà ben distinta. Chi le fondò e costruì? Che cosa vi avvenne? Quando furono prospere e potenti e quando decaddero? Nell'assenza di storia o meglio del senso della storia in India (gli indiani hanno il senso dei cicli cosmici, non quello dei cicli storici) tutte queste domande sembrano futili; e se ne conferma il carattere di magico trucco che il pensiero religioso dell'India attribuisce al mondo degli uomini con le sue glorie e le sue vicende. (Moravia, *Un'idea dell'India*, pp. 88–89)

Thus, diversity and otherness, and the reaction to them, seem to be represented in a comparable way in *Aracoeli, L'odore dell'India* and *Un'idea dell'India*. My analysis may therefore contribute to outlining the relationship between Elsa Morante's late works and the Indian/Eastern world, which in my opinion still plays an important role — as a reference point — in the author's cultural universe at the time when she is writing *Aracoeli*. At this point we can answer my first guiding question: are there Indian traces in *Aracoeli*?

In this connection, Concetta D'Angeli proposes a stimulating reflection. According to this scholar, in *Aracoeli* Elsa Morante, among the other meanings and paradigms related to the dimension of the journey, also attaches to it the derision of the journeys to India and the East that, during the 1960s, had become a fashion in some milieux of the Italian left wing. These journeys were perceived as the search for a spiritual and cultural identity, to be achieved through religions other than Christianity, as the latter had lost its guiding role.

D'Angeli identifies a symbol, appearing both in Morante's *Il mondo salvato dai ragazzini* and in *Aracoeli*, as the measure of the author's rejection of the fashion of the journeys to India that had marked her own generation. This symbol is represented by the stairs, which — in D'Angeli's opinion — undergo a kind of decline from *Il mondo salvato dai ragazzini* to *Aracoeli*. At the end of *Serata a Colono*, a section of *Il mondo salvato dai ragazzini*, the seven-door stairs appear. Every step of these stairs corresponds to a coloured door, which — according to D'Angeli — is a step on an existential path in which knowledge and wisdom are progressively acquired. The progression of the colours goes as follows: green, turquoise, red, yellow, white, and black. The last door is the door of emptiness. D'Angeli interprets the symbol of the stairs in *Serata a Colono* as a collective and shared path, meaningful to all human beings. On the contrary, in the passage of *Aracoeli* where Manuele explicitly recalls this symbol, the stairs, 'la scala', is said to be 'storta, zoppa e lunatica', and — D'Angeli states — it cannot but refer to a private, individual, unhappy destiny, where no meaning can be found.[24] The passage from *Aracoeli* referred to reads as follows:

> Così torna a lusingarmi senza fine il mito orientale della scala cromatica. La scala è discendente, ogni colore è una porta. In fondo a ogni rampa si lascia un grado dello spettro, e la porta s'apre. Finché, di grado in grado, si arriva alla porta del nero e di qui, spogliati, alla porta infima ossia suprema: la porta del vuoto. Ma la mia scala è storta, zoppa e lunatica. A ogni tratto, un sasso che mi fa inciampare; un intoppo che mi blocca; uno scalino rotto che mi fa rotolare in una frana; un incrocio o un segnale falso o un tranello che mi imbrogliano, mi sviano, mi rimandano indietro. Indietro e avanti e di nuovo indietro, senza

> regola né direzione. E infine mi ritrovo in capo alla scala, sulla bocca del suo pozzo vertiginoso. (pp. 1247–48)

As D'Angeli affirms, it is not easy to understand the last part of *Serata a Colono*, where the stairs appear.[25] She reminds us that Morante herself, in the above-cited passage from *Aracoeli*, explicitly refers to an oriental religious symbolism, even though she does not better define it. D'Angeli suggests that Morante may have used an indication that can be found in Simone Weil's *Cahiers*, an important source for the author. Simone Weil takes note of a Babylonian text describing seven doors: to each door one divests oneself of something. However, according to D'Angeli the colours associated with each of the doors in *Serata a Colono* recall those of the mandala, and the liberation interpreted as a cancellation of individuality points at a Buddhist context, possibly mediated by Beat poetry. This context would suggest a cathartic interpretation of the end of *Serata a Colono*, where tensions and contradictions seem to fade away. However, as D'Angeli herself points out, the final harmony of *Serata a Colono* remains ambiguous, and the reference to a poem by Hölderlin — 'O sacro Essere!' — at the very end of the text evokes a tragic dimension, a deep hiatus between the divine unchangeable peace and the human transitory condition.[26] Thus, the end of *Serata a Colono* would rather suggest self-destruction than liberation.[27]

I would like to add a couple of remarks to this frame. The colours associated with the steps of the stairs are not necessarily those of the mandalas, and I am not convinced that such colours are actually meant to recall these images. However, I agree that in the final passage of *Serata a Colono* there is a reference to Buddhism, even though, in my opinion, such a reference is not linked to the allusion to a final liberation conceived of as a cancellation of individuality, which would be the case in many branches of Hinduism as well, but to the explicit reference to emptiness, which is a main concept in various Buddhist traditions.[28] Except for these details, I agree with the general frame reconstructed by D'Angeli: the end of *Serata a Colono* is quite problematic and ambiguous, it is a tensional moment and not a releasing one.

It is exactly for this reason that I see some continuity in the use of the symbol of the stairs in *Il mondo salvato dai ragazzini* and in *Aracoeli*. The symbolism of the stairs remains ambiguous in both the texts, and in *Aracoeli* it may also be related to a path of knowledge — which is in the end the journey itself — even if it results in being slippery, deceptive, and obliges Manuele to change direction continuously. Furthermore, I find it interesting to note that the stairs symbolism also appears in a section of *Il mondo salvato dai ragazzini* entitled 'La commedia chimica', and in particular in a poem entitled 'La sera domenicale'. Here the stairs are not explicitly associated with an oriental world, and we do not find any allusion to a descent through a series of coloured doors or to the door of emptiness. It is worth quoting the whole passage:

> Non tentare l'itinerario
> storpio e rovinoso della scala, che per te è un'ascensione di secoli,
> e di sopra e di sotto c'è l'inferno.
> Il cielo decaduto è la bassa tenda cenciosa
> del lazzaretto terrestre. E il flauto mozartiano

> è un saltarello maligno, che ti ribatte
> fin dentro il bulbo dell'occhio la sua triviale mimica
> di un'aritmetica ossessiva che non significa altro. . .
> Nessun cielo ulteriore si scopre. Non s'apre il loto dai mille petali.
> Tu sei tutta qui. E non c'è altro.
> Assisti a questo. E cessa di chiamare
> amanti morti, madri morte.
> Denudàti, piú poveri ancora di te, loro non frequentano questa
> né altre dimensioni. Ultima loro dimora
> resta soltanto la tua memoria.[29]

I believe that this passage is very interesting in relation both to *Serata a Colono* and to *Aracoeli*. On the one hand, once again it shows that the stairs symbolism is not univocally connoted in a positive way in *Il mondo salvato dai ragazzini*. The very description of the stairs path as 'storpio e rovinoso' recalls the semantic area used in *Aracoeli*, where the scala is 'storta, zoppa e lunatica'. We also find here, a few lines after the stairs are mentioned, an allusion to the Indian Tantric tradition: the one thousand petals lotus, that is the highest *chakra*, the opening of which corresponds to the union with the Absolute, to the conclusion of the spiritual path of knowledge and transformation undergone by the *yogi*. The lotus of the quoted lines will not open, which confirms that in *Il mondo salvato dai ragazzini* the path of knowledge is ambiguous, and it may be as slippery and deceptive as it appears to be in *Aracoeli*. Moreover, I find that the lines following the reference to the lotus propose at least two themes that will become the focus of *Aracoeli*: the search for the dead mother and the centrality of memory. But, while 'La sera domenicale' forbids us to undergo the research path, *Aracoeli* is exactly an attempt to follow it, thus showing that *Aracoeli* can be read as a path of knowledge.

Of course, I do not think that the path of knowledge in *Aracoeli* is fully resolved in a positive and harmonious way. Yet, I believe that in the text there is a strain towards an integrity, which is researched in many directions, the most important of which is perhaps the union of opposites. It is quite evident that a series of opposites are coexistent in the text: the sacred and the profane Aracoeli, the blessed (in his early childhood, as a handsome baby) and the damned (after Aracoeli's rejection, as an ugly adult) Manuele, and so on. The indication that these opposites may be unified, integrated into one another, is suggested, for instance, when Manuele says that he loves both the chaste and the nymphomaniac Aracoeli as a hybrid.[30] But at least in one passage Morante explicitly refers to the possibility of this union, saying that perhaps it is 'our goal'. In this passage Morante also explicitly mentions the Indian (Brahmanical) tradition, which thus leaves here a trace, in the context of the reference to a series of intoxicating substances that may lead to the final union of opposites. Of course, this reference must also be read in relation to the use of hallucinogenic substances by Morante, mirrored in the frequent references in *Aracoeli* to Manuele's use of drugs. It is worth reading this passage:

> Gli dei non sono maciullati dalla macchina dei sensi. Sono integri. Passato presente e futuro — tenebre e luce — morte e vita — i multipli e gli addendi — i diversi e i contrari — per loro sono tutti uno. Forse il nostro traguardo è QUELLO. Né sarebbe lecito negare che il succo dell'integrità deificante possa

scoprircisi in qualche semplice prodotto della terra. Come in un grappolo d'uva stava nascosta l'ebbrezza, e il coraggio in una foglia di coca, e la quiete e l'estasi in un papavero, e in un fungo le rivelazioni brahmanniche dei misteri — e ogni specie di medicamenti e rimedi prodigiosi e guarigioni in povere erbe, semi impercettibili e cortecce muffe — si può supporre che davvero un qualche minimo germe o spora della vegetazione sterminata sia l'occulto portatore della nostra metamorfosi definitiva. Né si esclude poi che il Signore, nei suoi responsi, ricorra a simboli o metafore: il nascondiglio del 'frutto' segreto si potrebbe anche cercare, forse, in altri regni della natura. Potrebbe essere una pietra, un'ala d'insetto, una cenere d'ossa; o magari una parola inventata, un pensiero mai concepito da nessuno. . . Allora si vedranno le cose invisibili, e si capiranno quelle incomprese, e quelle perdute si restituiranno.
'Che le tenebre diventino tenebre luminose
e la luce diventi luce tenebrosa'.

(*Aracoeli*, pp. 1289–90)

Interestingly, Morante explicitly refers again to Indian culture in another passage where she plays with opposites, and with a transformation process. Manuele — after taking drugs — has a 'vision' of himself transformed into a beautiful Indian girl, perhaps a sacred dancer:

> Ero una fanciulla indiana bellissima (forse una danzatrice sacra?) vestita di stoffa leggera e preziosa, di tutti i colori dell'iride. E con passo allegro, quasi di ballo, scendevo verso la mia fossa. Due falchi neri, precedendomi in un volo basso, mi insegnavano la strada; e mi lasciavano sull'orlo della fossa già scavata, da cui divampavano pronte le fiamme della mia cremazione. In un salto, il mio snello corpicino spariva dentro le fiamme: le quali immediatamente si trasmutavano in fiori estivi, oscillanti sui lunghi steli. Ma questa era soltanto una prima metamorfosi: poichè subito i fiori, a loro volta, si trasmutavano in lunghe piume variopinte, per comporsi definitivamente a formare un uccello fantastico, di tutti i colori dell'iride. Una fenice! La quale, sollevandosi a volo, si dileguava in alto. [. . .] Rammento che non provai nessuna sorpresa a riconoscermi nella fanciulla indiana trasformata in fenice. Credetti, anzi, d'intendere che la parabola alludeva in trasparenza al vero tema occulto (ignoto anche a me stesso) d'ogni mia vicenda: come un oroscopo radioso leggibile in filigrana sulla cartaccia del mio povero calendario. E la mia fantasia drogata si lusingò, per una sera, di quella piccola epifania: tanto che oggi pure, qui a Gergal, la reminiscenza me ne riporta un sentore d'incensi magici. (*Aracoeli*, pp. 1214–15)

It is evident that here there is also a reference to Manuele's homosexuality, but the protagonist's comfort with himself as a girl suggests the possibility of unifying opposites, in this case male and female. Also, the phoenix myth evokes a positive conclusion of the transformation path, clearly alluding to rebirth and regeneration.

Interestingly, the Indian sacred dancer was originally a girl, 'married' to a deity, who took care of the temple and practised classical Indian dance and art, thus enjoying a high social status. Starting from the colonial period, the sacred dancer is also closely attached to immorality, as she has sexual intercourses outside marriage. Moreover, in modern India this practice often conceals exploitation in prostitution. Elsa Morante might have been aware of this perspective and in this case the Indian sacred dancer would also convey an indirect reference to the wild immoral sexuality that characterizes Aracoeli at the end of her life.

Like Aracoeli, in his journey Manuele challenges the civilized, logical world he comes from, in a constant search for an integrity that is to be found beyond any binary oppositions. In this perspective, the references to the Indian world may well represent a motif suitable to hint at transcending such oppositions, which — starting at least from Aristotle — are often recognized as a mark of Western culture. Considering the whole frame of the novel, the Indian traces in the novel allude to a union of opposites and seem connected to an attempt to integrate the Other represented by Aracoeli herself, in a sort of strain towards the alternative order that she embodies.

Notes to Chapter 14

1. Cf. Concetta D'Angeli, *Leggere Elsa Morante: 'Aracoeli', 'La Storia', e 'Il mondo salvato dai ragazzini'* (Rome: Carocci, 2003), p. 7.
2. Cf. D'Angeli, *Leggere Elsa Morante*, pp. 26–28.
3. Cf. D'Angeli, *Leggere Elsa Morante*, p. 29.
4. Cf. D'Angeli, *Leggere Elsa Morante*, pp. 27–29.
5. Adalgisa Giorgio, 'Nature vs Culture: Repression, Rebellion and Madness in Elsa Morante's *Aracoeli*', in *MLN*, 109.1, Italian issue (January 1994), 93–116 (p. 95).
6. Elsa Morante, *Aracoeli*, in *Opere*, ed. by Carlo Cecchi and Cesare Garboli, 2 vols (Milan: Mondadori, 1988–90), II (1990), pp. 1039–1454 (p. 1164). Further references to this edition will be given after quotations in the text.
7. Cf. *Aracoeli*, p. 1272.
8. I would like to point out here that Aracoeli was an illiterate, a feature which contributes to the characterization of her as a 'primitive'.
9. On the use of similes in *Aracoeli*, cf. Giovanna Rosa, *Cattedrali di carta: Elsa Morante romanziere* (Milan: Il Saggiatore, 2006), p. 320. The one just mentioned is not the only passage in the text suggesting the affinity between Aracoeli and animals. For instance, towards the end of the novel, when Manuele sees his mother for the last time at the hospital, we find another parallel between Aracoeli and an animal, as her face 'somigliava al muso triangolare di una bestiola' (*Aracoeli*, p. 1415).
10. As to Aracoeli's proximity to nature, at the very beginning of the novel Manuele also explicitly says that Aracoeli has a 'fisionomia intatta della natura' (p. 1050).
11. Giorgio, 'Nature vs Culture', p. 102.
12. Rosa, *Cattedrali di carta*, p. 330.
13. See Edward Said, *Orientalism* (New York: Vintage, 1979).
14. In this respect, many Indologists have argued in favour of Indian philosophy, aiming to reconsider the concept of philosophy itself in the light of Eastern thought. See, for instance, Carmen Dragonetti and Fernando Tola, *On the Myth of the Opposition between Indian Thought and Western Philosophy* (Hildesheim: Georg Olms, 2004); Johannes Bronkhorst, 'Perché esiste la filosofia in India?', in *Verso l'India. Oltre l'India: Scritti e ricerche sulle tradizioni intellettuali sudasiatiche*, ed. by Federico Squarcini (Milan: Mimesis, 2002), pp. 131–52.
15. Pier Paolo Pasolini, *L'odore dell'India* (Parma: Guanda, 2005); Alberto Moravia, *Un'idea dell'India* (Milan: Bompiani, 2005). Further references to these editions of Pasolini and Moravia's works will be given after quotations in the text.
16. Both Pasolini and Moravia's pieces on India were published by two Italian newspapers: Pasolini's pieces were published by *Il Giorno* between February and March 1961, while Moravia's were published by *Il Corriere della Sera* between February and July 1961.
17. As to these different approaches to India, I agree with the main critical literature on them, well summarized by Tonino Tornitore:
    > Pasolini è l'occhio discreto, Moravia è l'occhio sintetico sul continuo: il primo è catturato dal particolare, da cui egli deriva non solo le sue reazioni umane, viscerali, ma lo assurge a

emblema [. . .]. Insomma con Moravia si ha sempre la sensazione di guardare il mondo con il telescopio, e il dettaglio, l'aneddoto è sempre il tassello o il microcosmo di un panorama; con Pasolini guardiamo al microscopio, e si avverte, dietro all'osservatore che descrive, l'uomo che sente e che riconduce tutto un universo a un particolare minuto e soggettivo. (Tonino Tornitore, 'Moravia e l'India', in Alberto Moravia, *Un'idea dell'India*, pp. v–xxvii)

18. Enzo Siciliano, *Alberto Moravia* (Milan: Bompiani, 1982), p. 94.
19. For an interesting analysis of Pasolini's text in the light of post-colonial studies, one can refer to Luca Caminati, *Orientalismo eretico: Pier Paolo Pasolini e il cinema del Terzo Mondo* (Milan: B. Mondadori, 2007), pp. 11–29. On the same topic, now see also Giuliana Benvenuti, *Il viaggiatore come autore: l'India nella letteratura italiana del Novecento* (Bologna: Il Mulino, 2008).
20. Cf. 'L'esperienza dell'India: Un'intervista di Renzo Paris ad Alberto Moravia', in *Un'idea dell'India*, pp. xxxiii–xxxiv.
21. Cf. Pasolini, *L'odore dell'India*, pp. 40, 70, 61.
22. It is interesting to notice that this quotation is found in the context of a description of the Indian landscape, which never changes ('Ma un cambiamento vero non avviene mai', affirms Pasolini referring to the landscape, just a few lines after mentioning the crows). Yet, the whole passage strongly conveys the impression not only of a lack of spatial mutation, but even of temporal change. Luca Caminati also detects this characterization of India as ahistorical in Pasolini's text. Relating Pasolini's description of India to Homi Bhabha's analysis of the rhetoric devices mostly used by Western travellers in the Third World to report their experiences, Caminati affirms:
    Chi più da vicino ha cercato di scrivere una tassonomia delle strategie retoriche del narratore occidentale nel Terzo Mondo è il già citato critico post-lacaniano Homi Bhabha. In particolare il suo volume di saggi *Location of Culture* [. . .] individua e apre all'interpretazione alcune strategie retoriche come lo stereotipo, la ripetizione e l'a-storicità che sono ben visibili nelle pagine del libro. Questi 'esseri favolosi senza radici' sono bloccati, 'fissati', in un non-tempo mitico. (Caminati, p. 22)
23. Cf. Moravia, *Un'idea dell'India*, pp. 85–87.
24. D'Angeli, pp. 29–30.
25. D'Angeli, p. 138.
26. Cf. Morante, *Il mondo salvato dai ragazzini*, p. 96.
27. On the stairs symbolism interpreted by D'Angeli, cf. D'Angeli, *Leggere Elsa Morante*, pp. 138–39.
28. The term emptiness is a usual translation for the Sanskrit *shunyata*, which is a key concept especially in Nagarjuna's philosophy.
29. Morante, *Il mondo salvato dai ragazzini*, p. 28.
30. Cf. p. 164.

BIBLIOGRAPHY

Works by Elsa Morante

Collected Works

Opere, ed. by Carlo Cecchi and Cesare Garboli, 2 vols (Milan: Mondadori, 1988–90)

Prose Works

Qualcuno bussa alla porta, 'I diritti della scuola', 1–29, 25 September 1935–15 August 1936
Le bellissime avventure di Caterí dalla trecciolina (Turin: Einaudi, 1941). Reprinted with amendments as *Le straordinarie avventure di Caterina* (Turin: Einaudi, 1959)
Il gioco segreto (Milan: Garzanti, 1941)
Menzogna e sortilegio (Turin: Einaudi, 1948)
L'isola di Arturo (Turin: Einaudi, 1957)
Lo scialle andaluso (Turin: Einaudi, 1963)
La Storia (Turin: Einaudi, 1974). Available in English as *History: A novel*, trans. by William Weaver (New York: Knopf, 1977)
Aracoeli (Turin: Einaudi, 1982). Available in English as *Aracoeli*, trans. by William Weaver (New York: Random House, 1984)
Racconti dimenticati (Turin: Einaudi, 2002)

Poetry

Alibi (Milan: Longanesi, 1958)
Il mondo salvato dai ragazzini e altri poemi (Turin: Einaudi, 1968)

Essays

Pro o contro la bomba atomica e altri scritti, ed. by Cesare Garboli (Milan: Adelphi, 1987)
'Piccolo manifesto' e altri scritti (Milan: Linea d'ombra, 1988)
Diario 1938, ed. by Alda Andreini (Turin: Einaudi, 2005)

Translations

Katherine Mansfield, *Il libro degli appunti* (Milan: Rizzoli, 1945)

Other Works

ABELLÁN, JOSE LUIS, *María Zambrano: Una pensadora de nuestro tiempo* (Barcelona: Anthropos. Huellas de los saberes de la historia, 2006)
AGAMBEN, GIORGIO, *Profanazioni* (Rome: Nottetempo, 2005)
AGAMBEN, GIORGIO, and OTHERS, eds, *Per Elsa Morante* (Milan: Linea d'ombra, 1993)
ALIGHIERI, DANTE, *Opere minori*, 2 vols (Milan and Naples: Ricciardi, 1984–89)
—— *Commedia*, ed. by Anna Maria Chiavacci Leonardi, 3 vols (Milan: Mondadori, 1991–1997)

ANDREINI, ALBA, 'La Morante e il diario: autoritratto di donna e di scrittrice', in *Elsa Morante: La voce di una scrittrice e di un'intellettuale rivolta al secolo XIX*, ed. by Elisa Martínez Garrido (Madrid: Universidad Complutense de Madrid, 2003), pp. 9–22

ARENDT, HANNAH, *El concepto de amor en san Agustín* (Madrid: Ediciones Encuentro, 2001)

AUERBACH, ERICH, 'Sermo Humilis', in *Literary Language and its Public in Late Latin Antiquity and in the Middle Ages*, trans. by Ralph Manheim (New York: Pantheon Books, 1965), pp. 25–66

BARAŃSKI, ZYGMUNT, 'I trionfi del volgare: Dante e il plurilinguismo', in *'Sole nuovo, luce nuova': Saggi sul rinnovamento culturale in Dante* (Turin: Scriptorium, 1996), pp. 41–78

BARDINI, MARCO, 'Dei "fantastici Doppi" ovvero la mimesi narrativa dello spostamento psichico', in *Per Elisa: Studi su 'Menzogna e sortilegio'*, ed. by Lucio Lugnani and others (Pisa: Nistri-Lischi, 1990), pp. 173–299

—— *Morante Elsa. Italiana. Di professione, poeta* (Pisa: Nistri-Lischi, 1999), pp. 555–616

—— 'Realtà ed esperienza estetica negli scritti saggistici di Elsa Morante', in *Elsa Morante: La voce di una scrittrice e di un'intellettuale rivolta al secolo XXI*, ed. by Martínez Garrido (Madrid: Universidad Complutense de Madrid, 2003), pp. 23–36

BAROLINI, TEODOLINDA, *The Undivine 'Comedy': Detheologizing Dante* (Princeton: Princeton University Press, 1992)

BAZZOCCHI, MARCO, *Corpi che parlano: Il nudo nella letteratura italiana del Novecento* (Milan: B. Mondadori, 2005)

BELL, DAVID, *Paranoia* (London: Icon Books, 2002)

BENEDETTI, CARLA and MARIA ANTONIETTA GRIGNANI, eds, *A partire da Petrolio: Pasolini interroga la letteratura* (Ravenna: Longo, 1995)

BENEDETTI, LAURA, *The Tigress in the Snow: Motherhood and Literature in Twentieth-Century Italy* (Toronto: University of Toronto Press, 2007)

BENJAMIN, JESSICA, *Like Subjects, Love Objects: Essays on Recognition and Sexual Difference* (New Haven: Yale University Press, 1995)

—— 'The Rhythm of Recognition: Comments on the Work of Louis Sander', *Psychoanalytic Dialogues*, 12.1 (2002), 43–54

BENJAMIN, WALTER, 'Il narratore: Considerazioni sull'opera di Nicola Leskov', in *Angelus Novus: Saggi e frammenti*, ed. by Renato Solmi (Turin: Einaudi, 1995)

—— *Berlin Childhood around 1900*, trans. by Howard Eiland (Cambridge, MA: Belknap Press of Harvard University Press, 2006)

BENVENUTI, GIULIANA, *Il viaggiatore come autore: l'India nella letteratura italiana del Novecento* (Bologna: Il Mulino, 2008)

BERSANI, LEO, *The Freudian Body: Psychoanalysis and Art* (New York: Columbia University Press, 1986)

—— *The Culture of Redemption* (Cambridge, MA: Harvard University Press, 1990)

BOWLBY, JOHN, *A Secure Base* (London: Basic Books, 1988)

BROMBERG, PHILIP M., *Standing in the Spaces: Essays on Clinical Process, Trauma, and Dissociation* (Hillsdale, NJ: The Analytic Press, 1998)

BRONKHORST, JOHANNES, 'Perché esiste la filosofia in India?', in *Verso l'India. Oltre l'India: Scritti e ricerche sulle tradizioni intellettuali sudasiatiche*, ed. by Federico Squarcini (Milan: Mimesis, 2002), pp. 131–52

BUSI, GIULIO, *I simboli del pensiero ebraico: Lessico ragionato in settanta voci* (Turin: Einaudi, 1999)

BUTLER, JUDITH, *Gender Trouble: Feminism and the Subversion of Identity* (New York: Routledge, 1990)

—— *Bodies That Matter: On the Discursive Limits of 'Sex'* (New York and London: Routledge, 1993)

—— 'Melancholy Gender — Refused Identification', in *The Psychic Life of Power: Theories of Subjection* (Stanford: Stanford University Press, 1997), pp. 132–50

CAMINATI, LUCA, *Orientalismo eretico: Pier Paolo Pasolini e il cinema del Terzo Mondo* (Milan: B. Mondadori, 2007)
CAVARERO, ADRIANA, *Tu che mi guardi, tu che mi racconti: Filosofia della narrazione* (Milan: Feltrinelli, 1997)
—— *A più voci: Filosofia dell'espressione vocale* (Milan: Feltrinelli, 2003)
CESTARO, GARY, '". . . quanquam Sarnum biberimus ante dentes. . .": The Primal Scene of Suckling in Dante's *De vulgari eloquentia*', *Dante Studies*, 109 (1991), 119–47
—— *Dante and the Grammar of the Nursing Body* (Notre Dame and London: Notre Dame University Press, 2003)
CHIAVACCI LEONARDI, ANNA MARIA, '"Le bianche stole": il tema della resurrezione nel *Paradiso*', in *Dante e la Bibbia*, ed. by Giovanni Barblan (Florence: Olschki, 1988), pp. 249–71
CIVES, SIMONA, 'Elsa Morante: "Senza i conforti della religione"', in *Le stanze di Elsa*, ed. by Giuliana Zagra and Simonetta Buttò (Rome: Colombo, 2006), pp. 49–65
CIXOUS, HÉLÈNE, *'Coming to Writing' and Other Essays*, trans. by Deborah Jenson (Cambridge, MA and London: Harvard University Press, 1991)
CRITCHLEY, SIMON, *Infinitely Demanding: Ethics of Commitment, Politics of Resistance* (London: Verso, 2007)
D'ANGELI, CONCETTA, 'Il paradiso nella storia', *Studi novecenteschi*, 21 (1994), 215–35
—— 'Due donne appassionate: Elsa Morante e Simone Weil', in *Elsa Morante: La voce di una scrittrice e di un'intellettuale rivolta al secolo XXI*, ed. by Elisa Martínez Garrido (Madrid: Universidad Complutense de Madrid, 2003), pp. 61–70
—— *Leggere Elsa Morante: 'Aracoeli', 'La Storia', e 'Il mondo salvato dai ragazzini'* (Rome: Carocci, 2003)
—— and GIACOMO MAGRINI, eds, *Vent'anni dopo 'La Storia': Omaggio a Elsa Morante*, Atti del Convegno (Pisa, 24–26 gennaio 1994), *Studi novecenteschi* [Special Issue], 47–48 (June–December 1994)
DANIÉLOU, ALAIN, *Gods of Love and Ecstasy: The Traditions of Shiva and Dionysus* (Rochester: Inner Traditions, 1992)
DELEDDA, GRAZIA, *Cenere*, <http://www.liberliber.it>
D'ELIA, GIANNI, *Il petrolio delle stragi* (Milan: Effigie, 2006)
DESIDERI, FABRIZIO, 'Apocalissi profana: figure della verità in Walter Benjamin', in Walter Benjamin, *Angelus Novus: Saggi e frammenti*, ed. by Renato Solmi (Turin: Einaudi, 1995), pp. 309–39
DEVEREUX, GEORGE, *Baubo: die mytische Vulva*, trans. by Eva Moldenhauer (Frankfurt a.M.: Syndikat, 1981)
DICKINSON, EMILY, *The Complete Poems of Emily Dickinson*, ed. by T. H. Johnson (Boston: Little Brown & Co., 1960)
DI PASCALE, ANNA MARIA, 'Senza i conforti di alcuna religione', in *Vent'anni dopo 'La Storia': Omaggio a Elsa Morante. Atti del Convegno (Pisa, 24–26 gennaio 1994)*, ed. by Concetta D'Angeli and Giacomo Magrini, *Studi novecenteschi* [Special Issue], 47–48 (June–December 1994), 287–302
DRAGONETTI, CARMEN and FERNANDO TOLA, *On the Myth of the Opposition between Indian Thought and Western Philosophy* (Hildesheim: Georg Olms, 2004)
FONAGY, PETER, 'Attachment and Borderline Personality Disorder', *Journal of the American Psychoanalytic Association*, 48.4 (2000), 1129–46
—— MARY TARGET, GYORGY GERGELY, and ELLIOT L. JURIST, *Affect Regulation, Mentalization and the Development of Self* (New York: Other Press, 2005)
FORTINI, FRANCO, *Attraverso Pasolini* (Turin: Einaudi, 1993)
FORTUNA, SARA, *Il laboratorio del simbolico* (Perugia: Guerra, 2005)
—— and MANUELE GRAGNOLATI, '"Attaccando al suo capezzolo le mie labbra ingorde": corpo, linguaggio e soggettività da Dante ad *Aracoeli* di Elsa Morante', *Nuova Corrente*, 55 (2008), 85–123

―――― 'Allattamento e origine del linguaggio tra la *Commedia* dantesca e *Aracoeli* di Elsa Morante', in *Parole di donne*, ed. by Francesca Maria Dovetto (Milan: Aracne, 2009), pp. 271–303.

FREUD, SIGMUND, 'Trauer und Melancholie', in *Gesammelte Werke*, X (Frankfurt a.M.: Suhrkamp, 1999), pp. 428–46

―――― 'Three Essays on the Theory of Sexuality', in *The Standard Edition of the Complete Psychological Works of Sigmund Freud*, ed. by James Strachey, 24 vols (London: Vintage, 2001), VII, 125–245

―――― 'Instincts and their Vicissitudes', in *The Standard Edition*, XIV, 109–40

―――― 'Mourning and Melancholia', in *The Standard Edition*, XIV, 236–60

―――― 'A Child is Being Beaten', in *The Standard Edition*, XVII, 175–204

―――― 'Beyond the Pleasure Principle', in *The Standard Edition*, XVIII, 1–64

―――― 'Mourning and Melancholia' in *On Murder, Mourning and Melancholia*, trans. by Shaun Whiteside (London: Penguin, 2005), pp. 203–18

GADDA, CARLO EMILIO, *La cognizione del dolore*, in *Romanzi e racconti*, ed. by Raffaella Rodondi, Guido Lucchini, and Emilio Manzotti, 2 vols (Milan: Garzanti, 1990), I, 571–772

―――― 'Intervista al microfono', in *I viaggi la morte*, in *Saggi giornali favole e altri scritti*, ed. by Liliana Orlando, Clelia Martignoni, and Dante Isella, 2 vols (Milan: Garzanti, 1991), I, 502–05.

GARBOLI, CESARE, *Il gioco segreto: Nove immagini di Elsa Morante* (Milan: Adelphi, 1995)

GINZBERG, LOUIS, *The Legend of the Jews*, trans. by Henrietta Szold, 4 vols (Philadelphia: The Jewish Publication Society of America, 1968)

GIOANOLA, GIORGIO, 'Elsa Morante e la storia', in *Elsa Morante. La voce di una scrittrice e di un'intellettuale rivolta al secolo XXI*, ed by Elisa Martínez Garrido (Madrid: Universidad Complatense de Madrid, 2003), pp. 71–83

GIORGIO, ADALGISA, 'Nature vs Culture: Repression, Rebellion and Madness in Elsa Morante's *Aracoeli*', *MLN*, 109.1, Italian Issue (January 1994), 93–116

―――― *Writing Mothers and Daughters: Renegotiating the Mother in Western European Narratives by Women* (Oxford and New York: Berghahn Books, 2002)

GOETHE, JOHANN WOLFGANG VON, *Faust: Part I*, trans. by Peter Salm (New York: Bantam Books, 1985)

GONZÁLEZ ECHEVARRÍA, ROBERTO, '*Don Quixote*: Crossed Eyes and Vision', in *Cervantes' 'Don Quixote': A Casebook*, ed. by Roberto González Echevarría (Oxford: Oxford University Press, 2005), pp. 217–39

GRAGNOLATI, MANUELE, *Experiencing the Afterlife: Soul and Body in Dante and Medieval Culture* (Notre Dame: Notre Dame University Press, 2005)

―――― 'Nostalgia in Heaven: Embraces, Affection and Identity in Dante's *Comedy*', in *Dante and the Human Body*, ed. by John Barnes and Jennifer Petrie (Dublin: Four Courts Press, 2007), pp. 91–111

GUATTARI, FÉLIX, 'Everybody Wants to Be a Fascist', in *Chaosophy*, ed. by Sylvère Lotringer, trans. by Susanne Fletcher (New York: Semiotext[e], 1995)

HERRNSTEIN SMITH, BARBARA, *Poetic Closure* (Chicago: University of Chicago Press, 1968)

HEYER-CAPUT, MARGHERITA, *Grazia Deledda's Dance of Modernity* (Toronto and London: University of Toronto Press, 2008)

HULIN, MICHEL, *Mística salvaje* (Madrid: Siruela, 2007)

IDEL, MOSHE, *Kabbalah and Eros* (New Haven and London: Yale University Press, 2005)

JACOBUS, MARY, *First Things: The Maternal Imaginary in Literature, Art, and Psychoanalysis* (New York and London: Routledge, 1995)

JUNG, CARL G., 'On the Psychology of the Unconscious', in *The Collected Works of C. G. Jung*, ed. by Herbert Read and others, trans. by R. F. C. Hull, 20 vols (London: Routledge & K. Paul, 1953–79), VII (1966)

―――'Symbols of Transformation', in *The Collected Works of C. G. Jung*, v (1956)
―――*La simbología del espíritu* (México: Fondo de Cultura Económico, 1981)
KERMODE, FRANK, *The Sense of an Ending* (Oxford: Oxford University Press, 1967)
KIERKEGAARD, SØREN, *Philosophical Fragments*, trans. by Edna H. Hong and Howard V. Hong (Princeton: Princeton University Press, 1985)
KOFMAN, SARAH, *Nietzsche et la scène philosophique* (Paris: Union Générale d'Éditions, 1979)
―――*Paroles suffoquées* (Paris: Galilée, 1987)
KRISTEVA, JULIA, *La Révolution du langage poétique: l'avant-garde à la fin du XIXe siècle. Lautréamont et Mallarmé* (Paris: Flammarion, 1974)
LAPLANCHE, JEAN, *Life and Death in Psychoanalysis*, trans. by Jeffrey Mehlman (Baltimore: Johns Hopkins University Press, 1976, repr. 1993)
―――*New Foundations for Psychoanalysis*, trans. by David Macey (Oxford: Blackwell, 1989)
―――and JEAN-BERTRAND PONTALIS, *Vocabulaire de la psychanalyse* (Paris: Presses universitaires de France, 1967)
―――――'Fantasy and the Origins of Sexuality' (1964), in *Formations of Fantasy*, ed. by Victor Burgin, James Donald, and Cora Kaplan (London and New York: Routledge, 1989), pp. 5–34
LA PORTA, FILIPPO, 'The "Dragon of Unreality" against the "Dream of a Thing": On Morante and Pasolini', in *Under Arturo's Star: The Cultural Legacies of Elsa Morante*, ed. by Stefania Lucamante and Sharon Wood (West Lafayette, IN: Purdue University Press, 2006), pp. 290–309
LINGIARDI, VITTORIO, 'Dreaming Gender: Restoration and Transformation', *Studies in Gender and Sexuality*, 8.4 (2007), 313–31
LUCAMANTE, STEFANIA, and SHARON WOOD, eds, *Under Arturo's Star: The Cultural Legacies of Elsa Morante* (West Lafayette, IN: Purdue University Press, 2006)
LUGNANI, LUCIO, and OTHERS, eds, *Per Elisa: Studi su 'Menzogna e sortilegio'* (Pisa: Nistri-Lischi, 1990)
MAGRINI, GIACOMO, 'Un paragone con Lowry', in *Per Elsa Morante*, ed. by Giorgio Agamben and others (Milan: Linea d'ombra, 1993), pp. 153–66
MARIANI, ANDREA, 'cerchio', in *Enciclopedia Dantesca*, ed. by Umberto Bosco, 2nd rev. edn, 6 vols (Rome: Enciclopedia d'Italia, 1984), I, 919–20
MARSET, JUAN CARLOS, *El exilio andaluz en México*, Catálogo de la Feria Internacional del Libro de Guadalajara, ed. by Junta de Andalucía (Sevilla: Renacimiento, 2006)
MARTÍNEZ GARRIDO, ELISA, 'Bestiario, allegoria e parola ne *La Storia* di Elsa Morante: Un'altra via al sacro', in *Elsa Morante: La voce di una scrittrice e di un'intellettuale rivolta al secolo XXI*, ed. by Elisa Martínez Garrido (Madrid: Universidad Complutense de Madrid, 2003), pp. 85–107
MATT, DANIEL C., ed. and trans., *Essential Kabbalah: the Heart of Jewish Mysticism* (San Francisco: Harper, 1995)
―――*Zohar: Annotated and Explained* (Woodstock, VT: Skylight Publishing, 2002)
―――*The Zohar* (Stanford, CA: Stanford University Press, 2004)
MOI, TORIL, ed., *The Kristeva Reader* (London: Blackwell, 1986)
MORAVIA, ALBERTO, *Un'idea dell'India* (Milan: Bompiani, 2005)
MORENO SANZ, JESÚS, *Ciencia de la compasión: Escritos sobre el Islam, el lenguaje místico y la fe brahamánica* (Madrid: Trotta, 1999)
MURARO, LUISA, *L'ordine simbolico della madre* (Rome: Editori Riuniti, 1991)
NIETZSCHE, FRIEDRICH, *Die fröhliche Wissenschaft*, in *Kritische Studienausgabe*, ed. by Giorgio Colli and Mazzino Montanari, 15 vols (Berlin; New York: de Gruyter, 1988), III
PASOLINI, PIER PAOLO, *Trasumanar e organizzar* (Milan: Garzanti, 1971)
―――*Amado mio, preceduto da Atti impuri* (Milan: Garzanti, 1982)
―――*Petrolio* (Turin: Einaudi, 1992); available in English as *Petrolio*, trans. by Ann Goldstein (New York: Pantheon, 1997)

—— *Tutte le poesie*, ed. by Walter Siti (Milan: Mondadori, 2003)
—— *L'odore dell'India* (Parma: Guanda, 2005)
PHILLIPS, ADAM, *The Beast in the Nursery* (London: Faber and Faber, 1998)
PISCHEDDA, BRUNO, *La grande sera del mondo: romanzi apocalittici nell'Italia del benessere* (Turin: Nino Aragno, 2004)
PORCIANI, ELENA, *L'alibi del sogno nella scrittura giovanile di Elsa Morante* (Soveria Mannelli: Iride, 2006)
POZZI, GIOVANNI, *Alternatim* (Milan: Adelphi, 1996)
RASKIN, RICHARD, *'Nuit et Brouillard' by Alain Resnais: On the Making, Reception and Functions of a Major Documentary Film*, with a foreword by Sacha Vierny (Aarhus: Aarhus University Press, 1987)
RASY, ELISABETTA, 'La bestia che parla', paper delivered at the conference on 'Gender and Italian Literary History' held at New York University in February 2008
RATZINGER, JOSEPH, *Christianity and the Crisis of Cultures* (San Francisco: Ignatius Press, 2006)
RE, LUCIA, 'Utopian Longing and the Constraints of Racial and Sexual Difference in Elsa Morante's *La Storia*', *Italica*, 70.3 (Autumn 1993), 361–75
ROSA, GIOVANNA, *Cattedrali di carta: Elsa Morante romanziere* (Milan: Il Saggiatore, 2006)
ROSENBERG, DAVID, *Dreams of Being Eaten Alive: The Literary Core of the Kabbalah* (New York: Harmony Books, 2000)
SAID, EDWARD, *Orientalism* (New York: Vintage, 1979)
SALERNO, PAOLO, ed., *Progetto Petrolio: una giornata di studi sul romanzo incompiuto di Pier Paolo Pasolini* (Bologna: CLUEB, 2006)
SANDER, LOUIS W., 'The event-structure of regulation in the neonate-caregiver system as a biological background for early organization of psychic structure', in *Frontiers in Self Psychology: Progress in Self Psychology*, III, ed. by Arnold Goldberg (Hillsdale, NJ: The Analytic Press, 1988)
—— 'Thinking Differently: Principles of Process in Living Systems and the Specificity of Being Known', *Psychoanalytic Dialogues*, 12.1 (2002), 11–42
SASS, LOUIS, *Madness and Modernism: Insanity in the Light of Modern Art, Literature and Thought* (New York: Basic Books, 1992)
SCHOLEM, GERSHOM, *Major Trends in Jewish Mysticism*, with a foreword by Robert Alter (New York: Schocken Books, 1995)
SCRIMIERI MARTÍN, ROSALIA, *Despertar el alma: Estudio junguiano sobre la 'Vita nuova'* (Madrid: Ediciones La Discreta, 2005)
SERKOWSKA, HANNA, *Uscire da una camera delle favole: I romanzi di Elsa Morante* (Krakow: Rabid, 2002)
—— 'The Maternal Boy: Manuele, or The Last Portrait of Morante's Androgyny', in *Under Arturo's Star: The Cultural Legacies of Elsa Morante*, ed. by Stefania Lucamante and Sharon Wood (West Lafayette, IN: Purdue University Press, 2006), pp. 157–87
SICILIANO, ENZO, *Alberto Moravia* (Milan: Bompiani, 1982)
SILVERMAN, KAJA, *The Acoustic Mirror: The Female Voice in Psychoanalysis and Cinema* (Bloomington: Indiana University Press, 1988)
SITI, WALTER, 'Elsa Morante nell'opera di Pier Paolo Pasolini', in *Vent'anni dopo 'La Storia': Omaggio a Elsa Morante*, ed. by Concetta D'Angeli and Giacomo Magrini, Atti del Convegno (Pisa, 24–26 gennaio 1994), *Studi novecenteschi* [Special Issue], 47–48 (June–December 1994), 131–48
—— 'Elsa Morante and Pier Paolo Pasolini', in *Under Arturo's Star: The Cultural Legacies of Elsa Morante*, ed. by Stefania Lucamante and Sharon Wood (West Lafayette, IN: Purdue University Press, 2006), pp. 268–89
STELLARDI, GIUSEPPE, 'L'alba della *Cognizione*: Gadda postmoderno?', in *Disharmony Established: Festschrift for Gian Carlo Roscioni*, Proceedings of the first EJGS international

conference, Edinburgh, 10–11 April 2003, ed. by Emilio Manzotti and Federica G. Pedriali, *Electronic Journal of Gadda Studies*, 4.3 (2004) <http://www.arts.ed.ac.uk/italian/gadda/Pages/journal/supp3atti1/articles/stellaconf1/articles/stellaconf1.php>
—— *Gadda: miseria e grandezza della letteratura* (Florence: Franco Cesati, 2006)
—— 'La violenza in Gadda', *Electronic Journal of Gadda Studies*, 6 (2007) www.arts.ed.ac.uk/italian/gadda/Pages/journal/issue6/articles/stellarviol06.php
—— 'Amleto', *Electronic Journal of Gadda Studies*, 3.1 (2008) <http://www.arts.ed.ac.uk/italian/gadda/Pages/resources/walks/pge/amletostellardi.php>
STERN, DANIEL N., *The Interpersonal World of the Infant* (New York: Basic Books, 1985)
___ *The Motherhood Constellation: A Unified View of Parent–Infant Psychotherapy* (New York: Basic Books, 1995)
TISHBY, ISAIAH, ed., *The Wisdom of the Zohar: An Anthology of Texts*, trans. by David Goldstein, 3 vols (Oxford University Press: Oxford, 1989)
TORNITORE, TONINO, 'Moravia e l'India', in Alberto Moravia, *Un'idea dell'India*, pp. v–xxvii
VICTORIA, NELSON, *The Secret Life of Puppets* (Cambridge, MA and London: Harvard University Press, 2001)
WALKER BYNUM, CAROLINE, 'Faith Imagining the Self: Somatomorphic Soul and Resurrection Body in Dante's *Divine Comedy*', in *Faithful Imagining: Essays in Honor of Richard R. Niebuhr*, ed. by Sang Hyun Lee, Wayne Proudfoot, and Albert Blackwell (Atlanta: Scholars Press, 1995), pp. 81–104
WARNER, MARINA, *No Go the Bogeyman: Scaring, Lulling and Making Mock* (London: Chatto and Windus, 1998)
WEIL, SIMONE, *L'ombra e la grazia* (Milan: Rusconi, 1985)
—— *Lettera a un religioso* (Milan: Adelphi, 1996)
—— *Prologue à la connaissance surnaturelle*, in *Œuvres* (Paris: Gallimard, 1999)
WILSON, ANDREW, *Beautiful Shadow: A Life of Patricia Highsmith* (New York and London: Bloomsbury, 2003)
WOLFSON, ELLIOT R., *Luminal Darkness: Imaginal Gleanings from Zoharic Literature* (Oxford: Oneworld, 2007)
WOOD, SHARON, 'The Bewitched Mirror: Imagination and Narration in Elsa Morante', *The Modern Language Review*, 86.2 (April 1991), 310–21
ZAMBRANO, MARÍA, *Hacia un saber sobre el alma* (Madrid: Alianza Editorial, 1987)
—— *El Hombre y lo divino* (Madrid: Fondo de Cultura Económica, 1993)
—— *La agonía de Europa* (Madrid: Siruela, 2000)
ZAMPOLINI, ANNA MARIA, 'Aracoeli: Morte di Narciso', in Gruppo la luna, *Letture di Elsa Morante* (Turin: Rosenberg and Sellier, 1987), pp. 55–58

Filmography

All about Eve. Dir. Joseph L. Mankiewicz. 20th Century Fox. 1950
Cries and whispers. Dir. Ingmar Bergman. Cinematograph AB. 1972
Il Vangelo secondo Matteo. Dir. Pier Paolo Pasolini. Arco Film. 1964
Mujeres al borde de un ataque de nervios. Dir. Pedro Almodóvar. El Deseo S.A. 1988
New York Stories. Dir. Woody Allen, Francis Ford Coppola, and Martin Scorsese. Touchstone Pictures. 1989
Respiro. Dir. Emanuele Crialese. Eurimages. 2002
Suddenly, Last Summer. Dir. Joseph L. Mankiewicz. Horizon Pictures (II). 1959
The Women. Dir. George Cukor. Metro-Goldwyn-Mayer (MGM). 1939
Todo sobre mi madre. Dir. Pedro Almodóvar. El Deseo S.A. 1999
Un'ora sola ti vorrei. Dir. Alina Marazzi. Bartlebyfilm. 2002
Volver. Dir. Pedro Almodóvar. Canal + España. 2006

INDEX

abjection, *see* psychoanalysis
Achilles 24
Agamben, Giorgio 35, 40 n. 15
Alighieri, Dante 2, 4, 8-15, 18 nn. 4, 6, & 11, 19 n. 16, 92, 104-05, 127 nn. 30 & 34, 152, 157, 161
allegory 73, 92, 121, 132, 154
Allen, Woody 69
Almodóvar, Pedro 3, 64, 67-71, 88, 90
ambiguity 26-27, 34, 43, 51, 55, 73, 76, 78, 91, 112, 118, 120, 138, 153, 166, 172-73
ambivalence 3-4, 32, 34, 44, 57 n. 8, 62, 76, 78-80, 152-53, 161, 164-65
anamorphosis 2, 14, 23-25, 29, 36, 112
  see also vision
androgyny 12-13, 18 n. 15, 57 n. 8, 89, 93, 115, 141
anti-Fascism 110-11, 120
  see also Fascism, Resistance
anti-Semitism 131, 137
apocalypse 35, 37, 146, 155
archetypes 62, 96, 124, 126 n. 30, 127 n. 34, 131
Arendt, Hannah 122, 126 n. 19
Auerbach, Erich 10
Augustine 122-23, 126 n. 19, 151-52, 154, 157
Auschwitz 114, 137, 151, 159
  see also Shoah

baroque 3, 4, 24, 78, 80, 88, 89, 96, 104
Barolini, Teodolinda 11
Bassani, Giorgio 142 n. 5
Baubo 3, 78-80, 83 n. 26, 115
Bazzocchi, Marco 19 n. 20
Beckett, Samuel 87
Bell, David 40 n. 20
Benjamin, Jessica 66
Benjamin, Walter 130-31, 150
Bergman, Ingmar 69
Bersani, Leo 40 n. 21, 57 n. 19
bisexuality, *see* sexuality
body 8-10, 13, 16-17, 26-27, 31, 33, 39 n. 10, 49, 53, 59, 68-70, 75-77, 91-94, 94 n. 2, 131-34, 136, 137, 139-42, 142 n. 11, 143 n. 17, 149, 151-52, 154, 156, 162-63
  blood 91, 105 n. 8, 121, 125 n. 15
  breast 2, 8-11, 13, 31, 46, 57 n. 9, 67, 92, 94, 113, 161
  milk 10-12, 14, 46, 92,
  tears 16, 38-39, 62, 64-65, 81, 102, 124, 157

borders 5, 32, 114, 119-20, 122, 124, 131, 134, 162
Bowlby, John 66
Buddha 153
Buñuel, Luis 69
Butler, Judith 73-75

Cabbala 6, 132-34, 136, 139-41, 159
  see also Judaism
Cadel, Francesca 5
Callas, Maria 61 Fig. 3
Calvino, Italo 112
Campo, Cristina 23
Capote, Truman 69
Cavarero, Adriana 2, 18 n. 12, 26
Cazalé Bérard, Claude 6
Cefis, Eugenio 108-11
Cervantes, Miguel de 24–25
Cestaro, Gary 8-10, 18 n. 11
Christ 79, 82 n. 24, 92, 101, 141, 148-49, 151, 154, 158-59
  the Passion 92
  see also Virgin Mary
Christianity, *see* religion
Cixous, Hélène 12
  see also languelait
Colussi, Susanna 60 Fig. 1, 61
Communism 59, 110, 120
Congedo, Mimma 6
corporeality 1-2, 8-11, 13, 16-17, 19 n. 20, 25, 147
  see also body
Crialese, Emanuele 69
Critchley, Simon 39
Cukor, George 67

D'Angeli, Concetta 8, 124 nn. 2 & 4, 125 nn. 8 & 11, 126 n. 24, 127 n. 31, 161, 171-72, 176 n. 27
Dante, *see* Alighieri, Dante
death 3-6, 13, 26-28, 30, 33-35, 37-39, 40 n. 12, 42-44, 46, 52, 55, 59, 61, 66-67, 70, 75-81, 91-94, 96-99, 101-02, 105 n. 7, 106 n. 12, 108, 110-11, 114-15, 118, 120-21, 124, 125 nn. 8, 9, 11 & 15, 126 n. 17, 127 nn. 32 & 34, 130, 132-33, 138, 146-47, 150-52, 154-59, 159 n. 8, 160 n. 28, 164, 169, 173
death drive, *see* psychoanalysis
Delanious, Alain 115
Deledda, Grazia 27-28

desire 8-9, 11, 25, 30-31, 33, 35, 43-44, 73, 75-77, 89, 92, 100, 113, 116 n. 14, 140-41, 142 n. 11, 147, 162, 164
  see also love, sex
Deuber-Mankowsky, Astrid 3
Devereux, George 78, 83 n. 26
Dickinson, Emily 68
disturbance 1, 3-4, 6, 13, 29, 33-34, 37, 42, 44, 54, 56, 63, 67, 93, 97-98, 148, 154, 158, 165-66, 169
Don Quixote 24-25
doubleness 25-26, 35, 38, 45, 55, 63, 89, 118-19, 121, 124 n. 2, 136
dreams 5, 13-14, 22-24, 31, 42, 45-46, 56, 62, 68-70, 78, 83 n. 28, 94, 96, 99, 106 n. 12, 107-08, 116 n. 17, 131, 133-36, 138, 142, 143 nn. 15, 17 & 21, 146-49, 151, 156-57
drugs 134, 136, 148, 173-74

Echevarría, Roberto Gonzalez 24
Eden 10-12, 13-14, 134, 136-38, 140, 143 n. 17, 145, 149, 153, 155, 161,
  Garden of 10-11, 134, 136-38, 140, 143 n. 17, 149, 155
  language of 11-13
ENI (Ente Nazionale Idrocarburi) 107-09, 111, 115 n. 2

fantasy 3, 23-24, 26, 32-38, 42, 44-46, 48-51, 53-54, 56, 81, 120, 126 n. 27, 134-35, 143 n. 17, 147-50, 152-53, 157, 174
Fascism 16, 34-37, 77, 96, 108-14, 116 n. 14, 120-21, 131, 138, 152, 158
  in Italy 16, 34-37, 77, 96, 120-21, 131, 138, 152, 158
  in Spain 120, 152
  see also anti-Fascism, Nazism, Resistance
father 4, 5, 9-13, 15-17, 28, 42-43, 45, 49-50, 53, 64, 67, 74, 76-77, 79-81, 98-99, 103, 108, 113, 118-20, 123-24, 125 n. 9, 126 nn. 24 & 27, 127 nn. 30, 31, 33 & 34, 130, 131, 140, 144 n. 28, 146, 153-54, 157-59, 162, 164, 167
femininity 12, 27, 75, 78, 83 n. 24, 92, 127 n. 30, 139-40, 143 n. 17
  see also gender, motherhood
feminism 1-3, 19 n. 17, 27, 40 n. 17, 57 n. 14, 66, 79-80
Fortini, Franco 107, 115 n. 5
Fortuna, Sara 2, 18 n. 14, 32, 39 n. 9, 124 n. 4
Foscolo, Ugo 97
Franco, Francisco 77, 96, 120-21, 126 n. 17, 132-33
Freud, Sigmund 3, 12-13, 18 n. 11, 19 n. 19, 37, 39, 39 n. 10, 46, 49-51, 54-55, 57 n. 11, 13 & 25, 58 nn. 35 & 36, 66, 74-76, 90

Gadda, Carlo Emilio 1, 4, 96-98, 101, 103-05, 105 nn. 2, 3 & 5, 106 nn. 12 & 20
Garboli, Cesare 17 n. 1, 27, 39, 126 n. 24
Gardel, Carlos 71
Gaudì, Antoni 70
gender 1, 3-4, 10, 13, 23, 26, 64, 66, 74-75, 81, 89, 109, 111-13

gender studies 23
  transgenderism 4, 64, 67, 81, 89
Giorgio, Adalgisa 19 n. 17, 57 n. 14, 125 n. 14, 162, 164
Goethe, Wolfgang 79, 97
González Echevarría, Roberto 24
Gragnolati, Manuele 2, 32, 39 n. 9, 124 n. 4
Grieco, Agnese 4
Guattari, Félix 113, 116 n. 14

Hamlet 4, 24, 94, 103-04, 106 n. 20
heterosexuality, *see* sexuality
Heyer-Caput, Margherita 28
Highsmith, Patricia 25
Hölderlin, Friedrich 172
Holocaust, *see* Shoah
Holzhey, Christoph 3
Homer 161
homosexuality, *see* sexuality
humour 2, 38, 39, 69, 112, 114, 123, 148
  tragicomedy 44, 53, 56, 119, 121
hybridity 3, 16, 24, 45, 54-55, 63, 90, 164, 173

Idel, Moshe 141
identity 1-2, 5, 10, 20, 22, 25-27, 35, 40 n. 21, 47, 73, 87, 89, 109, 112-13, 124 n. 5, 147-48, 156, 171
  relational identity 1-2, 10, 20, 26-27
illness 13, 34, 48, 75, 79, 90, 94 n. 2, 97-98, 101-02, 106 n. 16, 121, 125 n. 15, 127 n. 32, 130, 164
India 6, 88, 92, 119, 125 n. 6, 136, 143 n. 17, 161, 165-71, 173-75, 175 nn. 14 & 17, 176 n. 22
Italy 5, 9, 16, 22, 27, 34, 36, 48, 74, 76-77, 80-81, 82 n. 24, 88, 96, 98, 105 n. 5, 107, 110-14, 116 n. 10, 119-22, 131, 138, 142 n. 5, 149, 152
  see also language, politics

journey 1-2, 5-6, 8, 11, 13-14, 32-33, 36, 42-44, 68, 81, 92, 97, 100, 108, 118, 120-24, 125 nn. 6, 8, 10 & 11, 127 n. 30, 132-34, 137, 139-42, 142 n. 11, 152, 161-62, 165, 167-69, 171-72, 175
Judaism, *see* religion
Jung, Carl Gustav 62, 66, 69, 126 n. 30

Kierkegaard, Søren 30
Klein, Melanie 12
knowledge 4-6, 17, 30, 38, 73, 82, 90-91, 107, 124, 134, 138-39, 145, 147, 155, 171-73
  see also Tree of Knowledge
Kofman, Sarah 77-78
Kristeva, Julia 2, 8-9, 11-13, 19 n. 19, 40 n. 12
  semiotic 2, 8-9, 12-15, 17, 19 n. 19, 40 n. 12, 45
  chora 8-9, 11, 19 n. 19, 40 n. 12
  symbolic 9, 12, 15-17, 19 n. 19, 35, 40 n. 17

Lacan, Jacques 12, 22, 31, 176 n. 22,
  symbolic order 4, 9, 15, 17, 19 n. 19, 35, 45, 54, 57 n. 14, 99, 101

language 1-2, 4, 8-10, 11-17, 19 n. 20, 22, 30-35, 40 n. 17, 45, 52-53, 69, 73-74, 76, 80-81, 88-89, 96, 100, 104, 124 n. 3, 141, 151-54
  language acquisition 8-10, 12, 15, 30-32, 45, 66
  languages:
    Italian 11-13, 45, 48, 88-89, 98, 152, 162
    Spanish 11-16, 19 n. 16, 22, 32, 45, 54, 65, 70, 73, 75-77, 88-89, 152
  language theory 2, 8-9, 12-13, 32
  languelait 12, 15, 32
  see also Eden, language of
Laplanche, Jean 3, 46, 50-54, 56, 57 nn. 11 & 13
Leopardi, Giacomo 93
Lingiardi, Vittorio 3, 56 n. 5, 90
logos 1, 90, 135
  see also language, religion
loss 12, 14, 17, 25-26, 32, 38, 40 n. 23, 55, 69, 70, 74-75, 78, 99-100, 102, 118, 121, 125, 131, 136, 157
  see also death, melancholia, mourning
love 4-6, 15-17, 20-21, 26, 28, 43-45, 54-55, 58 n. 35, 59, 61-63, 66, 70, 74, 76-77, 81, 90, 92, 94 n. 2, 97, 99-104, 106 nn. 11, 13 & 14, 110, 112, 118, 120, 122-24, 124 n. 4, 125 nn. 9 & 12, 126 nn. 19, 24 & 27, 132, 145-47, 149, 151-53, 156-59, 162, 164, 173
Lucretius 93
lullaby 13, 31, 88, 93
Luria, Isaac 139

Magnani, Anna 60 Fig. 2, 61
Magrini, Giacomo 19 n. 16
Mankiewicz, Joseph L. 67, 69
Marazzi, Alina 69
Martínez Garrido, Elisa 5
Marxism 111
masculinity 12, 45, 64, 74-77, 81, 125 n. 12, 139-40, 152, 162
  see also gender
masochism, *see* psychoanalysis
maternity, *see* motherhood
matricide 100, 103, 106 n. 12
Mattei, Enrico 5, 107-09, 111
Medea 63
melancholia 13-17, 35, 38, 53, 55-56, 58 nn. 35 & 36, 74-76, 78, 80, 163
memory 3-4, 11-12, 14, 16, 20, 22-24, 26, 28, 30-33, 35, 39, 40 n. 23, 42-54, 56, 56 n. 3, 57 n. 9, 58 n. 30, 65-66, 68, 70, 76, 80-81, 89-91, 98-99, 102, 104, 105 n. 4, 110, 112, 116 n. 11, 126 n. 24, 132-38, 143 nn. 17 & 21, 148, 150, 152, 157-58, 161, 163, 167-68, 170-71, 173
  see also oblivion
metamorphosis 11-12, 23, 33, 45, 75, 80, 112, 121-22, 139, 143 n. 17, 151, 173-74
modernism 20, 25
  see also postmodernism

Morante, Elsa:
  Alibi 151
  Aracoeli:
    Quartieri Alti 11, 13, 22, 32, 34, 36, 42, 45, 55, 58 n. 33, 98, 120, 146, 161, 164
    Totetaco 11-14, 31-33, 45-49, 55, 58 n. 33, 64, 81, 91, 94, 98, 120, 136, 140, 144 n. 27, 152, 155, 161-64
  Le bellissime avventure di Caterí dalla trecciolina 118
  Diario 1938: 134
  Il gioco segreto 142 n. 5
  L'isola di Arturo 1, 12, 27, 68, 93, 118, 124 n. 4, 125 n. 12, 140, 150, 153, 158
  Il mondo salvato dai ragazzini 6, 67, 70, 107, 111, 114, 146, 151, 171-73
  Menzogna e sortilegio 1, 12, 22, 27, 68, 118, 150
  Pro o contro la bomba atomica e altri scritti 25, 35, 147
  Lo scialle andaluso 5, 130-32, 140, 142 n. 5, 150
  La Storia 1, 12, 40 n. 17, 57 n. 6, 67-68, 101, 107, 114, 116 n. 16, 118, 123, 131, 146-51, 154, 158, 159 n. 8
  Racconti dimenticati 153
Moravia, Alberto 6, 131, 161, 165-66, 168-71, 175 nn. 16 & 17
Moses 153
motherhood 1-4, 8-16, 20, 22, 26-29, 31-33, 42, 44, 47, 55, 56 n. 5, 61-63, 65-71, 79, 92-94, 98-99, 101-04, 106 nn. 11 & 12, 118, 121, 131, 140-42, 146, 152-53, 157, 161
  mother and child relationship 1-4, 8-16, 20, 22, 26, 28, 31-33, 42, 44, 47, 54, 57 n. 9, 61-62, 65-66, 70-71, 76, 79, 88, 90-94, 98-104, 105 nn. 7 & 8, 106 nn. 11 & 12, 118, 124, 125 n. 8, 131-33, 136, 140-42, 142 n. 11, 150, 152-53, 156, 161, 163, 173
  see also matricide, suckling
mourning 38-39, 55, 69, 76, 78
  see also death, loss
Müller, Heiner 87
Muraro, Luisa 28
music 35, 44, 63, 87-89
  see also lullaby
Mussgnug, Florian 2
Mussolini, Benito 74, 120
mysticism 5-6, 43, 53, 88, 114, 122, 124 n. 3, 126 n. 20, 131, 140-42, 147-49, 151, 155, 159, 165, 167
  see also Cabbala
mythology 6, 16, 33, 63-64, 78, 80, 119, 124, 138, 145, 153, 161
  Aphrodite 63
  Arjuna 153
  Bacchus 79
  Demeter 63, 78-80
  Dionysius 78, 115, 124
  Hades 78
  Hecate 63

Juno 79, 82 n. 24
Kore 63
Kali 63
Medusa 63
Orpheus 160 n. 28, 161
Persephone 78
Selene 63
Shiva 115
Time 63

narcissism, *see* psychoanalysis
Nazism 113-14, 120, 131, 137-38, 148
Nelson, Victoria 37
Nietzsche, Friedrich 3-4, 78-79
normativity 3, 5, 9, 13, 17, 113

oblivion 44, 53, 55, 57 n. 9, 70, 112, 131, 147
Oedipus complex, *see* psychoanalysis
Orientalism 6, 124 n. 5, 161, 165, 171-72
Ortese, Anna Maria 20, 23
otherness 20-21, 23, 26, 28, 63, 89, 91, 99, 122, 126 n. 20, 162-64, 166, 168, 171, 175

pain 3, 33, 36, 38, 44, 46, 50, 61, 68, 71, 76, 89, 92, 94, 98-99, 106 n. 11, 124, 127 n. 30, 132, 145, 150
paranoia, *see* psychoanalysis
parody 1, 32, 35, 40 n. 15, 44, 96, 112, 114, 119, 124 n. 4, 149, 155
partisans, *see* politics
Parussa, Sergio 5-6, 158
Pasolini, Pier Paolo 1, 3, 5-6, 26, 59, 60-62, 64, 70, 75, 80, 107-17, 125 n. 11, 159 n. 8, 161, 165-70, 175 nn. 16-17, 176 nn. 19 & 22
Pavese, Cesare 112
phantasm 62, 70, 134, 136, 157
Phillips, Adam 32
piety 122-23, 164-65
Pirandello, Luigi 25, 96
Pischedda, Bruno 34
Plato 8
pleasure 12, 43-44, 50-51, 54, 56, 56 nn. 3 & 4, 57 n. 19
politics 2, 5, 34-36, 38, 40 n. 17, 74, 88, 96-97, 107-15, 116 n. 14, 119-20, 131, 133, 137, 147, 158
    anarchism 35
    Italian Civil War 107, 110, 120-21
    Resistance 110-12
        partisans 43, 57 n. 9, 77, 111-12, 116 n. 8, 158
    1968 movements 111
    Spanish Civil War 120, 149-50
Pontalis, Jean-Bertrand 3, 46, 50-54, 57 nn. 11 & 25
postmodernism 20, 64, 69, 96, 105 n. 2
psychoanalysis:
    abjection 28, 39, 74, 76-78, 86
    death drive 50
    early development 2, 9
    fantasy 3, 32

guilt 15, 38
idealization 55, 62, 76, 101
intersubjectivity 2, 27
libido 62, 76
masochism 38, 50-51, 53-56, 57 n. 19, 99, 118
mirror stage 22, 31
narcissism 2, 37, 39
Oedipus complex 3, 19 n. 19, 32, 45-47, 49-51, 54, 56, 57 nn. 6 & 16, 66, 74, 132, 156
paranoia, 2, 36-39, 40 n. 21
primal scene 11, 18 n. 11, 51, 53, 58 n. 30
repression 32, 36, 44, 49, 51-55, 110
sadism 50, 55, 58 n. 36, 98-99, 112, 138
schizophrenia 36, 66, 113

queer 3, 13, 15, 91, 93

Rasy, Elisabetta 23
Re, Lucia 19, 40
reason 3, 17, 47-50, 53-56, 93, 136
reincarnation 6, 132
religion 5-6, 76, 92, 101-02, 115, 117 n. 20, 125 n. 9, 145-59, 165-75
    Brahaminism 6
    Buddhism 6, 172
    Catholicism 59, 64, 79, 108, 113, 133, 165
    Christianity 3, 10, 61, 79-80, 92, 100-02, 106 n. 13, 126 n. 30, 133, 149, 151-52, 156-57, 159, 165, 168, 171
    Hinduism 172
    Islam 133
    Judaism 5-6, 132-34, 139-41, 145 n. 25, 151, 159
        Tree of Knowledge 138-39
        Tree of Life 134, 137-40
        Zohar 133-34, 137, 139-41, 143 nn. 15 & 17, 144 n. 23, 159
    paganism 3, 64, 79, 92, 133
    polytheism 3, 63, 69, 165, 168
Resistance, *see* politics
Resnais, Alain 137, 143 n. 19
resurrection 10, 14, 16-17, 124, 144 n. 28
Rosa, Giovanna 164, 175 n. 9
Rosenberg, David 141
Rossellini, Roberto 113
Russo, Mary 28

sacrifice 5, 28, 35, 45, 55, 61, 121-22, 124, 126 n. 15, 127 n. 30, 156
sadism, *see* psychoanalysis
Said, Edward 165
Sander, Louis 65-66, 71 n. 10
schizophrenia, *see* psychoanalysis
Scholem, Gerschom 160 n. 21
Seduction 3, 50-54, 56, 57 n. 9, 77, 79, 91
Serkowska, Hanna 18 n. 15, 57 n. 8
sex 13, 52–53, 78–79, 93, 97, 101, 109, 141, 163-64
    nymphomania 75, 79, 89, 92, 98, 121, 163, 173

masturbation 37, 56 n. 4, 80
oral 13, 101
sexuality 1, 3-5, 23, 45-47, 49-54, 56, 57 n. 16 & 19, 74-75, 77, 81, 107-08, 110-11, 113-14, 121, 127 n. 32, 162-63, 169, 174
  bisexuality 115
  heterosexuality 74-75, 81
  homosexuality 74-75, 77, 154, 174
Sgorlon, Carlo 27
Shoah 138, 158
  concentration camps 14, 137, 151
  see also Auschwitz
Siciliano, Enzo 165
Silverman, Kaja 31
Siti, Walter 75, 107, 109
Spain 1, 2, 5, 8, 11, 13, 22, 32, 43, 79, 88, 96-97, 116 n. 10, 119-20, 125 n. 6, 131-34, 146, 158, 161
  Almeria 21-22, 36, 119-21, 123, 125 nn. 8, 10 & 11, 126 n. 27, 132
  Andalusia 14, 42, 75-77, 80-81, 119, 121-22, 124 n. 5, 125 nn. 6, 8 & 10, 132-36, 140, 157, 164
  El Almendral 5, 15, 22, 32-33, 36-37, 54, 76, 79, 81, 119-21, 123, 125 nn. 6 & 9, 126 nn. 17, 24 & 27, 132, 136, 144 n. 21, 152, 159 n. 8, 162
  Gergal 126 n. 17, 132, 135-36, 143 n. 17, 174
  see also language, politics
Stellardi, Giuseppe 4
Stern, Daniel 66
subjectivity 1-3, 8-13, 15-17, 27, 34-35, 38-39, 40 n. 12, 43-44, 46-48, 50-52, 58 n. 36, 65-66, 73-74, 87-88, 96, 105 n. 7, 134, 136, 176 n. 17
suckling 9, 10, 13, 14, 18, 57 n. 9, 61
suicide 28, 33-34, 43-44, 53, 56, 56 n. 4, 69, 97, 115, 125 n. 8, 151, 156, 158
Svevo, Italo 96

tension 1-3, 5, 9, 14, 42-45, 56, 62, 65-66, 87-88, 103, 107, 133, 172
  aporia 6, 145, 158
  binary categories 13, 14, 17

coniunctio oppositorum 62
  dichotomy 13, 118-19, 124 nn. 2 & 4
  paradox 13, 16, 31, 36-37, 43-44, 50-51, 54, 56, 56 n. 3, 88, 94, 138-39, 148, 156
  unity vs. multiplicity 12, 45, 64, 124, 155, 173
  trauma 3, 4, 13, 17, 21, 28, 32, 51-55, 62, 66, 99, 101, 105 n. 7, 110-12, 150, 157, 168-69
Tree of Knowledge, *see* Judaism
Tree of Life, *see* Judaism

Unamuno, Miguel de 88

Venturi, Gianni 27
Victor Emanuel III 74, 76-77
Vidal, Gore 25
Virgin Mary 3, 63-64, 77, 79, 82, 92-93, 121
vision 2, 3, 11, 14, 20-27, 29, 31, 33, 35, 37-38, 54, 56 n. 4, 57 n. 9, 66, 80, 86, 88, 94, 96, 105, 111, 113-14, 116 n. 15, 119, 120, 133, 135-36, 138, 140-41, 143 nn. 15, 17 & 21, 145, 148-50, 152, 174
  see also anamorphosis
Virgil 10, 161
voice 6, 12, 31, 33, 36, 53, 70, 76, 80, 86-90, 97, 105 n. 7, 120, 132, 134, 136, 147, 149-51, 156-57

Warner, Marina 31, 39
Weil, Simone 6, 122, 126, 126 n. 19, 146-47, 149-51, 155-56, 159, 160 nn. 10 & 19, 172
West, Rebecca 2
Williams, Tennessee 69
Winnicott, Donald W. 66-67
Wolfson, Elliot 140
women's writing 23, 27
Wood, Sharon 27

Zambrano, Araceli 122, 126 n. 17, 159 n. 5
Zambrano, María 5, 122-24, 126 nn. 17, 19, 23 & 28, 159
Zampolini, Anna Maria 25
Zohar, *see* Judaism
Zola, Émile 75